Praise for

'A thundering good read is virtually the only way of describing Wilbur Smith's books'

IRISH TIMES

'Wilbur Smith . . . writes as forcefully as his tough characters act'

EVENING STANDARD

'Wilbur Smith has arguably the best sense of place of any adventure writer since John Buchan'

THE GUARDIAN

'Wilbur Smith is one of those benchmarks against whom others are compared'

THE TIMES

'Best Historical Novelist – I say Wilbur Smith, with his swashbuckling novels of Africa. The bodices rip and the blood flows. You can get lost in Wilbur Smith and misplace all of August'

STEPHEN KING

'Action is the name of Wilbur Smith's game and he is the master'

WASHINGTON POST

'A master storyteller'

'Smith will take you on an exciting, taut and thrilling journey you will never forget'

'No one does adventure quite like Smith'

'With Wilbur Smith the action is never further than the turn of a page'

'When it comes to writing the adventure novel, Wilbur Smith is the master; a 21st century H. Rider Haggard'

Wilbur Smith was born in Central Africa in 1933. He became a full-time writer in 1964 following the success of *When the Lion Feeds* and has since published over fifty global bestsellers, including the Courtney Series, the Ballantyne Series, the Egyptian Series, the Hector Cross Series and many successful standalone novels, all meticulously researched on his numerous expeditions worldwide. An international phenomenon, his readership built up over fifty-five years of writing, establishing him as one of the most successful and impressive brand authors in the world.

The establishment of the Wilbur & Niso Smith Foundation in 2015 cemented Wilbur's passion for empowering writers, promoting literacy and advancing adventure writing as a genre. The foundation's flagship programme is the Wilbur Smith Adventure Writing Prize.

Wilbur Smith died peacefully at home in 2021 with his wife, Niso, by his side, leaving behind him a rich treasure-trove of novels and stories that will delight readers for years to come.

For all the latest information on Wilbur Smith's writing visit www.wilbursmithbooks.com or facebook.com/WilburSmith.

Tom Harper is the author of thirteen thrillers and historical adventures including *The Orpheus Descent*, *Black River* and *Lost Temple*. Research for his novels has taken him all over the world, from the high Arctic to the heart of the Amazon jungle. He lives with his family in York. For more information about Tom's books, visit www.tom-harper.co.uk.

Also by Wilbur Smith

Non-Fiction

On Leopard Rock: A Life of
Adventures

The Courtney Series

When the Lion Feeds
The Sound of Thunder
A Sparrow Falls
The Burning Shore
Power of the Sword
Rage
A Time to Die
Golden Fox
Birds of Prey
Monsoon
Blue Horizon
The Triumph of the Sun
Assegai
Golden Lion
War Cry
The Tiger's Prey
Courtney's War
King of Kings
Ghost Fire
Legacy of War
Storm Tide
Nemesis

The Ballantyne Series

A Falcon Flies
Men of Men
The Angels Weep

The Leopard Hunts in Darkness
The Triumph of the Sun
King of Kings
Call of the Raven

The Egyptian Series

River God
The Seventh Scroll
Warlock
The Quest
Desert God
Pharaoh
The New Kingdom
Titans of War
Testament

Hector Cross

Those in Peril
Vicious Circle
Predator

Standalones

The Dark of the Sun
Shout at the Devil
Gold Mine
The Diamond Hunters
The Sunbird
Eagle in the Sky
The Eye of the Tiger
Cry Wolf
Hungry as the Sea
Wild Justice
Elephant Song

WILBUR SMITH

WITH TOM HARPER

WARRIOR KING

ZAFFRE

First published in the UK in 2024 by
ZAFFRE
An imprint of Zaffre Publishing Group
A Bonnier Books UK Company
4th Floor, Victoria House, Bloomsbury Square, London WC1B 4DA
Owned by Bonnier Books
Sveavägen 56, Stockholm, Sweden

A CIP catalogue record for this book is
available from the British Library.

Hardback ISBN: 978–1–83877–914–6
Trade paperback ISBN: 978–1–80418–427–1

Also available as an ebook and an audiobook

3 5 7 9 10 8 6 4 2

Typeset by IDSUK (Data Connection) Ltd
Printed and bound in Great Britain by Clays Ltd, Elcograf S.p.A.

Zaffre is an imprint of Zaffre Publishing Group
A Bonnier Books UK Company
www.bonnierbooks.co.uk

This book is for my love, Mokhiniso, spirit of Genghis Khan and Omar Khayyam, reincarnated in a moon as lucent as a perfect pearl.

This novel, like all of those published after his passing, originated from an unfinished work by Wilbur Smith. It was completed by Tom Harper, who was hand-chosen by Wilbur to co-create a story bridge from BLUE HORIZON to WHEN THE LION FEEDS in the famous Courtney family series. Wilbur and Tom worked on outlines that met Wilbur's rigorous standards. Wilbur's wife, Mokhiniso Smith, his long-standing literary agent Kevin Conroy Scott and the Wilbur Smith Estate's in-house editor, James Woodhouse, worked tirelessly with Tom to ensure Wilbur's vision was realised in his absence.

THE
COURTNEY
FAMILY
IN
WARRIOR KING

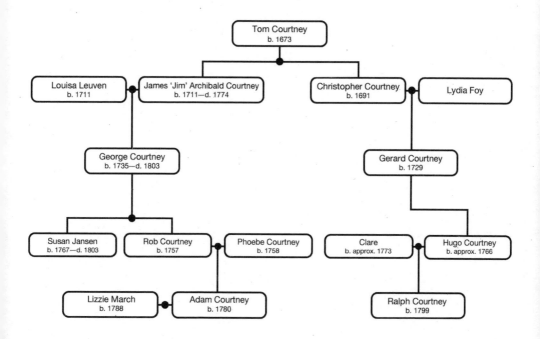

Tom Courtney
b. 1673

Louisa Leuven
b. 1711

James 'Jim' Archibald Courtney
b. 1711—d. 1774

Christopher Courtney
b. 1691

Lydia Foy

George Courtney
b. 1735—d. 1803

Gerard Courtney
b. 1729

Susan Jansen
b. 1767—d. 1803

Rob Courtney
b. 1757

Phoebe Courtney
b. 1758

Clare
b. approx. 1773

Hugo Courtney
b. approx. 1766

Lizzie March
b. 1788

Adam Courtney
b. 1780

Ralph Courtney
b. 1799

Find out more about the Courtneys and see the Courtney family tree in full at www.wilbursmithbooks.com/courtney-family-tree

ALGOA BAY, SOUTH AFRICA. APRIL, 1820

The continent was hidden. A thick sea mist rolled in off the bay, obscuring the ships at anchor and the canvas city that had risen on the shore two days earlier. It deadened every sound. Only the sea remained – the hush of waves breaking in the humid air. To Ann Waite, standing on the sandy beach, it was as if she had fallen off the edge of the world.

Ann needed to be alone. She hugged her arms against her chest, feeling the breasts that were swollen with milk to feed the baby that did not exist. She remembered the nightmare of the birth at sea: spread-eagled on a table; seamen going about their work just inches away; the old naval surgeon with his knives and rusty saws jangling on the wall behind him. She recalled the claustrophobia of the tiny compartment, deep in the ship, below the waterline. It had taken eighteen hours of labour for the baby to arrive, a girl whom Ann had named Susannah.

A day later, Susannah was dead. They buried her in the ocean in a canvas shroud, with a ballast stone to weigh her down.

The grief was so painful that Ann wanted to scream. Her daughter should have heralded the new life that Ann and her husband Frank had come from England to make in Africa. Instead, the voyage that began in hope had ended in death and despair.

Out in the fog, she heard the wailing of a baby. She must be imagining it. It was the sound that haunted her nightmares: a soul adrift, abandoned to danger, that she could not comfort or embrace.

Ann had never expected to find herself in Africa. Growing up in a small village in the Pennine hills of England, the continent had been no more real to her than the lands in fairy tales. Then the war that had begun before she was born had ended. Napoleon was beaten, but it did not feel like victory to the men who returned from the battlefields of Europe. Tens of thousands of men who

had known no profession except soldiering suddenly found themselves surplus to the requirements of the crown they had served
so loyally. Ann's husband, Frank, had been one of them. He had
found work as a hand-loom weaver, but wages had halved since
the peace and he could not earn enough to provide for the baby
growing inside Ann's belly.

Then, one morning, Frank had seen a notice posted in the bow
window of the general dealer. Free land – good, fertile land, the
notice promised – being given away by the government, with
tools, seeds and equipment for farming to be provided at cost. It
was in Cape Colony, at the southern tip of Africa.

Pulling his cap down, Frank had hurried home, a look of deter-
mination on his face.

Ann was hesitant, but Frank had fought at the capture of Cape
Town in 1806 and seen a little of the country. The land was ripe,
he promised her, a Garden of Eden where if you spat out a grape
pip, a vine would grow in front of your eyes. 'This is a godsend,'
he told Ann, falling to his knees. 'The answer to our prayers.
A place to make a home and raise our future family.'

Ann had yet to see the paradise she had been promised. Four
thousand settlers had answered the notice and taken passage on
the ships the government provided. They had been set ashore
in this bay of desolate sandhills and salt marshes, billeted in
tents among scrub and rocks while they waited for wagons to
take them to the grants the government had assigned them. Her
husband still clung to the hope that the country inland would
live up to its promise. Ann had lost faith. She had seen nothing
for six weeks but the dank inside of the ship and now this cursed
beach where the sun blistered their skin and the wind screamed
at them as if wanting to drive them back into the endless,
devouring sea.

She heard the cry again – the baby. The sound cut straight
to her heart; dark horrors invaded her thoughts. Was she going
mad? Many of the settlers had brought their children along with
them, and not all the babies born on the voyage had suffered
Susannah's fate. Though the sound seemed to be coming from a
different direction – out in the bay. The fog was so thick that Ann
had lost her bearings, only the sand beneath her feet seemed real.

The wailing grew louder – the infant crying at the top of its lungs, calling for help. As if its life depended on it.

Surely no parent could ignore that cry for long. Someone would find it soon and soothe the poor, scared soul.

The crying became more anguished. It was almost unbearable, but Ann was sure now that it *was* coming from out in the bay.

She ran to the water's edge. The fog was thicker here, but she could see a dark shape emerging and then disappearing in the spectral grey. She heard the mournful creak and grind of wood scraping rock.

'The baby must be on a boat,' she murmured to herself. But the ships had unloaded all their passengers and anchored far out in the bay. And if it was a boat, there should be other sounds: the screech of rowlocks and the grunt of sailors working the oars; the shouts of the coxswain, and perhaps the soothing voice of the child's mother. She heard none of those.

She had never encountered the sea before she left Lancashire. Its fathomless depths terrified her; she had spent the whole voyage in a state of muted panic. But now she was determined. Whether the baby was real or not, she was compelled towards the source of the crying.

Hoisting her skirts, Ann waded into the freezing water. The folds of her dress welling up; the incoming sea lifting her off her feet. The current was so strong that she lost her balance and found herself half-sitting in the water. A wave washed over her head as she tried to pull herself upwards, filling her throat as she called out in alarm.

'Help! God, please help!' Ann shouted, choking as another wave drowned her voice and the current took hold of her skirts, sucking her out to sea.

In the dunes above the beach, not even two hundred yards away, four thousand souls were starting the day – getting dressed, queuing for their breakfasts at the field kitchens, discussing the peculiarities of this new land. Yet they would not be able to hear her.

Desolate, terrified, half-drowning, Ann flung out her hands as the sea took her, desperate for any kind of purchase in the icy water. Sand and broken pieces of kelp billowed around her as the ocean's relentless power pulled her further from the shore.

Then she saw it – the prow of a boat.

It was trapped in a cleft between two rocks, the waves battering it, thrusting it to and fro. Ann could see that it would sink soon – already the water around it was full of splinters and broken timber.

The next wave drove her against the rocks. She thought she would be crushed, but then the baby cried again – it *was* in the boat! That cry filled Ann with fire. She would not let another child slip beneath the waves. A scream rose from her chest, just as it had during her hellish labour. She pushed against the rock on which she was pinned with all her strength, striking out into the deep water.

The waves drew the boat back, then threw it forward again, thrusting it towards Ann. As it came closer, she grabbed for the bow but she was still too far away – the gunwale agonisingly out of reach.

The next wave hammered Ann against the hull with such force that she feared her ribs would break. Grabbing the prow, she clung on as the sea tore at her skirts, leaning on the boat, hoping that somehow she would be able to lever it off the rocks.

The sea heaved around her, the waves ripping at the boat. Ann looked inside.

Three people lay there: a woman, a man and a baby.

The man lay across the main thwart, slumped in the bilge. The woman lay facing him. Long honey-coloured hair hung loose around her shoulders; her skin had been burned deep red by exposure to the sun and drawn tight on her bones from hunger, though Ann could still see that she had once been beautiful. She looked so peaceful – with her eyes closed and her hands folded in her lap – that one might have thought her asleep. But her chest did not move, and the grey pallor of death had already begun to creep in around her eyes.

The man was hideously disfigured. The right half of his face was a mess of raw scars where he had been badly burned, livid dead skin twisted like a clump of maggots. On the other side of his face, hair sprouted where his beard had tried to grow. He was dressed in a long tunic, heavily embroidered with golden dragons. A pistol was still tucked in his belt.

Neither the man nor the woman gave any sign of life. *They are dead*, Ann thought with horror.

Between them, the baby lay on its back, eyes closed, its small face puffed scarlet with the mammoth effort of screaming. It was a boy. He had been wrapped in a piece of sackcloth, but his frantic kicking had thrown off the covering and water leaching through the crack in the hull had soaked it. His skin was starting to turn blue.

Ann leaned all her weight on the boat, turning the bow a few degrees. It was enough. Suddenly, miraculously, the boat was free, sliding out from between the rocks and into the sea. Ann almost lost her grip, fighting to keep her head above the waterline as the current took hold.

The boy cried out again, but weaker this time. Ann wasn't sure how much time he had left.

Her feet touched the bottom. She could stand.

Ann let the morning tide carry the boat ashore, the waves nudging it up the beach until it came to rest. She knelt on the sand, exhausted, spitting out seawater, while white surf foamed around her and groped at her skirts.

The boy whimpered in the boat.

Adrenaline made Ann forget her exhaustion. Standing, she scooped the baby in her arms, unbuttoned the front of her dress and tugged the fabric apart to expose her swollen breasts. The baby's mouth puckered as Ann lifted his face to her breast. He found the nipple and clamped down so greedily that it made Ann gasp.

It felt as if a dam had broken inside her. The hot milk emerged with such force that it seemed to sear her flesh. As the milk flowed, she felt a long-awaited release and a series of deep shudders went through her.

Holding him close to her chest, Ann peered into the boat again.

It must have been at sea for weeks. It could not have come from the ships anchored in the bay, and as far as Ann knew there weren't any harbours nearby. It must have come from another ship, far out to sea, but why?

Ann stroked the baby's head, covered in a thin golden down. 'I suppose you are an orphan now,' she murmured.

'Who are you?'

The words rang out harsh on the empty beach. At the same time, a hand fastened around Ann's wrist like a talon and pulled her forward. She almost dropped the child in her fright.

The man in the boat was not dead. Amid the filth and gore that caked his face, his blue eyes were cold and sharp as they stared at her.

'Where is this?' His voice was a rasp. He stared around wildly, trying to penetrate the fog, then fixed his gaze back on Ann. 'Is this the Cape?'

'Al— Algoa Bay,' Ann stammered with dread.

His eyes narrowed threateningly. 'Tell me your name.'

'Ann Waite.'

'What are you doing here?' he demanded.

'I came with the settlers. On the ships, from England.' She pointed into the bay, but the fog still hid the anchored fleet. 'We arrived yesterday.'

The man let go of Ann and pulled himself unsteadily to his feet. His grip had left a deep red mark on her wrist.

'What is your name?' Ann asked. It was an innocuous question, but it took courage to ask it. Even in his weakened state the man blazed danger: she could feel it emanating from him like hot coals.

The man stepped out of the boat, and almost collapsed onto the sand, as if his legs were made of rope. He grasped the boat's gunwale to steady himself. The scars on his face twitched. 'Ralph Courtney.'

'Where did you come from?'

He ignored the question. A length of driftwood lay on the beach, bleached white by the sun. He picked it up and leaned on it as a crutch, scanning his surroundings.

'Is the navy here?' he asked.

Ann nodded.

'How many ships?'

She didn't know the precise number of ships. 'Twenty, perhaps?' she guessed.

He was still looking at her, but she seemed to have slipped out of focus, as if his mind was caught on a memory.

The baby suckled at Ann's breast. She knew she must return him to his father, though she could hardly bear the thought of giving up the child so soon.

'I am sorry for your wife,' she said.

'She was not my wife.'

'And the baby?'

'An orphan.' The words were expelled with a violence that made her cover the baby in her arms. Fury, hatred – but also something deeper, she thought. A kind of despair that had no other outlet but anger.

'You need help.' She spoke gently, trying to calm him, afraid of the lash of his tongue. 'Food and water.'

'No.' His throat was so parched he could barely grunt his words. 'I cannot stay.'

He leaned on his stick and began to hobble away down the beach.

'What about the child?' Ann called.

He looked back. With his head turned, she could not see the burned half of his face and it suddenly became clear to her that he was not much past twenty years old. He would have been a handsome young man, before his ordeal.

'His name is Harry,' he rasped. 'Keep him alive, if you can.'

Before Ann could ask what that meant, Ralph stumbled off into the fog.

Ann felt dizzy. She sat down on the boat's gunwale, cradling the child. He had drunk sufficient, and his colour had returned. He lay in her arms with his eyes closed, asleep. An occasional twitch of his face spoke of the dreams inside his little head.

If not for the child, and the hard wood of the boat under her, Ann would have thought she had dreamed the encounter. *Where had Ralph Courtney come from? What should she do now?*

'What are you doing?'

The voice startled her. She looked up guiltily, though she had nothing to hide. Her husband, Frank, had appeared and was staring down at her through his round, silver-rimmed spectacles.

'You should not wander away by yourself,' he scolded her gently. 'Who knows what savage animals may be roaming out here.'

Then he took in the boat, the dead woman, Ann in her soaking clothes – and the child. His face went white.

'What on earth . . .?'

'The boat washed ashore. I heard the baby crying.'

Frank's mouth opened as if to say something and his face seemed to twitch. He took off his glasses and rubbed them on his shirt, as if that would help him see more clearly.

'She came from a ship called the *Tiger*,' he said, pointing to the name painted along the bow. 'But there is no ship by that name in our fleet.'

He dug his finger into a crack in the gunwale where the wood had splintered. A round lump of lead came out of it.

'A musket ball. She has been in a battle.'

Ann stayed motionless and quiet. She held the baby tighter, her heart racing. *What would Frank say? Would he insist she gave him up?*

Frank looked at the dead woman, and then at the baby. He glanced at Ann and saw the fire in her eyes.

'We should report this.'

He was correct, of course. It was the right thing to do. The woman – the mother – must have a family; they would need to know what had happened to her. Yet Ann knew in her heart that they would not be found.

'If there is no family . . . If no one claims the child . . . I want to keep him.'

It seemed an eternity before Frank spoke. But he loved his wife, and – though he had not spoken of it – he grieved the daughter they had lost as much as he knew Ann did.

'If he is truly an orphan, then, my darling wife, we will keep him.'

Ann stood up and hugged him tight, so that the child was squeezed between them. 'Thank you,' she breathed. 'Thank you. We will raise him as our own. We will have a family after all.'

Frank did not notice the footprints in the sand that led away from the boat, punctuated by the round holes made by a make-shift crutch. Ann decided not to tell him about the man she had seen. Frank would want to find him, and that could only end badly for all of them. Ralph Courtney, she felt, was not a man who wanted to be found. Worse, Frank might insist that Ralph should take the baby back.

The fog was lifting; the tent city was coming into view. She could hear the chatter of the other settlers, while the smell of cooking made her realise how ravenous she was. In the sunlight, it was difficult to believe that Ralph Courtney was more than a figment of her imagination.

Maybe he never existed, she tried to convince herself, though the livid red welt where he had grabbed her wrist proved otherwise. She pulled her hand into the sleeve of her dress so that Frank would not see the mark.

It did not matter; Ralph Courtney was gone. She was sure that she would never see him again.

THREE YEARS LATER . . .

'Is there anything as sad as a flightless bird?'

A man sat on a boulder and watched a troop of penguins waddle towards the shore. His name was Marius Wessels. He stood several inches north of six feet, with broad shoulders and fat hands. His brown hair grew in an ungainly mop of curls, and – though he was only twenty-five – his fleshy features were creased like an old book. Yet when he looked at the penguins, his face lit up like a child's. None of them were more than two feet tall, but they carried themselves with dignity, their white chests thrust out and their useless wings dangling by their sides. Noble, but also rather pathetic creatures.

'They look at us and think the same,' said the man next to him, in thickly accented English. '*Hola, moegoes.*' His name was Jobe, a black man from one of the Bantu tribes of the African interior. He was almost as tall as the Dutchman, for his years of confinement had not bowed the pride in his bearing. His hair was cropped short; his arms were strong from two years of harsh labour. He wore an ivory bracelet on his upper arm.

'Maybe they look at you and think you're a cousin, hey?' Marius retorted, pointing to where Jobe's ebony skin was caked with white limestone dust. 'You're one of them.'

If the insult stung Jobe, he did not let it show. After two years in prison, he had learned to hide his feelings. 'If I was one of those birds, I would swim away.'

'You can try any time you like.'

Across the bay, the flat-topped peak of Table Mountain stood majestic against the blue sky. Five miles of open water stretched between them and the mountain, though from their viewpoint the horizon played tricks with distance so that it seemed little wider than a river. The bay's true extent was hidden – as were the currents, whales and sharks that lurked in its icy depths.

The place where they stood was called Robben Island, though it was not much of an island: barely a pimple on the face of the ocean. Even at its highest point, you felt that a strong tide might swamp it completely. It was a barren knoll covered in sparse, stunted trees and low scrub, unsuitable for any kind of life except penguins and seals. In the eyes of the Cape government, it was the perfect location for a prison colony.

'Up,' shouted one of the soldiers standing guard. 'Back to work.'

The prisoners took up their picks and hammers and returned to the rock face. Every day they had to break their quota of limestone. Once they had finished the day's labour, they were free to roam the island as they liked. Some fished; others tended little allotments they had made to supplement their rations. If the prisoners wanted to escape, let them try. They could leave the island easily enough – and a few days later, their corpses would wash up on the shore.

In the quarry, the prisoners worked in pairs: one to hold an iron spike, the other to drive it into the rock. Having a man swing a sledgehammer with stone-smashing force a few inches from his partner's fingers either ended in quick disaster, or fostered a certain trust between the pair. Marius and Jobe had been working together for six months, since Marius had arrived on the island. They resumed their accustomed positions – Jobe on the spike, Marius on the hammer. The dust made their eyes weep; the naked sun scorched their shirtless backs.

'When I am free,' said Marius, 'the heaviest thing I'll ever lift again will be a mug of beer.'

He swung the hammer. His exposed muscles rippled with the effort. A puff of grit and dust exploded from the rock.

'I will have a big house, and a fat wife, and fifteen children, and they will bring me a side of beef every evening for my dinner.'

Another strike; a crack appeared in the rock. 'I would be happy to go back to my people,' said Jobe with a grunt. 'And never see a white man again.'

'It's our country too, hey? You have to share it.'

'When you say "share", I think you mean "give",' growled Jobe.

'And when *you* say "share", you mean you will steal all our cattle, you black rascal.' Marius raised the hammer again. 'It's a big continent. There should be enough land—'

He checked his swing. A shadow had fallen over the quarry as the overseer rode up on his bay horse. The animal was an affectation: in the time it took to saddle it, the overseer could have walked anywhere on the island. But he was conscious of his status, and missed no opportunity to show it off. In the low society of the island, a man had to flaunt whatever privilege he could get.

Two soldiers stood beside him, holding a man between them. He was a stranger, a new prisoner, judging by how clean his clothes were. A young man, in his early twenties, clean-shaven and with angelic fair hair. More than one of the prisoners eyed him with undisguised desire.

The prisoner turned his head, and every lascivious thought disappeared. His right cheek, hidden until now, was a mask of snaking scar tissue. The hair on that side of his head still grew unevenly, while the eye regarded the world through a half squint.

The soldiers pushed him forward into the quarry. The overseer extended a white-gloved hand and pointed to Marius.

'Show him what to do.'

He rode off, his retinue of guards jogging behind him. The rest of the men returned to their work, occasionally glancing at the new arrival, who seemed indifferent to them. Jobe, relieved of his duty, leaned against a rock and rolled a cigar.

Marius sized up his new partner. The man had suffered some calamitous misfortunes in his life: burned, disfigured, and now imprisoned. Yet there was no trace of self-pity in his blue eyes, and the good corner of his mouth was set steady in a calm smile.

'What's your name?' Marius asked.

'Ralph.'

'English?'

The man shrugged. 'Mongrel.'

'A *brak*, hey? What are you here for?'

'Theft.'

'That does not usually get a man sent here.'

'It depends what you steal. In my case, it was the governor's daughter's virginity.' Ralph chuckled.

Laughter went around the quarry. The other men had stopped their work and were listening. It was contrary to reason that Ralph, with his savage scars, could have seduced anyone. But if you looked in his eyes, at the power and the confidence brimming within them, perhaps it was not such a fanciful idea.

'How long are you here?'

'They sentenced me to ten years. But I do not expect to be detained here more than a few days.'

More laughter, this time with a cruel edge.

'Everyone thinks that,' Marius advised him. 'But I tell you, there are only two ways off this rock. When the governor says you can go – or in a box.'

Ralph stayed silent. But the corner of his mouth twitched.

That night, the men lay in their bunks in the barracks. It was a small, square stone room, with two beds, one either side of a barred window, and a slop bucket in the corner. Ralph, Marius and Jobe took three berths; the fourth was empty.

Marius was scratching his initials into the stone wall with a nail, a painstaking business that had occupied him for weeks. Jobe sat on his bunk with a tallow candle, poring over a Bible. Ralph lay on his mattress, arms folded behind his head, listening to the rasp of the nail and the occasional guttering of the candle.

Marius paused his work and looked down from his bunk. 'Are you still dreaming about escaping, *brak*?'

'I was thinking about rain,' said Ralph.

'They still make you quarry in the rain.'

'I did not mean African rain.' Ralph's voice was distant. 'I spent the first half of my life in India, the second in China. When the rain comes there, it falls like bullets, and even on the wettest day the air is still warm as blood.'

'He's a bloody poet,' grunted Marius.

'I would like to feel cool rain on my face.' His hand crept to the scars on his cheek. 'I cannot stand the heat any longer. I want to be somewhere clean and cool.'

'And instead you're a prisoner on Robben Island. Life is a cruel mistress.'

Ralph ignored him. 'My grandfather had a house in Devon – in England. My father kept a picture of it in the house where I grew up. I used to stare at it for hours – I could not imagine a place so green. My father told me that even the summers there are cold.'

'Sounds bloody miserable.'

'When I get out of here, I will make my fortune, go to England, buy back that house and live out the rest of my life there.'

Marius snorted. 'By the time you get off this rock, your back will be broken and your fingers will be so sore you won't even be able to hold your own cock.'

'It cannot be so hard to escape.' Ralph pointed to the bars on the window. The iron was rusted, and the mortar that held them in place crumbling.

'I could pull those out any time I like,' Marius said. 'But where would I go then? It is not the cell that keeps us prisoners. It is the island. Those lazy guards only lock the door at night because they are afraid that we'll get out and murder them.'

'Do you never dream of being somewhere else?' Ralph asked.

'Me?' The question surprised Marius. 'I have had enough living by other men's rules, hey? When I get out, I will take my wagon across the Kei River and find some land of my own to farm. And I will be free.'

'That is Xhosa land,' said Jobe, looking up from his Bible. 'If you go, my people will kill you.'

Marius cracked his knuckles. 'I'd like to see those Kaffirs try.'

'You will get what you wish,' Jobe replied. 'If you cross the Kei.'

'And I will be ready.' Marius turned to Ralph. 'You know why our *swart* friend is here? He's a bloody prophet. Over on the eastern frontier, he tried to whip up the tribes, start a war against the white man.'

Ralph studied Jobe with new interest. In India and in China, he had learned many times never to underestimate a man because of the colour of his skin. Spending time in Cape Colony, it was too easy to see every black man as a servant or a slave. Yet looking at Jobe now, focusing on the man himself, Ralph could see the pride and intelligence in his eyes.

'Why did you want to start a war?'

'The British started the war.' Jobe's voice was rich with anger. 'When we fought back, they said it was our fault.'

'Don't you believe him.' Marius snorted. 'It was a cattle raid, nothing more.'

'Cattle that were grazing on land you took from my people.'

Marius was grinning, but there was a dangerous edge in his voice. Jobe was tensed like a warrior ready for battle. Ralph marvelled that the two men had shared a cell for so long and not yet killed each other.

'If you hate the British so much, why are you reading our scriptures?' Ralph asked.

The question deflected Jobe's anger from Marius, but only so he could scowl at Ralph. 'The word of Jesus does not belong to the white man.' Without looking at the Bible, he recited: '"The Lord has sent me to bring good news to the poor, to proclaim liberty to captives and to set the downtrodden free."'

'Liberty to captives would be a fine thing,' said Marius.

'Where did you learn to read?' Ralph asked.

Jobe stiffened, wary of any slight or insult Ralph intended. When he saw that Ralph was merely curious, his posture softened.

'When I was a boy, my mother worked for a white farmer. He beat her, and did . . . worse things.'

Marius looked as if he was about to say something flippant. The cast of Jobe's expression made him decide otherwise.

'When my mother died, I ran away. There was a mission station, and a preacher named John Weston. He found me and me the way of Jesus. The farmer came, and the missionary would not give me up. He said I was saved.'

'This is why we should not educate the Kaffirs,' said Marius. 'They twist a man's own religion against him.'

Ralph ignored him. 'How did you come from there to here?'

'John Weston went back to England. I returned to my tribe and tried to teach them the truth of Jesus Christ. I thought if they were Christians, the white men would not cheat and fight them.'

Ralph laughed. Jobe's jaw tightened with wounded pride.

'I was laughing at the way of the world,' Ralph explained. 'Not at you. I have seen how the British conduct their business wherever they go. Whatever they can find different in a people – the colour of their skins, their gods, their methods of government – that is what they will use against them. And if there is nothing that they can manipulate in their favour, they will simply take what they want at the mouth of a cannon.'

'There we can agree.' Marius picked up the nail and began vigorously scratching at the wall again. 'All of us know what it is like to have our freedom taken away by the bloody British.'

The three men lapsed into silence, each nursing his own personal dream of freedom.

'I will tell you where I would go,' said Marius suddenly. A light had come into his eyes; he leaned forward off the bunk. 'You like stories? Let me tell you this one.'

He took out his pipe and filled it with tobacco while the others waited. Only when it was lit and glowing did he continue.

'This was a few years ago. I was away hunting up on the frontier, past Grahamstown by the Fish River. One day, I was fishing at a drift when I saw a man on the far bank. A white man – stark naked. All he had was a hat on his head and a gun on his back.

'I helped him across the drift, brought him to my camp and gave him a blanket. He was a Frenchman, name of Du Toit. I asked him where he came from.

'"Cape Town," he says.

'"You've come the long way round, then," I say. "Cape Town's a thousand miles in the opposite direction."

'"That I have," he agrees. "I have been across the Karoo and the Orange River, over mountains, down to the ocean and now back here. You have not laid your eyes on sights such as those that I have seen."

'Of course I didn't believe him. "That must have taken you three years."

'"Five years," he says.

'"What were you doing there?"

'"Hunting."

'"And not a lot to show for it, hey?" Because this man is drinking my coffee with his *Jakob* hanging out . . .' Marius laughed. 'He gives me a look, like a man who swallowed a diamond and shit out a rock. "Ah, Boer, you have no idea. Now I have fallen on hard times, but six months ago I was the richest man in Africa. With my gun, I made myself a lord. Up there" – he points to the north – "there is every kind of animal and almost no one to hunt them. I had enough hides to carpet every street in Paris, feathers in every colour of the jewellery box, and ivory – a mountain of it. There is so much ivory up there, the natives use it to mend their fences, or else leave it lying in the dust."

'I did not believe a word of his tale, but he was a good story-teller and I was bored, so I asked him: "What happened then?"

'"A bad journey," he said. "It is one thing to accumulate wealth, but another to bring it out. The tribes between there and here are terrible people. They robbed me of everything I had, even the clothes off my back. They tried to murder me. If I had not had my gun, I would not have survived." By now, his head had sunk into his hands. "And that is how you see me now, this pitiful ghost of the man I was."

'He was so sad about it that I almost believed him. I gave him some of the food I had, which he ate like a horse, and brandy, which he liked even better. We sat by the fire, and he spun me yarns of the places he had been.' Marius drifted off, remembering. 'He was a good storyteller.

'Next morning, I woke and he had gone.' He sat back on his bunk, drawing on his pipe. 'That was the last time I saw him. But I will never forget his story. When I am free again, maybe I will go north and look for that land of his.'

The room fell silent. Each man stared into space, alone with his thoughts.

'Did he say how far this country was?' Ralph asked.

'Four hundred miles north of the Fish River.' Marius blew out a cloud of smoke. 'It must be lies, hey? If such a country existed, someone would have gone there by now.'

'Not if the Xhosa block the way,' said Jobe.

'*Ja.*' Marius sighed. 'And even if it is there, and you fought your way in overland, past the Xhosa, and piled up all the ivory you can dream of, you still have the same problem as the Frenchman. You are only rich if you can get it out.'

'What about by sea?' Ralph asked.

'Impossible. There is no harbour for a thousand miles after Port Elizabeth. You have no way in – and no way out.'

Ralph sat up so abruptly he almost banged his head on the bunk above. 'That is not true.'

'What?'

'There is a place a ship could anchor.'

Marius eyed him over the bowl of his pipe. 'I spoke to every sailor I could find and they all told me the same. Rocks, reefs and sandbars – that is all you find on that coast.'

'No.' Ralph's voice was quiet but unyielding. 'There is a bay, but a promontory hides the entrance. Sailors fear the currents close to shore, so they keep out to sea and never see it. There is a narrow channel that leads in, and even then you think you will run aground. Only a madman would risk it. But if you hold your nerve, you come into a bay where there is a landing and a safe anchorage.'

'You have been there?' said Jobe.

'No,' Ralph admitted.

'Fairy tales,' said Marius. 'How do you know this?'

'My father had a map. He went there. It's called Nativity Bay.'

Marius's face was screwed up with disbelief. But he did not say anything. Ralph spoke with such certainty that both Jobe and Marius felt it might be dangerous to contradict him.

At last Marius laughed. 'If you say so, Englishman. And maybe if we ever leave this godforsaken island, we will find a ship and go to this secret bay of yours, and if it exists we will all be rich men.'

'It will not be so easy,' warned Jobe.

Marius flicked a piece of plaster at him. 'No one invited you, Kaffir.'

'How will you speak to the people there? So they do not kill you?'

'The Frenchman said that there was no one there.'

Jobe rolled his eyes. 'No people? Or no *white* people?'

'We will need an interpreter,' Ralph agreed. 'All three of us will go – equal partners.'

'Partners?' Marius shook his head. 'You are mad, *brak*.'

'I mean it. We will make our fortunes.'

Again, there was an unquestionable sureness in Ralph's voice. To hear it, you knew not only that he believed what he said: you felt you had to believe it yourself.

Marius blinked. 'Very well. Partners. And when we have our fortune, we will make an equal split, hey?'

'An equal split,' said Ralph. 'Three ways.'

Jobe spat on his palm, then held it out. Ralph did likewise. After a moment's hesitation, Marius joined in. The three men gripped one another's hands in silence, each one of them contemplating his part of the shared dream.

Then sense reasserted itself.

'Stories and nonsense,' said Marius, pulling back his hand. 'They pass the time, hey, but what else are they good for? We are still stuck on this *verdoemde* rock.'

Ralph's eyes gleamed. 'I told you. I do not intend to be here for long.'

EASTERN CAPE

Ann Waite lay on her hard bed, listening to the insects chirping in the blackness outside. Her husband, Frank, lay beside her, drowned in a deep sleep. A few feet away, she could hear the boy, Harry, snoring in the stinkwood cradle which Frank had carved for him. Night after night he had sat up in front of the fire, working on Harry's crib. It was the one thing they owned that had been made out of love rather than from necessity.

Ann's aching limbs craved the sleep she had been deprived of, but she forced herself to stay awake. These moments in the dark were the only time she had to herself. She lay awake, hands clasped over her chest, and tried to count her blessings.

It was not easy.

The first time Ann had seen their new home, she'd thought that she had gone to Heaven. Standing in a copse of trees at the top of a hill, they had looked out across their grant: whitewashed stones marked the boundaries, where government officials had surveyed the property, stretching out of sight into the blue horizon. In front of them the grant fell towards a gully where the grass grew green and lush on the banks of a stream. 'So much land,' she had said, hugging the baby and gazing at Frank joyfully. 'This is Paradise.'

'Then that is what we will name it,' Frank had replied. 'Paradise Valley.'

It had not worked out that way. Reality intruded: she and Frank learned harsh lessons every day, through a thousand setbacks and disappointments. The stream in the gully dried up; for nine months of the year there was nothing but dust. They had a hundred acres, but more than half of it was so rocky that it was impossible to farm. Frank broke and blunted his tools trying to dig it out, and had to abandon the effort. The wide grassy fields were perfect for cattle, but the governor forbade them from owning any of the animals for fear of provoking raids by the Xhosa tribes across the nearby border.

Instead, they hoed the field at the top of the slope and planted wheat. Frank dug into the stream bed in the gully and found water not far below the surface. It was back-breaking labour, hoisting the water in buckets and carrying it up the hill day after day. The path from the well, past the house and up to the field, wore into a rut from uncountable journeys Ann made with those heavy buckets.

Frank grew thin and haggard, his eyes glazed with weariness. Each night he studied his agricultural manuals by the light of the single lamp they owned, but the manuals had been written for English farmers working soft English fields. Even the points of the compass were upended. A south-facing field turned out to not be so valuable here on the far side of the equator, where the sun reached its zenith in the north.

The hardships fell on them like the strokes of a chisel, carving new lines on their bodies. Worry, pain and hunger were their constant companions. But with every challenge they overcame, a new life took shape. They built a house in the hollow at the bottom of the hill. It was a modest dwelling. Their home in Lancashire may have been a draughty, leaky cottage, but that was a palace compared to where they lived now. It was a single wood-framed room, walled with clay and thatched with reeds. Back home, it would have been no better than a sheepfold. When they lit the fire, the house filled with so much smoke Ann worried Harry would choke; in the evenings, the wind cut through the cracks in the walls. But it was their own, built with *their* hands on *their* land. Ann made it as homely as she was able with the few odds and ends they had. She sewed curtains from the tent they had arrived with and brought in fresh wild flowers, yellow proteas and fire lilies. Frank cut turfs to build a wall around the house, and Ann began creating her own garden – larger than anything she could have dreamed of back home in England. She planted the enclosure with pumpkins, carrots and cabbages, together with wild herbs that she found in the surrounding countryside. From one of their neighbours, she managed to obtain a fig tree, which she planted by the wicker gate.

The land began – gradually, obstinately – to yield to their efforts. When the first green shoots of wheat emerged from the furrows,

Ann and Frank danced in the field, spinning Harry around so that he gurgled with delight. Week by week, they watched the crop grow. Leaves emerged; they rose tall, then drooped like limp flags.

From the uppermost leaves, buds emerged. Each one sprouted into a long ear, packed with kernels that would become the precious grain. Ann, always hungry, tried to imagine how much flour it would produce. Sometimes, in the evenings, she walked between the rows of wheat, now nearly chest high, running her hands through the silky crop. She imagined the grain milled to flour and turned to a hot, golden brown loaf; she thought how it would smell fresh from the wood-fired oven, a trickle of butter – if they could get some – running over their fingers as it melted into the bread. Her belly ached with interminable hunger, but she had to be patient. She put those visions aside, and focused her attention on Harry.

As the crop grew, so did the boy. He started to sit up, and then to crawl. His body filled out; he began to smile and babble. Harry was the reason she kept working from dawn until dusk. Harry was the reason she scratched at the earth until her fingernails bled and her shoulders ached. He was the most precious gift this land had given her.

The wheat turned from deep green to yellow, almost gold under the light of the African sky. The ears ripened to fat grains. Frank was often away during those long, scorching hot months, labouring on the farms of richer men so he could buy rice and millet to feed them until they could harvest their crop. For weeks at a time, Ann had to look after Harry, water the wheat, weed the fields and tend the vegetable garden herself. Her arms grew strong from hewing wood. Often at night she lay on her straw bed, Harry hugged close beside her, and listened to the lions roaring in the distance, wondering if the mud walls and wicker door would hold off those wild beasts if put to the test.

But there were some things she could not shut out.

One morning, she walked up the rutted path to the wheat field in her bare feet, cradling Harry to her breast. Frank was away. The sun had risen over the ridge, bathing the hillside in an ochre dawn. Every rock and blade of grass seemed to glow with a numinous light. The wheat had turned from gold to rose-red. She walked across the field, carrying Harry in one arm and letting her free hand caress the budding ears of grain. Surely they must be ready to harvest soon.

Then she glanced down, and saw her hand was stained crimson and her nightdress streaked with thick red smears as if she had walked through a slaughterhouse. Where had it come from? In mounting horror, she looked at the crops around her and realised that the red was on the wheat itself, a russet powder streaking up the stalks and over the leaves like rust on a piece of iron.

At first she could not think what it might be. Then she remembered a phrase she had read in one of Frank's agricultural manuals– words to make any farmer despair.

'Rust blight,' she murmured.

It was a fungus that grew on wheat. Uncontrollable tears washed down her cheeks. When she wiped them away, she saw that they left dark red smears on her hand.

There was no remedy for this. The crop was lost.

Frank returned that evening. He was heartbroken, too, but he comforted her as best he could.

'Next year will be better.'

She felt the knot of hunger tighten in her stomach. 'If we last until then.'

They survived on the kindness of others. On the voyage out, Ann had made friends with a couple called Simon and Margaret Armstrong. Although the Armstrongs had suffered many of the same hardships as the Waites, their land was better supplied with water, and the blight had not affected their crops. Ann tried not to feel jealous of her friends' good fortune.

Frank started to work on the Armstrongs' farm, and Ann helped Margaret with her laundry and housekeeping. It earned them enough to survive the winter, and to plant a new crop of wheat in the top field. But the following spring, the blight appeared again.

'How can it have happened twice?' Ann wept. She felt as if they were suffering the ordeal of Job, that God had decided to punish them for reasons she could not fathom.

But the rust was not their only affliction. Caterpillars ate their vegetables and lice infested the cabbages. Hot winds in summer made the beans wither. After two years, they had saved enough from Frank's labour to buy a cow for milk. The owning of cattle was expressly forbidden by the governor, but Ann told herself that it was just one cow and she knew of ten other families that had done the same. But then the rains stopped, the grass went brown, and the cow starved. They had no choice but to kill it, and the beast was so thin that there was hardly any meat left on its skeletal frame.

Ann's one consolation was Harry. He was three, now: a bouncing toddler who tore around the property with mischief permanently on his mind. Many times, Ann had to rescue him from a tree he had climbed too high, or bandage up a cut knee from the rocks in the gully. She marvelled at his energy, even as she was tormented by guilt at the fact that she could not feed him enough. Every meal she gave him almost her whole portion, but it was still not enough for the growing boy.

The third spring, planting the wheat felt like an act of defiance, an assertion of hope. Every morning, when Ann carried water up to the field, she felt sick with fear at what she would find. Surely it could not happen a third year in succession. *We have endured so much*, she prayed at night. *Grant us this one mercy.*

When the red marks appeared again, she barely had tears left to weep. They burned the field, and hoed the ashes into the earth. At the little church they attended, six miles away, some of the congregation brought baskets of food or loaves they had baked for the less fortunate members of the settler community. But even these good people kept a wary distance when they thought Ann was not looking. *The Waites are bad luck*, they whispered. *They are being punished by our Lord for something they have done. Better to keep a safe distance, and avoid the taint of it.*

Even as the drought stretched on, and their Indian corn failed, and their sack of rice shrank to nothing, there was one thought

Ann never voiced: *We should return to England.* Frank had given his heart to this plot of land. To admit failure, after everything they'd endured, would break him.

Ann felt disloyal even thinking about going home. She still loved Frank, though hardship, hunger and the constraints of a one-room house had tested their marriage. But once the thought of England had sprouted in her mind, she could not dislodge it. At night she dreamed of rain and green grass, and soft butter and roast meat. And tried to count her blessings.

The sound of thunder woke her. She listened to the echo roll around the valley. As it died away, she heard another noise, a sort of rustling, so long forgotten that at first she did not recognise it. Then, with a rush of delight, she knew what it was. Rain.

Rain meant hope. It was too late for their Indian corn, but she might get some vegetables out of the garden. If there were enough, maybe she could sell some at the market in Algoa Bay.

The fat drops drummed on the roof: not Lancashire rain that you hardly felt until your skin was soaked, but African rain that fell like stones and forced its way through the feeble thatch. She felt a drop wet her face, then another. Soon water was running down the walls and pooling on the earthen floor.

More thunder crashed around the valley. Would it wake Harry? The hammering rain sounded like a stream of gravel being poured from a great height. And there was a new sound, too, a low roar so deep it seemed to shake the earth, like a peal of thunder that never faded.

She reached out to Frank, lying beside her.

'Frank . . .? Frank . . .? Wake up! What is that noise?'

He lifted his head a moment, getting his bearings. 'It must be the stream flowing in the gully.'

'Will it reach us?'

He kissed her. 'It would take a flood of Biblical proportions to threaten us here.'

Still, she wanted her child beside her. She got out of bed and crossed towards Harry's cot.

She was halfway across the room when a flash of lightning tore open the sky, illuminating the cottage through the back window.

She looked out to see the landscape bathed for a split second in the electric blue light.

Then the night went pitch-dark again, even while her mind was catching up with what her eyes had seen. The hillside had vanished, and what looked like an ocean wave was bearing down on the house.

Frank had been right – only a flood like the one described in Genesis could reach them. And it had. It was as if God had decided to once again rid the earth of sinners.

A column of water burst through the window as if someone had opened a sluice gate. There was no glass, though if there had been it would simply have shattered. Ann took the impact of the water full in her face and chest and was thrown across the room. Holes popped open in the mud wall as the water broke through.

In the darkness, she felt the water rising frighteningly fast. The room was filling up.

Ann struggled to her feet, fighting against the water that poured over her, soaking her nightdress and pinning her down. She was back in the ocean the day she found Harry, the whole world moving against her. She had to find him.

The lightening flashed again and with horror Ann realised that the water had lifted Harry's cot and was carrying it towards the door. In a moment, it would be swept out into the darkness, down into the gully and smashed to pieces.

She threw herself across the doorway, bracing her arms against the frame. The wooden cot, now a raft, bumped against her. She was all that stood between it and the storm outside.

Harry had started to scream and move about – but that only unbalanced the cot. It tipped over; Harry rolled into the water, his cry choked off as he started to sink.

Ann lunged forward. She flailed desperately in the darkness, felt Harry's body in the water and snatched for him. She managed to grab the collar of his nightshirt and drag him back to her – but she had let go of the door frame. Without that to anchor her, the weight of the flood lifted her off the ground and carried her out of the door on a surge of foaming water.

A huge crash sounded behind her. The house vanished in an explosion of spray and mud and broken wood. The wattle and clay walls had buckled and the roof had collapsed, washed away on a tide of destruction.

'Frank!' she screamed, again and again, gripping her child tightly as the surging water tossed and spun her about. Something caught her, like a web or a giant hand. It held her up so that the onrushing current broke against her. Water forced its way into her mouth and down her throat. She thought she would drown. However hard she writhed and thrashed, she could not get free.

And then she could breathe again. The water drained away. Soon it was down to her ankles.

She opened her eyes, though it made little difference. The night was too dark to see anything. Feeling around with one hand while she clutched Harry in the other, she felt the prickle of branches, and realised that the flood had carried her into the fig tree she had planted by the garden gate. If it had not caught them, she and Harry would both have been carried away down the gully. She could hear the roar of water funnelling through it, a roiling cascade.

It was dark and still raining. She lifted Harry into the fork of the tree, safely above the receding water.

'Wait here,' she ordered him. 'Hold on.'

He wrapped his arms around the trunk. Ann waded up the slope, through the swamp that had once been her garden, to the remains of the house. She heaved on the broken timbers, hauling them away one by one. She called Frank's name until her throat was dry and hoarse.

'Where are you?' she screamed. 'Frank, my darling, where are you?'

As dawn was breaking, she found him at the bottom of the heap of turf and timber, face down in the mud, limp and unmoving. A mess of blood matted the back of his head where one of the beams must have struck him. Either it had killed him in an instant, or it had knocked him unconscious so he drowned.

She sank to her knees in the mud, tears mingling with the rain on her cheeks. A terrible void numbed her limbs.

'Mummy . . .?'

Harry had disobeyed her instructions, climbed down from the tree and followed her to the ruins of their house. He stood beside her now, staring at his father's cold, bloody body. She wanted to cover his eyes – but it was too late for that.

'Oh, my angel,' she said softly, feeling the tears hot across her cheeks. She threw her arms around him, pressing her body against his. 'He has gone to the Lord's house.'

Harry squeezed her back, trying to comfort her. The gesture filled her with a wretched sadness.

'What will we do?' he asked.

The question, from her tiny child, was so forlorn and so innocent that she could not answer. All she could do was hold him tight and sing him his favourite lullaby:

I won't be my father's Jack,
I won't be my father's Jill,
I will be the fiddler's wife,
And have music when I will.

In daylight, she could see the geography of the catastrophe clearly. Near the top of the hill behind the house there was a natural terrace. They had planted their wheat there – it was the most fertile land on the grant. Rainwater had flowed from the heights above, until the wheat field became a broad lake. When it overflowed, it was with the power of a massive dam breaking. The torrent had found the path that Ann had worn carrying water up to the field, which led the water straight to the house.

Ann gathered up the few belongings she had that were still miraculously intact. There was precious little, but picking through the wreckage of the house she found the single-volume collection of Daniel Defoe's novels – *Robinson Crusoe*, *Captain Singleton*, *The King of Pirates* – that had come with them from England. Frank had bought it for the son that he had hoped for, stories of fortune and adventure on the wild shores of Africa.

It was soaked and battered, but still in one piece. She laid it reverently on a stone to dry, as if it were the holy Bible.

Ann found one of the curtains that she had sewn from the tent that they had lived in when they had first arrived, and wrapped it around herself as a makeshift dress. Her nightdress had been torn into shreds.

She searched the wreckage for their tools – picks and axes and hoes and shovels – but the flood had washed them all away, so she could not dig Frank a grave. Tears and sweat streamed from her face as she pulled rocks from the sodden ground one by one, and piled them carefully over her husband's body. Even though she knew he was gone, an irrational part of her still worried about hurting him.

'Why did you put so many stones on top of Papa?' Harry asked. 'Won't it stop him flying to Heaven?'

'His soul has already gone,' she explained. 'This is to keep his body safe.'

She made a cross from two pieces of the shattered roof beams, tied together with a length of canvas torn from the curtain. She said a tearful prayer, stumbling through the words. She felt as if she was burying half of herself. Harry held her hand, but he did not cry.

She did not remember afterwards how long she stood at Frank's grave. Eventually, the tug of Harry's hand on hers made her realise that the day was wearing on. They had no shelter, and at nightfall the lions would emerge. At the best of times it was a long walk to their nearest neighbour: with the roads washed out by the storm, and Harry to carry, it would take hours. Ann gathered her meagre belongings and started walking, knowing full well that she could live on their friends' kindness for a night or two, maybe a week, but, after that, there was nowhere to go but Algoa Bay.

At the top of the ridge she looked back into the devastated valley, which had once been her land of hope and promise. The memory of the first time she had seen it came into her mind: *This is Paradise*, she had marvelled, then. Now, there was only devastation – storm-torn mud and the grave of the man that she had called her husband.

She picked up Harry, turned away from the past and walked towards the unknown.

ROBBEN ISLAND

A swarm of flies buzzed over the filthy foam that had accumulated around the corpse of a dead seal.

Three men stood on the beach, staring at it. They had delivered their quota of stone from the quarry and were free to go where they wanted on the small island. They had come to this cove, out of sight of the barracks and the cell block.

'At least the wind keeps the stink off, hey?' said Marius.

Ralph stepped forward and knelt beside the sea creature's body. Whiskers brushed his hand; dark dead eyes gazed up at him.

'It is like a dog with no legs,' said Jobe.

It was true. With its pointed snout, black nose and short fur, the seal resembled a hound sprawled in front of a fire. Now it was fly meat. A bloody gash in its side showed the marks of enormous teeth.

'What did that?' Jobe asked.

'Shark,' said Ralph.

It was an ugly wound. The seal must have had just enough strength to escape to shore before it died.

Marius looked out to sea. 'What makes you think a shark will not do the same to a man?'

Ralph didn't answer. 'Give me your knife.'

Marius pulled out the knife which he had hidden in his waistband. It was a crude tool: the blade was an old quarry chisel, its edge sharpened, the handle a piece of bone lashed on with twine. He handed it to Ralph, who stabbed it into the seal's tough hide, ripping open a line along the belly. Wet entrails oozed onto the sand. Even the wind could not disperse the stench now. Jobe wrinkled his nose.

Ralph looked up at the other two men. His arms were soaked to the elbows in gore. 'Are you going to help me?'

Reluctantly, the others joined in. While Ralph sawed the hide away from the blubber beneath, Marius and Jobe held the edge and peeled it away. Soon the seal was reduced to a bloody mass of fat and flesh.

'And how does this help us escape?' Marius asked. 'Do we dress up like *robbe* and try to swim to Cape Town?'

Ralph examined the skin they had taken. Removed from the animal, it was smaller than he had hoped.

'We will need more.' He ran his eye along the beach. Half a dozen of the creatures lay on the shore, sunning themselves or snoozing, but he knew if he approached them they would shuffle into the sea. Centuries of being hunted by the island's visitors had taught them to fear men. 'Also, we will need needle and thread.'

By this time the sun was setting. Soon the guards would come to round them up and lock them into their cells for the night. A sickle moon pricked its point over the horizon.

'We must be ready in two weeks.'

'Why two weeks?' Marius asked.

But Ralph didn't answer – he had already turned and was walking back towards the barracks.

Two weeks later a full moon shone so bright that you could almost make out the proteas growing on the flat summit of Table Mountain across the bay. Robben Island was little more than a shadow against the silver ocean, with a prick of light where a lantern burned in the barracks. The guards inside were playing cards, for there was no point patrolling the island. All the prisoners were locked up for the night.

A hundred yards from the barracks, Ralph wormed along on his belly, the rocky ground scraping his clothes. Behind him he heard a thump, and then a curse, as Marius banged his knee on a rock.

'You make more noise than an angry elephant,' said Jobe, from the rear.

'Why are we crawling anyway?' Marius asked. 'The guards are drunk. They are too busy scratching their fat bellies. They will never look for us.'

'And what would happen if one of them glanced out of the window at the wrong moment?' Ralph asked.

The full moon left them no place to hide, but they had to take the risk. Once they were on the ocean, they would need the light to navigate by.

The last two weeks had passed in a blur of furtive activity. Every moment that they were not in the quarry, Ralph and the others had worked to pull together the pieces of his plan. They had managed to kill and skin more seals, gather wood and steal a bodkin and a length of rope, which they had pulled apart into its individual fibres. They had lashed together a wooden frame, sewn the skins into a sheet and then stretched them over the contraption. At night, Marius had used his strength to one by one work the window bars out of the wall, replacing them carefully, so they looked untouched, but leaving them loose, so that they could climb out of their cell quickly when the time came.

They reached a shallow defile that led down to the shore. In the lee of the slope, they rose to a crouch and hurried to the beach. Ralph began pulling apart a mound of branches and seaweed piled against the rocks. Underneath the seaweed lay a long, grey shape: it looked like a giant cigar, but when they lifted it, it weighed hardly anything.

Ralph and Marius carried it between them to the water. In shape and length it resembled a small canoe, though the boat's sides were so narrow that a man could barely squeeze between them, while it appeared to be less than a foot deep. The hull rippled and sagged as it moved, like an old stocking.

The men set it down at the water's edge. From under the pile of seaweed, Jobe fetched two planks that they had carved into rough paddles and a leather beer tankard stolen from the guards' mess.

Marius stood over their strange creation. He prodded it with his toe and the side buckled. 'This is more like a coffin than a boat,' he complained. 'We will be eaten by sharks before we even get halfway.'

'They that go down to the sea in ships . . . these see the works of the Lord, and his wonders in the deep,' said Jobe. Ralph was unsure if he meant it as a vote of confidence – or a desperate prayer.

The three men stared at the boat, each thinking of his own survival. Now that they were being asked to trust their lives to it, they looked with a more sceptical eye. A flimsy wooden frame covered with a patchwork sheath of sealskins, sewn together using lengths of twine that had been unpicked from a rope – the whole thing greased with seal fat until it stank like a charnel house. Ralph was the best with the needle, but his work had been hasty, and the stitches were ragged, the seams uneven.

'I once served on a ship with a man who had crewed a Yankee whaler,' said Ralph. 'One of the places this fellow had sailed to was Greenland.' A shiver went through him even now as he remembered the old mariner's tales: the hoar-frost seizing the rigging; the way the harpoon point would bind to your skin if you touched it with your bare hand. 'He told me the natives in Greenland make their boats like this. You swear they should sink, but in fact they float like corks.'

'A cork in a bottle full of stones thrown into the sea, maybe,' said Marius.

'You are free to stay if you want.' Ralph snapped. 'Even these lazy guards sometimes get off their arses to go out for a piss. If they find us out of the barracks at night, we will be in solitary confinement until we rot.'

He waded out into the inlet, dragging the canoe with him. Jobe followed. A moment later, Marius came too. Ralph held the boat steady while the Dutchman climbed in. The moment his weight settled, it started to sink. Water bubbled through cracks in the seams. Marius howled and began thrashing about, trying to lift himself out. The boat capsized, tipping him into the water.

It was not deep. He struggled to his feet, shaking himself like a wet dog.

'Quiet,' Ralph hissed. 'You will bring every guard on the island.'

'I am not getting in that again,' said Marius. 'It will drown us all.'

Ralph did not respond. He flipped the boat over to let out the water, then righted it again. The frame was so light it was easy to handle. Carefully, he lowered himself in and tucked up in the stern.

'All she needs is a gentle touch,' Ralph said, more to himself than to reassure the other men.

Jobe got in the front. Marius hesitated.

'Trust in Jesus,' Ralph said to Marius with a grin. 'Did He not save the fishermen when their boat was sinking in a storm?'

Jobe glowered at him. 'That is blasphemy,' he said. 'And you are not Him.'

'Indeed not,' said Ralph. 'If I were, I could walk on water and there would be no need for this boat.' He raised his paddle, ready to go. 'Are you coming, Marius?'

With a grunt, Marius climbed into the boat again – more gingerly, this time. The seal pelts strained at their crooked seams; the vessel sank so low that the water almost came over its gunwales.

Ralph passed Marius the cup. He peered inside it.

'What is this for?'

'If you do not want us to drown, bale as if your life depended on it.'

It was a clear, bright, still night. The sea was calm, and the moon laid a path of shimmering iridescence across the water. Even so, the moment they left the cove the waves threatened to swamp the canoe. Ralph and Jobe paddled as fast as they could with their makeshift paddles, riding the long Cape swells, while Marius scooped out water and muttered prayers.

But gradually they mastered their craft. They learned to read her motion, to balance the tempo of their strokes, to keep her straight and upright. Even Marius managed to make his move-ments less panicked, though he could hardly keep ahead of the water seeping in. The vessel was still a beast – too low, too heavy, too slow, nothing like the graceful craft Ralph had heard described by his shipmate. But she kept afloat.

Jobe tipped back his head and let out a whoop of delight and laughter. Ralph glanced over his shoulder, but they were far enough from the island that no one could have heard them.

'We are free!'

The flat-topped bulk of Table Mountain loomed against the stars. Ralph kept it to his right, aiming for the beach at Blaauw-berg. It was the nearest landfall, and also safe as it was well outside Cape Town.

They paddled on. Ralph's arms began to ache from the effort; blisters rose on his hands, but he ignored the pain and kept going.

'Are we going backwards?' Marius asked. 'The mountains never get any closer.'

'Then do not look at them,' snapped Ralph. But it was hard to take his eyes off them. He continued staring, willing them to come nearer. 'And keep still,' he added, as the boat suddenly lurched over.

'I did not move,' said Marius. 'It was a wave.'

Ralph was about to retort that the sea was calm. But then he felt it – a ripple passing through the soft hull. A dome of white water began to bubble up on the sea to his left.

'Hold on,' Ralph shouted.

The sea erupted. A dark shape flew up out of the water like a cannonball – but infinitely more massive, as big as a ship. Droplets of water flew from its skin in a shower of silver, while its blubbery body quivered with the effort of hoisting itself into the air.

It climbed against the sky, blocking the moon; Ralph saw its long flippers extended wide as wings, as if it were about to take flight. For a moment, the enormous sea creature seemed to defy gravity and hang in the air.

It was a humpback whale. Ralph had seen them before, though that did not lessen the awe and terror of the sight. Even seen from the safety of the deck of a solidly built ship, the creature made brave men tremble. Here, there was nothing between it and Ralph except a thin layer of sealskin.

The whale could not stay upright for long – no more than a moment. Its back bent in the distinctive hump that earned it its name. Its flippers arced around; its body curved forward towards the water, glistening in the moonlight. For such a leviathan, it was a beautiful, miraculously supple manoeuvre.

But even with the grace of a ballerina, fifty tons of whale meat hitting the ocean caused more than a ripple. The sea exploded. Spray fountained into the air, while an enormous wave raced away in all directions.

Ralph knew it was coming and had already begun to react. He dug in his paddle and spun the canoe around, so that its stern turned to where the whale had been, just as the wave reached them. If it had struck them broadside, it would have rolled the boat over like a log; instead, it lifted them up and carried them forward on its crest.

'Paddle!' Ralph shouted. Not for speed, but to keep them upright. They wielded the paddles frantically, thrusting them far out to balance the boat. For a moment, Ralph thought they might capsize. But the wave slowed as it spread; the sea settled. Ralph's breathing began to return to normal.

'That was a monster, hey?' said Marius. His hand shook as he emptied another mug of water over the side. 'I thought we would go down like poor Jonah.'

'We were lucky,' Ralph agreed. He felt light-headed with relief and elation. The surge had pushed them far ahead, so that the Blaauwberg mountains seemed closer than ever. 'Hopefully we will have no more excitements tonight.'

As if to mock him, an orange light flashed from the mountain's flank. A few seconds later, a low boom came rolling across the sea. The boat lurched as all three men looked up, startled.

'That was a cannon,' said Ralph. The flash had come from Signal Hill, where a watch post overlooked the harbour. Surely they could not have seen Ralph's tiny canoe from there. As the minutes stretched by, he allowed himself to believe it had been something else: a ship in distress, or a false alarm.

Another cannon rang across the water, this time from Robben Island behind them. The signal gun must have alerted the guards. They had checked the cells and found one empty. Now there was no doubting it: they knew about the escape.

Ralph cursed his luck. The breaching whale must have caught the attention of the lookout on Signal Hill. He would have trained his spyglass on it, and seen the vessel lifted high out of the water on the wave. Surely a chance in a thousand – a bored lookout, the whale and a night so clear that you could see what the governor was eating for dinner from a three hundred yards through his dining room window.

Ralph listened to the night, trying to block out the noise the paddles made. Over to the right, he could see the glow of watch fires from the castle that guarded Cape Town. Had they heard the alarm? Would they be saddling up to come and catch the fugitives when they reached shore?

He was listening so intently, he almost missed the sound that mattered. A dull roar, ever present, getting gradually louder. The sound of surf. He peered forward and saw a line of white foam in the moonlight where waves broke on an empty beach.

'We are nearly there!' he exulted.

Dark points glistened like daggers in the water where rocks jutted out. Ralph and Jobe paddled with renewed energy, pushing the boat faster. The waves rose as they approached the beach, spilling more water into the boat. The cup for baling was pitifully inadequate. Marius pumped his arms like a madman.

And then suddenly they were overboard. Whether it was a rock, or a wave, or Marius's frantic motion – or whether the boat finally gave way at the seams – one moment Ralph was paddling, with the beach only twenty yards away; the next he was underwater, being spun about like a rag in a storm.

He kicked out and broke the surface, spitting salt water as he searched for his companions. Jobe had clung to his oar and was using it to keep afloat. But there was no sign of Marius – except a thrashing spout of foam away to Ralph's left.

Marius was a big, strong man but he could not swim. He splashed and kicked, got his head above water for a second, and then sank back.

With two strokes, Ralph reached the drowning man. He was welcomed by Marius's flailing elbow. He ducked under it, snaked his arm around Marius's shoulders and lifted. Even in the water, the Dutchman's weight was immense. While he writhed and struggled, Ralph could not support him.

If Marius could not keep still, he would drown them both. Ralph drew back his free arm and punched Marius hard in his face.

The Dutchman went limp. Before he could recover, Ralph hoisted him up and swam inshore with brisk scissor kicks. Soon his feet touched the bottom. Supporting Marius, he staggered out of the water and up onto the beach.

Jobe was already there. He pointed to their right. Firelight glowed from the end of the beach, beyond the dunes, moving fast. Ralph heard the jangle of harness.

'We will not enjoy our freedom long if we stand about looking at each other.' Marius was conscious again. Ralph stepped away, but the moment he let go the Dutchman staggered and sat down on the sand.

'Is he hurt?' Jobe asked.

'He hit his head on a rock,' said Ralph as Marius rubbed his face, bewildered.

The firelight was coming over the dunes.

'We must go at once!' commanded Ralph.

He took three steps towards the dunes – and stopped. In the soft sand, his footprints left a trail that even a child could follow.

Was this what it had all been for? To be tracked like a hunted animal. He would not even make fifty paces before he was caught. And then they would hang him. He could hear the unmistakable drum of hooves as the horses approached the three of them. Soon they would be in rifle range – and then he would not even have the chance to run.

He looked around his surroundings desperately. A little way along the beach, a stream flowed out from the dunes and debouched into the sea. At the sight of the stream, Ralph knew instantly what he must do next.

He looked at Jobe. 'Do you trust me?'

Jobe's eyes gave nothing away. 'Why?'

Ralph pointed down the beach. 'I want you to run.'

Jobe cocked his ear towards the horses. 'I will not escape.'

'No,' Ralph agreed. 'But while you distract them, Marius and I can make it to the dunes.'

Jobe's face was full of fury. Again, Ralph glimpsed the fierce pride in the man's soul. 'So, you escape and I go back to gaol?'

'No,' said Ralph. 'Either we all go, or none of us goes.'

Marius picked himself up and started to say something, but Ralph cut him off. He kept his gaze fixed on Jobe.

'How do I know you will come back?' Jobe asked.

'That is why you have to trust me,' said Ralph firmly.

Lieutenant Alexander Preston, commander of the watch at the castle, heard the cannon fire from Signal Hill and assumed it must be a ship in distress. But the night was still, and when he looked out from the castle he couldn't see a vessel that appeared to be in any sort of difficulty.

Then a runner came sprinting down the hill from the battery with an astonishing report. A boat had been seen sailing from Robben Island; a prisoner – or prisoners – had escaped.

'Are you certain it was not fishermen?' Preston enquired. But then a second gun fired, this time from Robben Island, confirming the messenger's report. The commandant must have been roused by the cannon fire and found some prisoners missing.

Preston could not see the boat, but the runner from the look-out post assured him it was making for the beach at Blaauwberg. Preston gathered his troop of cavalry and rode out.

Now he reined up on the promontory overlooking the beach. He gazed down intently, but saw nothing. The moon had gone behind a cloud. The pitch torches his men carried did not cast light more than twenty yards ahead. Beyond, and all around, the whole shoreline was in darkness.

He drew his sabre. If the fugitives had managed to escape the island, they might have managed to arm themselves too, Preston thought. He led the troop down an embankment and out onto the sand, letting the horses pick their way with care.

'Spread out,' he ordered. 'We will sweep this beach from end to end.'

At that moment, the cloud passed from the moon. Preston could see no sign of a boat, but in the distance, about a quarter of a mile away, he saw a lone figure silhouetted against the silvered sand.

He waved his sword. This would be as easy as coursing a hare, he thought.

'After him!' he commanded.

The troop spurred into a gallop. The moon guided them along the beach, giving the riders a clear run and their quarry no place to hide. The distance closed swiftly. 'It is too easy,' Preston murmured. Almost a waste of his time – no chase, no sport. Maybe the man would offer a bit of fight, give Preston an excuse to exercise his sword-arm. He was close enough now to see that the fugitive was a black man. Preston was flabbergasted that the man had had enough wit and courage to get off the island.

The man heard the horses pounding at his heels. It was evident he could not outrun them. He turned and dropped to his knees. Preston drew up in front of him and looked down on him as if he were a cowering dog, and Preston a god on high.

'Did you really think you could escape your black arse from His Majesty's justice?' He trotted his horse in a circle around the prisoner. The man was still dripping wet. 'How did you get here, you piece of filth?'

The man looked up sullenly. *He has an impertinent face*, Preston thought, *looking a white man in the eye as if they were equals*. No wonder he had ended up on Robben Island.

'Boat,' said the prisoner as one of Preston's dragoons dismounted and began to tie his hands.

'I see no boat.'

'Sank.'

It was plausible.

'Were there others with you?' Preston asked.

'Sir!' called one of his dragoons before the prisoner could answer, pointing at the dunes that rose behind the beach.

The trooper wheeled his horse away. A man stood on top of one of the hillocks, caught in the moonlight. Who was he? How had he got there?

Either he was a conspirator who had come to help the prisoner make his escape, or he was a confederate. The sight of him standing there, gazing down at the cavalry, was an insult, a silent challenge to Preston.

'You and you' – he pointed to the two men nearest – 'go and capture that ruffian now.'

As soon as they moved, the man vanished into the dunes. The troopers could not pursue him on horseback: in the dark, and with the uneven footing, they would risk breaking the animals' legs. They dismounted, leaving the horses untethered as there was no tree to tie them to, and followed the man into the dunes on foot.

Preston and the other three men waited. The pitch torches burned low, spooking the horses with their smoke until the flames guttered out. They waited in the moonlight, expecting any moment to hear shouts of victory or – more conclusively – the sound of a carbine.

Minutes passed. No sound came – just the sound of the waves breaking gently on the shore and the occasional nickering of the horses.

Preston started to get impatient. What were his well-trained men doing? Surely they could not have lost their target in the dunes in this moonlight. The fugitive would have left deep footprints, and he had not been far enough ahead to outrun them. The possibility of a single prisoner – soaking, hungry and exhausted – overpowering two armed men did not enter his mind.

He still had three armed men with him. 'All of you, go and see what they are doing,' Preston shouted impatiently. 'I will guard this filthy black swine myself.'

The troopers dismounted and followed the tracks that led into the dunes. Preston looked down at the captive. The man did not appear to intend any mischief – he knelt in the sand, hands bound, staring at the dunes – but there was a self-possession about him that offended the cavalry officer.

A white flash lit up the dunes. It blinded Preston for a moment, even as his ears were deafened by the sound of a shot. A few minutes later, two men came walking out of the dunes, dragging what looked like a corpse between them.

They let the body drop on the ground, mounted their horses and began to trot over to Preston.

Preston squinted. They must be his men – who else could they be? He could see their white crossbelts glowing in the moonlight, and the gleaming steel of their carbines. Yet they both looked bigger than any of his men, particularly the man on the right. And the man on the left seemed to be having difficulty controlling his horse.

At his feet, the prisoner started to move. Distracted, Preston glanced down, then jerked his head up again as he heard the drum of hooves. One of the troopers' horses had suddenly gathered speed, charging straight at Preston. The man was almost on him, so close that as he lifted his head out of shadow Preston could see his face with clarity.

It was not one of his troopers. It was a ragged-looking man, galloping towards him like a raging animal.

When they left Jobe, Ralph and Marius splashed up the little stream that flowed out from the dunes. The water and the soft sand slowed them, but it also covered their tracks well. At first Ralph had to help Marius walk, but the hard-headed Dutchman soon recovered his strength and strode ahead.

They crouched in the shadows among the dunes and watched as the dragoons reached Jobe.

'Maybe we leave him here, hey?' Marius suggested. 'The British don't know how many men they are looking for. They catch one, they think their work is done, they go home.'

'I gave him my word.' Ralph bent down and prised out three stones, each roughly the size of a nine-pound cannonball. He tossed one to Marius. 'Now hide yourself in that hollow, and wait for my signal.'

Marius hefted the rock. 'What am I meant to do with this?'

'Use your big, empty head and work it out. Now, be quiet.'

Ralph scrambled up to the top of the dunes. For a moment the sky was dark, and he feared the dragoons would not see him; but then the clouds parted and the moon illuminated him like a stage light. One of the dragoons pointed to him; two of them spurred their horses towards him.

Two was a good number. Ralph waited another second, then ran down the dune and threw himself prone in the sea grass. He waited, rubbing his fingers over the rocks he held, feeling every groove and whorl. He heard a horse's whinny, the thuds of men dismounting, and then cautious footsteps.

Wait. He had fought in enough skirmishes to know how a man's mind could play tricks, how time could become scrambled. He had to judge the right moment to strike. If he showed himself too late, he would lose his chance to disarm the cavalrymen. If he showed himself too soon, he would get a bullet in his head.

Ralph did not intend to die that night. He forced himself to lie still until he could hear the crunch of the dragoons' boots on the sand, their ammunition pouches thudding against their thighs as they walked. Then he rose out of the dunes and, in a single motion, hurled a rock with all his strength at the nearest man. The dragoon was taken by complete surprise, no chance to defend himself. The rock struck the side of his head and he fell to the ground instantly.

His companion turned towards Ralph, bringing up his carbine. As he did, Marius emerged out of the hollow where he had been hiding and snaked his arm around the man's chest. With the other hand, he smashed his rock against the man's temple. Ralph heard his skull crack.

Ralph ran to the two dragoons. The man he had felled was dazed but not unconscious; he had already started to move again. Ralph pulled off his crossbelts and used them to bind his hands and feet before he could fight back.

The man Marius had hit stayed motionless. Blood oozed from the side of his head.

'You only needed to knock him out,' Ralph said mildly.

'If they sentence me to seven years breaking rocks, they should not be surprised my arms are strong.' Marius glanced back towards the beach. The high dunes hid them well, and their attack had been so fast and quiet that the other troopers below had surely not heard it. 'Are there more?'

'Four more,' said Ralph.

'Too many,' Marius fretted.

'We'll let them come to us and take our chances.'

They stripped the dragoons of their carbines, then dragged them into the grass. Ralph kicked sand over the tracks to hide them. Then he and Marius returned to their cover.

Soon Ralph heard more men approaching. Three of them, more cautious this time, with their carbines already raised.

'Bill?' the leading soldier called. 'Where are you?'

'Something happened,' said a second man.

Ralph swore under his breath. The dragoon was pointing to scuff marks on the ground, where Ralph had not managed to hide his tracks well enough – the moon was too bright. The man peered into the surrounding dunes, ready to shoot.

'Come out,' he called. 'I know you're there.'

Ralph pressed himself even lower to the ground. He could feel his heart racing, thudding against the sand. He lined up the carbine through the grass, though he was reluctant to use it. All three of the dragoons were now looking in his direction, and he only had one shot.

He heard the click of a hammer being drawn back, and closed his eyes.

The sand muted the sound of the shot, but the flash lit up the dunes like lightning. Ralph saw the glare through his closed eyelids. The moment it had passed, his eyes snapped open.

Marius had shot one of the dragoons. The two survivors looked around wildly, swinging their guns left and right. The unexpected glare of the gunshot had temporarily blinded them. As Ralph sprang up out of the sea grass, he was just a blur of movement in the darkness to them. He slammed the butt of his carbine into the first man's face, pivoted, and put the barrel against the base of the other man's spine.

'I do not want to kill you, but I will if I have to,' Ralph cautioned him.

The young dragoon dropped his carbine and sank to his knees. He could only be eighteen or nineteen, Ralph thought. He had joined the army for glory and adventure, not to die chasing convicts on a godforsaken African beach.

Marius came up holding the hot, smoking carbine. 'We make a good pair,' he observed. Metal rasped on metal as he rammed another bullet home and primed the carbine. He put it to his shoulder and aimed it at the back of the kneeling dragoon's head.

'No!' Ralph snatched it away before Marius could pull the trigger.

'We killed two already.' Marius gestured to the man he had clubbed, and the one he had shot. 'They can only hang us once.'

'We are not butchers,' Ralph spat. 'It is enough unnecessary slaughter.'

Marius did not argue. They stripped, bound and gagged the two dragoons who were still alive, then donned their uniforms. The red coat was so tight across Marius's shoulders he ripped the seams while pulling it on.

They walked out of the dunes, dragging one of the dead men between them. They let him fall where the dragoon lieutenant could see, then mounted the horses and rode towards him. Ralph hoped the darkness was enough to disguise their distinctly un-cavalrylike horsemanship.

The officer wheeled to meet them. Ralph spurred his horse faster. The officer must have sensed that something was wrong; he started to raise his sabre, but Ralph's sudden charge had caught him by surprise and he was closing too fast. As Ralph cantered past, he swung the carbine's butt hard into the officer's ribs. The lieutenant was knocked out of his saddle. The sword flew from his hand onto the sand. Jobe ran forward and snatched it up. His wrists were bound, so he clasped it with both hands and advanced on the lieutenant where he lay prone on the sand.

'No!' Ralph shouted, leaping from his horse and stepping between Jobe and Preston. 'If you kill the officer, the British will never forget it. They will chase us all the way across the Orange River if they have to. We spare his life, perhaps they will let us go.'

Jobe lowered the sabre. Lying on the ground, Preston promised himself that if he survived, he would hunt these men to the ends of Africa if need be.

Ralph guessed that they did not have long before the garrison came to see what had happened to their men. Working in haste, he untied Jobe's bonds and used them to bind the lieutenant. They took Preston's sword and pistol and ammunition pouch, together with the carbines and cartridges they had stripped off the soldiers in the dunes. Then they mounted up, leading the spare horses on halters behind them.

They rode north-east, towards the looming bulk of the Hottentots Holland Mountains. But as soon as they were out of sight of the beach, and on hard ground where their tracks would not show, Ralph turned his mount's head east.

'This is not the way to the Orange River,' said Marius, riding beside Ralph.

'That was for the officer. With luck, the lieutenant will report what he heard, and they will waste precious days looking for us in the wrong part of the country.'

'Then where do we go?' Jobe asked.

Their plan had been to land unnoticed, steal into Cape Town harbour and cut out a small boat. Now that the castle was alerted, that path was impossible.

'We are going where we always said we would. To the land where ivory grows on trees and gold flows out of the ground.'

'You are a dreamer, *brak*. How can we go there now, with half the *rooinek* cavalry in the Colony chasing us?'

'We will find a ship. We just have to go a little further to find it.'

Marius stared at Ralph. Then he tipped back his head and laughed. 'You are a madman,' he pronounced. 'But I will go with you.' He kicked his horse's flanks, driving it to a gallop. Ralph spurred after him, came alongside and leaned out to grab Marius's reins.

'Save the horse's strength,' he advised. 'We have a long way to ride.'

ALGOA BAY

After the catastrophe at Paradise Valley, Ann and Harry had made their way to their closest neighbours, her friends, Simon and Margaret Armstrong. Margaret had immediately led them to the spare room, given them fresh clothes and more food than they had eaten in a month; for days she sat with Ann, holding her hand while Ann wept and grieved for Frank.

But after a week, Simon began to make comments about Ann moving on. He presented the idea compassionately, but there was a sharp point underneath his concern. 'Frank would not want you to live off our charity forever. It will be good for you to make a new beginning with your life beyond these lands.'

'This was my new beginning,' retorted Ann.

The thought of returning to Paradise Valley made her shake with dread. Even if she'd had the strength to rebuild the house and farm by herself – which she did not – she could not live there again. She looked to Margaret for support, but Margaret was suddenly mute. It was clear that a conversation had taken place between husband and wife and that Margaret had lost the argument. A decision had been made and there was nothing that Margaret could do to help Ann.

'God will find you the right path,' said Margaret warmly, but she didn't look up from her embroidery.

'I can earn my keep, if that is your concern,' Ann pleaded. 'I can wash and cook and clean, as I did before.'

'That would be unbecoming.' Margaret pointed out of the window, where a black woman in an apron was sweeping the yard. 'We have Kaffirs to do that for us now.'

Ann knew that her time with the Armstrongs was coming to an end. Her time living at Paradise Valley was over. 'Would you buy the farm from me?'

Margaret glanced at Simon. 'It is not yours to sell,' he explained. 'Because you did not occupy it for long enough, it reverts to the government.' He cleared his throat. 'I spoke to the land agent today, as it happens. He has agreed to transfer the plot to me.'

'So you see, you would not wish to stay with us in any event,' said Margaret. 'It would remind you too much of your loss, and your dear husband.'

Ann felt as if her skin was on fire. After all the hardships she had endured, all the sacrifices she had made, she was going to leave with nothing. She felt light-headed, the same emptiness she had felt when she saw the rust on the wheat. 'Then Harry and I will not impose on your hospitality any longer.'

'It is for the best,' said Simon, philosophically.

The Armstrongs gave her a small purse of money. Desperation outweighed Ann's pride and made her take it, though when she looked inside there was such a tiny amount that she wished she had refused. Her pride reasserted itself and Ann insisted that she and Harry would walk to Algoa Bay – a three-day trip by foot. Mercifully, a Boer farmer passed them on the road and let them ride into town in his ox wagon. It wasn't much faster than walking, but it did mean that they only spent a single night beneath the stars, huddled together for warmth, listening to the oxen pulling at the grass and the old farmer snoring after too much brandy.

When, finally, after a day and a half of travelling, Ann and Harry had reached Algoa Bay, Ann was astounded by how much things had changed. The last time she had set eyes on the bay there had been no buildings save the fort, and a few hundred tents hastily pitched on the foreshore. The town had been improved since then. The governor had named it Port Elizabeth, after his late wife. The government had built a customs house, and private enterprise had supplied a *winkel*: a building that managed to cram the functions of tavern, gaming hall, bank, brothel and general dealer under one small roof. A few thatched houses had replaced the tents. Otherwise, there was little to see. The only semblance of a port were the men who loitered by the longboats drawn up on the beach, ready to unload any vessels that called in on their way to or from India, which didn't happen often. This was the far eastern edge of British settlement in South Africa. Beyond it lay hundreds of miles of unexplored and uncharted coast, marked only by the wrecks of the vessels that had ventured too close.

But that day, there was a ship in the harbour. She was not like the great Indiamen that could sometimes be seen out to sea: she was a simple two-masted brig, with low decks and functional lines. A coastal trader; a beast of burden. To anyone with a nautical eye, it was clear she had many voyages behind her – and not too many ahead. The thick paint on her stern suggested she had carried various names in her life; now she went by *Farewell*. Her crew were busy hoisting aboard casks of gunpowder from the longboat moored alongside.

'Mummy, that big ship . . .' Harry, standing beside Ann on the foreshore, pointed at the ship. 'Where is she going?'

Her boy knew about ships from the stories Frank had read him from Daniel Defoe, and was fascinated by them. When Ann had told him they would actually see ships at Port Elizabeth, he had bombarded her with questions all the way to Algoa Bay. Ann had answered as much as she could, struggling to remember details of the voyage from England.

'I do not know where she is going, my darling.' Ann watched the ship with a yearning so strong she felt sick. She was desperate to be on it, to escape with her son and leave this unfortunate land.

But how would she afford it?

Ann went to the governor's office at the fort, where she and Harry queued in the sun for three hours to see someone, anyone who might be able to help them. Eventually, a minor clerk with bad breath and five different inkwells lined up in front of him on his desk received her. Even after hearing the account of her devastation, he exuded not an ounce of pity – he had been hardened by the stories he heard each and every day.

'The government has been more than generous, Mrs Waite,' he said, without looking up from the parchment in front of him. 'Tools, seed, land – everything that was promised. We cannot pay your passage back to England after incurring so much expense. We are not a charity. It is not our fault that your husband could not make his farm bear fruit.' He tapped the end of his quill against the cap of one of his ink pots. 'Of course, we are sorry for your loss.'

His callous dismissal made Ann flush with shame and anger. But emotion would not put food in Harry's belly, or a roof over their heads. The few coins the Armstrongs had given her would not even pay for a single night's lodgings. Ann had to think and act. She had no possessions except Frank's book of Daniel Defoe, and there was little value put on books in Port Elizabeth even if she had been willing to sell it.

Harry slipped free of her hand, ran down to the water's edge and started throwing stones into the waves. It was the place where he had entered Ann's life three years earlier, though he did not know it. Looking at him now playing with such joy, in his bare feet and the too-big smock she had been loaned by Margaret Armstrong, she ached with the need to keep him safe.

Ann looked down the beach. At the end, past the lightermen and the drying fishing nets, stood a low shack, the *winkel*. Ann knew from its reputation what happened there, and as a married Christian woman had never set foot in such an establishment.

Angry, frustrated, hungry and frightened, she walked towards it.

Ralph Courtney stood at his table in the corner of the *winkel*, one hand holding his drink and the other on the pistol in his belt. His hat was pulled down low to cover his face, though from under the brim his eyes missed nothing as they scanned the room. It was late afternoon, and the *winkel* was already half full, loud with talk and laughter.

It was a humble place: bare, lime-plastered walls and a rough earth floor. A few upturned barrels served as tables; more barrels stood on a shelf at the back. Otherwise, there was just the sturdy bar, and a stuffed leather chair in the corner from which Mrs Robinson – the *winkel*'s landlady, proprietor, and madam – presided. She kept a small dog curled up on her lap and usually had a pipe in her hand.

Marius stood by the door, monitoring every man who walked in. Jobe was outside, watching the road. They had arrived at Port Elizabeth that morning after a week's desperate riding from Cape Town, pausing only for new mounts whenever they could steal them. Ralph did not fool himself that he was far ahead of the soldiers pursuing them. Word spread fast in Africa, and three men breaking out of the inescapable prison that was Robben Island would be news all the way to the frontier.

He forced himself to relax and concentrate on what the man on the other side of the table was saying to him.

'I have sailed that coast a dozen times, and I would swear on the Book of Judgement that there is no harbour there.' The speaker's name was Thaddeus Conway, and he was the master of the ship in the bay. Like his vessel, he was nearing the end of his career. His coat was threadbare, his shirt dappled with red wine stains. His unkempt hair was neither fashionably long nor respectably short, while his two chins wobbled when he spoke.

'The bay is there,' said Ralph. 'I have seen it on a map.'

'Then show me the map.'

'It was lost,' said Ralph. His hand crept to the scars on his right cheek. 'My present circumstances do not allow me to retrieve it.'

'Alas.' The captain's expression spoke his feelings plainly: Ralph was a fraud or a fantasist, and either way there could be no profit dealing with him. He began to back away.

Before he could move, Ralph's hand shot out and grabbed Conway's wrist. 'I studied that map,' Ralph hissed. 'I know every bearing, every position and every sounding marked on it. I could find the bay with my eyes closed. All I need is a ship to take me there.'

Thaddeus Conway had spent more than thirty years at sea. He had risen from a fo'c's'le hand to be master of his own vessel, and fought his way up each rung of that ladder. He had bargained, haggled and argued against the most unyielding merchants to be found in every port from Aceh to Dahomey. Yet none of them had left him as uncomfortable as this man, with his ice-blue eyes and his horribly disfigured face. It made Conway even more certain that he did not want the man aboard his ship. But it also made him afraid to refuse.

'How much profit do you make in a season?' Ralph asked. 'And how many more voyages do you think your ship will make before her bottom rots?' He leaned closer. 'Do this, and you will be able to retire in comfort wherever takes your pleasure.'

'How much are you offering?' Conway asked.

'To take me . . . not much. I have three good horses outside. I will sell them to pay for my passage.' Ralph saw Conway losing interest again. 'You are sailing past where I want to go in any event. All I am asking is that you take me with you and put in to see if this bay exists. If it does not, then what I have paid will compensate you for your time. But if it does . . .'

He had let go of Conway's wrist. The captain did not pull away.

'That is virgin land,' Ralph continued. 'Ripe fruit ready for the plucking. You will leave us there and return six months later. By that time, either we will be dead – or we will be the richest men in Africa.'

For a moment, Conway seemed to be staring into the far distance. Then he blinked. 'How do I know you will honour the bargain?'

'Because everything that we find – ivory, hides, gold, gems – it will all be worthless until we put it up for sale in Cape Town. You are our only way out. When you return for us, you will be able to name your price.'

Ralph's eyes fixed on Conway's. He was so absolutely certain that the captain could not doubt what he said.

'The government forbids all settlement and exploration beyond the frontiers,' Conway pointed out.

'So they do.' Ralph shrugged. 'I was led to believe that you are a man who is not too *nice* about the letter of the law.'

Conway accepted the point. It was true that the *Farewell*'s registry papers would not bear close inspection; and there was plenty of cargo in his hold that – by some oversight – lacked the proper tax stamps.

Still, he hesitated. He was tempted by Ralph's proposition, fantastical as it was. But he had not survived three decades in the cut-throat waters of the Indian Ocean without a keen sense of danger. With Ralph, that sense was clanging like a fire bell.

'I do not even know your name.'

'Ralph Courtney!'

The name rang out in the *winkel*, clear above the din in the room. But it was not Ralph who had spoken. A woman stood facing him, staring in open-mouthed shock.

Ralph stared back. There were plenty of women in the world who might want to accost him, but of this one he had no memory.

She wore a tired, old-fashioned dress, and a small child trailed behind her. Her hands were calloused and scabbed; her bare arms covered in bruises. Obviously, she was a beggar who had pushed her way into the *winkel* in hope of a few coins. Ralph would not have given her a second glance.

But how did she know his name?

He looked at the boy. Was he part of the answer? A bastard Ralph had left behind? With his shock of dark hair, and his deep brown skin, he did not look like Ralph.

'You are Ralph Courtney,' the woman said. She tipped back his hat, revealing the burn marks on his face. 'I would know you anywhere.'

'A friend of yours?' Conway asked.

Ralph shook his head. The woman's eyes widened. 'Have you forgotten?'

'I do not think we have ever met.'

'On the beach – the boat – the day we arrived.' She clutched his arm, and though her hands were small her grip was desperate. 'I saved you.'

All the power in Ralph's gaze melted away. The scars on his face pulsed like a living organ. A curtain opened in his mind, though the window of memory was dim. After weeks in the open boat he had been half dead, his mind crazed by hunger and guilt. He remembered the woman's presence as a blur. He could not remember her face.

She knew his name. There was no other explanation.

'You were there,' he whispered. 'And him . . .' He looked at the boy, who was studying him with a frank and fearless expression. 'He was the boy.'

Ann nodded, a warning in her eyes. She had mothered Harry as her own son and never told him the truth about how she found him. She could not let him learn it now, this way.

'Help me,' she said. 'I have nothing. Three years ago, I saved you from the sea. Surely God has put you here now to rescue me.'

'I doubt that God has much interest in my movements,' said Ralph, collecting some of his poise. 'And I am not in a position to rescue anyone.'

'Please. If you have one ounce of Christian charity in your heart.'

'Not nearly so much.'

But Ralph's words were lost as the boy suddenly piped up: 'Who is that man?'

Ralph did not wait for Ann to answer. The other customers in the tavern had noticed their confrontation. His name had been spoken twice, and that was at least once too often for a man in his situation. If the news of his escape from Robben Island had not already reached Port Elizabeth, it would come soon enough, and then there would be a great deal of interest in the name of Ralph Courtney.

'Let us talk outside,' he said. He turned to Conway, who had listened to the exchange in astonished silence. 'Do we have a bargain?'

Conway had hoped Ralph might be distracted enough to leave him alone. But at the same time, Ralph's promises had ignited a fire in him. The captain wanted to refuse, but one phrase would not stop echoing in his mind: *The richest men in Africa.*

'We sail tomorrow.'

'I will be there.'

With Ann still clinging to his arm, Ralph steered her away from the table and through the door, with Marius and Harry in tow. He did not stop until they were on the beach.

'How did you find me?'

'I went to the *winkel* looking for work. I never dreamed you would be there.'

'It does not matter.' Ralph knew the real answer: it was fate. He had spent his life trying to escape it, but it always dragged him back to where he belonged.

Harry had squatted down on the sand and was excavating a hole with his hands. Ralph could not bring himself to look at the boy. Instead, he forced his attention on to Ann. She had been pretty, and would be still with decent clothes and a few meals to fill her out. Her long brown hair was tied back in a simple braid, and though there were lines in the corners of her eyes they only made her seem wise beyond her years. If she ever smiled again, her face would light up with beauty.

At the moment, her eyes held nothing but agonising pain. It was obvious she had suffered unbearably, but Ralph did not ask her about the course her life had taken. He could not let her become his responsibility.

'Three years ago you and I met in this bay, on this beach. We met under difficult circumstances. But that does not mean that we have anything in common. There is nothing between us now.'

'There is your boy!' Ann exclaimed.

Harry had gone off again and was running in circles to make himself dizzy.

'I told you before, he is not mine.'

'You saved his life.'

'We survived the same ordeal. That is a different thing. I gave him to you – he is yours now.'

Ann took a step back. A light had kindled in her eyes, the fierce glow of anger. 'How can you be so cruel?' she said. 'Have you never been desperate? Did you never find yourself with nothing – your home lost, your loved ones torn away?'

'Desperate?' Ralph echoed. 'You do not know what I have suffered. But I have survived.'

'Surely, not without the kindness of strangers,' Ann snapped at him, her face burning with rage.

'I have nothing to give you. The clothes on my back – that is all I own.'

'I heard you speaking to that captain. You have enough to buy a passage away from here.'

'I bought it on promises and hope.'

'And hope is more than I have. Take me and Harry with you.'

'You do not know where we are going.'

'It must be better than this place,' she said.

'It is a wilderness. A wild land, inhabited by wilder animals. Every day will be life or death.'

She laughed bitterly. 'You think I do not know about fighting an untamable land? About hardship?'

'It is no place for a woman.'

'If it is no place for a woman then it is no place for a man,' she retorted, with a steel that Ralph had not noticed before. 'There is nothing you can do that I cannot.'

Marius, who had been listening a little distance away, looked up the track, shifting impatiently.

'Maybe we should bring her with us,' he said. 'A cook would be useful.'

'And what about the child?'

'He would come too,' said Ann.

'No.' Ralph recoiled. He picked at the scars on his cheek. 'I will not have him with us.'

Ann stared at him. She could not fathom the hatred he seemed to have for the boy, but she could feel it blazing off him like the heat of a furnace. He would never yield to argument.

At that moment, Ann understood that if she wanted to get what she needed from Ralph, a passage out of Port Elizabeth, she would have to find another way.

'You have not heard the last of me,' she declared. She turned and walked away, Harry trotting after her.

Marius watched her go. 'Are you sure that was right?'

'I am not taking her and that child where we are going,' said Ralph.

'What if she goes to the governor? She knows your name, hey? What if she says she has seen Ralph Courtney and two of his friends here in Port Elizabeth? What if the governor sends some of his soldiers to investigate? I do not want to find myself breaking rocks on Robben Island again.'

'It is only one more day. Tomorrow, we will be gone,' said Ralph, but even he could hear the doubt behind his words.

A gust of wind blew spray in Ralph's face as he sat in the longboat and watched Port Elizabeth recede. 'I told you we would get out in time,' he said to Marius as he watched the settlement slumber in the mid-afternoon sun. 'The woman did not raise the alarm.'

The Dutchman was sitting on the bench beside him, looking unhappy. 'Say that again when we are out of sight of the English.' Marius had always hated being on the water, and his experience of escaping Robben Island had not altered his feelings towards it.

They had spent the last twenty-four hours waiting for the roar of the cannons from the fort, for the sound of soldiers going door to door, hunting for the men who had escaped Robben Island

and killed two of the governor's men. The sale of the horses had been easily completed – Ralph had taken the first price he was offered, a paltry sum – but then, as he watched the young, blond farmer lead the nags away, grinning at his good fortune, Ralph's heart had begun to pound in his chest. Surely, it was only a matter of time before word of his presence in Port Elizabeth reached the governor's ear? Too many people had heard his name in the *winkel*. It was not possible that Ann Waite hadn't given him away.

Ralph shuddered, thinking of the last time he had been in a boat in this bay: close to death, with a dead woman and a dying child for company. That had been an ending, the conclusion of the first part of his life. Now, with the *Farewell*'s crew rowing him out to the ship, he felt a new beginning. He saw now that the events in between were merely an interlude, nothing of significance. They had simply served to bring him back here, to open the next chapter of his life.

It would have been easier if he had not run into the woman, and the boy. Unease prickled his skin as he cursed the chance that had brought them together. Lady Fate, twisting her knife. They did not belong in this new life.

The longboat bumped against the ship's hull. The *Farewell* was a small vessel that sat low in the water even in ballast. With a full load, Ralph could almost see over her side when he stood. Two steps took him up the ladder and onto her deck.

Captain Conway intended to wring every penny of profit from the voyage. The cargo had filled up the hold and spilled out on deck, which was piled with chests and sacks. A hen coop took up much of her fo'c's'le, and a cow was tethered near her capstan. The crew would struggle to do their duties.

'I heard men in the *winkel* offering three to one that she does not return,' said Marius. 'And they had no takers.'

'Then let us hope we beat the odds.' Ralph had sailed aboard East Indiamen, Chinese junks, Bengal smugglers, Baltimore schooners and every craft in between. He had seen worse ships – but not many.

Conway approached, stepping around the cargo. He did not look happy to see his new passengers.

'Do you have your fee?'

Ralph handed him a small purse. Conway felt its weight and frowned. Ralph had sold the horses for a fraction of their value, but it was hard to find a buyer corrupt or simple enough to overlook questions about the animals' provenance.

'That is all I have. The rest will come when—'

Ralph broke off. His face went pale. He stared over Conway's shoulder as if he had seen a ghost.

'What are *they* doing here?'

Ann and Harry stood on the deck. A mound of cargo nearly obscured them – but the ship's size meant there was nowhere to hide. Ann met Ralph's gaze and returned it defiantly. Conway looked between them, puzzled.

'She came aboard an hour ago. She said you had engaged her as your cook.'

'You . . .' Ralph clenched his fists, as if trying to hold back something that threatened to burst out of him. 'You brought the child?'

'Do you know where we are going?' Jobe was more pragmatic. 'It is no place for women and children.'

'When the *trekboere* venture beyond the frontier, they take their families with them,' Marius countered. 'Some of our women are stronger than any man.'

'No.' Ralph was raging, almost out of control. 'I will not take them.' He stared at Harry, though if the boy felt the anger turned upon him it did not seem to trouble him. He tugged against his mother's grip like a dog straining on the leash, gazing at the ship with a look of wide-eyed wonder.

'It is not your decision to make,' said Ann, who had remained calm as the men discussed her like a bill of goods. 'Conway is the master, and he says who sails aboard his ship.'

A part of her marvelled to hear her own confidence. In the past, she would not have dared defy a man like Ralph Courtney. She would have submitted meekly, and afterwards regretted her cowardice. But she had changed for good. Working the land in the boiling sun had forged new steel in her; loss and grief had quenched it to something hard and adamant. Ralph's appearance in Port Elizabeth was a sign, she was sure of it, a lifeline out of her predicament. She would not let it go.

'Boat approaching!'

A sailor's cry broke the silence on the main deck. Conway glanced where the lookout was pointing. A longboat was pulling across the bay, with half a dozen men standing in the bow. They wore red coats, with white crossbelts and brass buttons gleaming in the sun.

'The garrison.' Ralph swore.

The news must have arrived from Cape Town that afternoon. In Port Elizabeth, it would not have been hard to pinpoint three strange men – two white, one black – who had arrived the previous day, even if no one remembered the name of Ralph Courtney from the *winkel*.

A smaller man, neatly dressed in a blue coat, sat on the thwart beside the soldiers.

'Who is that man?' Marius asked.

Conway took a spyglass from the rack and trained it on the boat. He swore.

'That is Mr Francis, the customs officer.'

'Do you know him?' Jobe asked.

'I have been doing everything I can to avoid him.' Conway turned to the mate. 'Put on all sail. We cannot let him get aboard.'

'He will be here before we can get the anchor up,' the mate protested.

'Then cut the cable,' said Ralph, realising the imminent danger.

Conway did not take kindly to strangers giving orders on his ship, but he had no time to argue. If the customs officer got aboard, he would find the ship unregistered, the name of *Farewell* as thin as a coat of paint, and cargo in the hold for which he had no tax certificates. Also, there was the small matter of his passengers.

Conway barked his orders. The crew raced aloft; sails dropped and snapped taut. The boatswain took a huge boarding axe and chopped the thick anchor cable like a tree trunk.

Harry clutched Ann's arm. His face was bright with excitement. 'Are we going away?'

'Yes.'

Once they were out to sea, Ralph would have no choice but to take them. Ralph Courtney was a brute, a ruffian – and now, it seemed, a criminal, too – but he was the best chance she had.

But perhaps they would not even reach the open sea. The *Farewell*, so heavily loaded, was struggling to get under way; the men in the longboat were maybe half a cable length off. If they captured the *Farewell*, they might arrest Ann as Ralph's accomplice. They would throw her in gaol – or worse, depending on the nature of his crimes.

Panic seized her. To bring Harry aboard a ship, bound for an uncharted land, with a gang of dangerous men she did not know: how could she have done it? Desperation had driven her to madness.

Ann ran to the side of the boat and looked down. All she saw was the churning sea. If she jumped with Harry now they would surely drown or, worse, be dragged under the ship first and then drowned. There was no way back.

White veins of foam spread from the ship's hull. The *Farewell* gathered headway. The chasing longboat slipped back. The men on the oars were strong, but they could not keep pace with a ship under full sail in a brisk breeze. They began to falter as they saw their effort was hopeless. In a moment, they would turn back.

The man in the bow, with a lieutenant's epaulette, snatched a rifle from one of his men and aimed it at the brig. A parting shot, no more; from a rocking boat, against a distant target, he could not hope to hit anything on deck.

Fire spat from the barrel. With a mother's instinct, even before the sound reached them, Ann threw herself over Harry and smothered him to the deck.

Harry writhed under her, but she did not release him – she was expecting more shots from the longboat. She looked up, feeling a warmth and a wetness spreading across her back. One of the crew – a large, sandy-haired man with a mermaid tattoo – stood above her. He must have been watching the chasing boat from behind Ann. Now he looked down with a quizzical expression, staring in shock at the blood that was pumping out of the hole in his chest and showering over Ann.

The shot had gone straight into his heart. He toppled over on top of her. Ann screamed, but the dead man's body muffled the sound. Her dress grew hot and sticky against her skin as his blood spread through it; his weight crushing her against her child. Harry cried out beneath her, the weight of the two adults pinning him painfully to the deck. He would surely suffocate. How was this man so heavy? How was there so much blood in him? Ann felt her strength failing. She could not breathe; she felt the sailor's death seeping into her.

Suddenly, the weight was lifted from her chest. Ann gasped instinctively as she felt the sweet sea air fill her lungs. She opened her eyes and saw Ralph, who had pulled the corpse away. Harry got up, bawling. She wanted to hug her boy, but her skirts were soaked with blood.

Climbing to her feet, Ann turned to Ralph. 'You must take me back,' she said.

Ralph gave her a cool look. 'Two minutes ago you insisted on coming with me.'

She pointed to the dead man. 'We must return to port so we can give him a Christian burial, and see justice done on his murderer.'

'His *murderer*?' Ralph said scornfully. 'Did you not see who was in the boat? The customs officer will swear that he was trying to enforce the king's laws, and all the other men will back him to the hilt. It is not so far from the truth, after all.'

'Then what do you mean to do?'

'I intend to follow my path. I will go to Nativity Bay and make my fortune.' He cast his eyes over Ann and Harry. A tremor went through the scars on his face as he took in the sobbing boy. 'It seems you are coming with us.'

Behind him, the ship's crew had swiftly bundled up the corpse in a hammock. The master said a few words, and then they hoisted it over the side. Ann watched it splash into the water, and wept at this reminder of the daughter she had buried on the voyage from England.

Every journey ends in death, a voice whispered in her mind. She knew she should not think this way, but the more she tried to silence the voice, the more insistent it became. The baby, her kind, loving husband Frank, now this innocent sailor. Each time, others had died and she had lived. How many more would have to die before she found peace?

INDIAN OCEAN

They beat up the coast, day after day. For many hundreds of miles, they saw nothing but barren land broken by black rocks shelving up in inaccessible cliffs. Occasionally at night they saw fires breaking the darkness, and Ralph wondered at the unknown tribes who lived there; by day, they saw no other ships, for most vessels would keep further out to sea. Conway was always alert to the least change in the wind.

'If we get caught in an easterly, we'll be smashed to pieces before you can say "spit".'

But there were no gales or storms. Instead, they had to contend with light, baffling winds that had them sailing on all points of the compass to try and make headway. They spent days changing course, setting and furling sails, but when Ralph checked the sextant, he found that they had made little progress and were only just advanced of their last position.

The *Farewell* was a small ship, and the space below decks was filled with cargo. The passengers had to find room on deck, cheek by jowl with the crew.

The dead sailor was quickly forgotten. His possessions were auctioned off the same afternoon he died. No one spoke of him. Once, when Ann mentioned him, Ralph furrowed his brow as if struggling to remember.

'Does a human life mean nothing to you?' she asked him.

'I have seen a lot of men die,' he answered curtly. 'Good men, some of them – and some not so good. You cannot mourn them all.'

Ann could not forget the sailor so easily. She was beset by nightmares. Every night she dreamed that he crawled into the ship, with blue stones for eyes and seaweed hanging from him like rags. Then she would see that it was not the sailor but Frank, risen from the grave where she had buried him. He slithered on top of her where she lay on deck, soaking her with seawater, pressing his black mouth on hers so that she could not scream until she woke.

In contrast to Ann, Harry was simply a happy, boisterous boy. By the end of the day he was too tired to be troubled by nightmares. He treated the ship as his own private playground. He darted down hatches and hid in the longboats; he turned newly coiled ropes into cat's cradles and put tarry handprints over the freshly scrubbed planking. There was a time when Ann turned her back and he climbed halfway up the rigging before anyone noticed, and had to be hauled down by the boatswain. He was fearless, mischievous and made twice as much work for the crew as they would have had otherwise, but he always had a wide smile on his face and delight in his eyes; they could not begrudge him his antics.

Ralph, meanwhile, seemed daily to grow more irritated by the boy. And somehow this made things worse. Harry seemed drawn to Ralph and the more Ralph tried to avoid him, the more Harry sought him out. He followed him like a shadow, fraying Ralph's patience. Once, when Harry darted under Ralph's legs while playing, Ann saw Ralph raise his hand to strike him – not a reproving cuff, but the sort of blow that would have laid a grown man out cold. Ann was too far away to intervene, and luckily Ralph mastered himself before he followed through, but Ann never forgot the raw hatred she saw on Ralph's face in that moment. As if he wanted to murder Harry.

She still could not fathom why the boy provoked such a reaction in Ralph. Was it a memory of their ordeal in the open boat? But Harry had been an infant – Ralph could not blame him for that. Had Ralph loved Harry's mother? Ann doubted it. She remembered his response when she had asked if the dead woman was his wife.

Ann could feel the rage emanating from Ralph. She had felt the same energy, the same anger when they had first met on the beach in Algoa Bay. She wanted to understand why Harry irked Ralph so, it was the only way that she could protect her son. But Ralph found ways to keep his distance, even on an overloaded tub like the *Farewell*. And in the evenings, when many of the men gathered around a guitar and a bottle of cheap brandy, he did not join in. Instead, he stayed aft by himself.

One day, Ann approached Marius. Of all the men aboard, he was the only one whom Ann felt she had come to know. Sometimes, in the evenings, he would drift back to where she and Harry had set up their little encampment on deck and sit with them for a while. The big Dutchman was affectionate to Harry, always ready with a kind word.

'He is a good boy,' he said one evening. Harry lay beside her, curled up asleep on a blanket, while Ann tried to read by the light of the binnacle lamp. 'I think he will be a sailor.'

Ann lowered her book. It was the volume of Defoe that had belonged to Frank. It comforted her to read it, though by now she almost knew it by heart.

'I fear Harry only gets in the way.'

'He is better than me, though, hey?' Marius gestured to the cow, tethered before the mast. 'I am like her. Boers are made for the land.'

Ann thought of the farm at Paradise Valley. 'I do not seem to be made for the land or the sea.'

Marius lowered himself to the deck, tucking up his awkward limbs, and sat beside her.

'You will find your place,' he told her. His brown eyes crinkled around the edges as he gave her a warm look. 'A pretty woman like you will always have somewhere to go.'

Ann's chest tightened. Was there something more than kindness in his eyes? She was very much aware of the fact that she was the only woman on the ship. Every day, a hundred times, she felt some man's gaze running over her. She hated it.

If there had been a suggestion in Marius's voice, she ignored it.

'Have you sailed with Ralph before?'

'Only once. The boat was not seaworthy – we almost drowned.' Marius grinned. 'Hopefully, this journey will end better.'

'How long have you been friends?'

'Friends?' Marius considered. 'We are . . . I do not know him well.'

The answer surprised her. She had assumed the two men were old friends. 'How long have you known each other?'

'Two weeks. A month.'

'How did you meet him?'

'In prison.'

The answer reminded her how little she knew of these men she had risked her life with.

'What was Ralph there for?'

'Theft.'

That was not so bad. A crime, to be sure, but a man might have many reasons to steal.

'And you?'

Marius looked at her intently. Again, she saw the kindly furrows of the lines at the corners of his eyes; the hangdog, slightly apologetic grin that was his natural expression.

'I killed a man.'

'Oh.' She did not know what to say.

'A British officer.' The grin grew wider. Perhaps he thought that would be reassuring.

'Why?'

Marius opened a tobacco pouch and began to fill his pipe.

'I will tell you. My family home was up on the frontier by the Fish River. My father was born there. So was I. Twenty thousand acres. Not an easy country, but we made it our own. Our land.'

He thumped the deck. 'Then the Kaffirs invaded. They drove off our cattle and burned our home. In broad daylight – can you imagine that? But that was not the worst.'

'No?' Ann asked.

His grin had faded. His lips were set hard, and a passionate light burned in his eyes.

'My father gathered up a kommando to cross the river and teach the blacks a lesson. Then, just before we departed, British troops arrived from the garrison at Grahamstown. We thought, "*Dank die Here*. They will protect us." Do you know what they did?'

He leaned forward and lit a spill from the binnacle lamp. Flame flared in the darkness.

'They turned their guns on us and forbade us to go. They said we could not cross the river, it would only start more fighting.' His voice throbbed with outrage. 'A man's property is taken, and his own government stops him from reclaiming it. What kind of justice is that?'

He touched the spill to the bowl of his pipe. The tobacco glowed red.

'The officer in charge was just a snot-nosed boy. Horrible pimples, so fat I thought they would burst all over me. He pointed his sword at my father and said he would cut him if he did not do as he was told. This boy . . .

'So I hit him.' Marius tapped his forehead above the bridge of his nose. 'Right here. You should have seen the surprise on his face, hey? He tried to get up, I hit him again. The second time, he did not get up.'

He flexed his fist, studying it with satisfaction. 'I pushed his nose so far back he could smell his own brains.'

Ann heard no remorse in his voice. The memory seemed to amuse him.

'Of course, they had to make an example. They arrested me, put me in a joke trial – the judge was the boy's father, for God's sake – and sent me to prison.' He blew out a long plume of smoke. 'But I taught the British a lesson that day. For the Boers, our land is our freedom, given by God. Try to take it from us, and we will fight you to the death.'

He reached out and put his arm over her shoulder. His massive hand fastened around her arm in a way that was perhaps meant to comfort her. 'You look cold.'

His touch chilled her. She wanted to shrug him off, but he was too strong for that. Instead, she gave him a forced, insincere smile.

'There is so much land in this country,' she said. 'Why can black and white people not share it in peace?'

'Such a pretty thought.' His hand slid up her shoulder and stroked her cheek. 'You are like all your countrymen. You do not understand the blacks.'

Ann's eyes turned to Jobe. He sat by the mast, apart from others, keeping both Marius and Ralph in sight. His dark skin blended with the night, and there was the occasional flash of a blade as he carved a new knife-handle from a length of bone.

'You treat him as an equal,' Ann remarked.

'We need each other,' Marius said thoughtfully. 'He wants to go back to his people. I need a guide to a new home.'

'I thought you were going to trade, not to settle.'

Marius pointed his pipe towards Ralph, who sat against the gunwale on the far side of the deck. His face was in shadow, beyond the orb of the binnacle lamp, yet Ann could feel the heat of his gaze fixed on her.

'That one, he wants to make his fortune and go back to England, to his never-ending rain,' said Marius. 'Me, I am an *Afrikaner*. I am here to stay.'

From across the deck, Ralph watched Ann and Marius talking. The sight made his chest squeeze tight, though he did not know why. Let Marius try his ham-fisted courting. Ann meant nothing to Ralph.

So why could he not stop looking at her?

Marius moved his hand towards Ann's face. Ralph saw her stiffen, her eyes darting as if looking for escape. She was like a bird, he thought, trapped by a child who could not decide if he wanted to make it his pet, or wring its neck.

She was not the woman she had been when she walked into the *winkel* in Port Elizabeth. Two weeks of ship's biscuit and boiled pork, basic though it was, had put colour in her cheeks. It made him realise how famished she must have been. Already, she looked ten years younger: you could see how attractive she might be, in happier times. She had a pretty face, and a neat figure that had begun to fill out again under her dress. For all the penury she had suffered, there was a trace of kindness in her eyes, a purity of soul that made you want to confide in her.

The cord in Ralph's chest pulled tighter. Back in China, he would have had a solution. The opium pipe would have calmed his nerves and obliterated his cares into blissful *nothing*. But he had learned – agonisingly – that it was only a temporary gift. When the opium wore off, a man's cares returned with a vengeance. It was like being tied to a stone that was falling into an ocean; and the release was always another pipe of opium. When he finally broke the habit, it had nearly killed him. Two weeks curled up on the filthy floor of a windowless cell below Kowloon Fort, slick with sweat as the convulsions tore through his body. The pain so deep inside him that it felt like it was in his bones. No sleep, even in the thick, humid darkness. Just the smell of his own vomit and the scuttling of the giant centipedes.

He wanted this woman. He needed her. That was why he kept staring at Ann. But it was more than just simple lust, a man's needs. He was drawn to her kindness, to her soul. Maybe, somehow, she could heal whatever was broken inside him.

He saw the boy Harry asleep on a blanket, close to Ann. Ralph's desire subsided as quickly as if he had been slapped in the face. The boy was living proof of the darkest moments of his life, the hours and days that even opium could not erase.

Will I ever be free of them?

Footsteps sounded on deck, breaking the chain of Ralph's dark thoughts. It was the master, Conway.

Ralph looked up. 'Yes?'

Conway had intended to say firmly that they could not keep close inshore any longer; they had searched for Ralph's hidden harbour for days without success and he was finished with risking his ship and his crew against uncharted coasts and shifting winds. But Ralph seemed to read his mind, and the speech he had prepared vanished from Conway's head. There was a demonic fire in Ralph's eyes that said he would not be defied, he would keep up the hunt until he had found what he had come for.

The master decided that he would broach the matter on the morrow. 'It was nothing,' he muttered uneasily. 'I only came to say good night to you.'

'Then good night,' said Ralph.

Not for the first time, Conway cursed himself for bringing Ralph and his companions aboard.

Across the deck, Ralph noticed that Ann had removed herself from Marius and was busying herself plaiting her soft hair. The moonlight illuminated the concentration on her face as she braided the three shiny strands together.

Pulling his gaze away from Ann, Ralph sought out Jobe. He had fallen asleep by the mast, his hat yanked down over his eyes. Ralph looked for Marius, but he could not see him. Perhaps he was also already slumbering somewhere on deck. Then Ralph turned away from the ship and stared out into the night like a man awaiting death.

The next day, the weather turned for the worse. The wind grew in strength until it was a harsh, keening thing that tore at the sails; grey clouds covered the sky, threatening to lash the *Farewell* with rain or hail. A bracing dose of rum gave Conway the courage to confront Ralph. 'We have no choice,' he said. 'If a storm blows up we will all be lost. I shall put out to sea and make for Delagoa Bay.'

Ralph's eyes bored into him. 'I did not pay you to take me to Delagoa Bay.'

'Look at the sea.' The waves had risen into choppy whitecaps, which made the heavily laden ship roll dangerously. It was obvious to Conway that a storm was coming – he feared Ralph Courtney, but he feared the ocean more. 'I am the master of this vessel. I have indulged your fantasies and fairy tales long enough. Your secret bay does not exist.'

'It is there.' Ralph went to the chart spread out by the binnacle. It was sparsely mapped, only a faint sketch of coastline and a row of x's plotting their daily course. Ralph put his finger on their last position. 'Twenty-nine minutes fifty-two seconds south. That is within seconds of the longitude I was given on my father's chart.'

'It is a hoax!' Conway pointed to the distant shore. 'There is nothing there.'

'I told you before – the entrance is invisible until you are nearly upon it. You are too far out.'

'And I will not go an inch closer.'

'You will lose your fortune.'

'Better that than destroying us all,' Conway declared.

Ralph's gaze swept across the deck, calculating the odds. He made no movement, but more than one of the crew found their fingers drifting towards whatever might aid them in a brawl – knives and belaying pins.

There were fifteen of them, and they were all loyal to Conway. Ralph had only Jobe and Marius by his side.

'I will not ask you to risk your ship,' said Ralph. 'But we are so close, it would be folly to abandon our search when the key to all our fortunes may lie only a league or so distant. Let me take the whaleboat inshore and see what we find.'

Conway studied the barometer. The mercury had already dropped an inch.

'Give me two hours,' said Ralph. 'That is all I require.'

A wave slapped against the hull and foamed over the deck. Conway knew it was reckless to linger; he was already too close to shore. But there was something about Ralph Courtney that was hard to resist, and Conway had a gambler's sense of possibility.

One last roll of the dice.

He turned the timer in the binnacle. Sand began to run through its narrow waist.

'Two hours. Not a minute more. If you don't come back, then I will leave you to the lions and the hyenas.'

They dropped anchor and lowered the whaleboat into the surging sea. The waves bounced the craft against the ship's side; Ralph had to leap from the deck and trust that the boat would be in the right place when he landed. Luckily, the *Farewell* was so heavily loaded that it was not far to jump.

Jobe came with him, along with six of the *Farewell*'s crew to man the oars. Marius remained aboard the ship. He would have faced a charging bull without hesitation, but the sight of the tossing whaleboat filled him with horror.

Ann and Harry stayed on the *Farewell* too. Ralph saw them watching from the rail as the boat pulled away, Ann clutching Harry tight for fear that a wave might lift him overboard. Again, Ralph felt the pressure on his heart, like a strap around his chest. But he had no time to dwell on it. The moment he stepped up to the mast and let the sail out, the canvas snapped taut and the whaleboat leaped forward.

'The wind is too strong,' protested one of the sailors.

Ralph bared his teeth. 'I have sailed a ship through a typhoon and lived to tell a tale or two. This is just a healthy breeze.'

The land loomed closer. Keeping one hand on the tiller, Ralph raised a telescope and scanned the shore for any sign of an opening. The crew watched him anxiously. They could see the tiller bucking and tugging in his grip, fighting against his control. If he brought them even a fraction too close to the wind, the boat would capsize; they would all be drowned long before the *Farewell* could reach them. But Ralph steered unerringly, while the spyglass in his hand stayed rock steady.

'There!' he shouted.

He could not contain his excitement. Ahead, a whale-backed hill rose up from the churning surf. Other hills loomed behind it, but close up you could see that this one stood apart, thrusting out into the sea.

'That is it,' he declared. He had seen it sketched on his father's map, its distinctive shape engraved on his memory. 'The channel should be a little to the right.'

He altered course. For long minutes, nothing changed. His certainty faded; he began to doubt himself. Perhaps the hill was not so distinctive, after all.

Then he saw it. A line of white water, very clearly an opening in the shore where the sea foamed over a bar. At once, he understood why the entrance had proved to be so elusive. The whale-backed hill stood on a promontory that ran almost parallel to the shore, angled out like a door that had been opened just a crack. From front on, it would appear closed: only when you were hard against the coast would you see the narrow channel that opened between the promontory and the mangrove-forested mainland. Even then, it was not clear if the opening would lead them any further, or if it was a dead end.

The boom slapped thunderously over as Ralph made his decision and leaned on the tiller. This was his chance. He knew that he was risking his life and the life of every man in the boat, but he had to explore the opening.

A cannon boomed behind them. Jobe looked back. 'Signal gun,' he said. 'Conway wants us to come back.'

Ralph ignored him, and kept the whaleboat pointed into the channel. If his memory of the map was accurate, then the land to their right should be just a narrow point, with a bay beyond. It was impossible to see clearly through the tangled mangroves.

The sailors shifted on their benches. 'We have to turn back,' said one, a veteran topman with a hatchet face. 'Conway won't wait. He warned us that he would leave without us.'

Ralph didn't even acknowledge the topman; he held his course. White water foamed ahead of them. Was it the bar to the river – or a reef that would rip them apart?

'Come about,' bellowed another of the sailors. 'Come about or you'll kill us all.'

'It is a sandbar,' said Ralph. 'We can clear it.'

The whaleboat was long and thin, with a shallow draught and a sharply pointed prow for slicing through the waves.

'There is nothing beyond it!' the topman shouted.

'There is,' Ralph said fiercely. He still could not see the channel, but he knew it must be there. 'A good heave on the oars will see us through.'

Suddenly, his world upended itself in a welter of water and flapping canvas. In the narrow channel, the wind swirled and chopped in unpredictable eddies. A gust had caught the sail like the slap of an open hand, knocking the boat over.

The gunwale tipped into the channel; water flooded over the side. For a moment, the whaleboat stayed balanced on its beam, caught in an impossible defiance of gravity. The crew hurled themselves to the far side, to right the boat before it was swamped.

With a splash, the vessel came down again. The topman let go of the halyard to loose the sail, while the rest of the men grabbed the oars and pulled frantically away from the white water, back towards the open sea.

'Captain'll hear of this,' the topman growled as soon as the boat settled and the men began to bale it out. 'You risked us all.' He stood, ripping his battered tricorn hat from his head and drawing a blade. 'I'm going to cut a hole in you and sink you in this godforsaken place!'

He started to try and make his way to Ralph, stepping over the rowing benches, shoving his shipmates out of the way.

'Easy, Ratray'. A big man with a broken nose pushed himself to his feet. 'Easy . . . Let's make the *Farewell* first. There'll be plenty of time for blood when we're on board.'

Ralph's immediate concern was not that of his shipmates. In that moment of disaster, when the world had stood on its end and he had been caught in mid-air, he had glimpsed the landscape beyond the whitecaps. He had seen the point where the mangroves ended, the channel leading in and open water beyond.

'There is a way in,' he murmured to himself.

Could the *Farewell* make it over the bar? *Possibly*, he thought. He knew his father's ship had entered the bay, years earlier. But Conway would never risk his vessel, certainly not as deeply laden as she was.

'We will wait for the wind to drop and try again,' Ralph told Jobe as the sailors settled themselves back at their benches, the topman still cursing. 'We will have to load up the whaleboat with enough supplies to last us for a couple of weeks.'

Jobe gave a grim smile. 'If Conway has not left us already.'

It was not an idle joke. Ralph could not tell how much time had passed. As he steered the whaleboat out of the channel, past the promontory and into the open sea, he expected to see the *Farewell*'s stern disappearing off into the horizon. But she was still there. Even Conway would not want to lose a boat and six of his crew.

The whaleboat heeled as she caught the full force of the ocean breeze blowing them back towards the shore. Ralph let out the main sheet a little. To reach the *Farewell*, it would be a long, arduous sail, beating into the wind.

Or maybe not so long. Ralph noticed that the *Farewell* was closer inshore than when they had left her. Perhaps Conway wanted to get the whaleboat inboard as quickly as possible so he could put out to deeper water again.

'Why does she sail without sails?' Jobe asked.

Ralph looked again. In the turbulent sea it was difficult to guess at distance and direction, yet he could see now that the *Farewell* was moving, without a scrap of canvas on her yards.

'She has dragged her anchor,' Ralph realised.

'That is bad?' said Jobe. For the first time since he had met him, he saw real fear written on Ralph's face.

'To be caught on a lee shore, loose from your moorings . . .' Ralph shook his head. 'I have done it once before.'

'And?'

'We lost the ship and half our crew. We were all below decks. By the time we noticed that we were being blown to shore it was too late.'

The *Farewell*'s crew were racing aloft, trying to put on sail so they could gain steerage way and bring the ship about. Ralph nudged the whaleboat's tiller, coming up as close to the wind as he dared. The boat heeled over; the men hung out off the side to keep her steady. A single wave could have flipped them over, but no one complained. Conway would need all hands to save the ship from the angry sea.

The whaleboat bumped against the *Farewell*'s hull. With the sea running high, Ralph had to scramble up the wet and slippery side, clinging to a rope, while water poured out of the scuppers into his face. Struggling to his feet, he saw Ann cowering by the mainmast with Harry and Marius, trying to keep out of the way. The crew had managed to set the topsails and braced them, while two men heaved on the wheel. They had to bring the ship around, away from the land and on to a tack that would take her out to sea. They had very little time. The shore rushed closer every minute.

The *Farewell*'s bow began to turn. The braces creaked; the sails stretched taut. Still the bow kept moving, ever so slowly.

And then stopped. Stopped dead.

Men hauled on ropes like the devil had come for them. The steersmen held the wheel as far over as it would go. It was not enough – the ship had lost steerage way. The bow began to slip back downwind, turning once more towards the shore.

'Put on more sail,' shouted Conway. 'We must gather speed and try again.'

'It is too late for that.' Ralph pointed to the line of rocks extending from the promontory. 'You cannot weather those.'

'You have left me no other choice, you madman!' Conway was screaming now. He knew he would lose his ship, yet he could not admit it. Instead, he turned all his rage on the man who should take the blame. He pulled back his fist to strike Ralph.

The blow would have laid Ralph flat if it had hit him. But Ralph pirouetted aside, so that Conway's fist sailed past his head. In the same movement, Ralph brought up his knee into Conway's stomach, doubling the captain over. Before he could recover, Ralph grabbed his shoulders and pushed him away. Conway stumbled across the deck, into Marius's waiting arms. He struggled to tear free, but Marius held him fast.

The crew had abandoned their efforts to save the ship and had turned towards Ralph. Did they mean to overpower him and throw him overboard? Some of them were certainly thinking of doing so. For the most, though, Ralph saw only fear and uncertainty on their faces. They needed leadership.

'There is one hope,' he said. 'We must make the channel and try our luck over the bar.'

'That's certain death.' It was the topman who had spoken, the hatchet-faced man from the whaleboat: Ratray. 'I seen it. She'll never clear the bar.'

Ralph pointed towards the rocks on shore. '*That* is certain death. If we go my way, we have a chance.' They were close enough now to hear the breaking waves. 'But only if we act at once.'

Even then, he thought they might rather fight him than obey. But every man aboard could see that Ralph's plan was their only hope. Recriminations could come afterwards – if they survived. They ran to obey Ralph's orders, even the topman, while Conway spluttered, helpless in Marius's grip.

The ship gathered pace as the bow turned forward again. The rolling eased, though it was a temporary reprieve. They were driving straight towards the coast.

A drop of rain stung Ralph's cheek. The storm was breaking, and the ship was moving too fast. Even with topsails reefed, he was carrying too much canvas for the delicate manoeuvre he meant to make.

'Ready a sea anchor,' he called.

Two of the men fetched up a long canvas cone. They fastened it to ropes and held it over the stern rail.

'On my command . . .'

Ann did not understood what was happening. A *lee shore*, a *sea anchor*, *wearing ship* – the expressions were gibberish to her. But watching in terror from the main deck, she could see a change in Ralph. It was as if the storm had transformed him into something more than a man. He stood with his legs planted by the wheel, riding the ship's bucking deck with confidence. The wind whipped his hair and rain poured down his cheeks, yet a strange stillness seemed to possess him. The light in his eyes was bright. His demeanour was that of a man who was, at that moment, exactly where he was supposed to be, doing exactly what he was born to do. Though he was fighting for his life, he seemed . . . happy.

Ann hugged Harry to her, folding him into her skirts, but to her astonishment her boy did not seem frightened at all. Instead, he tugged away from her, staring at the frantic activity in fascination.

'I want to help!' Harry demanded.

'No,' she told him. 'It's too dangerous.'

'Now!' said Ralph.

The sailors cast the sea anchor over the port side. The canvas filled with water, instantly helping to slow the ship's progress. She slewed around. Her spars shivered; her rigging groaned under the pressure, while her canvas bulged.

If it split, they would lose all power and be smashed against the shore.

'Braces,' Ralph ordered.

The crew hauled on the ropes; the yards swung around and the sails stretched tighter as the wind took them again.

A shudder went through the hull. From aloft came a crack like lightning. A piece of tackle tumbled to the deck and struck one of the chests, splitting it open. Loose canvas flapped above.

'We've lost the fore topsail,' came a cry.

Every man on deck held his breath. If they lost another sail now, they were doomed.

The sails flapped and crackled. Ann thought they would tear away – but they held. The ship gathered speed on her new course. Through extraordinary seamanship, Ralph had brought the *Farewell* straight into the narrow channel between the promontory and the land that he had scouted with the whaleboat. As they came into the lee of the hill, the shriek of the wind in the rigging dropped.

Ahead churned the line of white water where the whaleboat had turned back. The crew could see it now and every man knew what it meant.

'What will you do now?' shouted Conway. 'We have lost our anchor.'

'I do not mean to anchor,' Ralph exclaimed. 'I mean to go over the bar.'

There was no alternative. The channel was too narrow to let them come about, even if the ship could have endured such a manoeuvre. Unable to stop, unable to turn, they could only wait as the ship plunged headlong forwards.

'Ready on the braces,' Ralph commanded with new power in his voice. 'As soon as we cross the bar, we will need to turn to starboard.'

'Shall I put a leadsman in the bows?' the mate asked. 'To sound the depths?'

Ralph gave a grim laugh. 'If the water is shallow, we will know of it soon enough.'

Ann could not bring herself to look ahead. She called Harry to her from where he had been peering over the side at the landscape sliding past, the gnarled mangroves and white sand. 'Look, Mummy . . .' he said. A flash of grey moved in the trees. Across the water, she saw a wizened face watching her curiously. A monkey.

Then she was knocked off her feet. She fell, slamming her shoulder into the deck, grabbing frantically for Harry as the deck tilted over towards the foaming water below.

The ebbing tide had dropped too low for the heavily laden ship: she had driven onto the sand bar. The current turned her bow, so that the incoming waves hit her amidships and rolled her over. Boxes and barrels slid down the slope, knocking the men off their feet. The cow plunged into the water and vanished. A chest of tobacco hit Conway and carried him over the side into the sea. Others grabbed on to loose ropes or pieces of the ship, dangling like men hanging from a cliff face.

There was nothing for Ann to hold. The masts and ship's side were out of reach. She began to slide down the deck, towards the roiling surf, Harry tangled in her skirts. She threw out her hands.

Her fingers skidded over the planking, then caught the coaming around the main hatch, a wooden lip maybe two inches wide. The wood was wet, her soaked dress weighed on her like a coffin, but she clenched her fingers and gripped for her life.

Above the din of smashing wood and roaring sea, Ann heard a scream. She looked down. Harry was clinging on to her ankle, his mouth open in a terrified cry.

How long could he hold on? How long could she? Her fingers were slipping. She dug them into the wet wood, but her nails tore painfully away. She could feel herself sliding backwards.

Ann did not fear for herself. All her thoughts were for Harry. If she could not save herself, he would fall too.

Then a hand fastened around her wrist. She cried out, though whether with pain or relief, she didn't know. Ralph loomed over her. He stood balanced on the coaming like a cat, one arm gripping the torn rigging that now hung across the deck, the other reaching down to hold her.

She could not imagine how much strength it took. One-handed, he lifted her and Harry as if they weighed no more than a slip of paper, pulling them up to the ledge on which he balanced.

Before she could grab him, the weight that dragged on her leg suddenly broke free. Harry had lost his grip. He tumbled down the sloping deck like a loose cannonball.

'Harry!'

A scream rose in her chest as she watched him fall. If he hit the bulwark, he would break his neck. She wanted to dive after him, but Ralph held her arm fast, his fingers digging into her flesh.

Harry landed in the netting at the far side of the deck. It cushioned the impact, but the relief that Ann felt was short-lived. Water bubbled up around her boy.

'He will drown,' she cried hysterically.

For a split second, she saw Ralph hesitate. Did he really question whether or not to save a drowning child?

'I will go,' he said.

Ann's fingers were so sore that she could not hold on to the rope that Ralph handed her so she wrapped it around her arm.

Ralph let go of his handhold and slid down the sloping deck. He came to a stop against the far gunwale, knee-deep in water.

A knife appeared in his hand. With a few deft strokes, he cut Harry free from the tangle of netting. He lifted the boy out of the water by the scruff of his neck and grabbed on to a rope that hung down across the deck, one of the stays that had snapped when the ship went over. One-handed, he threw Harry over his shoulder, then turned the rope around his waist to belay himself. He began walking up the slanted deck, making it seem effortless. Ann felt her heart hammer in her chest as she watched Ralph rescue Harry – one false move and she would lose the one good thing in her life.

Reaching the gunwale, Ralph picked Harry off his shoulder and put him on the hull. Ann saw others scrambling to join him, hauling themselves onto the ship's broadside, which now faced the sky. Marius's face appeared above her.

'Give me your hand.'

She slithered over the edge of the ship and joined the others. Ralph passed Harry to her. The boy was soaked and shivering, yet even that could not keep the smile from his face. A part of him, Ann realised, thrilled at the adventure. He was not old enough to understand the danger, how close he had come to dying.

Ann looked down. The ship had rolled over so far you could see the barnacles and weed that crusted her bottom. Water surged through the holes that had opened in her planking, where her masts had torn free. The marooned crew clustered on the side like birds on a log, clinging to the channels and dead-eyes that covered the outside of the hull. The coast was only a few dozen yards distant, but the surf churned so high that there was no thought of trying to swim to shore.

The ship moved. Only a little, but it almost dislodged Ann. She started to slip but Marius, perched beside her, put out his hand and held her. The night before, she had cringed at his touch. Now, it was her best hope of survival.

She held Harry close. It was as if the ship was alive, shifting constantly with every ebb and surge of the sea. What if it righted itself? They would all be tipped into the water and crushed as it rolled over on them.

'Will we drown?' she asked Marius nervously.

He shrugged and pointed to Ralph. 'He is the sailor.'

Ralph sat with his legs drawn up to his chest, staring at the mainland. In the chaos of surviving, Ann had not looked beyond the water's edge. Now, she followed his gaze and saw green, densely forested hills. The trees came right down to the shore, their thick foliage dancing in the wind.

'We are safe enough,' Ralph said, the relief in his voice evident.

As if to show them that the gods of this place were not yet finished with them, a huge roller crashed against the hull. A wall of white foam sprayed up and drenched them. The ship moved again.

Ralph seemed unconcerned. 'The waves have carried us beyond the bar. We are on the sandbanks now. All this battering' – another breaking wave interrupted him – 'will only dig us in deeper. When the wind drops, we should have no difficulty getting ashore.'

Marius stared at him as if he were a lunatic. 'No difficulty, you say? And even if we do reach land, what then? Shipwrecked – no food, no supplies, no guns, and no way to leave?'

Ralph gave no answer. Ann remembered how she had found him, half-dead from weeks in an open boat. After that, maybe this was only a small setback.

'You have survived worse, too,' she reminded herself, squeezing Harry tight against her.

Even after the sun set, the storm did not abate. The barrage of waves continued all night, soaking and deafening the huddled survivors. For Ann it brought back memories of being trapped in the fig tree in the flood, certain she would die. Marius remained close by, always ready with a firm hand if she slipped. Jobe recited psalms. Ralph stayed so still, he might have been asleep – though surely no man could have slept that night.

Ralph had never before been a soothing presence to Ann. He was the opposite of reassuring, radiating danger and unpredictability from his core. Yet in the depths of the night, every time Ann felt panic begin to overtake her, she found her eyes turning to Ralph. His stillness gave her a strange calm, an anchor she could cling to.

By early morning the sea had calmed, though the surf still ran high. The beach around the bay was strewn with wreckage.

'Are you still so certain that we can go ashore?' Jobe asked, eyeing the breakers.

'I am.' Ralph pointed down.

The *Farewell*'s boats had broken free of their lashings in the wreck and fallen into the sea, but they had not gone far. Nestled in the lee of the *Farewell*'s hulk, they had been protected from the current and become tangled up in the shredded rigging. The whaleboat had been stove in but the two longboats bobbed beside the wreckage of the foremast just a few feet away.

Ralph stood, balanced on the edge of the *Farewell*'s hull, and dived into the water. Three strong strokes took him to the nearest longboat. He pulled it back to the ship, while the crew rigged ropes down the slanted deck so they could descend safely, and found pieces of wood to serve as oars.

The moment they emerged from the shelter of the wreck, they felt the force of the sea again. The boat wallowed over every wave; more than once, it seemed she would go over. The crew paddled with every fragment of strength left in their exhausted bodies.

But as they went further into the lagoon the waves calmed, until – with the grate of sand and a soft bump – the longboat ran up onto the beach. Men leaped out, almost capsizing her again in their eagerness to be ashore. They splashed through the shallows, staggered a few paces, then dropped to their knees, like the conquistadors of old landing in the New World.

Ralph stayed on his feet. He felt giddy, but neither from sea legs nor the elation of survival. *This was the place*. It was as if the lines on his father's map had risen off the page and become real. Brightly coloured birds called from the tall trees on the point, and were answered by chattering monkeys in the bush. Huge hippopotamuses wallowed in the mud near the water's edge.

What about other creatures? Were there people here? He scanned the beaches around the lagoon, and the undergrowth beyond, looking for any sign of habitation. He saw no one.

But that did not mean that they were not there.

A heavy clap on his shoulder almost knocked him to the ground. It was Marius. His eyes were wide.

'This is the place, hey? You were right. We got here.'

'But can we leave it again?' Jobe asked. He gestured to the ship, sprawled over near the mouth of the bay, and then to the crew spread out on the beach among the flotsam. Now that the initial joy of survival had passed, anger had begun to dawn on their faces as they considered the extent of their disaster.

Without a word, they drew together and fell in behind Ratray. Ralph, Marius and Jobe turned to face them, while Ann and Harry sheltered behind the three men. Even in the tumult of the shipwreck, several of the sailors had kept hold of their knives. Others carried pieces of driftwood or stones that they had picked up.

We have not been here a quarter of an hour, and already we are nearly at war, Ralph thought to himself.

Ralph had wanted this to be a new beginning, a blank slate where he could make himself anew, where he could begin to build the glorious future that he had always imagined. Instead, the violence that had cursed his life had followed him again.

One day, he thought, *there will be no more violence.*

But not today, he admitted.

He turned to face Ratray and the remnants of the *Farewell*'s crew.

'We must gather up everything we can,' he said, before Ratray could speak. 'Any tools or provisions that can be salvaged. I will need a crew to take the longboat back to the ship and see what is left in her hold.'

The crew stared at him incredulously.

'Who said you would give the orders?' Ratray asked.

'I am the man who saved your lives.'

'You killed Captain Conway and you damn near done for the rest of us, too.' Ratray's voice rose with anger. 'I say you're the last man to be in command.'

'I am sorry about Conway,' said Ralph. 'He deserved a better fate. It was no one's fault that the ship dragged her anchor. Once we were trapped on a lee shore, our only chance of survival was to run aground in sheltered water. Otherwise, we would have been dashed to pieces.'

He looked past Ratray, fixing his gaze on the men behind him. They were a mixed crew: English, Irish, Dutch, Portuguese; lascars from the Malabar coast of India and black Swahili-speakers from East Africa. But across thirteen different faces, the look in their eyes was the same. They were weary, hungry, and frightened. They did not have the energy to fight.

'You know I did the best that could have been done,' said Ralph. 'You may judge my character from my actions.'

He saw some of the men back off. They were sailors; they understood the treacherous nature of the sea. In Ralph they recognised someone with the strength that was needed to fight it.

Ratray felt the mood shift, too. He changed his angle of attack. 'Who says we should have a leader anyways? Ship's gone, and for sure we'll never see another penny in wages. I say we go our own ways, each man as he pleases.'

'As you wish,' said Ralph. 'I cannot compel any man to follow me. But you know how serious our position is.' He pointed to the wreck of the *Farewell*. 'She is almost beyond repair. No one knows where we were bound – no one knows that this place even exists. Overland, Cape Colony is five hundred miles away through an inhospitable country filled with dangerous tribes.'

He paused, letting the men think on what he had said.

'Our only hope is to build a ship from the remnants of the *Farewell*. We will launch her and sail her back to Port Elizabeth.' He saw some of the men staring at the wreckage on the beach, wondering how they could ever piece it together. *Better not to let them dwell on that now*, Ralph thought as he pressed ahead with his speech: 'And when we go, it will not be with an empty hold.'

He raised his voice. 'I came here to make my fortune. I have not changed my plan. By all reports, the country is virgin land, ripe for the taking. If I can salvage powder and shot from the ship, I will do what I intended and bring back enough ivory to make us all rich men. If you make me a new ship, every man who joins me will take a one twentieth share of our profit.'

For a moment, greed drove away the aftermath of the tragedy the men had suffered just a few hours earlier. On a normal voyage, a sailor would be lucky to get a fraction of one per cent. Even a captain would earn little more than a tenth of the profits.

'That's a pirate's share,' a voice called.

The men laughed; Ralph joined in, though his humour was forced. If he honoured his word, he had just promised away more than half his profits. The happy future that had been almost within his grasp had now receded.

I need them to build a new boat. There will be nothing at all if we do not escape from here.

Only one man stayed stony-faced. Ratray had listened to Ralph in silence. He took a step forward. His fingers touched the haft of his knife.

'You may gull some of us with your talk of riches,' he said. 'But even if every word you say is true, how long will it be before you have your new ship? Six months?'

'More likely a year,' said Ralph. 'Maybe more.'

Ratray spat on the ground. 'I say we'll not survive two weeks here. Either we starve, or a troop of blackies will come and slaughter us all.'

'What do you propose instead?'

'Take the longboat. Sail her to the Portuguese at Delagoa Bay.'

'That is almost as far as Port Elizabeth.'

'I will take my chances. And you all' – he circled round, looking at the crew – 'would do well to join me if you value your lives.'

Ralph could see the men were tempted. Again, he felt his fate hanging in the balance. He would not mourn the loss of Ratray, but if too many of the others joined, he would not have the hands he needed to build his ship.

He picked up a piece of wood and drew a sharp line in the sand between him and Ratray.

'You have a clear choice,' he told the men. 'Anyone who wants to take his chances in the longboat, stay where you are. But if you will trust to your wits and courage and throw in your fortune with me, step over the line.'

Had he misjudged it? He watched the crew's faces, riven with fear and uncertainty. Some glanced at the longboat, others at the waves breaking over the wreck of the *Farewell*. It was an impossible choice, likely to end in death either way. Why should they trust him over their own shipmate?

One of the men came forward. He shuffled past Ratray, scuffing his feet on the sand. Ratray growled as he stepped over the line.

'You always were a sneak, Marsden.'

The man shrugged. 'I'd rather die trying to get rich, than starve in an open boat.'

His words had a motivating effect. Two more men followed him across the line. Ralph saw more wavering. Ratray's face went deep red.

'This is mutiny,' he barked.

'Nonsense,' said Ralph. 'You said it yourself, the ship is lost and the bonds of discipline no longer apply. Every man is free to make up his own mind.'

Five more men came over. Now that Ralph had the weight of numbers, two others followed.

Ratray was left with three men. His closest messmates, Ralph guessed. They looked about uncertainly, weighing their choice.

Loyalty won – or perhaps it was fear. They planted their feet in the sand and folded their arms.

'Very well,' said Ralph. 'We will keep the longboats until we have salvaged what we can from the ship. The food we find, we will share equally, but you can take the water casks. There will be plenty of water here.'

He turned to Marius. 'Get a party to gather everything that has washed ashore. We will need spars and canvas to make shelters. Jobe, take two men and explore our surroundings. See if we are truly alone.'

'And you?' Jobe asked.

'I will return to the ship and see what gems can be prised out of her crown.'

Boarding the *Farewell* meant entering a world of topsy-turvy. The ship's side was her roof, and the deck had become an almost vertical wall, with a window where the main hatch led in. Inside, shafts of light shone through the holes that had been smashed in the hull. Waves washed through the wreck, while pieces of flotsam bumped and thudded against the timbers.

The ladder had been ripped away. Ralph lowered himself slowly through the hatch, feeling his way with his feet. Even when he dangled by his fingertips he did not touch solid wood. He would have to chance it.

He let go and landed with a splash on the side of the ship, which had now become her bottom. He felt sand under his toes as the water closed back around his chest; the water was deep but not too deep.

A face appeared in the hatch above. It was Marsden, the seaman who had been the first of the sailors to cross the line and who had come with Ralph in the longboat.

'Throw down a rope,' Ralph called.

The line sailed down. Ralph wrapped it around his waist and began breasting through the flooded hold. Much of the cargo had been washed away; some boxes had broken open and scattered their contents on the sea floor. Any food that was left would have been spoiled. The rice they carried had swollen and split the barrels and now floated on the water like a scattering of snow.

If any cargo had survived intact it could be retrieved later. For the moment, Ralph had a more immediate goal. He worked his way steadily aft, weaving through the debris. Further back, the hold had been divided into a series of tiny storerooms whose bulkheads had mostly survived. Ralph had to tug hard to open the doors in the sodden timbers. He found the sailmaker's locker, then the rope store. He marked them for later, but they were not what he was looking for.

A puff of sawdust blew out as he forced open the next door. The carpenter's store. To his relief the tools were all there. Saws, hammers, chisels, planes and drills. At that moment, they were more valuable than any quantity of food. They were the key to building a new ship that would let them escape with whatever treasures they might find.

There was one thing more precious still. It was behind the last door in the ship's stern. A heavy padlock fastened the door, and the timbers were fixed with copper nails that would not strike sparks.

The key to the lock could be anywhere on the seabed. Ralph took a hammer from the carpenter's store and pounded the door until it broke off its hinges. Inside were dozens of small casks, and a few large chests. The casks had been stored in racks on the walls; some had broken free and cracked, but several remained in place, held out of the water by the shelving. The acrid smell of sulphur filled the air.

Ralph waded through the water. He carried the casks of powder back to the hatch one by one, holding them above his head and passing them up to Marsden.

'Do we have guns?' the boatswain asked.

The *Farewell* had carried no cannon, but Ralph found three rifles and a pair of pistols in an iron-bound chest in the magazine. Those went up to Marsden, too, together with a leather bag of birdshot, a quantity of lead, bullet moulds and some damp cartridge paper. Then the carpenter's tools, some nails and a few scraps of sailcloth. There was a barrel of rum, still sealed, but Ralph left it where it was. He did not want to put temptation in front of the crew.

He was about to leave the hold when he saw something he had missed. A book, limp with water damage, caught in a nest of splinters on the underside of the deck. He would never have seen it if it had not splayed open, revealing a flash of white paper.

The *Farewell*'s crew were not educated men. So far as he knew, there had been only one book aboard, besides the ship's log: the volume he had seen Ann reading on deck so many times.

It was out of reach, and there was no pressing reason to salvage it. Yet he had seen the way Ann gripped the book, almost with reverence, the crease of concentration in her brow as she squinted against the bright sunlight, and the smile that curled at the corners of her mouth.

He jumped for the book. His fingers touched it, but it was caught so tight in the broken wood that it did not move.

You are wasting your time, he told himself.

He eyed the thick beams that supported the deck. With the ship on her side, they stood almost upright like tree trunks. The hooks for slinging hammocks protruded, undamaged. He could use them as footholds.

It was a precarious ladder. The first time he tried it, he slipped off at once. He tried again, hugging the timber as he planted his feet in the curves of the hooks. The water behind him was still clogged with debris. If he fell, he might crack his skull or break his back.

I must be mad, he told himself, even as he reached to try again.

The book was almost in his grasp. He had to stretch from his perch, gripping the beam between his knees, so he could lift it carefully away. The splinters scraped his skin, cutting his wrist and drawing blood. His knees began to slip. His hand closed around the book and he removed it from the snag.

He lost his grip, fell backwards, and landed in the water with a splash, banging his backside on a piece of floating wood. He spluttered to the surface, bruised and bloody, but with the book still in his hand.

He felt foolish. Then he read the title embossed in gold letters on the spine and laughed heartily. 'Robinson Crusoe.'

Perhaps it will teach us how to survive as shipwrecked mariners.

By the time Ralph returned to shore with Marsden in the longboat, drawing the second – laden with salvage – behind them, a camp was starting to appear near where the river flowed into the bay. The men had found one of the sails washed up on the beach and stretched it over a frame of branches and driftwood to make a tent. They had started a fire, and boiled a pot of water to make a salty stew from salvaged peas and pork.

Ralph had the powder casks stacked under the awning to stay dry. When Marius came to help him supervise the unloading, Ralph gave him one of the rifles he had taken from the hold.

'Keep this loaded.' He nodded towards Ratray, who was complaining loudly to his companions as they carried cargo from the longboats. 'Just because there are no natives here, does not mean we are free from danger.'

Marius took the rifle. With familiar ease, he scooped a handful of powder out of one of the casks and tipped it down the barrel, loaded a ball and rammed it home. Then he shouldered the weapon.

'I will be ready.'

Ralph still had the book in his hand, the leather binding spotted with blood from the cuts on his wrist. Harry was playing by the shore, throwing stones into the waves, but his mother was nowhere to be seen.

'Where is Ann?'

Marius pointed inland, into the long grass that grew on the flats around the river. 'She went up there.'

There were so many other important matters to oversee, but Ralph was impatient to give Ann the book. He wanted to see the pleasure and gratitude on her face when she saw what he had brought her. Also, he felt a prick of unease for her safety. Who knew what dangers might be hiding in that grass?

He loaded a rifle and slung it on his back. 'I will go and find her.'

Ann stood waist-deep in the river, savouring the cool water over her skin, and murmured a prayer of thanks to God for her deliverance. More than once in the last twenty-four hours, she had been certain she would die or, worse, lose Harry. Now, she allowed herself a few moments to savour her survival. She had stripped off her filthy dress to wash it. Naked, she could see the bruises that covered her body; the grazes and tears that the wreck had left. Some of them had formed in places where she still carried knocks from the flood at Paradise Valley, bruises layered upon bruises.

She worried about leaving Harry in the sailors' care. *It is only a few minutes*, she told herself. She needed the solitude. It was the first time she had been alone since . . . maybe since the morning she found Harry, she realised with a shock. On the farm there had always been Harry, and Frank when he was not away; then the weeks at sea, crammed aboard the *Farewell*, with Ralph Courtney's furious gaze making her feel like a bird in a cage. Now she was trapped on this shore, the only woman among a crew of desperate men.

She sank underwater, rinsing the salt from her long hair and combing it out with her fingers. She must not linger. She had seen fat hippopotamuses wallowing by the river mouth downstream; there might be crocodiles, or snakes. Even so, she gave herself a little longer, luxuriating in the peace.

The grass rustled. A branch snapped. At once, fear drove out the serenity she had felt. This was not a safe place. She waded to the riverbank and scrambled out, smearing mud on her clean skin. She lunged for her dress, which lay drying on a thorn bush.

The grass parted. It was Ralph.

Had he found her by chance? Had he followed her? The fear Ann had felt on the boat rushed back, the awareness of being a lone woman among rough men. Her body clenched; blood pounded in her ears.

'Please go away,' she said stiffly.

He did not move. 'You should not be alone away from the camp.'

'Go!' she insisted. 'Or did you come to spy on me while I was bathing?'

'Is that what you think I am doing here?' Ralph was still holding the book. It filled him with a sudden anger, to think that he had risked his life for such a ridiculous object. Why had he wanted to impress Ann? Why had he thought that she would be grateful? He had made himself look a fool.

He threw it on the grass and turned away.

'Do not be too long about your business,' he said over his shoulder. 'There is work to be done before nightfall.'

Ann pulled on her damp dress and buttoned it quickly. The solitude that had been a blessing now weighed on her like a crushing burden. Seventeen men and one woman, abandoned on a hostile shore, with no prospect of relief for months. What would they become?

How will I survive this place? she asked herself.

She was about to go when she saw the book Ralph had left. Frank's book, one good thing to cling to. It was a miracle it had survived the wreck. Perhaps she could take hope from that. She picked it up, hugging it to her chest.

Why had Ralph brought it? He must have found it in the wreckage, but why did he come so far to bring it to her? Perhaps . . .

Do not give in to fanciful notions, she chided herself. *Most likely he only came to peek at you bathing.*

Three fires burned on the beach that evening. The castaways had drifted into groups. Most of the *Farewell*'s men stayed together, while Ratray and his three companions made their own camp a distance away. Ralph, Marius, Jobe, Ann and Harry made up the third party. Marsden, the sailor who had emerged as the leader of Ralph's allies among the *Farewell*'s crew, joined them too.

Ralph was explaining their plan to Marsden. 'Inland, there are herds of elephant that have never laid eyes on a human being. Enough ivory to make us all rich.'

'It sounds a fine plan to me,' said Marsden. 'But it may be harder than you think.'

'What do you mean?'

'When we were in Delagoa Bay last year, I went to a tavern with a few of the men. There was a trader there, a Portuguese man named Da Costa. We got to talking, started spinning yarns. He'd been upriver into the country, not that it did him no good. He caught a fever that near killed him. But he still had the hunger.

'"This land is bigger'n you'll ever imagine," he says. "Where I been, I seen herds of elephant march from one horizon to the other. So much ivory you could build a palace from it."'

Marsden looked around, pleased to see the effect his story was having. Ralph, Marius and Jobe were leaning forwards, eyes bright with greed. 'The Frenchman,' Marius muttered. 'He is describing the same thing as the Frenchman I met.'

'Did he get any ivory?' Ralph asked.

'That's what I wanted to know,' said Marsden. 'I said to him, "If this place is so bloody rich, why are you drinking sour wine in a poxy flophouse like this?"

'He gave me a look so sad it'd break your heart. "No man can get it," he says. "The whole country is under the power of a mighty king. You cannot hunt without his permission, and he's got the people in such a terror that none of them will trade you so much as a glass of water."'

Marius stirred. 'That is not what Du Toit said.'

'Had your Portuguese traveller met this king?' Ralph asked Marsden.

'No. But everywhere he went, it was the same story. This king had conquered every tribe. A real tyrant, like a black Bonaparte, or Caesar. No one would trade. Then old Da Costa caught the fever, and had to scurry back to Delagoa Bay before it killed him.' Marsden poked the embers with a stick, stirring up a cloud of sparks. 'He'll be dead by now.'

Jobe had sat back with his eyes closed. Now he opened one eye and fixed it on Marsden.

'Did he say what is the king's name?'

Marsden frowned. 'Some savage mouthful. Chaka, or Shaka.'

Marius sucked on an empty pipe. His tobacco had been lost in the wreck, and it put him in a surly mood. 'Ten dollars says this Kaffir king is no more than a despot with a few spearmen. A taste of white man's lead will have him screaming for mercy.'

'We will not conquer a kingdom with three guns,' said Ralph. 'We must find a way to trade.'

'With what? We have no goods.'

'You told us there was no one to trade with. An empty land,' said Ralph.

'And you said there was a safe harbour where we could land as easily as at Table Bay.' Marius thrust out his arm towards the wreck of the *Farewell*. 'Who was more wrong?'

'My plan hasn't changed,' said Ralph. 'Except the means of our departure.'

'And if we get out?' Marius's temper was up; he was spoiling for a fight. He leaned forward, jabbing the pipe at Ralph. 'It was meant to be equal shares, one third each. Now you have promised more than half our profit to the sailors.'

'I did not have any alternative.'

'You should have discussed it with us first.'

'Before or after they murdered us?'

Jobe looked between them in disbelief. 'You are fighting about a leopard that is still in the tree,' he chided them. 'You must kill it before you quarrel over who gets the skin.'

His advice did not calm Marius. 'Nobody asked you, Kaffir.' He turned to Ralph. 'We brought him to translate, but there is no one here to speak to. Maybe we cut him out and have his share between us, hey?'

Jobe's eyes glittered. His back stiffened.

Ralph jumped up and stepped between them. Flames flickered at his back. 'There is enough in this land that will try to kill us without fighting each other. We swore an oath. Equal partners, equal shares.'

'Equal?' Marius sneered.

All three men were on their feet now. The sailors at the other fires had stopped talking and were watching the argument.

'If they see us quarrelling like thieves, they will never follow us,' Ralph hissed. Already, he could see a nasty smile spreading across Ratray's face in the orange firelight. Ralph felt his authority resting on a knife-edge.

Marius was in no mood to take the hint. 'If you say we are equals, why is it you who decides everything, hey?' he boomed. 'Who gets the money. Who gets the food. Who gets the girl.'

Ralph's anger turned to astonishment. 'That is absurd.'

'I have seen how you look at her. You want her for yourself.'

Marius stepped forward, fists raised. Ralph did not step back. The two men squared off against each other.

'Stop this,' said Jobe.

'Get out of my way.' Marius waved a fist at Jobe. 'Do you think I would not knock you down, too?'

'Stop this *now*,' Jobe insisted, and the urgency in his voice made Ralph pause. Jobe was not looking at Marius, or Ralph. He was pointing to the darkness under the foliage at the edge of the beach. Something was moving there.

'What is it?'

A giant shadow sprang out of the night. In a single bound, it crossed the sand to the second ring of men – those who had chosen to follow Marsden. The nearest, a seaman named Hobbes, was sitting with his back to the creature and had not seen it. He began to turn.

Not soon enough. In the firelight, Ralph saw a tawny coat and flashing claws, and curved fangs big enough to bite a man's head clean through. A pair of jaws opened wide, then clamped shut on the seaman's shoulder.

Hobbes screamed. The men around him leaped to their feet, but before they could make a move to help their shipmate, the creature ran back into the darkness, dragging the sailor with him like a doll.

Ralph snatched up a burning branch from the fire and moved to follow it. He took two paces – and stopped.

The animal that took Hobbes had come to hunt with a pack. Three lionesses stood revealed by Ralph's torch. Their bodies moved with a lethal swagger, their eyes glowing in the firelight.

Ralph needed a rifle – but the guns were with the powder under the awning, too far away. If he ran, and they chased him, he would be dead before he was halfway there.

'What are they, Mummy?' He heard Harry's voice behind him; the boy was the only person not terrified into silence by the big cats.

Ralph brandished his torch at the beasts. If they had been men he could have calculated his chances, guessed how they would respond. But there was no telling what these animals might do.

He walked towards them, sweeping the branch in wide arcs. The fire had not taken a good hold of the wood. If he swung it too quickly, he might put it out.

The lionesses stood their ground. Ralph kept advancing. *How close is too close?* he wondered. *At what point does bravery become suicide?*

One of the lionesses started to move. She circled around to Ralph's left. *She is outflanking me*, he realised. He swung the torch in wider arcs, but he could not face all of them at once.

The flames flickered. The lioness on his left took a pace towards him. Ralph jabbed the torch at her, but in his fear he moved it too fast. The flame went out.

The lioness crouched, ready to spring. Ralph held the log like a club, but it would be useless against those enormous teeth.

A deafening gunshot rang out across the beach. A blossom of blood appeared on the lioness's coat. The bullet had gone into her chest. She collapsed in shock, gasping for breath as her lungs filled with blood. The other animals, frightened by the noise, turned and fled.

Marius stepped forward, holding one of the rifles. A wisp of smoke trailed from the barrel.

'It was a good shot, hey?'

'Thank you,' said Ralph. Their eyes met. A truce, of sorts, was agreed. 'We should go after the man they took.'

Marius shook his head. 'He is dead.'

'How can you tell?'

'Because if he was alive, you would hear him screaming.'

Ralph knew Marius was right. But he could not abandon the sailor just like that. He took another burning branch and followed the blood-soaked track into the forest that fringed the beach.

Under the canopy, the darkness was thick and after ten minutes Ralph's torch had burned so low that he could barely see his way. He could hear lions roaring in the distance, but there was no sign of Hobbes.

In the dark, Ralph stumbled and fell, landing awkwardly. His torch hit the ground, showering sparks into the thick bush and briefly illuminating the sandy path.

Immediately in front of him was a human arm, torn from the socket. Ragged flesh and splintered bone covered the sand around Ralph and blood dripped from the leaves above him. It was a sailor's arm. He had only seen it for an instant, but there was no mistaking the anchor tattooed on the skin.

Ralph was sickened by what he stumbled across in the darkness. Hobbes had stood up to Ratray on the whaleboat, after they had almost capsized in the channel, he had talked him down and prevented an ugly confrontation. He had been a good man. But there was no point looking any further for him. He had been torn apart by lions.

Ralph wondered if the body part should be given a burial. He dismissed the idea. If he took it back to camp, it would undoubtedly draw scavengers. He left it where it was and worked his way slowly to the beach. The crew were gathered around the fire. Marius and Jobe had their guns at the ready, while the others held torches.

'Hobbes is gone,' said Ralph.

As he came closer he smelled liquor in the air. Someone must have found a rum cask from the wreck on the beach and broached it. Perhaps it was all that was keeping them from running into the darkness in mad panic.

'That's what's coming to all of us.' Ratray's voice came from the darkness, full of indignation and scorn. 'How many more will have to die before you see sense?'

'Tomorrow we will be better prepared,' said Ralph. 'We can build a barricade, and keep a close watch.'

'And then we'll die slower,' Ratray answered. A fine mist of rum sprayed from his mouth. A knife gleamed in his hand. 'I say the only way to survive is to strike out in the longboat.'

'We decided this before,' Ralph said.

'Maybe seeing Hobbes get ate changed some minds.' Ratray drew a line in the sand with the point of his knife. 'Anyone as still wants to stay here, cross the line. But anyone as thinks they stand more chance in the boat with me, you're more than welcome.'

'No,' said Ralph. 'We will all have clearer heads in the morning.'

Ignoring the knife in Ratray's hand took almost as much courage as facing down the lions. Ratray was drunk and Ralph knew just how unpredictable he could be even when sober.

'Morning won't save you,' Ratray called after him as Ralph turned and walked away.

Ralph squatted with his rifle, staring into the darkness at the dense African bush. 'I will keep the first watch,' he said firmly.

Sixteen men lay awake that night and listened to the darkness, terrified that the lions would return. One woman lay awake, too, also afraid, though lions were not the only beasts that haunted her thoughts. And one child slept peacefully, snoring loudly, exhausted after a day of excitement, dreaming of ships and a rocking sea.

The next day, as soon as the sun was high enough to make them feel a little safer, they re-examined their situation. Six men had changed their minds during the night and wanted to leave. Ralph did not even try to stop them. Now that Ratray had the majority of the sailors on his side, Ralph could not afford to provoke a quarrel. Ralph, Marius and Jobe stayed with the powder store, rifles primed, while Ratray's men loaded one of the longboats with provisions. By lunchtime, the boat was ready to cast off into the lagoon.

'Last chance,' said Ratray, sitting in the stern. He looked at the men who had chosen to stay with Ralph. There was Marsden – who had been the first to side with Ralph originally – and two others, a Dane and an Indian.

'We will be living like lords in Cape Town, while you are dying of scurvy on the ocean,' said Marius.

'More likely we'll be drinking grog with the most beautiful girls in Delagoa Bay, when you're nothing but white bones on this beach.'

'Then I will see you in Hell,' said Marius.

Ralph forced himself not to look at Marsden and the other men. He could not be sure that they would not change their minds as well. But no one moved. With a final glare at Ralph, Ratray gave the order and the boat pulled away.

'Ten to one, that is the last we see of them,' Marius declared as he watched the longboat wallow through the breakers.

Long before Ratray and his men disappeared from view – even crossing the lagoon to the promontory took them the best part of an hour – those they had left behind began to fortify the camp. The men excavated a ditch and piled the earth into a rampart which they covered with sharpened stakes. The task was monumental – hot work under the subtropical sun, with few tools. No one could be spared from the labour. Even Ann and Harry were kept busy, searching the flotsam for anything that could be reused in their temporary lodgings, while the men stripped to their waists to dig and chop.

'We should have Kaffirs for this work,' Marius complained.

Jobe, who was shovelling earth, looked up. 'You think it is easier for me?'

'You know what I mean. Your people are made for this climate, and for hard labour.' Marius thought for a moment, frowning. He wanted a metaphor, but his literal mind struggled to find it. 'Like oxen,' he said, finally.

Ralph saw the angry look on Jobe's face and hastily intervened. 'A man is a man,' he said. 'English, blacks, Indians.'

Marius shrugged his broad shoulders. 'Unless you have owned them, you would not understand.'

The big Dutchman walked away to fetch more timber. Jobe stared after him. His gaze drilled into Marius's back, until Ralph stepped in front of him and blocked his view.

'How can we have a partnership, if he thinks I am no better than an animal?' Jobe seethed.

'When he talks about blacks, he does not mean you. He sees you differently.'

Jobe's eyes smouldered. 'You have no idea what he sees.'

'We need more water, Jobe,' Ralph told him. 'We are all too hot. Come with me.'

It doesn't matter how impenetrable the walls are, Ralph thought to himself. It was not the animals lurking outside that he feared most. He knew that, in such a small group, isolated for months, the real danger was inside of them.

After two days of punishing work, they had erected three tents from what remained of the sails of the *Farewell* and completed a rough stockade around them. Using the remaining longboat, they had salvaged what they could from the wreck – Ralph had been wrong, not all the food has been spoiled – but now their meagre rations of salt pork and ship's biscuit were running low. And although they had seen duiker on the fringes of the forest, they'd had no time to hunt or fish. Ralph had tried to keep their spirts high, but the heat and humidity, the monotony of the work and the starvation diet were taking its toll.

As a final touch, Ralph stood a spar on its end in a hole he had dug in the middle of the camp, a makeshift flagpole, and hoisted the Union Jack – another thing that they had rescued from the *Farewell*.

Marius objected. 'This is not British land.'

'No,' Ralph agreed. 'But it stakes our claim if anyone else comes.'

'I will not have it. I came here so I would never have to live by British laws again.' Marius had gone red in the face; his big hands balled into fists. 'We are here to be free. If we must have a flag, make it our own.'

'He is right,' said Jobe. 'This is not British land and never will be.'

Marius gave him a suspicious look. The two men seldom agreed on anything, but he was happy to take support where he could get it.

'It is two to one.'

'I will sew you another flag,' said Ann quickly. The men were tired and fractious; she could see they would need little encouragement to fight. 'Our own flag, for our own country.'

'Our own country,' Marius echoed. 'Where all men are free.'

'I read a book about pirates, once,' said Ann.

Marius stared at her in disbelief.

'Why would a sweet girl like you read about that, hey?'

'It belonged to my husband. It said there was a pirate who founded a town on the island of Madagascar, where there were no laws and all men were equal. The place was called "Libertalia".'

'I have read that book, too,' said Ralph. 'Though I never found the town when I went to Madagascar. But it is as good a name as any. We will be the Republic of Libertalia.'

The Union Jack came down. Ann took scrap of canvas from their salvaged stock and Marius carved her a needle from a fish bone so that she could hem the edges and sew it into a flag. Ralph prised out oakum from between the planks of the wreck, and Jobe – who was the best artist – used the tar to daub a design on it. He drew an elephant's head, surmounted by two crossed muskets. When it was ready, they hoisted it to the top of the flagpole and watched it stream out in the breeze. Marius clapped Ralph on the back.

'The Republic of Liberty,' he said. 'We have our freedom.'

'Freedom,' Jobe agreed.

'Now all we need is to be rich,' said Marius.

Ann stared at him, anger in her eyes. 'How can you think of money when we aren't even assured of survival?'

'We have fresh water, weapons, enough game around to feed an army,' Ralph reassured her. 'We can live here for years if we have to.'

'But how will we ever get out?'

'We escaped from Robben Island with no more than a seal carcass and some driftwood. Here we have the frame of a ship, a full set of tools, and a whole forest's worth of timber.'

Far from reassuring her, Ralph's cool certainty infuriated Ann. Why would he not recognise their danger, or pretend it was not real?

'Do you think I am an idiot?' Ann asked.

'Be easy with her,' Marius said. He gave her an understanding smile. 'This would be difficult for any woman – and she has a child to worry about. It's not just her own security.'

Ralph shrugged. 'I did not ask her to come.'

A pointed silence stretched between them. It seemed to Ann they were always on the edge of violence. This time, it was Jobe who changed the subject.

'Putting up our flag, it does not mean other men do not claim this country. We should explore the interior.'

'Agreed,' said Ralph. 'We should find out what treasures this new land has to offer us.'

Next morning, before dawn, but after a hastily eaten breakfast of ship's biscuit, Ralph, Marius and Jobe left the camp. The land ahead was virgin; there were no paths, so the explorers followed the tracks that hippopotamuses and elephants had battered through the lush bush. Their rifles were loaded and each of them carried extra cartridges, but they did not come across a single large animal all morning. For miles, the land was wild and desolate, the terrain alternating between the same thick bush that surrounded their camp on the beach and swamp filled with flocks of pink-backed pelican.

After hours of exploring, they came to a river, deep-running and broad. On the banks they saw fat, shiny crocodiles sunning themselves, while hippopotamuses wallowed in the shallows. As the three men watched, a few waterbuck came down to the water to drink, but cautiously because of the crocodiles.

'We could ford it,' said Marius, doubtfully.

Ralph and Jobe were not ready to take such a mindless risk. Instead, they turned left and followed the riverbank upstream. Soon, the ground started rising, and trees became scarce. The river flowed through tight-knotted hills, which had to be navigated by strenuous climb after strenuous climb. In the far distance, Ralph could see mountains rising in a great rampart across the horizon.

'When do we find the elephants?' Jobe asked, wiping his forehead with the back of his arm. He was dripping with sweat. 'You said there are many.'

'That was what the Frenchman told me,' said Marius.

'At least he was right about the people,' said Ralph. 'We have not seen any sign of habitation.'

Near dusk, they learned why there were no people around. In a dell between two hills, they came upon a large circle of ash and beaten earth scarred into the landscape, two or three hundred yards across. A few heaps of half-burned timbers dotted the area like grave mounds.

It took Ralph a moment to realise what he was looking at.

'This was a village!' he exclaimed, looking at the other men to see if they agreed with him.

The piles of charred poles had been huts, set around a central circular compound. He counted over two dozen of them. If each one held a family, that was well over a hundred souls.

'What happened to the people who lived here?' Ralph wondered. 'Who did this?'

'Some wild savages, no doubt,' said Marius.

Jobe gave him a scornful look. 'Did you go to the Xhosa country after the British had conquered it? They burned our houses, killed the men and drove off the cattle. The women and children were taken as slaves. Every village looked like this.'

'The British have not been here, though.' Ralph looked over his shoulder. The sun was setting; shadows were lengthening. There was not a soul in sight, but whoever had burned the huts could be just over the next rise, watching them.

They had been walking for over twelve hours, but none of them wanted to spend the night with whatever spirits might still haunt the burned village. They found the strength to struggle up the next ridge as the dusk began to fall, and set up their camp on the hilltop.

'We will keep a close watch tonight,' Ralph said. 'If there is anyone out there, we will be sure to see them before they get within five hundred yards of us.'

But though lions roared in the hills, and the hippos grunted and chuffed in the river, no one came.

Ralph took the last watch, replacing Marius. The night was ice-cold, a sure sign that dawn was near. The stars were spread out above him, the Milky Way like a handful of diamond dust thrown across a jeweller's velvet cloth. Ralph inhaled deeply, transported back in time, seeing the sky of his youth, stars swirling across a different horizon on a different continent.

'Adam Courtney,' he whispered into the dark, running his hand over the scars that disfigured the left-hand side of his face. 'You haunted me for so long when you were alive, but you are dead. You cannot haunt me now.'

A different sky appeared above Ralph; the moon, fully dark, was visible only as a black absence in the star-filled heavens. This was the sky that haunted his dreams.

The sound of the ocean came to him, surging on, powerful and relentless. Ralph saw himself crouched in a boat's stern, staring ahead at the shadow on the water, where the *Tiger* rode under her topsails. This had been the moment he had waited half his life

for. He watched as his younger self pressed his thumb against the
the grapnel he carried, feeling the point he had honed sharp as a
needle prick his skin until it drew a bead of blood.

And then he was on board the Tiger confronting Adam Courtney across her lamplit deck.

'Do you not remember me?' Ralph asked.

'Should I?'

*'Perhaps not. I daresay there are many men whose fathers you mur-
dered.'*

*Adam peered more closely. Ralph held his gaze, challenging him to
remember. He watched Adam's face, scrutinising every twitch of his muscles like a sailor reading wind on water. Ignorance, then confusion. The
snap of realisation, eyes widening and pupils contracting. Memory; certainty; terror.*

'Ralph . . .?'

'I have been looking for you for a long time.'

*Adam went pale. His hand clenched three times around the hilt
of his sword. Perhaps he was remembering the small boy he had
thrown a cricket ball with in a garden in India. The boy whose mother
he had seduced, and whose father he had killed. 'I do not want to
fight you.'*

'You made your choice fourteen years ago,' said Ralph.

*A woman pushed through the crowd of sailors and came up beside
Adam. She had pulled on a shawl over her white night-gown, and her
honey-coloured hair was twisted in a loose chignon. She carried a sleeping
baby cradled against her chest. 'What is happening?'*

*'Stay back, Lizzie.' Adam stared at Ralph, though it was impossi-
ble to say if he was looking at his enemy, or into his own soul. Though
a score of men surrounded them, in the circle of lamplight Adam and
Ralph seemed to be the only people who existed.*

When the sun appeared on the horizon, a molten red line boiling
up through the morning mist, Jobe awoke to find Ralph on watch,
his rifle across his knees. But it seemed to Jobe that Ralph was
looking at a different sunrise, in a place where the lions weren't
still roaring and the hippos didn't grumble in the distance.

Jobe woke Marius, made a fire and boiled some water, mixing
in a handful of herbs from a pouch that Ann had given them.

Together, they drank the tea, passing the one cup they had in their possession between them, and ate their dry ship's biscuit.

As the sun rose higher in the clear African sky, Ralph suddenly pointed to the river. 'There's a drift,' he said, standing and stretching as if he was waking from a dream. 'We can cross.'

It didn't take them long to pack up their camp and douse the fire. Half an hour later they stood on the bank, looking out across the river. A bar of heavy gravel ran just under the surface, almost all the way to the other side. Maybe it had been washed there by a storm or had simply accumulated over time. Either way, it left them with only a short stretch of deep water to negotiate.

Ralph was eager to cross immediately, but Marius insisted on taking his time. He knelt in the water, peering closely at the bottom.

'Gold,' he said, and that one word was enough to make all three men forget any danger, hunger or discomfort. Jobe and Ralph waded over to Marius like children running after a pup. Ralph saw glittering specks shining among the mud and gravel of the riverbed.

They hadn't brought any tools with them, so Marius took a tin plate from their carry pack and used it as a pan. He scooped up a quantity of gravel and dipped it in the river, swirling the plate around so that the water slopped over the rim and washed out the mud inside, while the other two watched with fascination.

At last the pan was empty, except for a few golden grains spread across the bottom. Jobe's eyes widened.

'Is that . . .?'

Marius picked up a rock and pressed it against the largest of the grains. The pressure crushed it to a fine powder.

'Gold dust?' Ralph asked.

Marius's face clouded. 'Mica,' he said. '*God verdoem dit!*' He tossed the glittering grains back in the river to wash away. 'Fool's gold.'

They waded across the channel, Ralph and Marius holding the rifles above their heads as the water swirled around their waists, and carried on into another stretch of virgin territory. They managed ten miles that day, by Ralph's reckoning, and fifteen the next. Still they saw no sign of habitation.

'There is no ivory in these parts,' said Marius in disgust. 'No people, no game, no food – nothing.'

They had the means to feed themselves, and they hadn't encountered anyone who wanted to stop them exploring this land, but the hard African ground had shredded their boots and blistered their feet until they bled. Soon they would have to turn back.

They had reached the edge of a low escarpment overlooking another river. It was too dark to cross it. They made camp again, the three men taking the same places around the fire, like the points of a triangle.

'What was that?'

Jobe, always the most alert to their surroundings, had cocked his head and was listening to something in the night. Ralph had not heard it.

'We are being watched,' said Jobe. The fire glinted in his eyes.

'An animal?' said Ralph.

Jobe shook his head. He reached out and brought the rifle closer. His body remained still, muscles taut. Ralph reached for the second gun, but Marius already had it in his grasp.

In a single whiplash movement, Jobe spun around. His body uncoiled. He lifted the rifle to his cheek and fired it into the long grass around them. The flash split the night like lightning. Ralph was temporarily blinded, but over the echo he heard a cry of terror, then the crash of something stampeding through the long grass.

Without pausing to reload, Jobe sprang to his feet and ran in the direction of the footsteps.

'Wait,' Ralph called, but Jobe ignored him and bounded into the grass.

Ralph and Marius stayed by the fire. It was impossible to see anything beyond the ring of firelight; and even if they had seen a target they could not fire for fear of hitting Jobe.

'Is there a lion?' Marius asked.

Both men knew it could not be. The cry they had heard when Jobe fired was unmistakably human.

Footsteps approached from the direction where Jobe had disappeared, swishing briskly through the grass. Marius pointed his rifle towards the sound.

'Do not shoot.' Jobe emerged from the darkness into the fire-light. He returned to his seat and threw down the rifle. 'The man got away.'

'You're sure it was a man, hey?'

'I saw his footprints. And his blood.' Jobe held up his hand. His index finger was smeared red. 'He will not try again.'

He put the finger in his mouth and sucked the blood off it.

'Maybe there are no elephants here,' he said, 'But men there are, for sure.'

They kept watch all night. Marius and Jobe fell asleep when first light touched the hilltops, but Ralph was too hungry to join them. He stood up and went to the edge of the escarpment where he could look down at the river. In the stillness of dawn, its glassy surface was coloured coral pink. Waterfowl skimmed low over the water, while a riot of hoof- and paw-prints in the mud told of the animals that had come down in the night to drink.

Ralph went back to the camp and took his rifle, together with a handful of cartridges and the powder horn. Would that be enough? Marius slept with his rifle beside him, one arm thrown over it like a woman hugging her newborn. Ralph slid it out, careful not to wake Marius, loaded it with birdshot and slung it over his other shoulder.

He found a game trail that led down the escarpment to the river. A flock of ducks with bright red beaks paddled about on the water. Ralph picked up a stone and lobbed it so that it landed in the middle of the ducks. With squawks of alarm, they took to the air. One flew in front of him. He raised Marius's gun, tracked the bird and pulled the trigger.

The dead waterfowl landed with a splash in the shallows at the river's edge. Ralph went to retrieve it – but before he was half-way there a blur of motion streaked from the sky. A great eagle swooped down, talons outstretched, plucked the duck from the water and flew away towards the cloudless horizon.

Ralph gave a wry smile. 'I will have to find myself some bigger game,' he muttered to himself. The other ducks had returned to the river. It occurred to Ralph they must never have known a gun. They had not learned to be wary of its danger.

From downriver, Ralph heard a loud, wet snort: like the neigh of a horse, but deeper and more resonant. He turned towards the sound. There was a bend in the river about a quarter of a mile away, where over many years it had meandered across a gravel bed, changing course again and again, creating a series of deep, interlinked pools. A pod of three hippos stood shoulder-deep in one of the pools; Ralph could make out the curved hummocks of their backs and their flicking ears.

Ralph's pulse quickened. He reloaded Marius's rifle, with a bullet this time, adding as much powder as he dared. There was no cover along the riverbank, but he was standing downwind of the animals. He skirted along the bottom of the escarpment, clambering around the rocks that littered the ground.

He moved as stealthily as possible, but as he approached the hippos, something alerted them to his presence. With another snort, they moved away into deeper water and slid beneath the surface.

Ralph knew, from watching the creatures at Nativity Bay, that they could not stay underwater for more than a few minutes. He kept going downstream, tracking the bubbles that occasionally escaped to the surface. He lost track of time. He was caught in the grip of the hunt, where the sole measure was the beat of his own heart, where all that mattered was the next bubble and the moment when his prey would reveal itself.

Then, suddenly, a sleek grey back, one of the hippos, broke the surface. A head poked out: puffy pink eyes, mouse-like ears, and a long muzzle with drooping jowls like a basset hound. It peered at Ralph, then opened its mouth, wider than seemed possible, baring two huge canine teeth. A guttural growl sounded in its throat.

Ralph levelled the rifle and fired. His aim was perfect. The ball flew straight between the animal's yawning jaws and smashed through the back of its mouth.

The surface of the river turned into a churning froth of foaming bloody water. The hippo thrashed and rolled, beating the river with its huge legs. The other two animals had also surfaced. One – the smaller of the two – smelled the blood and tore away downriver. It galloped through the shallow water, then sub-merged again where the river fed another deep pool.

But the other animal – a big old bull with a latticework of pink scars across its hide – did not follow. It had seen Ralph. With a bel-low, it charged at him, pushing the water in front of it like a tugboat.

Ralph hadn't thought that the lumbering animals could move so quickly. The bull emerged from the river in a furious wave of weeds and brackish water, bounding forwards on its short legs at an unim-aginable speed. Its jaws opened wide enough to bite a man in two.

Ralph had the second rifle on his back, already primed and loaded. Throwing the first gun to the ground, he grabbed it, aimed and fired hastily. But shooting a charging hippo was not the same as taking aim from a safe distance. He snatched his shot. The bullet went wide, punching a hole through the animal's ear. That made it more furious. The ground trembled under its pounding feet. It was so close, Ralph could see the whiskery speckles around its muzzle and the pink flesh of its mouth.

In a misspent life, he had often faced danger. Men with swords, men with guns, men who had been ready to give up their own lives if they could only take Ralph with them. But he had never confronted anything like this: two tons of muscle coming at him as fast as a racehorse, tipped with teeth that would have shamed a tiger. And his gun was empty – he wouldn't even have time to tear the cartridge open before the beast was upon him.

But Ralph had learned that the key to survival was not weapons, or bravery, or even well-honed skill. It was timing. Timing was crucial. At the last possible moment, he threw himself to the left. He nearly misjudged it; he felt his shins slap against the hippo's shoulder as it charged past. A wind that stank of mud and musk blew over him.

He fumbled for the ammunition pouch to reload his gun. But there was no time. Again, the beast shocked him – this time with its agility. It skidded to a halt, legs splayed out, then whipped around, ready to charge at Ralph again.

Ralph had nowhere to go, no escape route. The crocodile-infested river was on his left and a wide escarpment to his right. If he tried to flee over the open ground, the hippo would overtake him within seconds.

The hippo lowered its head. Its small, puffed-up eyes watched Ralph with black menace.

Ralph brandished the gun like a club, jabbing it towards the animal, trying to buy some time by intimidating the beast, wondering if he could somehow jam his rifle in the hippo's mouth.

'*Imvubu!*'

A chilling cry rang out. Before Ralph could see where the sound had come from, a spear hissed through the air and struck the hippo on its flank. The beast growled with pain and turned to face the new threat. Ralph followed its gaze.

A figure stood at the top of the embankment, silhouetted against the morning sky. Ralph could not see him clearly from where he was standing, however, he was sure that the man was neither of his companions. A skirt flapped from his waist and he seemed to be wearing some kind of crown or helmet. He waved his arms and shouted unintelligible words: whether at Ralph or the animal, Ralph couldn't tell.

Blood gushed from the hippo's side where the spear had lodged in its flesh. The weight of the wooden shaft levered the wound open so that every movement the hippo made triggered another flash of pain. The old bull roared in agony. It lumbered across to a large rock and began rubbing its side against the stone to try to dislodge the spear.

This gave Ralph a chance to reload. He reached into the ammunition pouch and extracted two cartridges, bit off the ends and tipped both of them down the barrel of the rifle.

The spear clattered to the ground as the hippo knocked it free and turned back towards Ralph.

Normally, Ralph would have wrapped the bullet in a leather patch to help it grip the rifled grooves inside the barrel. But there was no time for that. Grabbing two bullets, he forced them into the barrel and rammed them home as quickly as he could. The hippo flared its nostrils, bared its teeth and let out a roar that Ralph felt like a punch to his stomach. There was no question that it was about to charge.

Ralph primed the rifle with his powder horn and immediately pulled the trigger – he didn't even aim as by now the beast was so close that accuracy did not matter. Two bullets exploded forward and struck the hippo between the eyes. Still it carried on, like a runaway wagon careering downhill, knocking Ralph aside and ploughing into the mud of the riverbank.

But even two bullets had not killed the hippo. It struggled to get up, tottering on its legs. It was dying, but it could still lash out in its death throes. Picking himself up, Ralph ran to the spear that the animal had dislodged on the boulder. It had a short handle, about three feet long, and a slim leaf-shaped blade that tapered to a sharp point. Ralph grabbed it, making his way to the riverbank and plunging it into the hippo's flank where he guessed the heart might be. Blood poured from the wound.

With a grunt, the hippo's head sank to the ground and its mouth fell open, revealing its giant pink tongue and the enormous teeth that had struck terror into Ralph. Its eyes closed and it kicked out at the mud one last time. Then it was still.

Ralph slumped to his knees. Now that the fight was over, the energy that had fuelled him suddenly drained away; he felt empty. His face was black with powder, his hands and shirt covered in the hippo's blood.

A whoop of triumph made him look up. Marius and Jobe were running down the riverbank – they had surely heard the gunshots.

'Look at you,' cried Marius, picking up the rifle that Ralph had discarded after his first shot had found its mark. There was a wild light in his eyes as he examined the dead beast. 'Mighty hunter, hey?'

Jobe was more pragmatic. 'Lucky you are not dead.' He had plucked the spear out of the hippo's side and was studying it. 'Where did this come from?' he asked.

'There was a man . . .' Ralph stumbled to his feet and looked back to the top of the escarpment where he had seen the figure. 'He saved my life.'

Now the skyline was bare. The man had vanished.

Ralph's mind was filled with questions. *Was he the same man who had crept up to their camp the night before? Was he an enemy? If so, why had he saved him from the hippopotamus?*

Ralph had to know.

'Hey?' Marius said as Ralph set off at a run. 'Hey? Where are you going?'

Exhausted from his battle with the hippo, it wasn't long before Ralph was dragging himself up the escarpment on his hands and knees, his rifle slung awkwardly over his shoulder. Jobe and Marius caught up with him, but the broken ground soon slowed them down too. The three men scrambled over the lip of the gorge, panting and sweating – and came to a halt.

The man Ralph had seen from a distance was still there – but he was no longer alone.

Ralph, Marius and Jobe stared, open-mouthed. Ralph did not know what he had expected – a lone hunter, maybe, or a ragtag raiding party. The multitude in front of him was neither.

There were over a thousand men, Ralph guessed. They were naked, except for kilts of furs around their waists, and barefoot, but every man carried a long shield of matching cowhide, and a short stabbing spear like the one he had used to kill the hippo. Though they could not have looked more different from British soldiers in their red coats and polished boots, their drill was as precise and disciplined as a guards regiment.

This was not a rabble. It was an army.

Ralph laid down his rifle, grinning like an idiot to try and look unthreatening.

'Put down your gun,' he said to Marius.

Marius's cheeks were flushed; sweat ran down his face as he took in the regiments in front of him. His eyes were wide with disbelief. 'Maybe we should give them a taste of our lead first. Teach them to fear us, hey?'

'We would be dead before you even began to reload,' said Jobe.

Ralph nodded in agreement. Shielding his eyes, he saw faces turning in their direction, countenances hardening as they took in the three figures on the ridge above them. 'And anyway,' he said, pointing to the man who stood at the front of the soldiers, most certainly their general. 'That man there saved my life.'

The general wore a square of fur, braided together from monkey tails, that hung from a belt around his loins. A circlet of rolled leopard-skin crowned his head, with two stiff pieces of cowhide sticking up from it like horns. Bushy ostrich feathers fanned out from this headdress, while around his upper arms and calves he wore thick puffs of white hair that looked as if it had been taken from a cow's tail. He carried a long oval shield in one hand, made from the same hide as those his men carried, and a short-handled spear in the other.

In Ralph's short life he had haggled with Parsi factors in the bazaars of Calcutta, exhausted the infinite patience of the Hong merchants in Canton, and bartered for his life with Chinese pirates. He had never faced odds like this, but he knew some things were universal, regardless of the colour of your adversary's skin or how he dressed.

Do not let them see you are afraid, Ralph told himself.

As casually as if he was walking through Garden Reach in Calcutta, Ralph strode forward to meet the men – arms wide, palms open, smile fixed, and his buttocks clenched tight.

He expected to hear one of those spears – or a hundred of them – whistle through the air and sink into his ribcage. When that did not happen, he kept walking. A thousand pairs of eyes watched him, but not one muscle moved. Their discipline was awe-inspiring.

When Ralph was ten paces from the general, he stopped and tapped his chest. 'English.' He gestured at the assembled soldiers. 'You?'

The general said something loud and defiant. The warriors behind him repeated it, bellowing out the words. Though none of them moved, the effect was like staring down a ship's broadside.

Ralph stayed motionless. He forced himself to remain calm, as if this was a sight he encountered every day, as if indeed he had grown rather bored of it.

The man opposite him had the natural air of a commander, the confidence that came from having your orders obeyed. Ralph thought of the king that Marsden had told him about back in Nativity Bay. *A black Bonaparte*, the Portuguese trader had said. Surely it would take a man like that to command this kind of professional army.

'Are you the mighty Shaka?'

The name had a dramatic effect. At once, the general and all his warriors banged their spears on their shields with a thunderous sound and bellowed the name like a battle cry.

'Shaka!'

Looking at the faces around him, Ralph could see the pride and the strength they took from the name; but also something more akin to fear. They shouted the name with a desperate edge, as if they were conjuring a god who might give them their hearts' desire but equally might cast them into a hell from which they would never be freed.

Ralph deduced that the general himself was not Shaka. But it was obvious that he and the army in front of them were somehow under his authority.

'Shaka,' Ralph repeated. 'Take me to Shaka.'

Ralph turned to see that Marius and Jobe were making their way towards him. The warriors lowered their spears as they passed. The general had obviously decided to humour his unexpected guests. Ralph felt like a condemned prisoner reprieved from the scaffold; his insides turned to water, but he did not let his relief show.

'Who are you?' he asked again, gesturing to the warriors standing before him.

Ralph was still puzzled. He knew the name of the king, but who were the people he ruled over: this kingdom that could put fearsome armies in the field, who could raze villages and strike terror far beyond their own borders.

'Who are you?' Ralph asked again.

Jobe repeated the question in Xhosa. By the way the general screwed up his face, Ralph guessed that he spoke a different language from Jobe, but that the two tongues were close enough to each other that the general understood Jobe's question.

The general gestured to his troops, then to himself, then spoke a name.

Ralph had expected the answer would be something long and intricate. Instead, the general said a single short word in which all the power and pride of a mighty kingdom seemed bound up.

'Zulus.'

NATIVITY BAY

After Ralph's party had set out into the bush, the camp at Nativity Bay sank into idleness. The *Farewell*'s broken hulk sat in the lagoon, blackening in the sun, and no one made any attempt to salvage timbers for a new boat. The men lazed in the stockade, sleeping in the sun or gambling with a pair of dice they had carved. Occasionally, they dipped into the rum barrel, or took potshots at monkeys with the rifle, but even Marsden seemed content to limit his activity to catching a couple of fish or listlessly constructing snares for the bushpigs they sometimes saw at the treeline.

For Ann, being inside the stockade was like being trapped in a cage. Every minute of the day, she was aware of being the only woman. The sailors seemed friendly enough, and treated her courteously, but she knew how they looked at her when they thought her back was turned. What if the time came when looking would no longer satisfy them? She could feel the constraints of civilisation rotting inside them, like meat left in the sun. They were violent men, used to a hard life and women who would sell themselves for a few coins. She and Harry were not safe.

But avoiding the sailors meant leaving the stockade – and that frightened her, too. As well as lions and hyenas, the rivers were full of crocodiles and hippopotamuses. She could see them from the stockade walls, low humps gliding through the water, and occasionally the flash of an enormous pair of jaws. What else might be out there, in the dark water and dense bush, that she could not see?

And yet, when it came to it, she would rather take those risks with Harry than stay cooped up in the fort. Every morning, before the men were properly awake, when they were still sleeping off the rum of the night before, she and Harry slipped out and went down to the beach. Over several days, they explored almost the entire perimeter of the lagoon, often finding more wreckage from the *Farewell*. If it looked useful, or valuable, they would drag it up the beach and leave it for the men to fetch later.

One day, while they were out walking at the far end of the lagoon, they saw something glinting in the sand. It was a piece of glass.

'Careful,' Ann warned Harry as he tried to pick it up, worried he would cut himself. But when she dug it out, she saw that it was not broken. It was a crystal goblet, clouded by years of abrasion but still, miraculously, intact. Even the design that had been etched into the side was legible. A long-barrelled cannon on a wheeled carriage, with a ribbon below sporting the initials *C.B.T.C.*

Ann was stunned to see such an object so far from the civilised world. She was certain that she had never seen anything like it aboard the *Farewell*. And anyway, how would it have made its way so far down the lagoon – they could barely make out the wreck from where they stood. *The edges are so smooth that it must have been here for years*, Ann thought to herself. *Maybe it washed ashore from another shipwreck, was buried under the sand for decades until the lapping waves revealed it again?*

She turned the goblet over in her hands. The fact that it had survived so long seemed significant, as if it had been waiting for her to find it. Maybe it was some sort of message. But that was just her imagination running away with her.

When she looked up from her little treasure, she found that Harry had run off. She saw the flash of antlers in the distance – the corkscrew horns of an impala – and Harry plunging into the long grass after it.

'Harry!'

She ran after him, following the narrow trail the buck had made. Her dress caught on twigs and tore on thorns while Harry, nimble and determined, disappeared into the thick bush.

Ann was terrified; her breath sawed in her throat as images of all the terrible things that could happen to her boy flashed before her eyes. *How could he have gone so far? How was it possible? The grass grew high here. What if there were predators? A three-year-old boy couldn't fight a lion.*

'*Harry?*' She called his name again and again, feeling the tears start to flow. '*Harry?*'

Running full pelt, her foot caught on something firm sticking out of the earth. She pitched forward and hit the ground, her hands coming up too late to break her fall. The impact knocked the breath out of her chest and she tasted blood where she had bitten her lip.

'Mummy?'

The sound of Harry's voice made her forget the pain in her chest. Harry stood over her, his face screwed up with deep concern.

'Are you hurt?' he asked, squatting next to her.

Sobbing with relief, Ann scrambled to her knees and pulled Harry close. He knew that he had scared her and would be punished for running off after the impala, but he also knew that his mother would forgive him anything if he was kind and gentle.

But he could not keep still for long. He pulled back – though she kept a firm grip on his hand – and pointed down.

'What is that?' Harry asked.

Ann rose slowly to her feet. The object she had tripped on was not rock, or wood. It was a lump of hard black iron, rising in a low mound out of the ground. It had been almost buried, protruding just enough to catch her foot and trip her.

She knelt and dug away the compacted soil with her hands. Harry joined her. By the time they had finished, they had revealed an iron cylinder fully nine feet long, tapering to a flared muzzle at one end.

'It's a cannon,' Harry announced in awe.

Ann was confused. *How could a cannon have come to be buried here? How long it had lain undisturbed? It looked as if it had just come from the foundry.*

'Mummy, was there a castle here?' Harry asked.

'I doubt it, my boy.' *How could there have been?*

'What about that?'

Harry was looking into the bush. Ann followed his gaze. At first, she could see nothing but the thick undergrowth. Then, like a morning mist suddenly lifting, she saw what Harry was pointing at. Patterns in the bush, straight lines under the twisting vegetation. Fragments of stone walls rising up like the bones of a carcass that had rotted away. Many were blackened by mould, or maybe by fire.

'Uncle Ralph said that no one ever lived here before,' said Harry.

'Well, that just shows you that even Uncle Ralph can be mistaken,' she said.

Ann knew she should go back, yet something about the ruins drew her to them. She knew that Harry wouldn't leave without exploring their find, but it spoke to her too. Termite mounds rose high around her like funeral monuments; the dust of floorboards and furniture long since devoured. Sometimes she caught the glint of metal: a brass hinge, a pewter bowl. In one place, she saw a full row of ivory keys from a harpsichord. The instrument had rotted away, but the keys remained laid in a row on the ground, so neat she almost felt they would make music again if she touched them.

Who was here? Where did they go?

They had walked so far that they had come out on the far side of what had once been a well-tended homestead. The bush had reclaimed the buildings, but she could still see how the estate had been laid out. Low scrub covered a flat area that must once have been cleared for a garden or crops, while further back stood taller trees, where the edge of the property must have been.

Ann gasped. Where the forest began, at the edge of the property, the undergrowth thinned out around five long mounds of rocks. There was no doubt as to what they were: the row was too even to be natural, each mound about the length and width of a man. Four were intact, but one had been pulled apart by an animal, and where the soil beneath the stones was scratched out, a white bone protruded from the earth.

It was a human bone. These were graves. At the head of each one, flat stones had been set upright as markers. Most had fallen down, but one remained standing, the traces of the letter 'G' still visible, scratched into it.

If she had found the graves by themselves, she would have guessed they contained mariners buried by a passing ship. But the cemetery belonged to the ruined house. This had been somebody's home. People who had cannons, and played the harpsichord. White people.

Did Ralph know about this? Had he been here before? Questions piled upon questions in her head again. *How had Ralph discovered Nativity Bay? Where did he get the map he claimed to have seen?*

Did he kill the people in the graves?

A chill went through her – she didn't want to believe Ralph capable of such an act but the thought would not leave her. Although the sun blazed brightly, there was a darkness at the edge of her vision. The glade seemed to close around her. Something evil had happened in this place – a family had been cut down, a house destroyed. Suddenly, she desperately wanted to be back in the stockade, with Marsden and the other men.

Harry felt it, too. 'I want to go home, Mummy,' he said.

'Yes.'

But Ann had frozen. She was staring into the bush beyond the graves. Harry followed her gaze.

'Who is that?' he asked.

A man stood at the edge of the clearing. He must have been there the whole time, observing them, yet until he revealed himself, he had been almost invisible.

The man stepped out of the shadows, spear raised. His dark hair was piled up above his head in a sort of intricately braided crown, and he wore a necklace of red beads around his neck. Otherwise he was naked, except for a thin pouch that covered his manhood.

He jabbed the spear at Ann, his face twisted in a terrifying snarl. The point darted at her, like a snake readying itself to strike. Ann snatched up a rock that had rolled away from one of the graves, but it did not deter him. He could see that she was not strong enough to hurt him with it.

She backed away. There was no point calling for help: she was too far from the stockade for anyone to hear her. But she would fight long enough to save Harry.

'Run,' she said. 'Back to the camp, as fast as you can.'

Harry did not obey. To her horror, he stood still, looking at the man with his head cocked to one side.

'Go,' she hissed, almost pleading.

The man took another step forward. Ann brandished the rock at him.

Harry began to move. But not down the path. Instead, he stepped forward towards the man, as if he had not noticed the spear.

'What are you doing?' Ann tried to snatch him back, but she was too slow. Harry was out of her reach, right under the point of the spear.

The man's fist clenched tighter around the shaft. He jabbed the spear at Harry; Ann screamed.

Harry stayed still.

The spear stopped inches from his face. Confronted with this unflappable boy, the man did not know what to do. The snarl on his face turned to a frown of confusion.

Harry reached into the front pocket of his smock, where he kept the shells and pebbles he collected from the beach. His hand emerged, clutching a piece of ship's biscuit that he must have squirrelled away.

He offered it to the man.

The man's eyes widened. Hesitantly, he reached out and took the biscuit. He eyed it for a moment, then popped it in his mouth. The biscuit was dry and hard – Ann heard it crunch so loud that she thought it would break the man's teeth – but the look on his face was sheer bliss.

'See how thin he is, Mummy,' said Harry. 'He is hungry.'

With his child's eyes he had seen what Ann had missed. The man was so gaunt every rib was outlined against his chest, his hips and collarbone pushing through his skin like ploughshares.

'What's his name?' Harry asked.

'I don't know. Maybe we can find out.' Ann pointed slowly to herself. 'Ann.' Then to Harry. 'Harry.' Then to the man. 'You?'

The man smiled, to show he understood. 'Mahamba.'

Ann repeated the name. She tried to think of something else to say, but her mind was blank. How could she make herself understood?

The man began to speak. The language was incomprehensible to Ann, a mix of rapid syllables and strange clicks. Was he thanking her? Asking for more? Warning her? She held out her hands in the universal gesture of ignorance.

'I do not understand you.'

Then, suddenly, she realised that his words were not for her. With a rustle of leaves, the branches around the clearing parted and a dozen more people stepped out. They, like Mahamba, wore almost nothing – only penis sheaths for the men, and a cloth band tied around the hips for the women, while the children were naked. All of them had hollow cheeks, pronounced bones and eyes dulled by hunger. When they stared at Ann and Harry, the hope in their eyes was painful to see.

Ann didn't need a translator to tell her what they wanted. Nor did Harry.

'We must give them food,' he said.

'We don't have enough for ourselves.'

Even as she said it, Ann knew how mean she sounded. Compared to Mahamba and his people, she and Harry must look fat. They had ship's biscuits and salt pork salvaged from the wreck, fish traps on the beach and the rifle for hunting.

Ann knew what it was like to be so hungry you could not sleep. To feel the hollow in your stomach every waking moment, as if your body was collapsing in on itself. One of the women had a baby in her arms, a shrivelled infant suckling on a withered breast. Ann understood her shame – a mother who could not feed her child. What she would have given, during those years in Paradise Valley, for a gesture of kindness.

She beckoned to Mahamba. 'Come with me.'

He stayed where he was. She beckoned again, then took Harry's hand and began walking slowly down the trail towards the camp. She glanced back encouragingly, but Mahamba hesitated. He looked to his companions and spoke briefly.

'Do come,' said Ann.

Harry took a more practical approach. He slipped out of her grip and ran to Mahamba, grabbed the man's hand and began tugging him towards the camp.

'Come with us,' he said.

Whether they were disarmed by the boldness of the child or whether they recognised that there was no point resisting Harry when he fixed his mind on something – they did not delay. Mahamba let Harry lead him down the path, with the rest of his people following.

Marsden, who was keeping watch at the stockade, leaped up in alarm when he saw Ann and Harry arrive with Mahamba's people.

'Please, Marsden, put the gun down,' she called. 'They are friendly.'

She was afraid that Mahamba and his people would run at the sight of the rifle, but they showed no concern. Perhaps they weren't familiar with guns and so had not learned to fear them.

The other sailors came running and looked in astonishment at the new arrivals.

'Who are they?' Marsden asked. He stood in the entrance to the stockade, the rifle held across his body, blocking the way.

'I encountered them in the bush,' said Ann. 'As you can see, they are starving.'

'We've not got enough food for ourselves, never mind a bunch of Kaffir beggars.'

'Of course we have enough,' said Ann.

Marsden peered at Mahamba's people suspiciously. 'Who's to say they're friendly?'

'If they wanted to kill me, they could have done it already,' Ann said.

She felt certain Mahamba meant them no harm, but how could she prove it? There was so much she wanted to ask him – about the country, his tribe, and the people who had lived here before. But at that the moment there was no way that they could communicate.

Maybe when Jobe returns he will be able to speak to them, she thought, hopefully.

But when would that be?

ZULULAND

The Zulus moved with a long, loping stride, mile after mile. Even Jobe struggled to keep up. Marius floundered behind, his perspiring face red as a beetroot.

'I thought you were a man of the land,' Ralph said, though he too was sweating.

'Walking is for Kaffirs and animals,' the Dutchman retorted. 'Give me a horse, or an ox wagon, like civilised men, and we'll see who looks *snarks*.'

The river where Ralph had killed the hippo seemed to be some sort of border. From the Zulu general, Ralph learned it was called the *Thukela*. They crossed it at a drift that the Zulus showed them, and came into a different land on the far side, a ripe and cultivated country settled with many villages, or kraals, as Marius called them. All of them were built on the same pattern, round huts in a circle between two rings of fences. The outer fence was for protection; the inner one formed an enclosure where the inhabitants kept their cattle. Around the villages were well-kept fields, some planted with corn and vegetables, others given over to pasture where young boys tended the cows and goats as they grazed during the day.

'Look at those heifers,' said Marius, admiring the cattle. 'Worth a pretty penny, hey?'

'Do not get ideas,' said Jobe.

'Spoken like a Kaffir.' Marius punched him on the arm, not gently. 'We are not all born cattle thieves like you blacks are.'

'No,' Jobe agreed. 'You are much worse.'

'Keep quiet,' said Ralph. 'Can you imagine what they will do if they think we have come for their livestock?'

It was obvious to him that cattle were the heart of the Zulus' society. Whereas an English village might be built around a church, every Zulu settlement was centred on the cattle pen. At each kraal the army visited, a cow was slaughtered and roasted and the meat served to the visitors. Ralph could not be sure if he and his companions were guests of honour, or prisoners, but they were certainly well fed.

'When will we ever see this Shaka?' Marius fretted.

Each time they approached a village, they wondered if this would be the king's residence. Ralph would go to the general and ask: 'Shaka?' But each time, the general shook his head with a smirk that said Ralph would know the capital when he saw it.

'But maybe you do not want to go there,' said Jobe. 'Who knows what sort of welcome we will get from King Shaka?'

'He would not dare touch a white man.' Marius spoke with an arrogant certainty, but there was an ember of doubt behind his words. They had come a long way into the Zulus' country: this was the fifth night that they had lodged together in a spare hut in a village.

The hut was dark – there were no windows, just a smouldering wood fire. It was a typical Zulu dwelling, a dome about fifteen feet across, made of saplings bent into a beehive shape and woven together. The roof was thatched with grass and covered with mats, with implements and baskets hanging from the walls. It smelled of smoke, cow dung and sour beer.

'How far do you think we have come?' Ralph asked.

The Zulus travelled on paths that followed the ridgelines of the hills. When Ralph asked the general how long the journey would be, the man had shrugged. It was clear that the journey was far and would take many days, but how far and how many days?

'Maybe fifty miles?' Marius guessed.

'How big this kingdom must be.' Ralph had assumed it would be no more than a few hamlets under a puffed-up warlord. But seeing the army that the Zulus could field, with its uniform equipment and rigid discipline, had shattered that delusion.

'The general said Shaka's kingdom stretches almost to the Portuguese port,' said Jobe. 'Lourenço Marques.'

'If that is so, it must be bigger than Holland,' said Marius.

'Have you ever been to Lourenço Marques?' Ralph asked.

Marius and Jobe shook their heads.

'It is a contemptible place. You would find more ambition in a graveyard. The Portuguese colonists make no effort to grow the trade, they just squeeze a few coins out of whatever is brought to them from the interior.'

'So?'

'Think about it. What we have discovered here looks to be the greatest empire in Africa. Yet the only way King Shaka can trade with the world beyond is through Lourenço Marques. That is why no one has heard of him.'

Light from the dying fire played over Ralph's face, knotting the scars on his cheek.

'Imagine if we could capture that trade from the Portuguese. The Zulus will have goods – ivory, gold, hides. We could ship it through Nativity Bay. We would make a fortune. Three fortunes.'

'I have a better idea,' said Marius. 'What if we became kings here ourselves? Overthrow this Shaka, take his kingdom and live like lords?'

'I say you should stick to stealing cattle,' said Jobe, lying back on his mat. The Zulus did not sleep on beds, but on woven grass mats. Instead of pillows, the guests were offered carved wooden headrests. 'Then you might escape with your life.'

'A white man is worth a hundred Kaffirs.' Marius's voice was sharp with anger.

'And if Shaka has ten thousand men? Or a hundred thousand? What will you do then?' Jobe stared at the ceiling, keeping a relaxed pose, but Ralph could see the tension in his jaw, the anger he was holding in.

'Enough,' said Ralph. 'Even if I could make myself a king here, I would not do it. I came to get rich.'

'And him?' said Jobe, pointing at Marius. 'What does he want?'

'A place where I do not have to listen to uppity Kaffirs.'

For a moment, Ralph thought Jobe would fly at Marius. The Dutchman wanted it; his biceps were already flexed. Instead, Jobe guffawed with laughter: a sound that stung Marius more than any punch he could have thrown.

'If you do not want to listen to "uppity Kaffirs", I think you are going to the wrong place.'

The following morning, when they started their march, Ralph increased his pace so he could reach the front of the column. He forced himself on until he and Jobe caught up with the general. The general's name was Hamu. His powerful physique, high cheek-bones, shrewd eyes and confident air of command would have sin-gled him out as a leader in any situation, but by the way people bowed to him at every kraal they came to, there was no doubt that he ranked high in the Zulu hierarchy. The men addressed him as *induna*, which Ralph took to be a title like lord or general.

Hamu saw him approach and offered the traditional Zulu greeting. '*Sawubona.*'

'*Yebo, sawubona,*' Ralph answered, instantly exhausting all the Zulu that he had learned so far. 'Is today the day we will meet Shaka?'

Jobe translated. Hamu smiled and shook his head in a regretful way that might have meant 'no', or that he couldn't say, or that he did not understand the question. The Zulus, in Ralph's brief experience, were evasive when it came to precise answers.

'Tell me about Shaka,' Ralph said, pressing on despite Hamu's silence. Every time he heard the name, he felt the awe and power in the way men spoke it. But behind the name there must be a human being, and he wanted to know what to expect. 'What kind of man is he?'

Hamu considered the question. He frowned at Jobe and spoke a few words.

'He says, "Why do you want to know?"'

'Shaka is a great king. He will be offended if I do not know of his exploits when I meet him.'

He could see the answer made sense to Hamu.

'What do you want to know?'

'How did he become the king?'

Hamu thought for a moment, then nodded. 'I tell you.'

Shaka was the first-born son of a king – but illegitimate. The Zulus, Ralph gathered, were even less enamoured of bastards than the English. Shaka's mother, Nandi, had been expelled from the court, and the boy sent to grow up as an outcast. His life had been at risk from the day he was born. He had survived on the charity of relatives, terrified that his father would one day choose to have him killed.

It was not hard for Ralph to imagine himself in Shaka's place. Fatherless, an outcast boy living off the kindness of strangers. He could conjure up the looks the Zulu matriarchs would have given Shaka and his mother: pity to their faces, but scorn and judgement when their backs were turned. Women would have avoided being seen with Nandi. Boys would have hit her son with sticks and pelted him with stones. Shaka would have taken the beatings in silence. But he would not have forgotten.

In those days, Hamu explained, the Zulus were not an empire – not even a kingdom. They were a family of tribes, loosely linked by common ancestors. Sometimes they fought among themselves, stealing cattle and carrying off each other's women. But this was no more than family squabbling.

It was the custom among them that at the age of sixteen, all the boys joined a regiment for a few years to serve the chief, fighting in times of war or labouring during peace. These had been times of war – and this was where Shaka's military genius asserted itself. He quickly became the commander of his regiment and made himself indispensable to the king.

Before Shaka, the Zulu way of war had been largely ceremonial: a charge, a volley of thrown spears, then submission and a tribute from the side which had come off worse. Few men died. Under Shaka, war became an uncompromising battle for survival. He took away the throwing spears and allowed his men to keep only one short-handled stabbing spear apiece. The tactics he built upon this were simple and brutal. Engage the enemy in close quarters, combat and slaughter him. Kill or be killed, became his war cry.

Shaka's deeds reached his father's attention. The king came to visit his estranged son. In a great ceremony, the two were reconciled; the king presented Shaka with a spear in honour of his accomplishments in war.

'That night, the king died.'

'The same night?' Ralph wasn't sure he'd understood correctly. Jobe nodded.

'How did he die?'

'Sleeping.'

Hamu was looking away, his jaw clenched. Ralph did not probe further.

'So Shaka became king?'

Hamu shook his head 'Shaka have brother.'

'What happened to him?' Ralph guessed the answer before Hamu spoke. Even so, it made him wince.

'He too died.'

Hamu cupped his left forefinger and thumb, then rammed his right fist through it. It took a moment for Ralph to realise he was miming a man being impaled through his rectum.

'Then Shaka king.'

As the story continued, Ralph realised that the Zulu realm was not something Shaka had inherited: he had dreamed it into being, and then created it through the force of his will. He had transformed his people: their way of war, their lands, even their way of life. His armies had spread over the country, far beyond the traditional Zulu heartlands. They had conquered some tribes and added them to their empire. Others, they obliterated.

'Does Shaka have a queen?' Ralph asked.

'No wives. No children.'

'Then who is next in line if Shaka dies?' Marius asked.

He had lumbered up the column to join Ralph and Jobe, though the effort had almost killed him. He did not trust them speaking to the Zulus without him.

'You cannot ask that,' said Jobe. 'Even to think that the king will die . . .' He shook his head. 'You cannot ask it.'

'Then what other family does the king have?'

'Dingane.'

'Who is that?'

'Half-brother.'

'This Dingane is lucky to be alive, hey? Men do not have long lives in that family.' Marius gave a sly wink. Jobe did not translate what he said.

'And maybe one night if old Shaka dies in his sleep,' Marius continued, 'then—'

He broke off. They had come to the top of a ridge. Standing in the shade of a euphorbia tree, they looked down into a valley. A river wound through it, sparkling in the afternoon sun. And on the far bank, on an eminence at the top of a slope that faced east over rolling hills, was a city.

Ralph had seen many Zulu settlements on the journey from the Thukela, and this was like every one of them, and yet nothing like them at all. Built on the same circular plan, like a giant wheel, but almost a mile across. Smaller circles – each big enough to be its own village – surrounded it, like moons orbiting a planet. At the heart of it, through a brown haze of smoke from cooking fires, Ralph could see the central cattle enclosure, a vast open circle of trampled earth surrounded by so many huts that he couldn't tell where one ended and the next began.

The top section of the circle, furthest from the gate, was divided from the rest of the city by a stout wall. This uppermost segment was in turn divided into three: a smaller cattle enclosure; a labyrinth of huts; and, in between, an open stretch of ground containing a single hut. It was built far larger than any of the others, at least three times as high, commanding the entire compound. It had to be Shaka's palace.

'KwaBulawayo,' said Hamu.

'*God verdoem dit.*' Marius stood, staring at the Zulu capital. Ralph knew what he was thinking. Any idea that the three of them might go to war with this kingdom was laughable.

Jobe also gazed on the city. But unlike Marius, the sight did not intimidate him. A strange light had come into his eyes. *Did he admire the Zulus?* Ralph wondered. *Or did he envy them for creating the power that he had always dreamed of?*

As for Ralph, when he looked across the valley to the great kraal it was the people who struck him the most – boys herding cattle, blacksmiths smelting metal, women cooking outside their huts. After the teeming, ancient civilisation of India, he had thought Africa would be an empty land, a blank canvas where he could wander freely. That, he could see now, was blind arrogance. There had always been people here. Their buildings were grass huts and wattle fences, rather than pagodas and temples; their wealth was in livestock, not gold and jewels. But they would fight for their land as fiercely as the men he had met in China, or Singapore, or Madagascar.

Ralph, Jobe and Marius followed Hamu down the slope, forded the river, then climbed towards the great enclosure. Ralph studied the outer fence. There was no sign of ivory palings, as the French hunter had promised, just thorn trees and saplings woven together. But it was solid, with no way through apart from a narrow, well-guarded gateway at the bottom of the slope. Long logs lay on the ground, where they could be quickly slotted into an upright frame to bar the entrance. Or, Ralph thought, to prevent anyone escaping.

They entered a long passage with high walls. Through the gaps in the woven panels Ralph could hear laughter and singing; the clicks and hums of Zulus speaking to one another; the clatter of clay pots and the clack of looms. A whole city existed on the far side of the wall, but it was hidden from him. He saw flashes of colour through gaps in the fence, like birds glimpsed in a thicket.

The passage ended at the mouth of the central cattle enclosure. At this time of day, the cattle had been driven out to graze, so the entire ground was empty. Even though it was only beaten earth surrounded by a woven wooden fence, the colossal scale of it reminded Ralph of the square outside the emperor's palace in Peking. Crossing it, he felt like a mouse scuttling across a bare field, naked under the eyes of circling predators.

'How many cattle must they keep here?' Marius muttered in astonishment.

On the far side of the enclosure, a gate led into another courtyard, the royal area that they had seen from the opposite hillside. In the centre stood the hut that Ralph had identified, twenty feet high, its thatch fastened with criss-crossed ropes so that it looked like a woven basket that had been turned upside down.

Scores of men were gathered outside. They wore ostrich plumes in their hair, great cloaks of animal skin, and necklaces of beads and claws. *These must be the* indunas, Ralph thought, men like Hamu who were the lords and generals of the Zulu empire. He searched the crowd for Shaka, thinking the king must surely stand out. But the crowd was so thick he was invisible.

The *indunas* glared at Ralph and his companions.

Ralph had visited rulers before. As a child, he had accompanied his father to the opulent courts of Indian rajahs and queens; as a man, he had penetrated the great palace of the Chinese emperor in Peking. But none of them had been as intimidating as this. Those potentates practised a remote form of rule: they proclaimed their superiority by becoming distant, untouchable statues. Here, the power was immediate and as real as the taste of dust in his mouth.

Hamu spoke a few words, then gestured to Ralph.

'Announce yourself,' Jobe whispered in his ear.

Ralph still couldn't see the man he was supposed to be addressing.

'My name is Ralph Courtney,' he said. His voice sounded small and feeble against the towering silence around him. It died away as Jobe repeated his words. 'I have come from the great king over the water, King George, to visit King Shaka, whose reputation is known across the world.'

A thought struck him: *I should have brought gifts*. You did not come before a king empty-handed. Many of the high-ranking Zulu *indunas* wore strands of glass beads for decoration. Running his merchant's eye over them, Ralph could see they were poor-quality, uneven and dull. Probably they had come from the Portuguese at Lourenço Marques. He could have impressed Shaka with the quality of the British equivalent. But this journey had not been planned and so he had nothing to offer, nothing to show his respect for this great king.

The silence stretched longer.

'Fire off the gun,' said Marius, beside him. 'That will make them notice us.'

'Are you mad?'

Ralph could feel the tension around them. They were like exotic animals brought into a ring for display. If they showed their teeth, the Zulus would surely put them down.

'We should sing for him,' Ralph said.

Jobe and Marius stared at him incredulously.

'Sing?'

'Sing *what*?'

'"God Save the King".'

He knew they would not like it. Marius and Jobe might disagree on almost every subject under the sun, but they were united by the belief that King George was a foreign tyrant, occupying their homeland and trampling their freedoms. Both men had gone to prison for defying the king's law.

Before either man could object, Ralph started bellowing the words as lustily as an English sailor on St George's Day. The others were forced to join in, or they would seem disrespectful to Shaka.

God save our gracious king, long live our noble king . . .

Ralph made them sing all three verses. The Zulus watched. Some swayed a little in time with the music; a few smiled, but most observed impassively. One man in particular caught Ralph's attention. He stood near the centre of the gathering, studying them with penetrating eyes. He had a fleshy face, with a prominent chin and a small mouth; a very fat stomach which drooped over the belt around his waist; and hair growing in thick tufts over his body. An ugly man, and the way that he stared at Ralph was uglier still. Could this be Shaka?

'Tell Shaka that is a song we sing in England in praise of our king,' he told Jobe, when they had roared out the last refrain.

Perhaps the song had worked. Like clouds parting before the sun, the assembled chiefs drew back to reveal the man in their midst. He had been sitting on a carved wooden chair, but as the crowd divided, he leaped up and approached the visitors.

For a moment Ralph struggled to believe that this was the man whose name alone could inspire such fear. He was strong, true: sturdily built, with powerful legs and broad shoulders. His skin was deep ebony black and gleaming with oil. He wore a kilt of braided monkey tails, and a two-foot high crane feather like a diadem in his head-ring, which was garlanded with red lourie feathers. But he was not particularly tall, and his face was remarkably ugly. His forehead bulged out, his cheeks were sunken and his two front teeth protruded.

His eyes fixed on Ralph, and suddenly Ralph had no doubt that this was the man he had heard of. The eyes were deep brown, so dark that the pupil and the iris seemed to blend into one bottomless hole. To look into them was to lose your bearings, to feel yourself being sucked into their depths.

Shaka focused on the mesh of scars on Ralph's cheek. Ralph had long since become used to people staring at his disfigurement, but under Shaka's gaze it felt as if he was back on the *Tiger*, the fire raging around him, filling the rigging with billowing smoke, the burning spar pinning him to the deck. He felt every thread of tissue like a hot wire, until he was desperate to cover it with his hand, or turn his face away.

He is testing me. He wants me to show weakness.

Ralph fought the urge to submit. He focused his mind on the pain he had felt that day, drawing strength from it. He tilted his head so that Shaka could see the scars more clearly, displaying them proudly.

A smile played at the corner of Shaka's mouth. He said a few short words that made his men erupt with laughter.

'What did he say?' Ralph muttered to Jobe.

'He said, "At last he has found a man who is uglier than him."'

Ralph grinned, to show he could take the joke. The scars began to cool again. Ralph waited for the inevitable next question: how he had got the injury. He wondered which version of the story he should tell.

But Shaka had lost interest. When he spoke again, he said: 'What is the name of the king of England?'

'George. King George.'

'Is umGeorge king of all white men?'

'Yes,' Ralph said, before Marius could contradict him.

'You have seen umGeorge?'

Ralph had never in his life set foot in England. 'I have. He lives in a great palace.'

Shaka considered this. Ralph felt the power in his eyes: calculating, weighing.

'As great as KwaBulawayo?'

What should Ralph say? He had seen pictures of Windsor Castle in the illustrated newspapers, and the extraordinary pavilion that King George had built himself in Brighton. Set against those magnificent buildings, Shaka's kraal was a farmstead. Did he risk King Shaka's wrath by saying so? Or should he try to intimidate him, impress him with the achievements of the white king?

'umGeorge builds his palaces of stone,' he said neutrally.

'Ha!'

Shaka waved his stick at Ralph.

'He says umGeorge is very foolish,' Jobe translated. 'A palace made of stone would be very heavy. How does he move it when he wishes to establish a new kraal?'

Ralph had no answer – nor was one expected. Shaka's thoughts had moved on.

'Did umGeorge send a message for King Shaka?' Jobe asked, fixing Ralph with a look that said *I hope you know what you are doing*.

'He . . . ah, seeks friendship with King Shaka, and trade between our peoples,' Ralph improvised. He sensed Marius stiffen beside him and prayed the Dutchman would keep his mouth shut.

But Marius could not tolerate being a spectator. He stepped forward, holding himself proudly, his eyes full of defiance.

'Tell Shaka that King George has a mighty army, very power-ful.' He shook the rifle he was carrying. It was lucky the Zulus did not know what it was, Ralph thought – but perhaps they guessed, or had heard of such things. They eyed it like a ser-pent. 'Tell them that if they do not give us land, and the right to settle and hunt and trade, King George will be very angry. He will send his army. He will burn their kraals, scatter their people and make slaves of them all if they do not give us what we demand.'

'Do not tell them any such thing,' said Ralph, before Jobe could open his mouth.

'You translate what I said,' Marius retorted.

The Zulus waited. They had heard Marius's speech, and though they did not understand the words, the threat in his voice was clear. The silence stretched as Jobe looked between his two companions. At last, he muttered a few words.

Shaka's answer was brief – and apparently hilarious. The assembled Zulus roared with laughter, stamping their feet and banging their shields with their spears. Even the fat man Ralph had noticed earlier, with the piercing eyes, could not help his mouth twitching.

Marius's face went red. 'What did he say?' he demanded. Jobe also was struggling to contain his mirth and this made Marius even more furious. 'If he is insulting me—'

'He said: "Can a lion be threatened by a baboon?"'

Marius's mind was not made for metaphors. He frowned a moment, then erupted as Shaka's meaning became clear. 'Did he call me a baboon?'

'*Enough.*' Ralph stepped forward. 'Tell King Shaka that the lions are stronger when they hunt as a pack. All we ask is friendship, to our mutual gain.'

The laughter had stopped. The fat man Ralph had seen earlier said a few words. He stood almost beside Shaka, in a place of honour, and although they looked very different, there was a kinship in their demeanour. Ralph guessed he must be the brother that he had heard about: Dingane.

'What tokens of friendship do they offer?' Jobe translated Dingane's question.

Ralph had nothing to give except the gun in his hand – which he could not surrender – and the small shoulder bag he had brought from Nativity Bay. He felt the weight of eighty thousand Zulus staring at them – and one above all, that unignorable presence bearing down on him from the throne.

'We brought many gifts for King Shaka. Great gifts, worthy of such a mighty king.'

He ignored the incredulous look Jobe gave him and carried on. 'A storm wrecked our ship—' He broke off; Jobe was struggling. 'What?'

'They do not have a word for ship.'

'Our gifts were lost in a storm,' Ralph amended. 'All I have to offer King Shaka is . . . this.'

He reached in his bag and pulled out one of the teeth that he had taken from the hippos he had killed at the river. Ralph had found time to go back and take some trophies after their first meeting with Hamu, but he was painfully aware of what an inadequate gift it made for a king. Staring into the charging beast's jaws, unarmed, each tooth had seemed as big as a tree. In Shaka's court, it appeared no better than a toothpick.

Shaka gestured to one of his men to take it from Ralph and bring it to him. He studied it carefully, examining the ivory like a jeweller testing a diamond for flaws, turning it in his hands. He pulled a face, eyes wide, mouth hanging open in wonder.

Then he tipped back his head and laughed. All the *indunas* joined in, battering Ralph's pride.

The meeting had become a disaster. The tooth was so small it was insulting; better to have given nothing at all. Shaka walked around the group, showing the tusk to his men so they could heap more scorn on it. Ralph could see Marius swelling with fury.

If Ralph could not retrieve the situation, it would end one of two ways. At best, Ralph and his companions would be driven away in ignominy. At worst, they would not leave at all. Many of the Zulus carried fighting sticks, polished hardwood with bulbous ends, like maces. One blow would split a man's skull open. Several of the *indunas* were already fingering their weapons. A word from Shaka and their lives would be over.

'Offer him the rifle,' said Jobe.

'Are you mad?' said Marius. 'I will die before I put a gun in a Kaffir's hands.'

'Maybe you will die if you do not.'

'*Quiet*,' Ralph hissed.

The chatter among the *indunas* was getting louder, taking on a life of its own, becoming dangerous. Shaka had turned away. That was even more frightening than being the focus of his attention. With a man like Shaka there was nothing worse than being unimportant, for him to lose interest.

Shaka walked back towards his throne. He moved with the grace of a dancer, a deliberate, swinging gait, swaying from side to side with each step. The monkey tails of his kilt rippled and parted like curtains in a summer breeze, revealing the sculpted buttocks beneath. The most eloquent riposte to Ralph's pretensions.

Unless . . .

'There is something else,' Ralph said, loudly enough that it broke through the laughter and chatter. The *indunas* went quiet. Shaka turned back and looked at him.

'umGeorge sent medicines to cure what ails King Shaka.'

Jobe and Marius stared at Ralph in disbelief.

'Careful what you say,' said Marius.

And indeed, Ralph's words drew a sharp response from Shaka. He whipped around, jabbing his finger at Ralph and subjecting him to a fierce lecture.

'Shaka says, you do not know what hurts him,' Jobe translated.

'I do,' said Ralph. He tried to sound confident, though inside his nerves were burning like quickmatch. 'He is suffering from pains in his backside.'

The moment the words were translated, he knew he had hit the mark. Shaka advanced towards Ralph, his face a mask of incredulity and wonder.

'He says you do *abelumbi* witchcraft,' said Jobe. 'You are *abathakathi.*'

'What is that?'

Jobe spoke briefly to Hamu, clarifying the meaning. 'Wizards.'

Ralph could have explained that he was not a wizard. He could have said that he'd had an opportunity to study Shaka's posterior under the swinging tails of his kilt, and had noticed the many half-moon scars on his buttocks. The marks were too regular to be from an accident, and he had noticed that the Zulus – unlike some other African tribes – did not practice ritual scarring. Shaka's doctors had been bleeding him, Ralph guessed; and where else would you bleed someone except where the pain was?

In the time they had been travelling, he had witnessed the Zulus eat milk, yoghurt and beef, but though the fields were full of ripe crops, he had not seen anyone touch them. And that kind of diet, he knew, would surely lead to constipation.

Shaka was speaking again. 'White man's medicine nothing,' Jobe translated. 'Zulu medicine very good, very powerful.'

A man came out of the crowd. All the Zulus looked exotic to Ralph, but this man was extraordinary even by their standards. His face was painted white, and he wore black feathers in his hair that fanned out around his head. His hair hung over his face in plaits, with strange charms woven into them: bones, scraps of fur, and bulbous balloons made of animal bladders. The Zulus shied away from him as he moved through the crowd, trying not to catch his eye.

'This is the *sangoma*,' said Jobe. 'The doctor.'

'A witch doctor, you mean,' Marius muttered.

'King Shaka says, "What can you do that this man cannot?"'

'I will show him.'

Ralph rummaged in the bottom of his bag and found a glass jar he had taken from the *Farewell*'s medicine chest. The assembled chiefs eyed it suspiciously. The sangoma mumbled to himself.

'What is that?' whispered Marius.

'Brandreth's Vegetable Universal Pills,' said Ralph. He tipped two into his palm and offered them to Shaka. The king squinted at them, then pointed to Marius.

'He eats first,' said Jobe.

'He is not sick,' said Ralph.

'He eats first,' Jobe repeated. 'He will show it is good medicine.'

Marius looked at the pills almost as sceptically as Shaka. 'What will they do?' he asked.

'No harm,' Ralph reassured him. He put the two pills in Marius's meaty hand. 'Swallow them.'

Marius did nothing.

'Swallow them,' Ralph said again. He was still smiling, but steel had come into his voice. 'If you do not, the Zulus will think I mean to poison their king. And then what do you suppose they will do?'

Reluctantly, huffing with indignation, Marius took the pills. Shaka watched him closely. Marius gulped them down dry, then forced an insincere smile.

The Zulus waited. The sangoma drew back, as if the pills might have some dread power from which his own magic might not be able to protect him. Shaka watched Marius with such focus that even the Dutchman seemed to shrink under his gaze. Then, suddenly, the king snatched the bottle from Ralph's grip and tipped it upside down. Half a dozen pills spilled out into his hand. Before Ralph could stop him, he had swallowed them all.

Shaka spoke. 'He says, tomorrow he will know if the medicine works,' Jobe translated. 'If the medicine is good, Shaka will be pleased.'

He did not need to say what would happen if the medicine was not good.

Shaka returned to his throne and the knot of *indunas* closed around him until all that Ralph could see of the king was the red crane feather waving in the air.

Hamu's men escorted them out of the kraal and through a maze of narrow passages that criss-crossed the royal section. Every hut was guarded by a Zulu warrior with tall ostrich plumes in his hair, their short stabbing spears held across their chests.

'Where are they taking us?' Marius fretted.

'If Shaka wanted to kill us, he would not do it in a dark alley,' said Ralph. He had already started to grasp a little of how the king's mind worked. 'Everything he does is calculated to demonstrate his power. He would make an example of us.'

'Very reassuring.'

A small rear gate let them through the outer fence onto the hillside. At the top of the slope, a little distance from KwaBulawayo, stood a cluster of round huts. Perhaps they were guest quarters, for when they went inside there was no sign of personal belongings. Hamu gestured to the sleeping mats and headrests and spoke a few words.

'We stay here until tomorrow,' Jobe translated.

'What will happen tomorrow?' Ralph asked, though he could guess the answer. It depended on the pills he had given Shaka.

Hamu gave him a grim smile. Then they were left alone.

They stared at one another in silence. None of them could quite believe what they had witnessed – the spectacle, the power, the theatre.

'What in God's name have you just done?' Marius asked. 'What were those pills?'

Ralph threw himself down on the sleeping mat. 'They are only a cathartic. He will shit like an elephant tonight, and tomorrow he will feel mighty relieved. And so will you,' he added, ignoring Marius's look of disgust.

'You had better hope those pills work on Shaka, hey?' Marius curled his fingers in a crescent, then rammed his fist through it. The same gesture that Hamu had made to describe the fate of Shaka's brother. 'Otherwise, it won't be *his* arse that's on fire.'

A little while later a woman entered the hut with a pot of sorghum porridge. Nervously, she placed the food on the ground in the centre of the hut, but the three men were already asleep, snoring deeply on their mats.

Ralph crouched on the deck of a ship on fire. A woman floated in the water below, her skirts billowing around her. She was drowning. Ralph reached out to take her hand, but the waves carried her beyond his reach.

He had to rescue her.

He lunged for her again, and again the waves carried her away. The mainmast crashed down in a tower of flame. Over the din, he heard a baby crying.

'Elizabeth,' he called.

But when she looked up, he saw the woman was not Elizabeth but Ann.

He woke with a start to a lingering ache in the scars on his cheek, and the sight of Marius stooping to go out through the hut's door. Ralph rubbed his eyes.

'Where are you going?'

'To take a piss.'

The moment Marius stuck his head out of the door, a challenge rang out. With a few crude gestures, Marius managed to communicate what he needed – but when he returned his face was dark.

'There are twenty blacks on guard outside.'

Jobe rolled his eyes. 'What did you expect?'

'I did not come here to be made a prisoner.'

'I do not think you have a choice.'

Again, Ralph saw the hostility between the two men, like a fire that had taken root underground. It was always there – smouldering under the surface, ready to erupt into violence at any time.

'Shaka will send for us when he is ready,' Ralph said. 'Until then, we wait at his pleasure.'

It was a long wait. The hut was tall enough for Ralph to stand up in, but for Jobe and Marius it was impossible, and Marius was not made for sitting still. He was constantly twitching, swelling with impatience until Ralph thought he might burst through the roof.

'Who does he think he is, keeping us penned in here like wild animals? Someone should teach him a lesson in manners.'

'Someone should teach you manners,' snapped Ralph. The waiting was wearing on him, too.

'We are King Shaka's guests,' Jobe reminded them.

'He does not treat us like guests,' said Marius.

'Then perhaps you should try being more charming,' said Ralph. 'Or if you cannot do that, keep your mouth shut.'

'Or maybe I should send him a message.' Marius jumped to his feet again. Before Ralph could stop him, he had snatched up one of the rifles, lunged for the door and pushed himself through.

'Does he think he can shoot his way out of here?' Ralph asked. *That would be insanity. Shaka's men will massacre us all.* Ralph and Jobe dived after him.

They heard the deafening report of the gun. Ralph crawled through the low door, blinded by the sunlight after so long in the dim hut. Through his ringing ears he heard shouts of panic and alarm. What had Marius done?

As his eyes adjusted, he saw the big Dutchman silhouetted against the sky, holding the rifle aloft in a defiant pose. A dog barked furiously. Half a dozen Zulus made a loose circle around Marius, spears ready – but they kept their distance. Smoke hung in the air.

'What are you doing?' Ralph shouted. 'You will get us all killed.'

Marius waved the rifle at him. 'They would not dare.' Firing the gun seemed to have released something inside him. The grin was back on his face. 'That was just to get their attention.'

'You have certainly got that.' A dozen herdboys had gathered at the kraal's gate and were peering through the fence. Down below, Ralph could see that a file of warriors had left the palace compound and begun climbing the hill towards them. In their midst was a man with two tanned ox tails standing up like horns from his headdress, a leopard-skin shawl over his shoulders.

'You do not need your little pills to impress Shaka,' said Marius. 'He will come to the sound of a gun.'

'That is not Shaka,' said Jobe. Now that the group was closer, he could make out the man in the headdress. 'That is Dingane, the king's half-brother.'

Ralph felt a tremor go through him. Shaka might be terrifying, but his power was that of a lion in its pomp, fully on display. Dingane's strength was more like that of a coiled snake.

They waited. The dog settled down and began scratching itself. The boys outside chattered excitedly among themselves, then fell silent as the procession entered the kraal. Dingane's warriors fanned out, angling their spears towards the men in the middle. Dingane strutted forward, his pot belly wobbling like a jelly as he moved.

'How is King Shaka this morning?' Ralph asked.

Jobe translated, but Dingane acted as if neither man had spoken. He barked a few staccato words.

'He wants to see the gun,' said Jobe.

Ralph felt Marius stiffen beside him. The Zulu guards saw it, too. They edged closer, their spears jabbing forward like adder tongues.

'I will get mine,' Ralph said.

He ducked into the hut and brought out his own gun, together with his ammunition pouch and powder horn.

'You will get us killed if you put that in the hands of a black man,' grunted Marius, through clenched teeth.

'Not as quickly as you would.'

Ralph offered the rifle to Dingane. The prince tipped back his head in distaste, but he allowed one of his lieutenants to take it and hold it up for his inspection. He closely studied the barrel, the trigger, the flintlock and the pan. Ralph could see him puzzling over the firing mechanism. With a little experimentation, the two men managed to pull back the hammer to full cock.

The hammer snapped forward and struck a spark. Dingane leaped back, while his lieutenant gave a yelp and dropped the weapon in the dust.

Dingane scowled and spoke. Jobe translated. 'He says, "Do all umGeorge's army have firesticks?" Guns.'

'Yes.'

Dingane spoke again, something that made the men around him cat-call and shake their spears in the air.

'The firestick is no good,' Jobe translated. 'The Zulus have the *iklwa*, the stabbing spear. Firesticks only frighten birds and children.'

The words were bold enough. But while the guards hooted with laughter, there was no mirth on Dingane's face. He was watching Ralph closely. Daring him.

'I will show him how my rifle scares the birds.'

A flock of vultures was circling overhead. Ralph picked up the rifle that had fallen on the ground. Methodically, ignoring the ring of spears around him and Dingane's impatient gaze, he loaded the gun and primed the pan. He cocked the hammer and put the rifle to his shoulder.

He knew how much was resting on this one shot. If he missed, Dingane would delight in his humiliation. Ralph would seem weak; they would be lucky to escape alive.

Ralph ignored the mounting pressure. He was a hunter: nothing existed except the weapon and the target. His breathing slowed. Nestling the stock against his cheek, he tracked one of the birds with the bead of the gunsight.

Smoke and fire erupted from the gun. Shouts rose from the watching Zulus. Then their surprise changed to fear and wonder as the vulture dropped to the centre of the kraal. They went quiet, looking to Dingane to see what he would do.

The dog padded over and picked up the vulture's carcass in its jaws. The bird was too big for the dog to carry. It dragged its trophy back to the fence and began chewing on its head.

Ralph held out the gun to Dingane. 'Would you like to try?'

Dingane waved the gun away with a jerk of his head and said: 'Can a firestick kill a man?'

Ralph nodded. 'We use them in battle.'

'Kill him well?'

Ralph wasn't sure what he meant. 'It is a very effective weapon.'

A smile spread across Dingane's round, fat face. 'Show me.'

Did he want him to shoot another vulture? Ralph began to reload the gun. Dingane watched critically, pointing to all the apparatus – the patch, the bullet, the cartridge and the powder – and providing a commentary in Zulu.

'What is he saying?' Ralph asked Jobe.

'In a battle, before you are ready you will be dead.'

Ralph rammed home the bullet. He wished he could have explained infantry drill to Dingane, how three ranks of men armed with muskets could form an unbreakable line. Instead, he only had the one weapon, and a crowd of sceptical Zulus willing him to fail.

The ramrod rattled back into its slot below the barrel. Ralph primed the pan, cocked the hammer and lifted the gun towards the sky.

A harsh command rang around the enclosure. Dingane raised his hand to stop Ralph.

'What does he want?'

The prince spoke in his remorseless monotone. 'Not birds,' said Jobe. 'A man.'

Ralph stared at him. 'What?'

The look on Jobe's face was grim. 'He says: "Kill a man."'

'That would be murder,' Ralph protested. 'Surely Dingane does not want me to kill one of his people?'

Dingane gave a sideways look to two of the guards and jerked his head. They stepped out sharply and grabbed one of the boys watching by the gate.

'No!' Ralph cried.

The boy was not yet ten years old, with a shaven head and round, frightened eyes. He pulled against his captors, but they were too strong.

Dingane pointed to the gun, then to the boy, then to Ralph. It needed no translation.

'You must not do this,' Ralph said. 'Please.'

The guards dragged the boy into the centre of the enclosure, about fifty yards away. They held him by his arms, standing as far apart as they could, while his begging cries echoed around the hilltop. He writhed in their grip, but he could not escape.

Dingane clicked his tongue impatiently. The men around him pushed forward. The spear blades seemed to ripple in the sunlight, a naked threat if Ralph disobeyed.

The boy had stopped struggling. He raised his head, staring across the open ground that separated them. Ralph met his gaze impassively. What comfort could he offer?

Once before in his life, he had stood over a child, prepared to kill him. And the decision he made in that moment had altered everything that came after.

He raised the rifle in a sudden quick motion. He could not give himself time to think, or he might change his mind. He sighted the gun, curled his finger around the trigger and fired.

Again, the noise of the gun brought gasps from the crowd, and squeals of alarm from the boys at the gate. A hundred yards away, the dog that had been chewing on the vulture bled out its life into the dirt from the hole that Ralph's bullet had made.

The dog was so far from the boy that no one could doubt Ralph's intentions. In the centre of the enclosure, the boy dropped to his knees in relief. He was saying something, but the words were drowned out by Dingane's voice, loud and angry behind Ralph.

Ralph turned to face him. The prince's face was twisted with fury.

'He told you to kill the boy,' said Jobe.

Ralph shrugged. 'A man will die as easily as a dog.'

'Then why didn't you shoot the bloody Kaffir?' said Marius. His head jerked wildly. 'You see what you have done?'

Dingane's razor-sharp eyes ran over Ralph, as if he wanted to skin him alive.

'King Shaka—' Ralph began.

That was the wrong thing to say. At Shaka's name, Dingane's face turned to thunder. He extended his arm and screamed a short, brutal command.

'They will kill us all,' Marius cried.

He grabbed Ralph's ammunition pouch and began frantically reloading his rifle. Ralph could have done the same, but there was no point. At this range, Dingane's taunt was all too true. *Before you are ready, you will be dead.*

But the guards hung back. Perhaps the gun still had some hold over them; perhaps they feared what Shaka would do if they executed his guests. Their hesitation outraged Dingane. The tall stalks on his headdress wobbled back and forth as he shouted and harangued the men.

A warrior sprang forward, the ox-tail hairs billowing around his biceps. He drove his spear at Ralph's belly. Ralph parried with the rifle. He caught the spear behind the haft, deflecting the blade across his hand. A line of blood appeared across his knuckles, but Ralph did not feel it. He spun around, inside the Zulu's guard, and smashed the butt of the rifle into his face.

The man went down. But the others had seen that without ammunition, the rifle was no better than a club, and that was a weapon they did not fear. Ralph could never defeat them all. He saw Dingane watching him as the guards advanced. Even now, his face showed but the merest hint of emotion; he looked like a man anticipating a moderately satisfying meal.

Then Dingane disappeared in a puff of smoke as an explosion burst from behind Ralph. To a man, the Zulus flung themselves to the ground with cries of fear. Turning, Ralph saw Marius with the rifle raised. While Ralph was fighting, he had managed to reload the gun.

If he had shot Dingane, that would be the final nail in their coffin. The Zulus were already rising to their feet, ready to avenge their leader.

But Dingane was still standing, unhurt. Fifty yards away, the herdboy was lying on the ground, clutching his chest. Blood oozed from between his hands.

The bullet must have gone straight through his heart. The child's eyes went wide, frozen in shock. They seemed to hold on Ralph for a moment, indicting him. Then the boy slumped backwards and fell in the dust.

'What have you done?' Ralph screamed at Marius, though he could hardly hear the words for the ringing in his ears.

'What you should have done the first time, hey? I saved our bloody lives!'

'He was a child.'

Ralph had his own rifle in his hands. For a moment, anger burned so hot in his heart he wanted to smash it into Marius's fat, complacent face.

Again, he felt Dingane's eyes on him. The prince had not moved. Even his face had maintained the same expression.

He wants Marius and me to fight, Ralph realised. *He feeds on division and conflict.*

Ralph lowered the gun, forcing himself to control his breathing. 'You see,' he said to Dingane, spitting out the words through gritted teeth. 'A man will die as easily as a dog.'

The Zulus drew back. Dingane tipped his head and stared at him through narrowed eyes. Ralph had the feeling that they had passed a test, though the thought sickened him.

'Better him than us,' said Marius.

Having witnessed the power of Marius's rifle, Dingane returned to the city. The Zulu guards still ringed the compound, but they did not make the visitors go back into the hut. Perhaps they feared what Marius and Ralph would do to each other if they were forced inside that little space together. Instead, the men paced around the cattle enclosure like a pair of angry bulls.

'How could you do that?' Ralph raged. 'You shot a defenceless child.'

'I saved our lives, because you didn't have the balls,' said Marius. 'Shooting the bloody dog? Did you think that would satisfy that bloodthirsty Kaffir?'

Ralph turned to Jobe. 'What would you have done?'

Jobe's face gave nothing away. 'If the king's brother says so, it must happen.'

Marius nodded. 'You think you are better than me?' he said to Ralph. 'That you have scruples, morals, that bullshit? The only reason you are alive right now is because that boy is dead.'

Is that true? Ralph remembered the look in the boy's eyes, helpless and uncomprehending. *I have been a man without a conscience, a man who will hurt anyone to get what he wants. I will not be that man again*, he told himself.

'It would be better if we had not made Dingane our enemy,' said Jobe.

'He does not have to be our enemy,' said Marius.

'Did you see how he looked at us?'

'Did you see how he looked at the king?' Marius lowered his voice. 'There is no love lost between those two. The brother understands the power of our guns. Maybe we could do him a good turn, earn his gratitude.'

'No!' Ralph shouted. He glanced at the watching guards. He did not think they could understand what was being said, but if they guessed . . . 'Are you mad? Whatever bad blood there is between the brothers, we cannot take sides.'

Marius did not react. He seemed to take pleasure in having provoked Ralph again. A sly smile spread across his face.

'Where there's two men wanting the same thing, you always end up taking a side.'

'We will not discuss this,' Ralph insisted, longing to be out of the cattle pen and away from Marius.

You came here to make your fortune, he reminded himself. *You cannot cut and run, just because it does not fall in your lap like an apple at the first time of asking.*

He saw the bloodstain the boy had left in the dust. Was that an acceptable price?

Marius had crossed to the far side of the kraal and was leaning on the fence, looking down into KwaBulawayo. A vast crowd was streaming into the city. Many were warriors, with their matched cowhide shields and stabbing spears. They marched into the great enclosure, lining up in ranks facing towards the palace, the ostrich feathers in their hair waving like a field of wheat.

'There are thousands of them,' marvelled Marius.

'Tens of thousands,' Ralph corrected him.

When they had first met Hamu, Ralph had been amazed that the Zulus could put a regiment of men in the field. Now he saw that Hamu's men were just a fraction of Shaka's immense power.

A shiver of fear went through Ralph. 'Why would they gather so many men together?'

'It is *Umkhosi*,' said Jobe. 'A ceremony. The first crop. To celebrate the harvest.'

'How do you know that?' Marius demanded.

'I heard the guards speaking.'

'So it is just bad luck that we arrived when the king has gathered his entire army together?'

Ralph could see the suspicion written on Marius's face, fear that this was some plot against them. But that was arrogance. The king did not need to muster his full power because three shoeless explorers had stumbled into the kingdom.

Another delegation of Zulus was approaching their kraal from the city. This time, Ralph saw Hamu leading them.

'Whatever it is,' he said, 'we are about to find out.'

Hamu brought Ralph and the others down the hill to a side gate, along a narrow passage and into the inner courtyard. Shaka sat on a wooden chair in front of the great domed house, surrounded by the usual crowd of *indunas* and retainers. He had his head tipped back. Two attendants flanked him, one holding a small hollowed-out gourd, the other a tiny spoon. The spoon was dipped into the gourd, then held to Shaka's nostril. The king inhaled deeply.

'He is taking snuff,' said Jobe.

Ralph had been prepared for the Zulus to have many different rituals and habits, things that were outside of his understanding, but this he had not expected. The snuff seemed to agree with Shaka, though. He gave a prodigious sneeze. The crowd nodded approvingly. The servant with the spoon pushed it up Shaka's nostril, scooping out a great quantity of mucus.

Without looking around, Shaka began to speak. It was only when Jobe started translating that Ralph realised the words were for him.

'King Shaka had a good sleep last night. The pain inside him is gone.'

Ralph tried not to let the relief show on his face. 'I am glad to hear it. I was certain that umGeorge's medicine would work.'

Shaka did not acknowledge the point. He seemed reluctant to admit in front of his men that Ralph's pills might have had any benefit.

There was a silence. For the Zulus, this was normal. In their society, it was the height of bad manners to speak without time for reflection first. For a white man, it was difficult not to be disconcerted by it.

And Marius was not known for keeping his mouth shut.

'Tell him what we did with the rifle, hey?' he said. 'Tell him we are powerful wizards.'

Ralph tasted bile. He saw the dead herdboy bleeding into the dust.

'We will not speak of that.'

It seemed Shaka did not wish to speak of anything. The audience was already over. Shaka rose from his throne and advanced into the great cattle enclosure. While they had been talking, the warriors Ralph had seen from the hill had continued to flood in. Now, the whole space was filled with men and women. The men were warriors, fully armed and wearing the Zulu equivalent of parade dress uniform. The women were bare-breasted, with only thin strips of hide tied around their hips, and brightly coloured strands of beads worn like crossbelts across their chests.

'They love those beads,' Ralph observed, noting the size and colours they favoured, calculating how many beads it took to make each piece. Many of the necklaces were fashioned from carved wood or dried berries, though some of the most beautiful girls wore glass.

Shaka took up a position at the top of the kraal, facing his people. The *indunas* spread out around him. Hamu gestured to

Ralph and his friends to stand by him, only a few yards from Shaka. Ralph did not miss the symbolism.

'It seems we are in Shaka's good favour,' he said to Marius, with a flush of satisfaction. The medicine had done the trick.

'Or maybe he wants us where he can keep an eye on us,' the Dutchman retorted. Being here in the great enclosure, with so many Zulus, put him in a bad humour. He kept touching his hand to his shoulder, feeling for the rifle that wasn't there.

The soldiers drew back to the perimeter, making a vast circle. Young girls brought cattle in to the centre, parading them around the ring like prize racehorses. Ralph noticed that the herds had been separated by the colour of their skins, matching the shields of the soldiers around them. Caramel brown, white, black and spotted: each seemed to belong to a particular regiment.

After the herds had been presented, there was dancing. Young women came out, formed in companies like the men. Instead of spears, they carried thin staffs, which they waved in perfect rhythm to the beat of the song. They advanced towards the men, retreated, and advanced again, like waves on a seashore. Many were strikingly handsome.

'Look at that *poesje*,' Marius exulted. 'I'd take some of that, hey?'

Jobe glared at him.

'You know how long it's been since I had a woman? First prison, then the ship, and only that frigid little English bitch to look at.' He did not notice the way Ralph stiffened at the mention of Ann. 'Now I have ten thousand black girls shaking themselves at me. How is a man to resist?'

The Zulus danced and sang in the great kraal until sunset; then they lit bundles of rushes and held them aloft so that the whole ring was lit by fire. The dancers lifted their legs high, bent their backs and stomped forward with outsized, exaggerated motions. They raised their spears and stabbed them down, singing all the while. Shaka came down from his throne and danced with them, stabbing at the ground as if he was finishing off a defeated warrior.

'Your people have grown strong,' Ralph said to Jobe.

He meant it as a compliment. He had not expected the reaction he got from Jobe: a clench of his jaw, and a flash of anger in his eyes.

'They are not my people,' said Jobe. 'Do you not see how they look at me?'

'No.'

Ralph had grown up in India, where white faces were always a minority. But there it was a privilege, casually assumed and easily forgotten. Here, in front of many thousands of black men and women, a prisoner in all but name, he had felt the whiteness of his skin in a new way – these people looked at him like he had a disease. He had assumed Jobe would blend in; had envied him for it.

'They are as different from me as a Dutchman from an Englishman,' said Jobe. 'To them, I am *amaLala*.'

'What is that?'

'A cross between an Irishman and a Kaffir.' Marius chuckled at his own wit. In his sly way, he had understood faster than Ralph. To a proud nation like the Zulus, the less powerful peoples next door would be the butt of jokes and scorn, maybe even contempt. That human habit was ingrained deeper than the colour of a man's skin.

'But you can speak their language,' Ralph pointed out.

'When I speak, they laugh.'

Despite the energy of the dance, a tense atmosphere hung over the kraal. Ralph had the feeling that he was being watched, but at the same time no one would meet his eye. Except one person: a young woman, standing back from the *indunas* among the attendants and serving girls. She was probably in her mid-twenties, wearing nothing but a thin hide girdle. She had high cheekbones, smoky eyes and hair twisted into short, spiky braids held up by a beaded headband. A small leather bag hung on a string around her neck. When she caught Ralph's gaze, she held it.

Ralph narrowed his eyes, as if to say: *What are you looking at?* But her face remained expressionless. Then Ralph noticed the slightest upturn at the corner of her full lips.

What is she thinking, behind those smoky eyes? Ralph was intrigued. The tens of thousands of Zulus around him seemed to recede and the torchlight spiralled in and wrapped her in its light.

Then suddenly she vanished. Without any warning, the top of the kraal had been plunged into darkness.

'What the hell is this?' said Marius.

All the torches had been extinguished at once, as if a blast of wind had blown them out. But the night was still.

In an instant, Ralph forgot about the woman. Around him he heard murmurs of alarm sweeping through the crowd.

'Stay close to me,' he hissed to Marius and Jobe. His senses were on high alert. He was acutely conscious he was unarmed, surrounded by thousands of men with spears.

Did Dingane plan this? Was this deliberate? Did he have men poised to strike Ralph down for his disobedience in the kraal? He began pushing through the darkness towards the place where he imagined the throne would be, hoping that no one would dare to attack him in front of the king.

Unless Shaka himself had engineered this moment.

Light flared on the edge of his vision. Someone had managed to rekindle a torch, and as the dry grasses flamed, Ralph saw Shaka. He had collapsed to his knees, while another man who Ralph did not recognise stood over him, holding a short stabbing spear.

The shock of the moment paralysed everyone. Ralph was first to move. He lunged forward, hurling himself at the assassin. Long shadows flickered over the ground; the few yards between them stretched like miles.

The assassin saw the movement. He turned, caught for a second between finishing the man at his feet and pivoting to defend himself.

His mission was paramount. He tensed his arm and brought the spear down.

Ralph was still a yard short of him. The king threw up his arm to defend himself, but flesh was no match against steel. The blade sank deep into his side, passing between his ribs below his armpit.

The assassin's shriek of triumph was choked off as Ralph cannoned into him.

The force of his charge knocked the man to the ground. The spear, still in his grip, was jerked out of the wound. Before the assassin could turn it against Ralph, Ralph grabbed it with both hands. For a moment, the two men wrestled it between them.

Something flew over Ralph's head, ruffling his hair. An object smashed into the assassin's head, the impact so violent that his temple was inverted. The man went limp.

Hamu stood over them, holding one of the knob-ended fighting sticks.

'Thank you,' said Ralph. But Hamu didn't hear him. The murmurs in the crowd had risen to mournful shrieks as those nearest saw what had happened. Men and women hollered and wailed, one word cutting through the chaos: *Shaka*. They surged forward towards the fallen king, a shadow army in the flickering torchlight. If they came any closer, they would crush Shaka underfoot in their grief.

Ralph and Hamu ran to the king and lifted him between them. Ralph had to fend off the crowd with his arm, or he also would have been trampled, while Hamu swung his stick to clear the way.

'Where are you going?' Above the din, Ralph heard a voice shouting in English. Marius pushed through the crowd, his bulk acting as a shield against the wave of humanity pressing in.

'Shaka is wounded.' *Or is it worse?* The king hung limply; Ralph could not tell if he was alive. 'We must get him to safety.'

'Are you crazy? They will say *we* did this.'

'I tried to save him.' Ralph was yelling at the top of his voice, but even so he could not tell if Marius understood him. 'They saw that.'

'They saw you standing over the king with a spear in your hand. What do you think they will say? A dead king, and a white man's hand on the weapon?'

Ralph could not think with all the noise. Hamu's guards had managed to fight their way through and had pushed back the crowd, making a corridor to the royal quarters. Hamu had already begun to drag Shaka away. Ralph had to follow or let go of the king.

He took two steps. Instantly, human bodies filled the space he left, marooning Marius in their midst.

'Get Jobe and find me in the palace!' Ralph called, though he doubted Marius heard him. Then the crowd and the darkness swallowed them both.

They left the great enclosure and entered the palace area. Guards barred the entrance behind them, but to no avail. Hundreds of women lived in the royal quarters, and they crowded the narrow passageways between the huts, emitting a cacophony of despair as if they could not bear to be alive.

Hamu shouted something in Ralph's ear. Ralph looked at him blankly. He could see the impatience on the Zulu's face; he was desperate to make himself understood, but without Jobe, there was no way they could speak to each other.

Hamu brought two of his men over. One shouldered Ralph aside and took up Shaka's weight. The other tugged Ralph away. Ralph looked uncertainly at Hamu, but an impatient flick of the general's eyes told him what was expected of him: *Go.*

Ralph obeyed. The escort led him through the back gate, up the hill to the kraal where they had stayed, and gestured that he was to go in.

Now I wait, Ralph thought. Hamu had seen him attack the assassin, but to the rest of the watching Zulus it would have appeared as Marius said: *They saw you standing over the king with a spear in your hand.* First, they would see if Shaka lived or died. Then they would decide what to do with Ralph.

The wicker gate that covered the door rustled. Ralph looked up, expecting that the guards had found Jobe and Marius, too. But it was not his companions. It was the guard who had brought him.

He pointed to Ralph's bag, hanging from a peg on the wall.

Ralph squinted. 'What do you want with that?'

The two men stared at each other in mutual incomprehension. The guard pointed to the bag again, then through the door towards KwaBulawayo. He said a short word that sounded urgent. When that made no impression, he repeated it three times more.

'You want me to bring this?'

Understanding dawned. Hamu had not sent Ralph to the hut to wait. He wanted him to fetch his medicine bag.

'There is nothing in there for Shaka.' He had seen how deep the spear had gone between Shaka's ribs. If it had not pierced his heart, it would surely have punctured a lung. Ralph had nothing that could help a man with a wound like that.

But the guard had his orders. He took the bag himself and shoved it into Ralph's hands. Ralph had no choice.

As they ducked out of the hut, Ralph looked down at KwaBulawayo on the hillside below. Most of the city was dark, with only a few patches of light where torches had been relit. Yet the sound swelling out of it across the hills was chilling, as if the city had become a necropolis, and the dead walked its streets, gibbering mournfully.

Ralph did not want to go back. He could feel the hopelessness of his situation closing around him. If he refused to treat Shaka, he would be condemned as a traitor. If he did treat him, and the king died, Ralph would be cast as the murderer.

The guard led him down the slope at the loping run that the Zulus used on the march. As they re-entered the palace compound, Ralph saw that the women were still there. A few torches burned dimly, illuminating faces streaked with tears and blood where nails had torn skin. The guard moved forward, taking Ralph's hand to make sure that he didn't lose him in the throng, but it became harder and harder to push through the crowd of women.

The palace door was shut, and the crowd around it packed solid. Ralph's escort did not try to get through. Instead, he skirted the edge and carried on into another part of the complex, to a small compound of four huts surrounded by a high fence. It seemed almost deserted.

The anguish around Shaka's great house had been frightening, but the silence here was even more unnerving. Should Ralph have run? Had he been blamed after all, as Marius said? Was this a place where he could be tortured until he confessed?

The guard gestured him into one of the huts. The smell of blood wafted out as Ralph lifted the flap above the door; bile rose in his throat.

A fire smouldered in the hearth. By its glow, Ralph could see Shaka lying on a rush mat on the floor. His eyes were closed; the leopard-skin cape he had been wearing was matted with blood.

Two men knelt beside the king. One was Hamu, holding him still. The other, moaning softly, looked very different: if Ralph had been superstitious, he might have believed it was a ghoul come to take Shaka's spirit. It was the sangoma, the witch doctor. His long hair hung like a curtain over his eyes, while the feathers and gourds he wore rattled every time he moved. He was holding a spear close to his face, sniffing at the point. Blood dripped from its leaf-shaped blade. He was examining it, either for poison or for signs that a fragment might have broken off.

It was the weapon that had been used to stab Shaka. As Ralph's eyes adjusted, he could see a gash on the king's left arm, where he had tried to defend himself, and blood still running from the wound in his ribcage. If the spear had struck his heart – as the assassin surely intended – then Shaka would already be dead. But if it had pierced a lung, death would be slow but inevitable.

The witch doctor put down the spear. He drew out a handful of dried leaves from a little bag and threw some of them on the fire to make a sweet, dry smoke. Crushing the rest in his hands, he stirred them in a pot with water to make a paste. He smeared it around the wound, working it into the gash. Shaka grunted in pain and blood ran from his mouth as the man's fingers probed his flesh.

Hamu spoke sharp words to the witch doctor, who responded defiantly. Ralph watched helplessly as the two Zulus argued. By the way the witch doctor kept looking at Ralph, jabbing his finger and spitting out angry words, Ralph had the uncomfortable feeling that he was the subject of the argument.

Hamu pointed to Shaka, then Ralph's bag, and then Ralph himself.

'You want me to treat Shaka?'

While they argued, the wound had started to bleed again. The king's breath had become shallow. Ralph was not confident Shaka would survive the hour, let alone the night.

'There is nothing more I can do,' said Ralph. 'He has done everything I could.'

It was true. The sangoma might look like an outlandish demon, but beneath the paint and the costume, he was probably as competent a doctor as Ralph. He had cleaned the wound, purified it with his herbs and – judging by the smell in the air – purged Shaka's stomach.

Ralph's words made no impression on Hamu. The *induna* repeated the gestures, while the witch doctor glared at Ralph and muttered under his breath.

Ralph had to do something to protect himself – even if he tried to save Shaka and failed, it might be enough to buy their freedom. If he did nothing, then his fate was assured.

Hamu was staring at his bag as if it was a magic amulet. Ralph opened it and rummaged inside. There were a few pieces of smoked meat, some cartridge papers and bullets, and a few jars he had taken from the *Farewell*'s medicine chest. The remaining Brandreth's Vegetable Universal Pills, a bottle of peppermint essence, and a small box of camomile tea. This was what he had to cure a dying king.

He took a step towards Shaka's sickbed. The sangoma sprang up, the feathers in his hair flaring out like a cobra's hood, but he could not defy Hamu's authority. More guards had arrived, and though Ralph could see that they were wary of the sangoma, afraid of his powers, it was evident that they would eventually escort him from the hut by force if they had to – disobeying Hamu's orders held a more certain outcome.

The sangoma knew when he was beaten. He gathered his medicines and made his exit, shouldering roughly past Ralph – then stopped abruptly and turned on his heel. Ralph had been watching the witch doctor leave, but now, suddenly, they were face to face. The sangoma rolled his eyes so that his pupils disappeared, hissing and chattering wild words, spraying spittle over him. Ralph did not understand the words, but he could feel the curse in his bones.

Wiping his face, Ralph tried not to let Hamu see him shaking. *It is nonsense*, he told himself, *a fit of petulance from the witch doctor to frighten the man who had taken his place*. Though in the close hut, with herb-laced smoke still filling the air, he struggled to believe his own story.

With a final volley of invective, the sangoma spun about and left.

Ralph knelt beside Shaka. A black pot hung on the wall, and there was a ewer of water standing on the floor that the sangoma had used. Ralph filled the pot with water and placed it on the fire. Hamu watched closely. When the water had boiled, Ralph threw in a handful of leaves and let them infuse. A sweet, floral smell filled the air. Hamu sniffed it suspiciously.

'Good medicine,' said Ralph. He could only hope that the Zulus did not know – or would not recognise – the scent of camomile tea.

Hamu did not look convinced. Herbs and infusions were no different from what the sangoma had used. Ralph would need to make more of an impression to gain the Zulus' respect. He racked his brains for anything else he could use.

It was a desperate thought, but Ralph had no other options. He took out one of the rifle cartridges from his bag, tore open the paper and tipped the black powder onto the wound on Shaka's side. Hamu squinted at the black paste it made with the blood. Ralph waved him back.

'Be careful.'

Ralph snapped a small length of dried grass from the hut's ceiling. He held its tip into the fire to light it, then touched it quickly to the powder on Shaka's wound. It erupted in a sudden puff of flame. Shaka convulsed, his eyes fluttered open; Hamu screamed. Some of the guards moved towards Ralph, but Hamu gestured them back. The smell of sulphur and charred flesh filled the air.

Ralph doubted his efforts had achieved anything – not any medicinal effect, at least. The heat from the explosion had been so brief it would not have cauterised the wound. But nor did it seem to have made it any worse. And the Zulus in the hut were looking at him in terror.

He washed the wound carefully with the camomile tea. He had no bandages, so he cut strips off his shirt that he soaked in the tea and bound over the wound. Shaka whimpered and rolled on his sickbed, clutching his side. Each time he coughed, more blood came out of his mouth. Soon blood had oozed through the thin bandages.

I must close that wound, Ralph thought. He needed a needle and some kind of thread, but when he tried to mime this the Zulus looked blank.

I will not be able to save Shaka if we can only speak through dumbshow.

'Jobe,' he said. 'Find Jobe. Bring him here.'

Hamu recognised Jobe's name and barked a command to one of the guards waiting by the door. The man went out.

Ralph became aware of a noise outside: hundreds of voices, maybe thousands, swelling in shrieks of lamentation. The crowd had discovered where Shaka was hidden and had surrounded the hut. As well as the crying, the walls of the hut flexed and bent as if they were in a gale. The mourners might crush it in their desperation to be near the king.

'Tell them to get back,' said Ralph. But the guards did not understand.

There was movement by the doorway. A woman entered and, surprisingly, Ralph recognised her. She was the woman he had seen in the enclosure, eyeing him as he watched the dancing. She crawled through the entrance, still with just the thin strip of cloth around her hips, and the bag hanging from her neck.

She stood. Her bearing was dignified and resolute: her back was straight and she held her head high.

'You speak me,' she said.

Ralph's mouth dropped open. He stared at her like a simpleton.

'You speak English?'

'Yes.'

'How?' he said, but explanations could wait. 'What is your name?'

'Thabisa.'

'Thabisa, I need a needle and thread. As thin as possible. Do you understand?'

Thabisa frowned in concentration as she spoke haltingly to Hamu.

One of Hamu's men disappeared and came back with a thin bone needle and a length of gut.

'They must hold him,' Ralph told Thabisa. 'Tell them to hold him down. And he will need something to bite on, something wooden or leather.'

Thabisa related Ralph's requests to Hamu, but even though it was clear that he passed on Ralph's instructions to his men, they were reluctant to come forward.

Ralph had no choice. He instructed Thabisa to hold the wound together and began to sew. Immediately, the king bellowed in pain, rolling away from the needle, ripping the thread from Ralph's hand.

Hamu charged forward and gripped Shaka firmly. Seeing their leader manhandle the king gave his men confidence, and one by one they placed their hands on Shaka, pinning him to the floor while Ralph began to put a neat line of stitches along the length of his wound.

Shaka yelled out at the men who held him, screaming what could only be curses at them, clawing at the floor until he finally passed out.

At least that old sawbones did me one good turn, Ralph thought, remembering the ship's surgeon who had taken him on as an apprentice. On the first day, he had showed Ralph three items: a saw, a needle and a bottle of rum. 'These are all we have to help a man, and I will teach you to use all three liberally.' He had been as good as his word.

He could not save my mother, but perhaps he will save King Shaka.

Working by lamplight in the cramped orlop deck of an East Indiaman turned out to be good practice for sewing up a man in a Zulu hut. Ralph finished the stitches quickly and tied off the knot. He glanced up and saw Thabisa's eyes watching him. It was remarkable behaviour. In his time with the Zulus, Ralph had noticed that almost all of them – apart from high-born men like Shaka and Hamu – shied away from meeting his gaze directly. His white skin seemed to make him hard to look at. Yet this young woman watched him fearlessly. He wondered again by what miracle she had learned English.

Hamu interrupted, his voice low and urgent.

'He say, does King Shaka alive?'

Or will he die?

'Maybe.' Ralph shrugged.

The blood in Shaka's mouth was a bad sign, but at least it was dark – not bright and fresh. That was some reason for hope.

'I have done what I can. Now we have to wait. If he survives until sunrise, then his body has accepted the medicine.'

Ralph sat beside Shaka, the stench of blood and the screaming of the Zulus outside filling his senses. There was little he could do other than change the dressings and pray.

After a few hours Hamu left, but Thabisa stayed with him. When Ralph called for fresh water, she went to fetch it, but mostly she positioned herself next to him, staring at Shaka with such intensity that Ralph wondered if her life, too, hinged on the king's.

'Are you his wife?' he asked. It was the darkest part of the night. The wailing outside was louder than ever.

Thabisa shook her head. 'Not wife. *Isigqila.*'

'What is that?'

'Slave.'

It was a simple word, a single syllable, yet it changed everything. A word that swallowed a person's identity, that attempted to negate their very existence. Ralph was about to speak, but he saw a warning in her face that made him think again.

'How is it you can speak English?' he asked.

She frowned. It softened her features: two dimples appeared at the corners of her mouth, while her eyes looked down. It was a sorrowful look that made Ralph want to comfort and reassure her.

'Old. Old story.'

Her accent was strong and her voice was quiet. It was difficult to hear her over the din outside. Ralph leaned closer to her.

'We have time.' Ralph looked at Shaka. He lay still, breathing lightly. 'Tell me.'

So Thabisa told him her story.

She was not a Zulu. She had been born to a tribe called the Tembu, in a village to the south and near the sea. She called the place *eThekwini*, which – when Ralph prompted her – she translated as 'the place of the lagoon'. From her description, Ralph realised it must be Nativity Bay.

A tremor of foreboding passed through him.

'Family live there. Big house.'

Ralph's jaw tightened. He tried not to show it. 'A Tembu family? Or Zulu?'

'*Abelumbi.*'

'What tribe is that?'

She reached out and put her hand on his chest. Despite the circumstances, Ralph felt a sudden spark of heat. How long had it been since he had felt a woman's touch?

'*Abelumbi* you,' she said.

'A white man?' The heat in his chest cooled to ice. 'A white family lived at Nativity Bay. They taught you English?'

What were the chances of him meeting this woman here?

He listened as she went on, feeling the chill spreading through his veins. Her family had worked for the white family as cowherds, labourers and servants, and been paid in kind with food and trade goods. Thabisa's mother had worked as a cook, and she had helped her in the kitchen. She liked the family she worked for. Their children treated her like a sister, particularly the youngest daughter. They played together, and she learned to speak their language.

'What were their names?' Ralph asked.

'Gert. Susan. Mary. Peter. Rachel.' Even after so many years, Thabisa could recite the names by heart.

'What happened to them?'

Her face clouded. 'Men attack.'

'Zulus?'

'No Zulus. No Shaka. *Abelumbi*.'

'White men killed the family?'

'Yes.' Even now, the memory brought tears to her eyes.

'What did you do?'

After the battle her family had returned to their village in the woods by the headland. They had lived as their people always had, herding cattle and cultivating their fields. Not an easy life, but no different from any other.

Then the Zulus came.

'Five summer ago.'

They were on their way to a different war – Thabisa's village was a stop on their way. They killed the men, burned the huts, and took the cattle and the women as plunder. Thabisa was taken to KwaBulawayo and put into the *isigodlo*.

'What is the *isigodlo*?'

'Shaka House.'

The palace.

'And you were a . . .' He tried to remember the word she had used. '. . . Iza-gila?'

His pronunciation made her laugh. Her face lit up, and her eyes sparkled with mirth.

'*Isigqila*.' She made him repeat it. There was a sound in the word, a sort of click of the tongue while simultaneously swallowing, that Ralph could not replicate.

'And an *isigqila* is a slave?'

Her face went grave again. Her smiles were like the flowers that bloomed in the wet season: there for a brief moment, and then when they had gone there was emptiness.

'Yes. Slave.'

It was obvious from looking at her what those duties involved. Her compact body was well muscled, with strong legs and limber arms from fetching water, hewing wood, carrying food and sweeping. But there was also her flawless skin and smoky eyes. A beautiful woman like her would draw the attention of the king, or other men in the palace. As a slave, she would have no rights or protection. He could guess what they would make her do.

'Does it not trouble you, serving the people who killed your family?'

She shrugged. 'What choice do I have?'

'If I were King Shaka, I would have married you.'

Whether she did not understand the compliment, or whether it embarrassed her, she didn't respond. Instead, she said: 'King Shaka, no wives.'

Hamu had said the same about the king. Although Ralph was ignorant of the Zulus' culture, he had seen that they were not averse to matrimony. At every kraal they had visited on the journey from Nativity Bay, they had been presented to the headman and his wives, who often numbered as many as five or six. Yet their king, who could have his pick of the most beautiful women in the country, had none.

He glanced at Shaka. Even asleep, possibly dying, the energy coiled in his powerful body was almost palpable. Surely a man like that would have appetites. Did he not possess human needs? Or did maintaining his grip on power take all of his time and energy? Ralph remembered the story Hamu had told him of Shaka's ascent. The father and brother who had stood in his path, both dead; the half-brother Dingane, loitering by the throne, watching everything. Perhaps Shaka had decided that family was an impediment, that any heir he fathered would become a rival. Easier to take your pleasure with concubines and slave girls, and bury the bastards where no one could find them, than have an heir.

Was Thabisa one of Shaka's courtesans?

That was a question to which Ralph did not want to know the answer.

In the hut, as the fire began to die, Ralph realised that he had lost all sense of time. He looked across at Thabisa, who was asleep on a grass mat, her breathing slow and steady.

Ralph thought about the differences between them. Both had seen their families die in violence. But while he had dedicated his life to revenge, she simply accepted her fate.

He wondered who was more free.

Suddenly a girl entered with fresh water, and daylight spilled through the door. Desperate for light and fresh air, to be away from the metallic stink of Shaka's blood and the pungent odour of the king's shit, Ralph crawled outside.

The scene in front of him was terrifying. Shaka's women had gathered around the hut, confined so tightly by the surrounding fences that they could barely move. They must have been grieving all night. The few clothes they wore were torn, their bodies bruised and scratched. Some bled around their eyes from rubbing them so much, as if they had shed all their tears and were now forced to cry blood.

Ralph struggled to his feet. He was starving – it had been twenty hours since he had last eaten – and exhausted. He needed to eat and sleep, but he could not leave Shaka's side. His life was now bound to the king's. And although he had done his best to attend to Shaka's wounds, there were other ways that the king could yet die. Ralph doubted that the would-be assassin had acted alone. There were certainly other conspirators waiting for an opportunity to finish what the assassin had begun. If they could be discreet, who better to blame than the white wizard who had been treating the king?

Was it a coincidence that the assassination had been attempted the day after Ralph's party arrived? *Maybe they meant to blame me all along.*

A shudder went through the crowd. Shouts rose above the wailing as a troop of Zulu guards entered the compound, pushing the women aside until they had cleared a passage to the hut.

A man appeared and started to make his way towards Ralph, a phalanx of bodyguards following him. It was Dingane, waddling with the weight of his fat belly, his eyes half-closed, seemingly oblivious to the women around him. He approached the door of the hut as if he meant to enter.

Ralph stood in his way. He planted his feet and squared his shoulders, so that even if the prince did not understand what Ralph said, his body language was unmistakable.

'You cannot come in.'

Dingane hesitated. It was beneath his dignity to acknowledge Ralph, but he could not ignore him. His scowl deepened. He snapped a command to one of his guards, a huge captain with a string of claws around his neck. The man stepped towards Ralph, lifting his spear while more men fell in behind him.

Ralph could not fight Dingane's entire entourage. Besides, he had no right to: Dingane was Shaka's half-brother. Who was Ralph to keep him from the king's sickbed? Yet still he would not yield. Dingane was the heir to the kingdom. To Ralph's mind, that made him the most likely man to have planned the assassination – and most likely to want to finish the job.

The flap covering the door behind him lifted as Thabisa crawled out. Hamu had also heard the commotion and the *induna* emerged from one of the other small huts in the compound. He appraised the situation in a single glance and spoke firmly to the guard captain. The captain answered fiercely and Dingane's guards fingered their weapons. The women around the enclosure ceased wailing as the voices of the two men became loud and aggressive, watching to see what would happen next. The only person unmoved by it was Dingane, who acted as if he had not even noticed the confrontation happening in front of him.

Ralph glanced at Thabisa. As a slave, she had more to fear than anyone. Ralph had seen only the previous morning how casually Dingane could order a person killed. Yet Thabisa stood tall, her face as calm and impassive as ever.

The argument between Hamu and his opponent grew more heated. But as brave and loyal as he was to Shaka, Hamu could not defy a prince.

Ralph was certain that if Dingane reached Shaka's bedside, the king would die. And after that, those who had tried to save him would not live long.

'I must speak to Dingane,' he said to Thabisa. 'Tell him what I have to say.'

Thabisa stepped forward.

'The medicine I have used is very strong,' Ralph said. Thabisa translated. 'If they go inside, it may make them sick.'

Dingane's lip curled. Ralph could see he did not believe him. But could he be sure? Even on the march to KwaBulawayo, Ralph had learned that the Zulus had a powerful reverence for magic. They believed it was everywhere, always waiting to enchant or curse the unwary.

Dingane took a step away from the hut. He and the captain spoke to each other in low voices, then addressed Hamu.

'He say, want see spear hurt Shaka,' Thabisa translated.

'What for?'

Ralph had examined the weapon and seen no marks or special decoration. What could Dingane discover from it?

Dingane spoke again.

'Bad ones put magic on spear,' said Thabisa. 'Dingane take bad magic from Shaka.'

Maybe the prince believed that, or maybe there was something on the spear that might identify the conspirators. Something that Dingane did not want to be found.

Ralph glanced at Hamu. In the *induna's* eyes, he saw the same calculation: that there was nothing to be gained from refusing Dingane a second time. Hamu nodded to Thabisa, who fetched the spear from the hut and presented it to one of the guards.

The prince examined it. He ran his finger over the blade, which Ralph noticed had been wiped clean. With a venomous look at Ralph, he turned and waddled away. The guards followed in his footsteps.

You have just made a very dangerous enemy, Ralph thought as he watched Dingane make his way out of the compound. It reminded Ralph of the words he had spoken to Marius and Jobe: *Whatever bad blood there is between the brothers, we cannot take sides.*

Despite his best intentions, he had chosen where he would stand.

There had been a time when the most important substance in Ralph's life was opium. Every day had revolved around the pipe and the wait to feel the drug curling through his lungs into his veins. It had begun as a release from his pain; by the end, the opium itself was far crueller than what it was meant to cure.

Ralph had broken the habit, but the process had plunged him into a black hole of infinite depth and anguish. A part of his soul had stayed trapped there forever.

The days following Shaka's stabbing were an echo of that dark time. He could not eat – the nausea was unbearable. Sleep, too, was impossible – he was haunted by visions and apparitions every time he closed his eyes. His hands began to tremble so much that he could hardly tie the bandages.

Yet he never left Shaka's side.

Shaka awoke on the morning of the third day convinced that he was dead. He remembered the assassin standing over him and stabbing down with his *iklwa*, remembered Hamu and Ralph carrying him away from the crowd, but whatever medicine the sangoma had given him after the attack, to keep him sedated, had filled his head with vivid dreams. He had ascended to sit with the ancestors, and this could only mean one thing – he was dead.

But the more vehemently the king proclaimed that he had joined the ancestors, the more Ralph began to hope. There was no longer any blood in Shaka's mouth and the wound in his side had begun to heal. The spear tip must have missed the king's lungs and heart, perhaps by no more than the thickness of a blade of grass. It was nothing short of a miracle.

The sangoma's drugs were strong and took many hours to leave the king's body. On the fourth day after the assault, Shaka managed to sit upright. On the fifth day, having realised that he was still alive, he pronounced that he might, after all, continue to live.

'You save me,' he said to Ralph. Thabisa squatted in the corner and translated. 'Good medicine.'

Gunpowder and camomile tea, Ralph thought.

He had probably done more to save Shaka by distracting the assassin. The split second that the killer hesitated, as Ralph charged towards him, might have been the fraction of an inch between the spear tip and Shaka's heart.

Ralph had come here to make his fortune. He had arrived at the court empty-handed – and he had saved Shaka's life. The fates that had brought him here had given him an extraordinary opportunity.

'You powerful doctor,' Thabisa translated, her voice sweet and mellifluous. 'You great man.'

It would be easy to accept Shaka's compliment. But Ralph was wary: he knew he was walking a knife-edge. Saving the king's life had earned him gratitude, but it had also put Shaka in his debt, and that was an uncomfortable place to be. Even in his short time in KwaBulawayo, Ralph had glimpsed Shaka's way of interacting with the world. Anything that limited his power, anyone he could not control, was a threat. And the king would not tolerate threats.

'I am not great,' Ralph said humbly. 'I have merely helped a great man.'

The answer pleased Shaka. The king looked emaciated, but the power in his eyes when he fixed them on Ralph was overwhelming.

'Why you come see Zulus?'

There was no reason for Ralph to lie. 'To get rich.'

This, too, pleased Shaka. He could understand that desire. It gave him power over Ralph.

'And your friends? Big man like sea cow.'

'Sea cow?'

Ralph needed a moment to realise that the king was talking about Marius. For five days he had been so consumed by Shaka's wellbeing that he hadn't thought of his companions at all.

'Do you know what has happened to him, and my other friend?' He turned to Hamu. 'Are they safe?'

Hamu gave him a crooked look. 'Safe.'

'What they want?' Thabisa asked, reminding him he had not answered Shaka's question. 'Your two friends.'

'They want to get rich like me.'

He saw the doubt on the king's face. Shaka had seen the way that Marius talked and behaved. The sneering condescension would have needed no translation.

'Only this?'

'Only that.'

A week after the attack, they moved Shaka back to the great hut. As his strength returned, so did the trappings of power. More attendants moved in and took over his care; Ralph was pushed back to the edge of the room, where the domed walls came down to the floor. The intimacy of those first days receded like a dream.

Ralph still did not leave the king. He waited at the fringes, eyes hollow with exhaustion. He could not pretend to himself that he was safe: any relapse, any sudden change in Shaka's health, would be laid on him. So he watched.

The king talked earnestly to his *indunas* for hours.

'What are they talking about?' Ralph asked Thabisa. She had become his shadow, always by his side.

'Fightings.'

He presumed that she meant that they were swapping old war stories. Nothing to do with Ralph.

'Why don't you go to your quarters and get some rest?' Her eyes had dark rims, and her skin had turned sallow and dull.

She shook her head. 'Stay here. Stay with you.'

'As you wish.'

He thought she was being obstinate. Then, as her arm brushed his, he realised she was trembling.

She is as bound to my fate as I am to Shaka's. And she did not even have a choice.

He put his arm around her and cradled her to him. Her body was rigid, but after a few minutes in silence he felt her soften into him. Her head touched his shoulder. Soon, he heard gentle snoring.

The next day, Shaka arose from his sickbed. The attendant Zulus exclaimed with praise and delight.

The king seemed to have aged ten years in a week. Standing naked, his skin was grey and his shoulders bent; his once-powerful legs were thin and slack. He tottered on his feet. Even when Hamu handed him his knobkerrie, Ralph feared he might collapse.

But Shaka wanted to show his people that he was still alive. They had seen him killed, had seen the assassin stab him in the heart, and yet he lived. He had awoken thinking that he had joined the ancestors; now he was going to make his people believe he was a god. Leaning on the knobkerrie, Shaka looked for Ralph. Their eyes locked, and though Ralph knew just how much the wound had weakened the king, the light in his eyes was strong. His head seemed to tilt at a defiant angle as he said a few words.

'He go out,' Thabisa translated.

'You should rest,' Ralph warned him. 'You are still very . . .' *Weak* was the word he meant to say, but you did not call a king weak. '. . . sore.'

'Shaka strong. Need go out. People see, people not afraid.'

Young women came with water and bowls. One held a lumpy orange paste. Shaka scooped up a handful and began scrubbing himself with it.

'What is he doing?' Ralph whispered to Thabisa.

'Washing.'

'What is he using?'

Instead of cleaning Shaka's skin, the paste left streaks of fat across it.

'Cow.'

'He washes himself with *beef?*'

Another servant poured water into a black stone basin. Shaka dipped his hands, then began washing off the beef paste. When he was clean, he took reddish ointment from a bowl and rubbed it all over himself. As he worked it into his body, his skin took on a new, healthy lustre. Finally, he took fingerfuls of grease from a third bowl. It was butter, Ralph realised, thick and rancid, with such a terrible smell that he struggled not to gag. But as he slathered it over himself, it made Shaka's skin shine like polished metal.

Shaka walked to the door, still naked, and crawled out. Everyone followed. The floor of the inner courtyard had been polished to a sheen like green jade. Shaka stood in its centre, while attendants dressed him. First came the kilt of monkey tails, then a string of billowing ox-tails that they fastened around his chest. Ralph saw him wince as they tied it over the wound. He had obviously requested the ox-tails to hide the bandage.

More ox-tail bands were added to his arms and legs. A necklace of lion claws and red beads was fastened around his neck, and copper bracelets on his forearms. The attendants fitted his head-dress, which bristled with bunches of scarlet and green lourie feathers, and two tall blue crane feathers rising above them all.

Shaka was invincible again. Even the knobkerrie he leaned on carried menace, a weapon rather than a sick man's crutch. Shaka's shoulders straightened, his head tipped back, and he cast an imperious glance around the courtyard. As one, the attendants and *indunas* squatted low and bowed their heads.

'*Bayete,*' they murmured – the royal acclamation.

On the far side of the enclosure, Ralph saw Dingane among a knot of *indunas*. The prince was so fat that when he bowed he had to lean on one of his men for balance. As Dingane straightened up again, Ralph saw him glance in his direction. Even from across the courtyard the hatred on his face was obvious, his eyes hooded like a cobra's.

If he was not my enemy before, Ralph thought, *he is now.*

Shaka processed to the main gate of the *isigodlo*, where the palace complex opened into the great enclosure. As he stepped out in front of his people, Ralph heard an eruption of noise, a roar of victory followed by a wave of ululation.

People see, people not afraid. Was it a shout of delight, or of terror?

The crowds which had gathered after the attack had not gone away during Shaka's convalescence. In fact, they seemed to have grown. The people filled the main enclosure, swaying and singing with hoarse voices, songs of grief that turned to shouts of jubilation as soon as Shaka emerged.

Shaka took his place at the head of the enclosure. The earth at the top end had been embanked slightly to create a dais, elevating the king above the crowd. The *indunas* and attendants filed in behind the king, arranging themselves in the lee of the embankment.

Shaka began to address the crowd. The feathers in his hair rippled in the breeze, his furs swung as he swayed and moved. Everything proclaimed: *I am alive*. But he spoke in a low tone, almost mumbling, creating a vacuum that seemed to suck in his audience.

Every other sound in the kraal ceased; no one moved. Even the cattle were silent.

'What is he saying?' Ralph whispered to Thabisa as she came up behind him.

'He say, umGeorge send *abelumbi* help him.'

'He is thanking me?' Ralph felt a surge of relief, though when he checked the crowd, he realised that no one was looking at him. The aura of strangeness he carried as a white man still seemed to frighten them.

A group of boys came out from the palace compound carrying a heavy burden between them. It was a pair of elephant tusks, each one so big it needed four youths to carry it. They climbed the embankment and laid them on the ground before Shaka.

They must be a hundred pounds each, thought Ralph, marvelling at their size.

Shaka beckoned Ralph forward. Ralph made his way up to the dais and squatted, Zulu fashion, in front of the king, while Shaka spoke over his head.

Shaka pointed to the tusks, then to Ralph.

'These for you,' said Thabisa, who had accompanied him. 'He make you rich man.'

Ralph forgot his exhaustion. He glanced at Thabisa.

'How do you say "thank you" in Zulu?' he whispered.

'*Ngiyabonga.*'

'*Ngiyabonga,*' he repeated, bowing low to Shaka.

His reaction – and his attempt to speak Zulu – delighted the king. *He is like a father who spoils his children so he can glory in their gratitude*, thought Ralph, though he guessed that there was another side to Shaka for those the king deemed ungrateful.

A twitch of Shaka's head told Ralph that he was dismissed. He stepped back, making his way down into the crowd behind the embankment. He could feel Dingane's eyes on him. He may have made a powerful enemy – but for now, he was untouchable.

Shaka spoke again, and this time his words were louder and more forceful. He jerked his head and jabbed his arms. The plumes in his headdress waved as if caught in a fierce wind. The watching Zulus began to pound the ground with the butts of their spears, underscoring his speech with an urgent rhythm.

Ralph edged away. Shaka's wounds had not weakened his hold over his people. He was whipping them up as expertly as any actor or conductor, playing with their emotions. Ralph could see the Zulus' faces gripped with a terrible intensity.

Shaka swayed and shook like a man possessed by demons. He bellowed out a tirade in staccato sentences, and each time he drew breath his audience roared its approval.

Ralph followed the emotion in his speech – he could not understand a word, but he could tell where it was going. Blood would be spilled, copious amounts of blood.

A side gate to the right of the enclosure burst open. A company of warriors emerged, dragging a group of men between them. They hauled them up on the dais in front of the crowd, holding them by their arms, spears pointed at each man's throat.

Six of the condemned men were Zulus, naked except for their penis sheaths. The other two were Marius and Jobe.

Ralph remembered what Hamu had said when he had asked about his friends: *Safe.* He had assumed that Hamu had meant that they had gone back to the kraal, outside the city – their lodgings since they had arrived in KwaBulawayo. But there was more than one way a man might be made 'safe'.

Marius and Jobe were barely recognisable. Their bodies were bruised and streaked with blood; Marius had a purple ring around his right eye, and his nose was bent at a crooked angle. Jobe's left arm hung limp.

Dingane clambered up the embankment and confronted the captives. He too had been dressed for the occasion, Ralph saw. He wore a necklace of beads around his neck – blood-red baubles that glowed in the sunlight – and embroidered crossbelts that fell either side of his belly, so that it seemed even more enormous. He carried a spear, like any other Zulu *iklwa*, except that it had a bulbous pommel at the end, which he jabbed at the prisoners while he spoke.

He seemed to have taken on the role of prosecutor. His voice had none of Shaka's subtle modulations. He did not play to his audience, nor did Ralph think he was trying to persuade them with arguments. He hurled a barrage of accusations at the African prisoners, bludgeoning them with angry, short sentences.

'What is Dingane saying?' Ralph whispered to Thabisa.

'These men Ndwandwe.'

'What is Ndwandwe?'

'Other tribe. Not Zulu. They try kill Shaka.'

Ralph studied the captives. They made an unlikely group of would-be murderers. Stripped naked they were gaunt, their arms so stick-thin it was impossible to believe that they could even wield a blade. They looked at their feet as if they already knew their punishment.

'How does he know they are guilty?' Ralph had seen one man stab Shaka – and he had had his skull broken by Hamu.

'Not Zulu spear. Ndwandwe.' Thabisa cupped her hands together, mimicking the shape of the bulbous butt of the spear in Dingane's hand.

Ralph had seen the weapon that wounded Shaka. 'That is not the same spear. The one the assassin used had no pommel on the end.'

He glanced at Thabisa and saw the warning blazing in her eyes: *Do not contradict Dingane.*

Ralph had no experience of Zulu justice, but the outcome of this trial was not in doubt. If he remained silent, Marius and Jobe would die at Dingane's hand. Could Ralph help them? Or would he get himself killed, too?

'What is he accusing my friends of?' he whispered to Thabisa.

'He say Jobe Ndwandwe spy.'

'Jobe is not Ndwandwe,' Ralph objected. 'And Marius would never conspire with the Ndwandwes.' Or any black man, he might have added.

Dingane spoke again.

Thabisa pointed to Marius and mimed aiming something into the air. 'He firestick. Big noise.'

Ralph remembered how Marius had fired the gun into the air that first morning in KwaBulawayo, letting off his frustrations at being confined in the hut. A few hours later, Shaka had been stabbed. To the Zulus it must look as if he had been summoning some kind of black magic. Or it was a prearranged signal.

Ralph could have cursed the Dutchman for his stupidity.

The fact that I saved Shaka's life does not matter, he thought bitterly. *Or, worse, it counts against us. This is Dingane's way of punishing me.*

Up on the dais, Shaka leaned forward to listen to his half-brother. Ralph could not tell if the king agreed or disagreed with what Dingane had to say, but the longer he spoke, the more impatient Shaka seemed to become. Under the gleaming grease and splendid headdress, Ralph could see him beginning to tire from spending so long on his feet in the blazing sun.

He will let them die.

Marius was a brute. Jobe wanted to drive the white man out of Africa. If life had taken a different course, Ralph would have had nothing in common with either of them. But fate had drawn them together, and they had sworn an oath to one another.

Dingane had finished his case. He stopped talking and turned towards Shaka, awaiting judgement. Marius and Jobe could see what was coming. Marius's face had lost its colour, while Jobe scanned the crowd behind the dais, looking for Ralph with mounting desperation.

Ralph was distraught. He had no evidence to prove their innocence. Maybe there was nothing he could say that would persuade Shaka to spare them.

But if I do not speak now, it will be too late, thought Ralph, urging himself to speak.

He had this choice before in his life – to act to save someone; or to save himself. Even with hindsight, he could not say which choice was better.

Ralph stepped forward and began to make his way back up the embankment, Thabisa hurrying behind him. Shaka was lifting his stick to pass judgement as Ralph dropped to his haunches and bellowed at the top of his lungs: '*Bayete!*'

Shaka looked down at him, surprised and angry. Ralph was not supposed to interrupt this moment.

'*Nkosi*, my friends are innocent of any plot against you,' he said as Thabisa translated. 'They are as loyal to King Shaka as I am. Everything I have done to heal you, it is as if they did it with their own hands.'

The king glared at him.

'In my country, a man is given a chance to prove his innocence. umGeorge does not condemn a man just because his brother says so.'

Dingane's expression became more poisonous. But Shaka hesitated. The reference to his brother had caused him to think again.

'How they show they good?'

'They will take an oath of loyalty to the king.'

Shaka considered this. Then he spoke a few words.

'Salute like Zulu.'

Ralph glanced at Thabisa. 'He wants me to salute him?'

She pointed to Marius. 'Him.'

A smile played across Shaka's lips. He understood human pride – and delighted in humbling it. He pointed to the ground so there could be no doubting what he meant. He wanted Marius to prostrate himself.

Jobe dropped to his knees. It stung his pride to kneel before any man, black or white, but not so much that he would part with his life. Marius, however, remained motionless. The guards began to approach, but Shaka ordered them back with a flick of his fingers.

'If you do not do this, they will kill us all,' Ralph said to Marius.

'And bow before a Kaffir?'

'Bow before the man who can spare your life.'

The whole enclosure – tens of thousands of people – had gone still. Under the heat of the sun, Marius's face flushed crimson.

Ralph could see that Shaka was losing his patience. The stubborn, bull-headed Dutchman would not bow before a black man. Ralph had spoken in his defence, and that would give Dingane the pretext he needed to place Ralph's neck in the same noose.

The guards began to move forward, spears ready. Marius flexed his arms. He would not fall without a fight.

Ralph could not watch. Squatting on his haunches, he bowed his head and stared at the dust.

Dust thou art and to dust thou shalt return. To anyone who had grown up in India, like Ralph, they were words that became ingrained from the endless round of funerals. To a child, standing at the graveside, hearing dry earth rattle on yet another coffin lid, the lesson was unmissable: *this will be your end, too.* Ralph had never imagined it would be the red dust of Zululand that took his bones.

At that moment, as if the gods themselves heard Ralph's prayers, a scorpion skittered across Ralph's shadow. He saw the tiny claws, the tail curled up over its back with the pointed stinger on the end. Its body was a cloudy brown, like a drop of blood in water.

Ralph did not know what species it was. Size, he knew, made no difference: the tiniest creature could contain the most lethal poison, and a large one might hurt no worse than a bee sting.

Its sting might be a swifter death than what Dingane would do.

Shaka had started addressing his people again, no doubt pronouncing Marius's death sentence. The Zulus stamped their feet and shouted their approval, while the guards raised their spears and circled around Marius.

Ralph reached down and, with a flick of his wrist, scooped up the scorpion from the dust and flicked it towards the big Dutchman, just as he had once scooped up cricket balls in their garden in Holkar. It sailed through the air and landed on the back of Marius's leg.

The disorientated scorpion gripped its enemy with its claws and plunged in its venomous stinger.

Marius bellowed in agony. He grabbed for his leg, but before he could reach it all the strength drained from his limbs. His body went limp; he collapsed onto the dais and lay still.

Shaka broke off in surprise. The Zulu guards leaped back, as if they feared the taint of witchcraft. The crowd went silent. For a moment, it felt as if the whole city held its breath. The buzzards circled overhead, and the unseen scorpion scuttled away, but there was no other movement.

Shaka looked down at Ralph. His intuition told him Ralph must have had something to do with it, but he could not work out what. His piercing eyes dug into Ralph's face, commanding answers.

'He bowed before you,' said Ralph.

Shaka frowned as Thabisa translated. He glanced at Marius.

Then he tipped back his head and roared with laughter.

In an instant, the mood changed. The assembled Zulus followed their king's lead and began to laugh. Ralph found himself laughing, too, almost on the edge of hysteria. Even the other prisoners, the Ndwandwes, risked a few tentative smiles, thinking perhaps that Shaka's good humour meant they were reprieved.

They hardly had time to realise their mistake. At a sign from Dingane, the guards seized the prisoners. Each put one arm around a captive's neck, the other around his forehead, and gave a quick, well-practised twist. The neck snapped; the head lolled on to the chest. The guards threw the dead men on the ground as the Zulu crowd surged forward with a roar. Every man carried a bulb-ended knobkerrie, like Shaka's. They gathered around the corpses, fighting and jostling to batter the bodies to pulp.

Ralph stood and pushed his way through to where Marius lay. The Dutchman was still, but when Ralph put a finger to his neck he felt a pulse – he had simply fainted from the pain. Jobe joined him, and between the two of them they managed to carry Marius off the dais and into an open space between a pair of huts. Behind them, the Zulus dragged the corpses of the executed men out of the city.

Marius blinked his eyes open and stared at the sky, his pupils dilated.

'Where the bloody hell have you been?' he grunted to Ralph. And then, wincing: 'And what did you do to me?'

'A scorpion stung you.'

Marius stared at him, struggling to focus. 'What?'

'It was the only way to make you bow.'

'A scorpion? *God verdoem dit.* How did you know it wouldn't kill me?'

'I didn't. I still don't. We will find out if you will live in a few hours.'

'You *rooinek* bastard—'

He lunged at Ralph, but he was too weak. Ralph stopped the punch and held Marius's fist, bending low so that their faces were inches apart.

'Shaka would have killed us because of your stupid pride. If you had died it would be no more than you deserved.'

Jobe nodded. 'Ralph is right.'

Marius twisted towards him. 'And a hell of a lot of use you were,' he snarled, the pain of the scorpion sting evident on his face. 'Why didn't you try to speak to Shaka, one Kaffir to another?'

'Because to them I am as worthless as you,' said Jobe.

'What matters is we are alive.' Ralph released Marius's fist and stood. 'For now.'

Would Shaka be content with the Ndwandwe men he had executed, or would his attention return to Ralph and his companions?

Hamu was striding towards them, with Thabisa two paces behind. The *induna*'s face was grim. He looked down at Marius, clearly unimpressed that he was still alive, then pointed to him and to Jobe and spoke a few words.

'They go,' said Thabisa.

'Go where?'

'eThekwini.' She said it as if Ralph should know what it meant. He racked his brains, trying to remember all the strange words he had heard in the past fortnight, and then it came to him: the place of the lagoon.

'We are to go back to Nativity Bay?'

'They go. You here.'

'You want me to stay?'

'Shaka want you stay.'

'What is she saying?' demanded Marius. Still groggy from the poison, and unable to conceive of a black woman speaking anything other than her native language, he had not realised that Thabisa was talking in English.

'Shaka has released you,' said Ralph. 'You and Jobe can go back to Nativity Bay.'

'And you?' Marius's voice was instantly hot with suspicion.

'Shaka wants me here.'

'So you can get rich by yourself, hey?' Marius propped himself up on his elbow. Jealousy had driven the dull haze from his eyes. 'Make yourself King Shaka's pet while we rot by the sea?'

'We made a partnership,' said Ralph. 'Everything shared equally. And all the ivory in the world will not fetch me much profit if I cannot get it to market. The only way to do that is if you go back to Nativity Bay and build us a boat. Your shares will be safe enough. Safer than I will be,' he added.

Marius grunted, pulled himself to his feet and brushed the dust off himself. He leaned towards Ralph, swaying slightly on unsteady feet. 'Just remember . . . I came here to get rich. And if you try to cheat me . . .' He smacked his fist into his open palm. 'A scorpion sting will seem like nothing against what I will do to you.'

NATIVITY BAY

Mahamba and his people – the tribe was called Chunu, Ann learned – settled into a small camp outside the walls of the stockade. Ann marvelled at how they built it. Instead of hewing logs and sharpening stakes, as the sailors had, the Chunus gathered thorn bushes and put them in a rough circle to keep out the wild animals, then bent saplings into arches and thatched them to make simple huts. Ann gave them as much food as she could from the stores, which they supplemented with roots and fruits they gathered from the forest.

'Why don't they fish?' Harry asked innocently one day. He was fascinated by Mahamba's people, and spent hours following them around – to the discomfort of the Africans, who tried to avoid the whites with an almost superstitious aversion.

Ann hadn't considered the question. 'Maybe they don't know how.'

'But they live here.'

'I think they came here from somewhere else.'

It was more than a fortnight since they had met Mahamba, but she still knew almost nothing about him or his people. Where did they come from? What had happened to put them in such a distressed state?

Ann looked to the north curve of the bay, where a herd of hippos were wallowing in the estuarine mud. With a start, she saw two people had emerged from the forest. Both were tall men, one broad, the other more slightly built.

She recognised something familiar in those shapes. She squinted, shielding her eyes from the sun.

'It is Marius and Jobe.'

But why were there only the two of them? was Ann's first thought. *What had happened to Ralph?*

She ran barefoot across the sand, Harry following behind, and reached them before they were halfway across the beach. Their clothes were ragged, their bare feet bruised and swollen. Both men looked as if they had been in a fight – and come off second best.

'Where have you been?' Ann asked. And then: 'Where is Ralph?'

'Not coming back,' said Marius.

She gasped.

'Ralph is alive,' Jobe reassured her. 'He stayed with Shaka.'

The questions tumbled out of her. 'Who is Shaka? What did you find?'

'It's a long story.' Marius turned to the stockade. 'It needs a drink to tell it.'

The tale was indeed extraordinary. The sailors listened with wide eyes to Marius's description of King Shaka and his capital, and what had happened to Shaka and Ralph. Marsden kept glancing out through the cracks in the palisade fence, as if he expected a thousand Zulus to appear on the beach at any moment.

'After we left KwaBulawayo, the Zulus escorted us to the river. We followed the coast from there back here,' Marius concluded.

'And Ralph is still there?' Ann asked.

'*Ja.*'

'Will he be safe?'

'Shaka is a brute,' said Marius. 'He kills men like swatting a fly.'

He said it casually, as if he did not see or did not care about the impact his words had on Ann.

'Ralph saved the king,' said Jobe quickly. 'He is safe for now.'

'Maybe safer than we are.' Marius suddenly leaped to his feet. 'Who are they?'

He stared out through the open gate. Mahamba and his people were coming across the beach. They had disappeared into the forest the moment Marius came. Now, seeing that he belonged with the party in the stockade, they had emerged to examine the new arrivals.

'They are with us,' Ann explained.

'The devil you say.' Marius snatched up the rifle and strode to the palisade. He hollered over the wall, 'Are you Zulus? King Shaka, hey? Zulus?'

Mahamba stopped dead. Fear shaded his face: at the sound of 'Zulus', he turned to bolt back into the bush.

Ann shouldered past Marius and ran out to Mahamba.

'It is all right,' she said. 'He is with us.'

But Mahamba was not looking at Marius. He was staring at Jobe in something like terror.

'Zulu?' he whispered.

Until an hour ago, 'Zulu' meant nothing to Ann. Now, having listened to Marius's story, she could imagine why the name would strike fear into Mahamba. She understood why his people had ended up so famished and desperate.

'Jobe is not Zulu.' She turned to Jobe, who was watching from the stockade. 'Can you speak with him?'

Jobe spoke a few words. Mahamba frowned, concentrating. Jobe repeated himself, more slowly, and this time Mahamba replied.

'I can understand him,' said Jobe.

'Can you find out where he comes from? We found them in the forest nearby. They were starving – they needed our protection.'

Before Jobe could speak, Marius's voice broke in. 'I don't know why you care.'

Ann braced herself for another fight, for Marius to tell her that they did not have enough food to spare on charity, let alone (as he would put it) for Kaffirs. But he said none of that. A sly look passed across his face, some secret thought.

'But I suppose we can use them,' was all he said. He pointed to the wreckage of the *Farewell* out in the bay. 'Ralph thinks he can persuade Shaka to give us ivory. Our job is to repair that boat so we can get it away from here.'

He turned away, as if bored by the conversation. 'Now how much more of that rum did you rescue?'

Next morning, Marius strode across to Mahamba's camp. He had a rifle in his hands, and Jobe in tow. He barked a series of orders that brought the Chunus running out to line up in front of their kraal.

Marius pointed to four of the strongest men. 'You – come with me. Bring your spears.'

Harry stood beside Ann, watching. 'Where are they going?'

'I do not know,' she said.

Marius turned back with his usual crooked grin. 'Hunting. Big game.' He winked. 'You want to come with me, little one?'

Harry tugged on Ann's hand. 'Can I?'

'No.'

'*Please.*'

'It will do him good, hey? Make a man of him.'

'He is staying with me,' Ann said firmly, in a tone that told both Marius and Harry it would be unwise to argue.

Marius tipped his hat and turned away. 'As you like.'

He led the Chunus along the beach towards the river mouth, where the hippos bathed. Ann tried to distract Harry, but he fidgeted constantly. She knew how big and strong and important Marius would appear in the little boy's mind. It would be easy for the boy to hero-worship a man like that.

A gunshot echoed back down the beach. Harry leaped to his feet with a squeal of excitement, raced away from Ann and ran down to the foreshore.

Two more gunshots sounded from the river mouth.

'They shot a hippo . . . hip . . . hippobotomus.' Harry danced from leg to leg, beside himself with excitement. 'I saw it go splash!'

Sure enough, a little while later the file of men came trudging back up the beach, covered in gore from butchering the animal. Marius led the way, carrying two huge teeth, still bloody at the roots where they had been hacked out of the animal's jaw. The others carried hunks of meat and fat that had been cut from the carcass. They were singing as they walked, bodies swaying in a rhythm. The women who had stayed in the kraal ran out to meet them. They built fires and began cooking the meat: boiling some as stew, roasting other pieces over the coals, and hanging the rest up to cure in the smoke. It was a prodigious amount of food, probably the most they had seen in many months.

Marius strode over to the stockade and threw down the ivory teeth. Each one was longer than a man's arm, curved like a scimitar blade and wide as a log. Marsden and the other sailors ran over and picked them up, whooping with joy as they felt the weight.

'This is the first money down on our fortunes,' Marius declared.

As well as the tusks, he had brought a long strip of the hippo's flesh. He sawed off a gobbet with his knife and tossed it to Harry.

'Eat that, little man. It will make you big and strong like me, hey?'

'Don't eat it,' Ann said immediately. 'It is not cooked.'

But she was too late. Harry snatched the morsel and stuffed it in his mouth. He gave a happy, blood-smeared grin.

'Good boy,' said Marius.

'You should not have eaten that,' Ann scolded Harry furiously. 'Raw meat can make you ill.'

'It makes me strong,' he retorted. 'Like Marius.'

Ann couldn't help herself. In a rush of blood she slapped Harry's cheek.

At once a wave of guilt crashed over her. *What made me do that?* Harry was a gift who had come to her in her lowest moment, and she treasured him. She had never hit him before.

Harry gazed at her in shock, blinking back tears. She moved towards him – to hug him, to make him feel better, to make things right between them – but Harry's face immediately screwed up in fury.

'Go away. I don't want you.'

His words cut to her heart and stopped her dead. Harry turned and ran down to the water's edge, while Ann watched through a veil of tears. She could not explain why she had done it. Marius had shown the boy kindness, and though his manners were rough he had not mistreated her in the time she had known him. Yet there was something in him that unsettled her, that made her protective hackles rise.

Harry needs a father, and I do not want it to be Marius.

Marius had left the stockade and wandered back to the Chunu kraal. Smoke rose from their fire, ripe with the smell of charred meat and sizzling fat. One of the women came out carrying seared pieces of meat on a wooden platter. She knelt in front of Marius and presented it to him, head turned away.

The woman stayed kneeling in front of him as he ate, while the rest of Mahamba's people gathered around at a distance.

'Very good,' said Marius, smacking his lips. The woman understood his meaning. She smiled.

'*Yebo, baba.*'

'*Yebo, baba,*' the other Chunu echoed. Only Mahamba did not join in.

'Now go and get more,' said Marius. He pointed down the beach, then to the hippo meat cooking on the fires. 'More meat.'

The Chunu hurried to do as he said. Marius turned towards the stockade, where Jobe had been watching.

'What does "*yebo, baba*" mean?' he asked Jobe.

'It means "Yes, Father".' Jobe's voice dripped with distaste.

'I like how that sounds.' Marius looked pleased with himself. 'Maybe a phrase you should learn, hey, Jobe?'

'I came here to be free.'

'And so did I.'

Marius sat in the shade and took up a piece of hippo skin. With his knife, he scraped away the flesh until the hide was stripped clean, then trimmed the edges so that the piece tapered to a point. When he had finished, he rolled it up tight.

Holding it by the thick end, he studied it with satisfaction. Then he flicked his wrist and snapped it forward. The hide made a crack like a gunshot as the sharp tip lashed through the air.

He had made a sjambok, the biting whip that the Boers used to drive cattle. It was a vicious tool, able to lay a man's skin open with a single lash. Ann shuddered at the sight of it.

Letting the whip dangle from his wrist, Marius returned to the Chunus' kraal. The men had gone back to the hippo carcass, but a few of the women remained, tending the cooking. They looked up at him, nervous at the sight of the whip in his hand.

He gave a broad smile. 'From now on, you work for your living, hey?'

They could not understand what he said. But he had fed them, and he was smiling, and that was enough. They smiled back happily.

'*Yebo, baba.*'

KWABULAWAYO

After Marius and Jobe had left, Ralph climbed the hill back towards the kraal where he was lodged. Lights were coming on in KwaBulawayo below, as the women lit torches and fires. To the west, the sun was sinking behind the hills, painting a gilded stripe across the horizon. Hamu walked beside him, head bowed, while Thabisa followed three paces back. Behind her, a group of boys struggled under the weight of the ivory tusks that Shaka had given Ralph.

I am alone now, Ralph thought. He felt exhilarated, more free than he had in years. *I have earned Shaka's trust. Now all I have to do is turn that to profit.*

He glanced at the boys carrying the tusks. The ivory in their hands glowed almost gold in the sunset. *That is a handsome down payment. But how to get more?*

'What will Shaka do now?' he asked. Thabisa translated.

'Shaka dance *amaGaqa*,' said Hamu.

'Shaka is going to dance?'

'Before the next moon.'

Hamu's mouth was set in a firm expression that said this was something important. Ralph waited for him to say more, but the *induna* clearly felt he had said as much as he needed to.

'*AmaGaqa* dance for war,' explained Thabisa.

'So Shaka will go to war? In the next month?'

Hamu gave a grim smile.

'Who will he fight?'

'Ndwandwe.'

That was the tribe that Dingane had accused of planning the attack on Shaka, the people whose distinctive spear he had presented as evidence.

'You saw the spear that stabbed Shaka,' Ralph said to Hamu. 'Was it a Ndwandwe spear?'

Hamu appeared to misunderstand the question. 'Ndwandwe must be punished,' he said.

They had reached the gate of the kraal. The boys took the ivory into Ralph's hut, but Hamu lingered by the gate.

'You bring firesticks,' he said.

'Rifles,' Ralph corrected. 'The word is *rifles*.'

'Bring. Come.'

'Where to?'

'Ndwandwe.'

'You want me to come to war?'

'Shaka want. For fight.'

'I am a merchant, not a soldier.' He saw Thabisa frown, struggling with a word. 'What?'

'What is "merchant"?'

'A man who trades. A man who brings you the things you do not have and exchanges them for things he does not have.'

'Shaka want you.'

'A merchant does not trade himself. He trades goods, like beads, or ivory.'

'Zulu not need.'

Ralph stared at Hamu. Like most of the great men at the Zulu court, the *induna* wore a necklace of coloured beads around his neck. Ralph pointed to it. 'Where did you get that?'

'From Shaka.'

'But where did he get it?'

'Shaka give everything. Give beads. Give ivory.'

'These beads are not made by Zulus. Shaka must get them from someone else.'

Hamu shrugged. 'Shaka have.'

And in those two words, Ralph realised the fundamental truth. You did not trade with a king like Shaka: you served him. You did not earn a profit; you were rewarded. As long as the king had goods to give you, you did not worry how he came by them.

Over to the west, the sun had sunk behind the hills. The sky had gone dark, and the air was grey with twilight. Ralph smelled blood in the atmosphere, blown from the city where cattle had been slaughtered. For a moment, he had thought he was free. Now he saw how wrong he had been – he was chained to Shaka.

It still might make him rich, if Shaka rewarded him for his service.

'I will come and fight the Ndwandwes,' he said.

Hamu returned to the city, leaving Ralph alone in the outer kraal. Ralph stood alone in the dark, watching the stars come out one by one above him. He felt as if he had made some deep, irrevocable decision, committed himself to a path, but what that decision was and where the path would lead, he could not say.

Turning, Ralph crawled through the door of the hut and flopped onto the straw mat. After so long at Shaka's side, and the drama of the ceremony, all he wanted now was to sleep.

Sleep would not come. His thoughts would not cease. Memories raced through his head as he tossed and turned on the hard mat. As a boy, he had often struggled to sleep, especially after his father died. He remembered endless nights in the monsoon heat, his mother sitting at his bedside and mopping his forehead with a damp cloth. He wished Ann was here now to soothe him.

Memories became dreams. The picture of the house in Devon came into his mind, a grey house against green hills, and soft rain pattering on the windows. In his mind, he strode towards the front door, rain running into his eyes. Ann waited on the doorstep, and when he leaned in to kiss her, her mouth was warm as the sun.

Something rustled by the hut's door. Someone was coming in. In an instant, Ralph was awake, his dream forgotten. Had an animal got into the kraal? One of the Zulu servants? Or was it one of Dingane's men come to kill him?

Footsteps padded across the floor, light and steady. Ralph reached out for his knife, but he had been so tired that he had not put it where it should be. He was defenceless.

Before he could move, the intruder threw itself on Ralph. Ralph thrust himself upwards, trying to dislodge his attacker, grabbing for their wrists, expecting a knife.

He heard a shriek as he rolled the intruder over, and an exclamation in Zulu as he pinned them beneath him. Words he could not understand – but a voice he recognised.

'Thabisa?'

He felt the contours of her body: smooth legs, the small curve of her waist, the heat from her belly and her nipples brushing his chest.

'Why you here?' she demanded.

'This is my hut,' he said indignantly. 'Why are you here?'

'Sleep here.'

'You are going to stay here? Did Shaka send you?' She nodded. Shaka must have decided he wanted to keep a close eye on Ralph.

'You could have looked before you threw yourself on me,' Ralph said.

Thabisa was unrepentant. 'You wrong side.'

'This is my bed.'

'No. My side here.' She stretched her arm towards the other side of the hut. 'You side there.'

'Says who?'

'Says always. Woman here. Man there. Man only come woman side when want . . .' She said a Zulu word that Ralph did not know.

'What is that?' he said.

'*Hlobonga.*' She repeated the word. She giggled, but did not say more. Perhaps she did not know the words to explain. Then, suddenly, she was moving under him, arcing her back, wrapping her arms around him and tucking her feet over his thighs, pulling him down on her while she kissed his face and neck.

The brush of her bare skin against his was electrifying. Desire overwhelmed Ralph. He reached his hand down, guiding his manhood towards the opening between her legs. But she grabbed his hand and pulled it away, squeezing her thighs together so he could not enter her.

'No.'

Ralph was confused, and not a little frustrated.

'No – like so.'

Pushing him back into a sitting position, she lifted his hips up and forward, so that his sex pressed against the lips of her womanhood, the tip against her belly. Closing her legs, she trapped him between the tops of her thighs, resting her legs against his shoulder.

Before Ralph could react, she began to move under him – a rocking, undulating motion that sent shivers of pleasure through him. She gripped him between her thighs, tugging expertly. Her skin was slippery and smooth. Their bodies moved in rhythm. She clutched at his hair as her climax took her, thrusting herself hard against him until he too could no longer hold himself back.

Afterwards, Ralph lay on top of Thabisa in a blissful state, half awake and half dreaming. The heat of her body pulsed through him; their sweat mingled. He thought he could stay there forever.

Thabisa put her hands against his shoulders and pushed him aside. Again, Ralph felt disconcerted.

'Is something wrong?'

Thabisa didn't answer. She moved to the door, as if she meant to leave.

She lifted the flap, but did not go out. By the moonlight that flooded in, she found a small hollowed-out gourd hanging on the wall, and a stick that had been carved into a sort of spatula. Sitting down, she used the stick to scrape up all the sweat and semen that was smeared over her belly and put it in the gourd. She worked fastidiously until not a drop remained on her skin.

When she had finished, she took the gourd outside, made a small hole, and buried it in the ground. Ralph watched her, mystified.

'What was that for?' he asked when she returned.

'*Abathakathi.*' She saw he did not understand. 'Danger.'

'How is my' – he was not sure what word to use – '*seed* . . . dangerous?'

'Magic.'

'It is magical?'

'Bad people use anything from you body. Seed, hairs, skin. Make *umbulelo*, bad magic. You go sick. You die.'

'Who would want to use black magic against me?'

But the moment Ralph asked the question, he knew the answer. In Shaka's court, he already had plenty of enemies. That they might use his bodily fluids to curse him seemed far-fetched, but perhaps no more extraordinary than curing a wound with gunpowder and camomile tea. Nothing about his situation was normal.

For now, all he wanted was to lie with Thabisa again. He put his hand out to pull her close to him, but she pushed it away and pointed to the other side of the hut.

'You side.'

Clearly some Zulu rules were non-negotiable. The expression on her face was as commanding, in its way, as Shaka on his throne. He crawled across the floor to the sleeping mat laid out on the far side of the hut.

He fell asleep with the afterglow of sex still warm in his veins, and a profound sense that there were many things about the Zulus that he still had to learn.

NATIVITY BAY

Now that Marius and Jobe were back in Nativity Bay, the castaways turned their attentions to the shipwreck. They could amass all the ivory and hides imaginable, but without a way to get it to market it would be worthless.

'But what the bloody hell do we do with the boat?' Marius wondered, staring at the sunken hulk in the bay. 'I'm not a ship-wright, hey?'

'If her keel's sound, we can work from that,' said Marsden. 'First thing's to get her on dry land.'

With the longboat, they rowed out to the wreck and fixed ropes to the stumps of her masts. They ran the lines back to shore, and wrapped them around the largest, strongest trees above the beach as makeshift pulleys. Then the hard work began. They hauled until the ship righted herself, adjusted the ropes, and slowly dragged her in to shore.

Marsden and the other sailors stayed on the *Farewell* to check the lines, while Mahamba and the Chunus wrapped the ropes around themselves and did the heavy work of hauling. The sun was high and hot: soon their naked bodies streamed with sweat. Although they had enjoyed a better diet since arriving in Nativity Bay, they were still dangerously undernourished.

'We should have oxen for this,' said Jobe, wiping his forehead.

'Nonsense,' Marius retorted. 'Ten Kaffirs are as good as any ox.'

The ship was heavy with the tons of water inside her. Every yard they moved her was an ordeal. They managed to pull her halfway to shore, before the receding tide stranded her on a mudbank.

'Keep going,' Marius shouted. 'You have not finished.'

Mahamba threw down the rope and spoke angrily to his companions.

'He says they are tired,' Jobe translated. 'They will do it tomorrow.'

Marius's face, already flushed from the heat, went dark. 'You bloody well do it now, hey?' He pointed to the hawsers. 'Get on those ropes and start hauling.'

'They are tired,' said Ann.

'They are nothing but a bunch of lazy Kaffirs.' Marius turned to Mahamba, but the African stared him down, eyes narrowed, and head tipped back in defiance.

The sjambok quivered in Marius's hand. 'Don't look at me like that, you filthy black.'

Mahamba kept staring at Marius. Then, disdainfully, he turned his back and walked away.

The whip whistled through the air so fast Mahamba did not hear it. The tip seemed to brush over his bare back as light as a feather. A thin red line spread across his shoulders, quickly opening into a bloody welt.

Mahamba stumbled forward with a cry of pain. He spun around, just in time to meet the second lash face-on. It cut open his cheek half an inch below his eye. A fraction higher and it would have taken his sight.

Even that did not bow him. The warrior he had once been still lived inside him. As Marius drew back his arm for another strike, Mahamba charged.

With a spear in his hands, he would have ripped Marius open from his navel to his throat. But Mahamba was unarmed, malnourished and exhausted from his labours. Marius had the advantage of a foot in height and a hundred pounds in weight.

Marius lashed out with the sjambok again – but, in his haste, he did not manage to crack it. Mahamba was able to snatch the hide out of the air. He turned it around his arm and jerked Marius towards him.

As Mahamba pulled, Marius let go of the whip, so that the African lost his balance and staggered back. With a single stride, Marius closed the gap. His clenched fist struck Mahamba a stunning blow. Mahamba's knees buckled; he collapsed on the ground.

Marius picked up the whip and stood over Mahamba. 'You think you can touch a white man, hey?' He kicked him in the ribs. 'You think you can shirk your labour?'

Mahamba groaned and curled himself into a ball, but that was no protection. Marius brought the whip down on him, again and again, until his body was a skein of bloody slashes.

'Stop,' Ann screamed. 'You will kill him.'

Marius's gaze met hers, daring her to come close.

You think you are too good to feel the taste of my whip, his eyes seemed to say. He brought the sjambok down again.

There were eight other Africans in the clearing. *Why didn't they act?* Ann wondered. Even unarmed, they might have rushed Marius and brought him down just through weight of numbers. What power held them back?

Then she realised they were looking not at Marius, but at Marsden. He was standing at the edge of the clearing, with a rifle cocked in his hands.

Marius stepped away. At his feet, Mahamba lay in a heap of blood and loose flesh. The whip had flayed him to the bone.

The other Chunus stood back, stricken. They wanted to tend their chief, but Marius's presence held them off. He pointed the whip at each man in turn. One by one, they bowed their heads.

Last of all, the whip pointed to Jobe. The two men's eyes met. Ann, looking over Marius's shoulder, saw the hatred burning on Jobe's face. Neither man spoke, but she sensed a struggle of wills being fought between them under the silence.

'Tell them to go back to work,' Marius said.

Jobe looked at him in disbelief. 'You want me to tell them to work for *you* – after what you have done?'

'To work for us,' said Marius. 'We are still partners, are we not?'

'Are we?'

Marius shrugged, as if he hardly cared. 'For sure. A Boer does not break his promise. Even to a Kaffir.'

Jobe's jaw tightened – but he did not take the bait. He spoke a few curt words to the waiting Chunus. They trooped back to the ropes, put the straps over their shoulders and bent their backs to haul on the boat again. Marius walked alongside, barking orders and flicking his whip so that it cracked in the air close to their ears.

The Chunu women lifted up Mahamba and carried him to the kraal. Ann wanted to follow, but one of the women gave her a glare of such hatred that she did not dare. Marius had drawn a line between the races. By no choice of her own, Ann was on the wrong side.

Nothing more was said. But after that day, everyone understood that Marius was the undisputed leader of Nativity Bay. The *Farewell*'s hull was warped up onto the beach, sawpits were dug, and trees felled for timber. Marsden directed a crew of Chunus in hacking away the broken timbers and cutting replacements.

Their camp became more permanent. Marius had the Chunus build a house to his specifications, a wattle-and-daub hut with roof beams made from spare ship's timbers and thatch cut from the reeds by the river. Nobody asked who the house was for: they did not need to. When it was complete, Marius moved in by himself, while Ann and Jobe and the sailors stayed in their tents and lean-tos.

Ann moved her tent closer to Jobe's, and stayed as close to him as she could every day. She was not sure if he welcomed her presence, but he did not object. He guessed what she was afraid of. Perhaps he, too, feared what Marius might do to him if he had the chance.

They spent most days on the edge of the lagoon. Ann found peace in the breaking waves, and security in having wide open sand all around her so she could see who was approaching. Jobe had built a fish trap by sinking stakes into the seabed and weaving branches between them to make an enclosure. At high water, the sea filled the traps and fish swam in. As the tide receded, the fish were stranded in the traps, swimming in ever more frantic circles until the water drained away and they were left flapping on the sand.

'They are like us,' said Ann, half to herself and half to Jobe. The tide was full, a spring tide that covered the tops of the posts. It would be hours before it receded low enough to retrieve the catch. Yet the fish were already caught. She could see their dark shapes swimming in circles, butting their heads against the walls, unaware that their deaths were already ordained. The sight always made her melancholy. 'Trapped in a place we never expected to be, our hopes dwindling day by day.'

Jobe gave her one of his inscrutable looks.

'Do you think we will ever escape this place?' she asked.

'If we have a boat.'

Further along the beach, the *Farewell*'s frame stood on the sand, held upright by the props that Marsden had wedged against her ribs. They did not have enough men to sail a ship her size, so Marsden was in the process of cutting her down. It seemed to involve disassembling her almost completely, stripping her back to her frame and then reducing even that. The sight made Ann despair of ever leaving.

'Marius does not seem in any hurry to go,' she said.

He had set some of the Chunus to clear ground around the stockade, and plant it with roots and seeds from the forest.

Jobe grunted. 'That is the way of his people. They are hungry for land like a python for food. They swallow everything they find.'

'I thought you – the three of you – came here to hunt and trade.'

'That is not what is in his heart.'

Ann stared at the water. The trapped fish made the surface boil as they thrashed about, trying to find a way to escape. The castaways would eat well that evening.

'What is in your heart?' she asked.

Her conversations with Jobe rarely stretched further than talking about baiting traps and drying fish. He was so self-contained, it felt almost like an affront to ask anything personal. Sometimes she felt that the difference in their races was an unbridgeable gulf. Then she would angrily remind herself that he was a man like any other. But the gulf remained.

For a moment, his eyes narrowed. 'I want what you want. Like Ralph, like Marius.'

Ann gazed at him, trying to read the truth in his eyes. 'To live in freedom?'

He nodded.

'Here?'

'In my country. With my people.'

'Without white people taking your land and your cattle?'

He nodded again.

'It is strange that it's so difficult,' Ann mused. 'We all want to live in peace, free from trouble. Yet in the getting of it, we lose what we seek.'

'Because the white man wants the black man's land,' said Jobe.

'Are the races so different? It was not the white man who displaced Mahamba's people from their homes. It was the Zulus.'

'They are not my people.'

'It is such a big country. It seems a tragedy that there is not room enough for everyone.'

'"Wait on the Lord and keep His way, and He shall exalt you to inherit the land: and the wicked will be destroyed."'

As usual, a faraway look came into Jobe's eyes when he recited from the Bible. Ann wondered who he meant by the wicked.

'What is that?' she said suddenly.

Looking out over the lagoon, her eye had caught something moving against the blue sky beyond the mangroves on the point. Almost like a wisp of cloud, but too low and travelling too fast. It reached the end of the point, seemed to hover in space, and then grew larger.

It was a sail. The prow of a ship nosed around the end of the point. Ann wondered if she was dreaming. She stared at it for long moments, waiting for it to disappear. The hope was so painful she could hardly bear it.

'Mummy, a boat!' Harry, playing by the water's edge, had seen it, too. He ran to Ann, took her hand and dragged her to the shoreline as if he meant to swim out to meet it.

How could it have found them so soon? What were the chances of another ship coming? It could only be Providence. At last she and Harry could leave this place. She dropped to her knees and murmured a heartfelt prayer of thanks to the Lord.

'We are saved,' she breathed.

The ship glided on. Ann remembered the bar at the mouth of the bay. Did the ship's captain know about it? Was his ship light enough to clear it? Or would she be wrecked, as the *Farewell* had been? It would be too cruel if their rescuers suffered the same fate as the castaways they had come to save.

By now the whole ship was visible: a low, sleek vessel, with a single flat deck and black-painted sides. She approached cautiously, carrying just a few small sails at the tops of her masts.

A plume of white water splashed up by her bow. Ann waited for the sound of tearing timbers, cracking masts and snapping rigging;

the sounds that still haunted her nightmares. But the ship glided on. The splash had been a lead line taking a sounding. Her stern passed over the white line of water that marked the bar. She was safe.

The tension that had gripped Ann drained away. She leaped up and down, shouting and waving. Up the beach, Marsden, Marius and the others ran down to join her, bellowing in excitement.

'What is she?' Marius asked. 'Where is she from?'

'Maybe the governor from Port Elizabeth with soldiers to arrest us,' said Jobe.

'No,' said Marsden. 'She's a Yankee ship.'

'How can you tell?' Ann asked.

'She's Baltimore-built. A clipper.'

As soon as he had spoken, a flag broke from her masthead. The Stars and Stripes of the United States.

'She is far from home,' Ann said. Though of course they were all far from home.

'They trade in these waters,' said Marsden. 'Picking up the East India Company's leavings, carrying cottons and opium and . . . ah, other cargoes.' He and Marius shared a look that Ann could not decipher.

The clipper anchored in the middle of the bay and lowered her whaleboat. Men shinned down her sides and took up the oars.

'Fetch the rifles,' Marius said to Marsden.

Marsden stared at him as if he was crazy.

'They've come to rescue us.'

'How do you know that, hey? What if they want to take our land? We must be ready to defend it.'

Marsden could have pointed to the nine-pounder cannons mounted on the clipper's bow – or the boat pulling towards them, loaded with twenty strong men. The idea of Marius resisting them with a ragtag band of castaways and two rifles was insane.

But Marsden did not dare defy Marius. He ran back to the camp, while the whaleboat pulled steadily closer. The rowers bent on their oars, backs to the beach, while two men sat in the stern facing forward. One wore an old-fashioned tricorn hat that seemed to indicate some level of rank. The other wore a red kerchief tied over his skull, his dark hair tied back in a sailor's queue.

At that distance, Ann could not make out his face – yet something about him seemed familiar.

The boat came ashore. The sailors held her steady while the two men in the stern disembarked and splashed through the shallows. The man in the hat, who was evidently the captain, strode up the beach, while the rest of the crew fell in behind him. The man in the red kerchief was obscured by the crowd.

The captain's clothes were fashionably cut, cinched in sharply to an hourglass waist. His trousers were pressed, his boots buffed to a shine and the gold buttons on his coat gleamed. He was young, fresh-faced and clean-shaven, but he carried himself with the devil-may-care arrogance of a man who had seen much of the world and feared nothing.

It crossed Ann's mind that in his confidence and self-possession, he was not unlike Ralph Courtney. But where Ralph seemed to carry a melancholy deep inside him, in this man she saw only ambition.

He tipped his hat. 'Archibald Sterling, Master of the *Nanticoke*, out of Baltimore.'

His eyes flicked over the castaways. As his gaze landed on Ann, she felt a sudden hollow feeling inside her. It was not a lecherous look, or threatening; in fact, it was empty of emotion. She felt she was being appraised or valued, no more significant than tradable goods or a piece of livestock.

Whatever calculation the captain made, it took less than a fraction of a second. His gaze moved on to Marius, where it lingered longer.

'I guess you must be Marius Wessels,' he said.

Marius's jaw dropped. 'How do you know my name?'

'Your friend told me all about you.' The captain stepped aside, so that the man in the red kerchief could come forward.

'S'pose you thought I'd be dead,' the man said. His hatchet-sharp features twisted in an unpleasant smirk. 'Truth to tell, I didn't think I'd be seeing you neither.'

He laughed, enjoying the castaways' shock. It was Ratray – Ann remembered his name – the topman from the *Farewell*. The last time she had seen him, he had been rowing out of the bay in the longboat to take his chances on the ocean.

'How did you get back here?' Marsden had returned with the rifles. He stared at Ratray as if he was looking at a ghost.

'And it's nice to see you, too.' Ratray gave an ironic bow. 'Thinking maybe you threw in your lot with the wrong side, eh? Should've stuck by your shipmates.'

Looking at the group of men behind him, Ann saw several more faces she recognised – members of the *Farewell*'s crew who had left in the longboat. All of them, she noticed, had knives, while Ratray sported a sturdy pistol in his belt.

'We took the boat up the coast,' he continued. 'Easy it weren't – short rations, fearsome thirsty – but we bore it stoutly. Ain't that right, lads?'

The men around him nodded.

'Then, two weeks out, we saw a sail. This fine ship here.' He jerked his thumb at the clipper. 'Storm had driven her close inshore. Lucky for us, Captain Sterling keeps a sharp-eyed look-out. He don't like chance meetings.'

Several of the men laughed, as if at a private joke.

'He brought us aboard and treated us like proper gentlemen. Gave us food and water, and passage to Lourenço Marques, where they was bound. When we anchored, some of the lads put ashore to find another ship home. But Charlie Ratray had another notion.'

He tapped the side of his head, grinning.

'Obviously I'd be coming back to see my old shipmates, soon as I had the chance.'

'If you cared that much about us, why not bring the *Nanticoke* here right away?' challenged Marsden. 'You must have lost two months going to Lourenço Marques and back.'

'Oh, I tried to persuade him.' Ratray's voice dripped insincerity. 'But he had to collect what you might call a perishable cargo. Couldn't waste no time. On his voyage back, though, he was willing to put in so I could see you.'

'You're lucky we're still alive.'

'Am I?' Ratray bared his teeth. 'You look well enough to me. Even got some darkies to fetch and carry for you, I see.' He nodded to the Chunus gathered by the line of trees. 'But where's the scar-faced fella, Ralph Courtney? What happened to him?'

'He went exploring,' said Marius.

'Why did you come here?' Marsden asked. 'Was it to rescue us?'

'This ain't a rescue.' Ratray spat a wad of tobacco onto the beach. Brown spittle stained the white sand. 'Them as wants can make arrangements with Captain Sterling here, if he'll take 'em. He's plenty of passengers already, but I'm sure he can squeeze in a few more.'

Again, sniggers from the crew that Ann did not understand. She could not see any passengers on the clipper's deck, only a handful of sailors standing by the hatches. They all seemed to be armed.

'Then what are you here for?' Marsden asked.

'I heard a man once said this could be the richest land in Africa. Place a man could make his fortune, an' another fortune atop of that.' Ratray put his hands on his hips, not far from the handle of his pistol. 'Reckon I'd like to see if he was right.'

There was an implication in his words that Marius did not miss.

'This is our land. We claimed it by right of settlement.'

Ratray rolled his eyes. 'I don't want this poxy land. All we want's to live free and a fair shake.' He nodded to Sterling. 'Captain here's a man of means. He's willing to venture a few dollars on our success.'

Marius rounded on the American. 'You will not take one tusk from this place. Not one.'

Sterling raised an eyebrow. 'I did not come here to steal from you. But . . . perhaps we could discuss a trade that would be to both our benefit.'

'He'll offer fair terms,' Ratray added. 'There's enough here that we can all be rich men.'

'What do you have to trade?'

'How about guns?' Ratray grinned as he saw desire light up in Marius's eyes. 'I know what you salvaged from the *Farewell*. Not more'n three rifles, an' I only seen two so far. We brought enough guns to fight off the whole East India Company.' A second boat had put out from the *Nanticoke*, the men on board rowing strongly for the beach, piled high with casks and boxes. 'Captain Sterling would happily trade them to you, for the right price.'

Marius frowned. 'Then what do you want from us in return?'

Ratray gave a sly smile. 'Nothing it'll hurt you to part with, I promise you that. But we can talk of such things later. For now let's have a drink, like old shipmates.'

The men began to disperse. Sterling's crew brought supplies ashore, while Ratray's companions built a small camp a little way around the lagoon from the stockade. It was obvious that they expected to stay some time. A rum cask was broached, and soon songs and laughter rang out along the beach.

Ann and Harry remained in the background. Ann needed to speak to Captain Sterling, to beg her passage back to England, or at least to Port Elizabeth or somewhere else where she could find an English ship, but she hesitated. Week after week she had prayed for deliverance: now, against all hope, God had answered her prayers. The *Nanticoke* would take her away from Nativity Bay, away from hardship and her constant terror of Marius. Finally, Harry would be safe.

Yet she was wary. Maybe it was the look of the sailors who had come ashore, hard-bitten men with surly faces and scarred hands. Or maybe it was the captain, whose glittering dress made him seem as bright as the Devil. Perhaps it was the smell she caught drifting from the ship each time there was a gust of wind: a rank and foetid stench, as if all the sewers in London had been emptied into her hold.

This place was evil – or if it had not been before, Marius had made it so. Ratray's arrival would only make it worse. Competition and greed would surely lead to fighting. She had to get Harry away before it corrupted him further.

The smell of perfume wafted up the beach. It was the most incongruous scent, so strong it almost masked the stench of the ship.

It was Captain Sterling's eau de cologne. He had come up and was standing by her, waiting expectantly.

'I'm sorry?'

He tipped his hat again. 'Mr Ratray informed me there was a woman and a child here. Said you'd appreciate a passage at the first opportunity. Where do you call home?'

Where indeed? She no longer knew herself.

'Manchester,' she murmured.

'I'm not going by way of Manchester,' he said. 'But I can transport you as far as Cape Town. Our hold will be taken up with the cargo, but I dare say we can find you a berth on deck.'

'Thank you.'

For some reason, she found herself thinking of Ralph. As much as he frightened her, it was not the same as the fear she felt when she was with Marius or Ratray. All three of them were ruthless, but Ralph was not callous.

'It is because he has been gone so long,' she murmured to herself. 'He is as iniquitous as the others; you have simply forgotten what he is like.'

But she would still have felt safer if he had been there with her.

KWABULAWAYO

The Zulus were going to war. No one could mistake it. When King Shaka went on campaign, he did not gather a brigade or a division. He took the entire strength of his nation, fifty thousand men or more, whose marching feet raised a column of dust higher than the surrounding hills.

First came the regiments with their matched shields, which they carried rolled up on their backs; then the baggage porters, boys as young as six with sleeping mats and wooden headrests for the warriors; then women and girls with baskets on their heads full of beer, corn and milk. And of course, no Zulu army could be complete without its cattle. Ralph did not try to count the herd that followed behind the army. As the dust cloud announced their coming, so a great trail of manure marked their passing.

They marched for days. They crossed lines of rugged hills that gave way to sweet, rolling valleys: sometimes thickly forested, other times grassland stretching flat to the next line of hills. Close to KwaBulawayo, the land was well settled, with frequent kraals and many cattle, but as they went further the settlements became more sparse.

After a week's march, they crossed a broad river.

'What is it called?' Ralph asked. Thabisa, who had accompanied him, translated.

'uThukela,' said Hamu.

'Thukela?' Ralph repeated.

That was the river that he had crossed when he first entered the Zulu kingdom with Marius and Jobe – where he had killed the hippo. But that had been near the coast, to the east. So far as Ralph could tell, they had marched mostly west since leaving KwaBulawayo, heading ever inland. These must be the upper reaches of the Thukela, and even up here it undoubtedly still formed some kind of border for the Zulus. On the far side, the regiments unrolled their cowhide shields and slotted poles into the frame to stretch them taut. They could no longer travel without fear of being attacked.

'Where does the river rise?' Ralph asked.

Hamu pointed further west. Far on the horizon, Ralph glimpsed a rampart of mountains, their ridgeline stretched so straight it seemed to have been ruled across the sky. Even at such a distance, Ralph felt a shiver of awe at the sight.

'And what is beyond that?'

Hamu shrugged and turned back to the march. How could he know? Why should he care? The mountain range made an impassable barrier, and the Zulus did not think of going beyond it.

On the far side of the river, the country was lush and green. Trees shaded their passage, while broad meadows provided plenty of grazing for the cattle. Water was abundant from the springs that bubbled up everywhere. It was a fertile country, yet there was not a human soul to be seen. Sometimes they observed the beehive domes of kraals rising above the grass, but by the time they got there, the Ndwandwes had abandoned them.

Will we ever bring them to battle? Ralph wondered.

Many of the warriors seemed to treat this more like a holiday than a military expedition. Unlike being at home, they were spared routine chores, and given beef to eat every day. If the campaign ended, they would either return to their homes and drudgery or they would be dead. Neither option encouraged them to force the issue with the Ndwandwes.

After two days, the landscape changed. The undulating hills flattened out into a wide, open plain, punctuated by steep hills – the Dutch word for them was *kopjes* – that thrust up like the peaks of a sunken mountain range. The ground became sterile and barren. The trees thinned and in some places there were no trees at all. By day there was no protection from the sun, and at night they had to use dried grass to roast their beef. The meagre fires were no protection against the bitterly cold night. In the mornings, the ground was frozen.

The end of the plain was dominated by three high kopjes linked together to form a ridge. Smoke was rising from the summit. Shading his eyes against the sun, Ralph saw the domes of huts, and pinpricks of light where the sun glinted on metal. Later, he was able to make out the silhouettes of figures lined up along the ridge, watching the Zulu army approaching.

The place was called eZindololwane, the Zulus said. It was where the Ndwandwes had decided to build their stronghold, and Ralph could find no flaw with their logic. The slopes of the kopjes were too steep to charge. Even if a man made it to the flat plateau of the main ridge, he would not be safe. The summit of the central hill was an upthrust crown of rock, fronted by an almost sheer cliff. Any attacker would have to try to scale it, while the defenders hurled rocks and spears down on him.

The Zulus sang as heartily as ever as they marched towards the ridge. But watching their faces, Ralph saw them exchange anxious looks at the heights ahead. They too could see that it was almost impregnable.

EZINDOLOLWANE

Shaka's army made camp half a mile from the kopjes. For three days, they waited. Shaka was in no rush to attack, and the Ndwandwes showed no inclination to come down from their stronghold. Perhaps Shaka hoped that the sight of his army laid out before them would intimidate them into surrender – but if the Ndwandwes drew any conclusions looking down on the besiegers, it was that the siege could not be sustained for long. Each day, more of the camp followers slipped away as the food they had carried or the cattle they had herded were consumed. Each day, the army shrank, while the kopjes seemed to grow higher and higher.

The mood in the camp soured. Fights broke out. There were no songs. Every morning, the Ndwandwes drove their cattle out to pasture on the flanks of the hill, as if to taunt their enemies, while the Zulus were forced to watch impotently.

On the fourth day, Shaka gathered his *indunas* for a council of war. He sat on his throne, which had been carried all the way from KwaBulawayo; Dingane positioned himself at his right hand, while the other chiefs stood about in their furs and feathers and beads. Ralph, still dressed in the rags he had washed up in at Nativity Bay, felt like a pauper. Thabisa was behind him, his constant companion, whispering a translation.

Dingane spoke first. 'They mock you, brother.' He shook his arm, as if outraged, though his narrow eyes remained as cold as ever. 'How long will you let them disgrace you?'

Shaka's face flashed with anger. Even for a prince, Dingane's words were a bold provocation.

'The hill is too steep,' Hamu countered. 'If we attack, we will lose many men and still not defeat the enemy.'

A few men nodded, but most stayed impassive. It was not wise to speak before you knew what the king thought.

'If we keep the mountain surrounded, they will starve eventually,' suggested one of the *indunas*.

'Not while they have their cattle up there,' Dingane retorted.

The discussion continued, while the sun crossed the sky. Ralph did not understand everything that was said, for Thabisa could not translate quickly enough. Instead, he tried to follow the progress of the argument through tone and body language. He noticed the captains kept glancing at Shaka, but the king stayed as regal and uncommunicative as a statue. Only his eyes moved, missing nothing.

He wants men to commit themselves, Ralph thought. Always testing their loyalty, never letting them feel safe. Observing every hesitation, every catch in the voice, to be noted and remembered later.

The sun was already sinking towards the kopjes when Shaka finally stirred. Standing, he stepped down from the throne; the *indunas* fell silent. The only sound was the clink of the beads he wore, and the swish of the feathers in his headdress.

'What did the Ndwandwes do?' he asked, rhetorically.

'They tried to kill King Shaka.'

'What should be their punishment?'

'Death!' shouted the *indunas*, stamping their feet. 'We should destroy them! No two bones should be left together!'

Shaka shook his head, his face a mask of disappointment. 'My *indunas* speak bravely. But who will be the man to climb that mountain and bring down the Ndwandwes?'

Dingane spoke. Before Thabisa could translate, Ralph felt all eyes in the council turn on him.

'What did he say?' he whispered.

'Let *Abelumbi* punish Ndwandwe.'

Dingane advanced towards Ralph, his stomach protruding from between his crossbelts like a pregnant lioness's belly. He carried on speaking in the same uninflected voice he had used against Marius. With Thabisa murmuring the translation behind him, Ralph had the dizzying experience of his senses being disconnected, as if his ears had fallen a few seconds behind his eyes.

'Make him prove loyalty,' said Dingane. 'He come KwaBulawayo, Ndwandwe try kill King Shaka.'

'I saved King Shaka's life,' Ralph said. But by the time Thabisa had translated, Dingane had moved on.

'Maybe *Abelumbi* good magic. Maybe *Abelumbi* bad magic. Climb mountain. Fight Ndwandwe.'

Ralph could see the summit of the kopje, its high walls dark against the sinking sun. If it was well defended, you might conquer it with an artillery battery, but not with anything less.

He turned to Shaka. 'I saved your life,' he said again. '*I* do not need to prove anything.'

Dingane clicked his tongue and gave a little hiss. Shaka remained silent. A crease of concentration lined his forehead. He turned from Dingane to Ralph, and back again, calculating rapidly. Loyalty to his brother against gratitude to Ralph, how his decision would be received by the *indunas*, and the most important question: how would it affect his power?

He had brought his army far beyond the frontiers of his kingdom to punish the Ndwandwes. If he retreated, he would lose face. If he attacked and lost, he would be humiliated. Dingane offered him a way to split the dilemma, to fight without being blamed for the loss.

Looking up at the high kopje, thinking of the warriors waiting on its summit, a shiver went through Ralph. The delight on Dingane's face made it clear that the prince thought he had condemned Ralph to his death, and Ralph was not sure he was wrong.

Is this my fate, to die in this remote wilderness, fighting for a country that is not mine?

The unfairness of it made his bones ache.

But Ralph had learned many times that fate was never fair. Better to embrace it than try to avoid the inevitable.

He stepped forward into the circle of *indunas*.

'I will fight the Ndwandwes.'

A rosy dawn light licked the top of the kopje, though the slopes below were still in darkness. Ralph stared at it, mapping out the contours against the dawning sky. This was where he would be tested.

I thought saving Shaka's life would make my task easier, he mused. *Instead, it has only brought me greater danger.*

The kopje took the form of a crowned hat. From the valley, it rose moderately steeply to the first ridge, the grassy plateau where the Ndwandwes grazed their cattle. That would be almost impossible to assault. But even if an army managed this, they would simply put themselves in greater danger. For any man who reached the ridge would be an easy target for those throwing spears from the second summit, the crown of the hat where the Ndwandwes had built their kraal.

On three sides, the cliffs that led up to the central summit were almost sheer, virtually impossible to climb. Only on the west side was there a defile that allowed access from the left flank of the ridge: narrow, steep, and easy to defend. That was how the Ndwandwes must go up, and where they drove their cattle down to graze.

Shaka could call on fifty thousand men and yet he had not tried to take the Ndwandwes' stronghold. What chance did Ralph have, with the two hundred men he had been given?

Hamu gestured to the left flank of the hill. 'We go up that way.'

Ralph nodded. He did not know if Hamu had volunteered to accompany him on this assault, or if Shaka had ordered him, or if this was another part of Dingane's revenge, but he was glad to have the *induna* by his side.

'I will hide in those broken rocks at the base of the summit,' Ralph said. 'When the Ndwandwes bring down their cattle to pasture them on the ridge, I will use my rifle to scare them towards you. You will round them up, and then we will all get off the mountain before the Ndwandwes counter-attack.'

I have become a cattle raider, Ralph thought ruefully.

It was not a glorious vocation, but under the circumstances it seemed like his best chance of survival. Rather than try to attack the summit, they would steal the Ndwandwes' cattle. The Zulus valued the livestock so highly that it would count as a triumph. And the Ndwandwes could not survive in their stronghold without their cows. At the very least, stealing the Ndwandwes' cattle would restore morale in Shaka's army; at best, he might declare victory and go home while Ralph and Hamu stayed behind with a small force to wait for the Ndwandwes' surrender.

Ralph waited while Thabisa finished translating. He and Hamu had gone over the plan three times already, but it was vital they both understood it. Once they were on the mountain, they would not be able to communicate. When Ralph had asked Thabisa if she would come with him, she had stared at him as if he was an idiot. It was clear that custom dicatated that a Zulu woman had no place on a battlefield.

Hamu's men lined up in a double file, while the eagle feathers in their headbands waved gently in the breeze. The *inyanga* went along the rows, carrying a gourd and an ox-tail. The gourd held some kind of magic concoction. He would dip the ox-tail into it, then flick it at the men to sprinkle them with the liquid. Ralph could see them growing in confidence as they rubbed it onto their skins, standing taller and speaking more loudly, throwing taunts towards the Ndwandwes on the mountain.

'Medicines,' said Thabisa. 'Stop get hurt.'

'Let us hope it works.'

Hamu had hand-picked the men who would join them on the assault from his own regiment, strong warriors who carried their spears and their white cowhide shields with easy familiarity. Seeing them joke and spar together, Ralph recognised the camaraderie of men who had fought together for years.

He checked the priming on his rifle, and made sure that the buckle of his cartridge wallet was undone. He had enough powder for twenty shots. After that, his only weapon would be the traditional Zulu knife that Hamu had given him.

Hamu waved his men forward. 'We have waited long enough. The time has come.'

The darkness in the valley hid them as they loped through the long grass to the base of the hill. The Ndwandwes had not posted pickets, relying instead on the heights to protect them. Hamu's company reached the foot of the slope unchallenged and began to climb.

Even in the grey pre-dawn light, Ralph felt exposed. The air was so still, every noise he made sounded loud as a gunshot. While the Zulus seemed to glide over the ground like wraiths, his feet crunched on the dry earth. He stood on a loose rock, dislodged it, and sent it tumbling down the slope. A wild pheasant, startled, took flight on its noisy wings, whirling out of the grass.

Ralph paused. Even in the darkness, he could feel Hamu glaring at him. He crouched low, craning his neck to look up, waiting for a sign from above to say that the Ndwandwes had heard him.

The seconds passed slowly as the bird wheeled in the sky, then glided back in to land. Ralph began to breathe again.

They continued on. As the slope began to level off, Ralph smelled the warm, rank odour of cow dung. They had reached the first plateau, the meadow where the Ndwandwes grazed their cattle, just in time. A line of pink light was rippling down the face of the high summit as the sun began to rise. Soon the plateau would be flooded with bright sunlight.

The Zulus ran forward, scanning the ground for any bush or hollow that would hide them while they waited for the herdboys to bring the cattle down. If the Ndwandwes saw them too soon, they would be massacred. Their only chance was to surprise the herdboys and drive the cattle off the mountain before the Ndwandwes realised what was happening.

This is not a good plan, a voice whispered in Ralph's head. But it was the best they could come up with. If he returned without the cattle, he could imagine what Dingane would do to him.

The sun was climbing. On the plateau, light touched the tips of the grasses. Ralph threw himself on his belly and crawled forward, trying to find shadows that would cover him. Insects chattered in the scrub; ants skittered across the cracked earth.

Soon he felt the sun prickling his back. He had to find somewhere more sheltered. He wormed further forward, as slowly as he could, his nose almost pressed into the earth. He began to sweat. The rifle on his back thudded against him every time he moved, and he was glad he had wrapped the barrel in cloth so that the sun would not reflect from it.

A shadow fell over him. He raised his eyes from the ground to see what it was.

Two bare feet stood planted in front of him. His first thought was that the herdboys had come down early, that they had already brought the cows to pasture. But as his gaze travelled up the firm pair of legs, the short kilt of ox-hide and the well-muscled torso, Ralph realised that the feet in front of him definitely did not belong to a herdboy.

The man wore his hair in small braids that flopped down so Ralph could not see his eyes. He was holding a spear with a distinctive wooden bulb at the end of the handle. A Ndwandwe spear.

The man stared. Perhaps he was surprised to see this strange, pale-skinned creature crawling through the grass at his feet. Perhaps, for a fleeting moment, he wondered who Ralph could be.

But then he recognised an enemy. With an exultant yell, he drew back his spear to strike.

Ralph had no time to get up, let alone unsling the rifle from his back. He could not reach his knife, which was trapped under his body. In desperation, he pressed the balls of his feet into the earth, sprang forward and sank his teeth as deep as he could into the Ndwandwe's shin.

The Ndwandwe's battle cry turned into a howl of pain. Ralph's tackle had carried him backwards and knocked him off his feet and in a second Ralph was on top of him. For a moment, the two men wrestled on the ground, Ralph's mouth filled with dust and blood. The spear tip glinted as the Ndwandwe tried to bring it round, but Ralph hugged him tight, keeping him pinned so that he could not get enough space to wield it.

Ralph managed to get a hand to his knife. He drew it, beat aside the spear tip, and – before the Ndwandwe could retaliate – plunged it into the man's heart.

He leaped to his feet, unslinging the rifle. Looking around, he could see that their plan had failed. All over the plateau, men were rising out of the grass: Ndwandwes. Not herdboys, but hardened warriors, fully armed and ready for battle.

It was a trap. Behind Ralph, scores of Ndwandwe warriors came charging up the slope. They must have hidden in a gully while the Zulus passed; now they had cut off the retreat. Ralph looked for Hamu. He stood in the centre, shouting orders, trying to get his men to regroup. They were strung out in a line across the plateau, skirmishing hand to hand. There was no thought of capturing cattle anymore. They would be lucky to escape the mountain alive.

Something hissed through the air and stuck, quivering, in the ground between his feet. A javelin, much longer than the Zulus' *iklwa*. Looking up, Ralph saw men lined up on the heights above, launching spears on their enemies below.

What am I doing here? Ralph wondered. *Standing on a desolate hillside, in an unknown kingdom, fighting an enemy I have no reason to hate.* It was a pointless way to die.

In a fury, he lined up the rifle's sights on the nearest Ndwandwe and pulled the trigger.

The battlefield was transformed in an instant. As the man Ralph had targeted went down in a spray of blood and brains, the Ndwandwe warriors threw themselves to the ground in terror. It was as if Ralph's thunderous weapon had somehow killed every Ndwandwe on the kopje.

The Zulus took full advantage, leaping forward and butchering their enemies where they lay.

'Wait!' Ralph shouted as the Ndwandwe warriors in front of them began to turn and flee.

The Zulus were so eager to attack that they were running towards the summit, closer to the enemy and away from safety. Some had not noticed the Ndwandwes' rearguard closing in behind them. As soon as the Ndwandwes recovered, the Zulus would be trapped even further from their lines.

'Wait!' he shouted again. But if the Zulus heard him, they did not understand; and even if they had understood, they would have ignored him. He ran after Hamu. He had to show the *induna* the danger.

Already, the tide of battle was turning again. The routed Ndwandwes had started to regroup, supported by the spearmen on the summit – a curtain of wood and iron had begun to fall on the Zulus. They were pushed back into a knot around Hamu, fighting off the Ndwandwes, while javelins rained down from the heights. Ralph shouldered his way through until he found the *induna*.

'We have to go back,' he shouted. He pointed back down the slope. 'We can fight our way through.'

Hamu shook his head grimly. A spray of blood spattered his right cheek; his eyes were dark with fury. He swept his spear in an arc at the men surrounding them, stabbing it again and again and again until Ralph understood. *Too many men*. Any retreat would become a rout, then a slaughter.

Down below, in the valley, Shaka must have seen what was happening. Ralph could see the army assembled at the foot of the mountain, watching the fighting on the plateau above.

Why don't they come?

If the Zulus advanced now, they could cut down the men who had been deployed to block their retreat, break the ring of men around Hamu's company and rescue them. But they did not move. Perhaps Shaka feared another trap, that the battle was only bait to get him to commit his army. Perhaps Dingane was down there whispering in his ear, telling him to wait, watching the battle through those hooded eyes.

The thought infuriated Ralph. He reloaded the rifle and fired a second time. Again, the Ndwandwes reacted as if every one of them had been hit.

Ralph grabbed Hamu's shoulder. 'If we are going to die, at least let us die on the attack.'

Hamu didn't understand. Ralph pointed to the heights, where the Ndwandwes' spearmen stood lined up against the sky. Their comrades below had pressed the Zulus so close, they could not throw their weapons now for fear of hitting their own men.

'We go there.'

Hamu nodded. He shouted orders to his men, while Ralph reloaded. This time, Ralph aimed over the heads of the men around him, up to the warriors on the summit.

He fired. A long shot, but his aim was accurate. The man he had targeted let out a scream and toppled off the cliff.

The sight stunned the Ndwandwes. The men on the heights retreated from the cliff edge, afraid of more gunfire, while those on the plateau shrank back. The gun still had its power to shock. To men who had not seen it before, it must have appeared wonderous. Ralph had reached through space and killed a man by some invisible magic. Who could be safe?

Even the Zulus were frightened by it. But Ralph was with them: if he wielded god-like magic, it was on their side. They charged forward, spears raised, cutting a path through the Ndwandwes towards the defile that led up to the summit.

They could not reach it. More Ndwandwe warriors were charging down the path from their stronghold. Hamu's men would never be able to cut through all of them. The press of bodies turned the Zulus away, tight against the foot of the cliffs on the south face of the kopje.

Now their situation was worse still, surrounded by the Ndwandwes with their backs to the cliff. No way out. In desperation, Ralph scanned the cliff for a path they could use. The rock face was sheer – but as they moved around its base he saw a place where rainwater had carved a channel running down from the summit. It was steep and narrow, more a fissure than a gully. But a man could climb it if he had the strength.

Above, the Ndwandwes' defenders had advanced again to the cliff edge, throwing down rocks onto the trapped Zulus. Ralph saw one strike a Zulu clean on the top of his head and crush his skull.

Reloading the rifle, Ralph fired another shot, almost straight up in the air. He could not see if it hit anyone, but again the noise and the mysterious power of the explosion drove the Ndwandwes away. The rocks stopped falling.

'Guard my back,' he said to Hamu.

Of course the *induna* could not understand, even if he heard Ralph over the screams and howls of battle. Ralph could only trust that, as a soldier, he knew what was required.

Ralph started to climb. Hamu followed with a handful of warriors, while the rest of his men crowded around the base of the cliff to protect their rear. The cleft was steep. Ralph needed both hands to haul himself up over the smooth rocks; in some places, it narrowed so tight he had to sling his rifle awkwardly across his chest, brace his back against the sides and force his way up.

Ralph pushed on, to a place where the cleft flattened out to become a cliff. They were near the top of the kopje now and there were no more handholds. But Hamu was behind him. The *induna* braced himself in the gully and made a stirrup with his hands, lifting Ralph until he could reach the top. Pulling himself over the lip, Ralph reached back to give Hamu a hand up.

Looking down, he could see that the Zulus were tight-pressed against the foot of the kopje, besieged on three sides by the Ndwandwes. How much longer could they hold on?

Ralph reloaded his rifle as one by one Hamu's men made their way onto the summit. He had fifteen cartridges left and no way of knowing if they would be enough. All he could hope was that the gun would keep the Ndwandwes running.

In front of him, the ground sloped gently upward, covered in a thick carpet of loose stones. Clearly, when it rained the water from the top of the kopje ran through this cleft. The natural rock walls on either side made a perfect channel. As Ralph looked up to where the slope levelled off among a cluster of boulders, a head appeared above one of them. Ralph aimed the rifle, and saw the surprised expression still fixed on the man's face as the bullet split open his forehead. By the time the body hit the ground, Ralph was already reloading.

All his instincts told him to keep low, to find cover from where he could take potshots at the defenders. But he would not beat them that way. Eventually, the mystical power of the gun would wear off and they would overwhelm him.

He drew a deep breath and touched the scars on his face. *You have confronted impossible odds before*, he reminded himself. *You survived.*

Ralph rushed forward, scrambled up onto one of the boulders and stood, rifle raised, looking out on to the mountain top.

The summit was flat table-land, larger than it had seemed from below. The Ndwandwes had built a kraal, some twenty huts around a cattle pen surrounded by a thorn hedge. Nor was it just a warriors' camp. Ralph saw women tending cooking fires – ignoring the battle raging below them – and children pressing their noses against the hedge to watch as the Ndwandwe soldiers ran back and forth.

In that moment, standing on the boulder with the wind whipping his hair and the world spread out beneath him, Ralph had a dizzying feeling of omnipotence. To his right, he could see back down towards Zululand. To his left, the line of mountains he had seen on the march now seemed close enough to touch.

Then, suddenly, he was just a man again. A lone attacker, a perfect target silhouetted against the sky – and there were hundreds of Ndwandwe warriors in front of him, staring up at him in shock. One of the men dropped to a crouch and launched his spear at Ralph. Ralph was surprised by how quickly it flew. He ducked, almost too late. The spear grazed his shoulder. Before the next one came, Ralph levelled his rifle and shot the man dead.

It was the first time the Ndwandwes on the ridge had faced the rifle close up. The tongue of flame that flashed from its muzzle, the cloud of smoke that enveloped Ralph, and the resounding thunderclap of its explosion, terrified them. They had laid their trap, confident that the Zulus would be massacred down on the plateau. Yet here the enemy was, on the summit, a man with a weapon the like of which they had never seen in their lives: a weapon not even the ancestors could have imagined. Some turned away and ran. Others took hesitant steps backwards. Ralph tore open another cartridge with his teeth and tipped the powder down the barrel. He did not even bother to ram home the bullet: that was not important. He primed the pan, cocked and fired again. The noise and the fire did all the damage he needed.

The Ndwandwe army started to flee. Hamu and his men emerged from the gully and pursued them, pricking them on with their spears. Ralph reloaded and fired again.

He could have remained there, watching the rout safe from on top of his boulder. But his blood was hot; the power of the gun coursed through his veins. He could not let go of the fight. He leaped from the boulder and joined the Zulus, driving the Ndwandwes off the summit.

A few of Hamu's men broke into the kraal. They took burning logs from the cooking fires and threw them onto the thatch of the huts. The dry wood and straw caught like a haystack, making a ring of fire. Thick smoke billowed, shrouding the battlefield and adding to the chaos. Ralph saw a cow charge through the crowd, nostrils flared, bellowing in panic. Any man in its way was knocked down and trampled into the earth.

There was a single, narrow path off the mountaintop, and the Ndwandwes could not all squeeze onto it at once. They pushed and barged each other: some toppled off the cliffs and fell screaming, while those at the rear made easy prey for Hamu's men.

But some would not give up. Around the battlefield, pockets of the bravest or most desperate Ndwandwe warriors tried to regroup and fight the Zulus. Some still had their spears and shields, while others picked up rocks and hurled them. Ralph was grateful for the smoke: if they had seen how few men Hamu had, or if they had joined forces, there were enough of them to have driven the Zulus back over the cliff. Ralph kept back, firing into the knots of men who resisted. The sight of one of their comrades collapsing as if by magic was usually enough to break their resolve.

He felt something strike him from behind, but ignored it. He fired again. His hand went to his ammunition wallet for the next cartridge.

The wallet was empty. He had used all his bullets. But instead of dry leather, he felt something wet and sticky in the bottom of the bag. When he pulled out his hand, he saw it was covered in blood.

He became aware of a dull ache in his back where he had felt the blow. He craned around.

A spear hung out of his back. Blood streamed from the wound and ran down his leg. Ralph was surprised he had not felt the impact more. Even now, seeing the full horror of the wound, did not connect it with any sensation in his body. As if in a dream, he grabbed the spear shaft, trying to tug it free, but it would not come.

Hamu came running out of the smoke. He shouted something that Ralph understood to mean 'Stay still'. Ralph obeyed. Everything seemed unreal. Despite the weapon lodged in his back, he still did not feel any pain.

Hamu pushed Ralph on to his knees and stood over him. Without warning, the *induna* plunged his finger into the flesh alongside the spear tip. Now Ralph felt it, like a hot iron jerking about inside him. He screamed.

With a gush of blood, the spear tip came free. Hamu tore one of the ox-tails from his kilt, balled it up and pressed it into the wound to staunch the bleeding. He threw the spear aside, onto the ground where Ralph could see it. Up close, Ralph noticed it had a barbed tip, like a harpoon.

That was why I could not pull it out, he thought.

He felt his consciousness slipping away. He had to stay alive, had to fight – but he could not resist the tide of exhaustion overtaking him. His face felt hot under the sun, yet his body shivered with cold.

From nowhere, an image burst into his mind: Ann, standing alone on the beach by the lagoon, hundreds of miles away. She turned to look at him and held him with her eyes.

Then pain, exhaustion and blood loss overwhelmed him, and the world went dark.

NATIVITY BAY

A grey heron surveyed the lagoon from its hunting perch – a wooden stump that had once been the *Farewell*'s bowsprit. Even at low tide, the spar protruded but a few inches from the water: the next storm would most likely bury it completely. For now, it made a perfect perch for the bird, which stood so still that if it had not occasionally twitched its head you might have thought it was carved from the same wood as the bowsprit.

Ann watched the bird from the bluff. The heron captivated her: its poise, its stillness, the beauty of its slate-blue colouring. She found its presence comforting and came here almost every day to spend time in its company.

Behind the heron, the *Nanticoke* sat in the middle of the lagoon. It was a handsome ship, but for some reason Ann felt a shiver every time she looked at it. Ever since the ship had arrived, her men had been busy below decks, making some kind of repair. The sounds of hammering and sawing had drifted out of the hold from dawn until dusk. The wind brought the smell of tar, sawdust and lye from her decks.

Soon the ship would set sail again – and Ann and Harry would be aboard her. Ann still wondered if she had made the right decision. She did not trust Captain Sterling, with his sharp eyes and dangerously good manners; and she was not naive to the perils of putting herself aboard a ship in the company of two dozen strange men.

Will Ralph return before I leave? To her annoyance, she often found herself thinking of him. It felt wrong to go without saying goodbye. He had slipped into her life four years ago on the beach at Algoa Bay, as unexpected as a ghost, and now she would leave him the same way.

Would he care? She wanted to think so. But that was just foolishness.

In a blink, the heron slipped off its perch into the water. Its long neck stabbed forward. When it pulled back, a tiny fish wriggled in its beak. With two gulps, the bird swallowed it whole. Even a moment of repose was only the prelude to the next kill.

Ann got up. The calm she craved had slipped away; best to get back to camp.

'Harry!' she called.

She knew he would not be far away. At first she had fretted that he roamed so freely in this wild place. She had worried about the hippos and crocodiles that lurked by the water, the lions in the bush. But he had proved to have surprisingly sharp instincts, almost a sixth sense for danger. He kept away from the riverbanks in the middle of the day, when the crocodiles were sunning themselves; and from the deep pools where the hippos lay submerged. He seemed to be able to sniff out the game paths where lions had passed, or know where the jackals hunted. Once, Ann had seen him playing in a meadow of long grass. Suddenly, he had stopped and looked up at a tree on the edge of the clearing. Following his gaze, Ann's heart nearly stopped. A leopard lay on a low branch, almost hidden in the dappled shadows. Its paws hung limp over the branch, while its head was turned sideways as if on a pillow.

Ann had to bite her fist to keep her composure. But Harry had shown no fear. He backed away, slowly and silently, until he reached the far side of the clearing and wondered why his mother was crying.

Now, at Ann's summons, he came trotting out of the thick bush on to the bluff.

His face was streaked with mud, the tear in his shirt that she had darned that morning had reopened, and blood oozed from a gash on his knee.

'I found a calemion on a tree,' he said. He could not say 'chameleon'.

He held it out, a puffy lizard squeezed into his cupped hand. Its flesh was a cloudy, almost transparent colour, tinted pink where it touched his skin and with a green tinge along its spine. Ann thought it must be terrified.

'Can I keep it?' Harry asked.

'Let it go,' she said gently.

'I won't hurt it.'

'I know. But it wants to be free.'

Harry bent down to the ground and opened his hand, watching as the chameleon lurched slowly into the brush.

If only I could escape so easily, Ann thought. *Change my colours, and live unnoticed.*

They walked back to camp, off the bluff and round into the bend of the lagoon. The stockade they had made on their first day still stood, though the only house inside it was Marius's. Everyone else had made their homes beyond its gate, preferring to keep a safe distance. Ann's home was a lean-to hut, logs laid against a ridge pole and woven through with grass to keep the rain out.

Whoever thought that one day our house in Paradise Valley would seem like a mansion? she marvelled.

Ann made a fire and put some water on to boil. Marius had kept the cooking utensils they had salvaged from the wreck for himself, but the Chunus had made her a broad pot with a tapered mouth, sculpted from river clay. As the water began to simmer, she added fish and herbs to make a stew.

Approaching footsteps started her, but it was just Jobe. The smell of food often brought him to her hut. He came so regularly that she always prepared an extra portion. He sat cross-legged by the fire and took the bowl that Ann offered him.

'What will you do when I am gone?' she asked.

'Wait for Ralph. Try not to kill Marius.'

She laughed, though she couldn't tell if he was joking. She wished he had not mentioned Ralph. She was trying to avoid thinking about him.

'Will Ralph return, do you suppose?'

'He escaped the prison on Robben Island. If anyone can survive King Shaka, and come out a rich man, he will.'

'Then you will be rich, too.'

It felt absurd, imagining any of these ragged castaways ever making their fortunes. The best that could be imagined was that they would eke out a wretched existence, no better than she had in Paradise Valley. The worst . . .

She thought of the graves by the ruined house. People had lived here, they had died, and now they were no more than bones.

Marsden was coming up the path. 'Boss wants you at the stockade,' he said to Jobe.

Jobe gave him a contemptuous stare. He had objected when the men started referring to Marius as 'boss', and he still refused to refer to him in this way, but the title had stuck.

'What does he want me for?'

'He's got something to say. Needs you to translate.'

The Chunus had trooped in from the village and the fields and gathered inside the stockade. Ann was surprised to see that men from the *Nanticoke* had come, too. They stood around the perimeter with guns and axes in their hands.

'They look like the guards on Robben Island,' Jobe muttered.

Marius stood in the gateway. As the Africans arrived, he directed them to one side or other of the enclosure: men to the left, women and children to the right. Some of them looked frightened, but most of their daily work saw them divided by gender – it was not unusual for them to be split up in this way. If any man wanted to complain about being separated from his wife and children, Marius's sjambok made him think again.

Ann hung back. Five years previously, she and her husband Frank had attended a meeting at St Peter's Field outside Manchester. They had gathered to protest against the corrupt parliamentary system that let landowners live in luxury while honest people starved. It had been a good-natured affair: women in their Sunday best, children playing.

Then the hussars had arrived. They had ordered the crowd to disperse, and – when the crowd did not oblige – they had lowered their sabres and charged as if they were facing a corps of Bonaparte's infantry. Twenty minutes later, eighteen civilians lay dead and hundreds more were wounded.

Ann and Frank had escaped with some bruises. But she had not forgotten the horror of it, the disbelieving moment when she realised that the cavalry meant to attack, that innocence and good intention were no protection. Now, she felt something of that brutal purpose in Captain Sterling's men. They looked at the Africans with the same pitiless contempt as the hussars: not as human beings, but as quarry.

The last of the Chunus were almost inside the stockade. Ann's feeling of dread grew stronger: she wanted to warn the Chunus that something terrible was going to happen, but she did not know how, and Marius would surely silence her if she tried. She glanced at Harry. She had to protect him at any cost.

'Come with me, my boy.' She took his hand hastily and pulled him into a rough lean-to that the men used for storage. There was no door, but a pile of salvaged barrels would at least conceal him from anyone passing. 'Wait here,' she said, hoping for once he would obey her.

Harry seemed to sense the menace in the air. He ducked down obediently. 'Mummy, aren't you staying?' he asked from behind the barrels.

'No, my heart.'

Ann longed to keep him safe and sit out the danger until it had passed, but she could not hide in ignorance while others might be suffering. She had to see it for herself.

'Stay here and be good.'

She went back to the stockade. Twenty yards behind it, a spreading tree grew on a low hill that allowed a view over the palisade wall. Ann hid behind the tree and looked out.

The stockade was full. Every African in the settlement must be there, perhaps the first time they had all been gathered together. Ann had never realised how many there were – well over a hundred. They crowded into the open space in front of Marius's house, while the armed sailors stood around the perimeter. Ann saw Ratray and Marsden, and Captain Sterling in his immaculate frock coat. Jobe was there, too, standing at the front next to Marius, who had climbed onto a crude platform made from a plank stretched between two barrels. It put him almost on eye level with Ann. She shrank back, but he had not seen her behind the tree. He was surveying the assembled Africans with an unpleasant smirk on his face.

'Tell them they have done good work,' he said to Jobe. 'Tell them I am pleased with them.'

Jobe translated what Marius had said. Some of the Chunus smiled tentatively, but most were more worried about the armed men around them.

'In fact,' Marius continued, 'I am so pleased that I am going to send them to work for other men. They will go on that boat' – he pointed to the *Nanticoke* – 'across the sea to another country.'

His words died away without translation. Jobe was staring at him with murder in his eyes. Everything that Ratray had said – the sly jokes and euphemisms, the references to 'passengers' and 'perishable cargo' – suddenly made horrifying sense.

Perhaps Ann had always known it. Perhaps, deep in her subconscious, she had understood it; but against all judgement she had looked away, refusing to believe it. Maybe some betrayals were simply too enormous to imagine.

The *Nanticoke* was not a merchant ship. She was a slaver. And now Marius would make the Chunus her cargo.

The last to know, inevitably, were the Africans. They stood uncertain and afraid, waiting for Jobe to translate what Marius had said.

'Tell them.' Marius poked Jobe hard in the ribs with the toe of his boot. 'Tell them, or I'll put you on that ship, too, hey?'

For Jobe, this was the bitterest betrayal of all. But he was unarmed, and surrounded by men who would happily put a bullet in him. He was alive and free for one reason – his use to the slavers as an interpreter.

He raised his head and spoke a few short words.

A shudder went through the crowd. Some cried out; others clasped their neighbours. One or two of the women started to weep, and in turn their children started crying agonisingly.

But a few men decided on a different tack. Mahamba was one of them. The beating Marius had given him had broken his authority, but it had not taken away his pride. He stood in the front rank, staring at Marius with undisguised loathing. When Jobe spoke, he did not flinch. Instead, he launched himself at Marius.

He moved so fast that the big Dutchman had no time to react. He was knocked backwards off the makeshift platform onto the ground. Before he could get up, Mahamba sprang onto him.

Marius was the bigger man. He could wrestle Mahamba off him in seconds. But the Chunu chief raised his arm, revealing a stone clasped in his hand: big enough to smash Marius's skull, with jagged edges as sharp as an axe.

A shot rang out from the palisade. Mahamba slumped. Blood gushed from the hole that a bullet had punched clean into his heart. The stone fell from his hand and rolled at Jobe's feet.

Jobe looked down. Marius was pinned under Mahamba's body. In three paces Jobe could be on top of him. But there were armed sailors on every side, all watching Jobe. He would be dead before he was within striking distance.

Jobe left the stone where it lay. Better to live now, and take his revenge later. But others among the Chunus felt differently. Better to die now than submit. Following Mahamba's example, they charged their captors.

They would surely have overwhelmed the white men, but their advantage was also their weakness. With so many people crammed into the stockade, those who wanted to fight struggled to reach their opponents, while many of the crowd had no appetite for battle but only wanted to flee.

More shots were fired, deafening at such close range. Smoke billowed into the compound. Cries became screams; fear turned to panic. The crowd surged back towards the gate.

They could not get out. The gates were closed, and Ann saw with horror that they had been barred from the outside, buttressed with heavy logs so that they would not shift even under the press of a hundred Africans. Mothers lifted their children above their heads, holding them up to save them from being trampled. A sailor reached out and took one of them, as if to help it over the palings and to safety, then tossed it back into the compound as casually as throwing a ball. The child vanished in the melee.

What could Ann do against so many men? If she revealed herself, she would put both her and Harry in danger. But she could not stand by and watch as women and children were condemned to death, or worse.

She ran from the tree, across the open ground. Two sailors had been stationed outside the gate, but their attention was on the people inside, so they did not see her coming. Ann was able to get right up to the gate. The timbers propped against it were blocks salvaged from the *Farewell*'s stern post, each one so big she would struggle to put her hands around it. She grabbed one as best she could and heaved with all her strength.

It did not budge. It was too heavy and the people pushing on the gate had driven it into the ground. If they had stepped back, they would have released the pressure on it, maybe given Ann a chance, but they did not know that, and Ann had no way of telling them.

Ann beat her fists on the wood in fury. She wrapped herself around the beam, rocking her weight to try and shift it.

One of the sailors had seen her.

'Hey,' he shouted. 'Hands off that.'

The sailor came lunging towards her. He hit her with all his weight, crushing her against the prop and squeezing the breath out of her.

The timber moved. Ann's frantic heaving had pushed it loose; now, the sailor's weight piling in on top of her dislodged it. It fell with a thud that made the earth tremble – so thunderously that the second prop was also shaken loose.

It toppled over, just missing Ann. The sailor was not so lucky. The heavy beam fell on his legs and crushed them, mangling the limbs into grotesque shapes. Ann scrambled free, ignoring his screams. The other sailor stood a few yards away, staring at her and his crippled shipmate.

But without the props, there was nothing to hold the gates shut. They burst open like a breached dam, letting the Africans pour out. The sailor, still pinned under the piece of timber, was trampled under their feet. His companion fared no better: he was knocked down and trampled, too, as the Chunus fled in every direction.

Ann joined the rout. Again, she was taken back to St Peter's Field, running with the crowd like game before the beaters, heart bursting, knowing that if she did not keep up, she would be killed. Gunshots sounded behind them as Marius's men fired indiscriminately into the crowd. A woman cartwheeled past Ann and collapsed. Ann wanted to help, but there was nothing to be done. She was caught in a river in spate; her one thought was to run.

She reached the lean-to. Harry had come out from his hiding place and was staring in shock at the fleeing Chunus. Ann scooped him up in her arms and kept running.

She did not stop until she had run far into the bush, until she could no longer hear the sound of Marius's voice. The Chunus had scattered. She and Harry were alone.

Ann saw she had come to the clearing Harry had found months earlier, with the ruined house and the five graves. A dread hung over the place, the memory of unspeakable things. They could not linger here.

'Can we go home now, Mummy?' Harry asked.

'No, my darling. We have to go further.'

'Where?'

'Where we can find a new home.'

Night was falling; soon it would be dark. She could not run forever; she could not go back; she could not fight the slavers alone.

But Marius and Ratray and Sterling would not stop until they had fulfilled the devilish bargain they had struck. They would organise hunting parties to round up the Chunus and bring them back. Some might escape, but there were pregnant women and children who would not get far, and husbands and fathers who would not abandon them. Ann could not leave them to their fate.

Ann knew of one man and one man alone who might be able to stop Marius. But he was a hundred miles away in the heart of an enemy kingdom – if he was still alive.

She had no alternative. She hoisted Harry on to her back and began striding north, towards the river crossing and the hills beyond.

'Where are we going?' Harry asked again.

'We are going to find Ralph.'

EZINDOLOLWANE

Ralph woke to the sight of stars. Lying on his back, looking up at the night sky, he could see the Southern Cross, the luminous trail of the Milky Way, and thousands more tiny pricks of light. Somewhere in the distance he could hear singing.

Images washed into his head, like waves lapping a beach. Shaka's bedside. The march. Climbing the mountain; the narrow gully; reaching the summit and facing down the Ndwandwes. Blood dribbling down his leg. Hamu kneeling over him.

The pictures seemed so fantastical that he could not be sure if they were memories or dream fragments. But there was a dull ache in his back that flared into a bright stabbing pain the moment he tried to move. That was real.

There was something else he had to remember. Something important. Standing on the boulder, that moment of lightness with the world at his feet, invincible as a god. And . . .

Ann?

The thought took him by surprise. She had not been there. She was hundreds of miles away.

Warmth rippled through him as, in his mind, he beheld her face. Her dark hair tied back, a few loose strands flying in the breeze; her pert chin and parted lips; and the humour in her eyes.

In those closing moments on the mountain, when he had thought that he would die, he had thought of her.

Ralph had faced death many times. Every other time, it had come with an empty feeling, a feeling that he had failed, and that had been the impetus that kept him alive and made him keep fighting. But this had been different. He had not thought of failure. He had thought of Ann.

A torrent of emotion broke over him, washing away the darkness and hate that had choked him for so long. He felt it with the force of a spiritual revelation, the purest emotion he had experienced since his mother died.

He desired her, body and soul. He desperately wanted Ann Waite.

Then he remembered Harry. The boy was a reminder of the darkest parts of Ralph's past, a living, breathing monument to his guilt. If he lived with Ann, he would have to confront that every day.

The scars throbbed in his cheek again.

'I saved his life,' he said to the stars. 'Is that not enough?'

The stars withheld their judgement. But out of the darkness, an unexpected voice said: 'You are awake.'

Ralph had thought he was alone. He turned in the direction of the voice, grunting as pain shot through his side.

'Who is there?'

It was Thabisa's voice. She squatted on her haunches, a few feet away, her skin grey-blue in the starlight. She must have been there all along. Behind her, he saw the familiar shape of the mountain silhouetted against the pale sky.

'What happened in the battle?' he asked.

Thabisa shrugged, as if to say that that was men's business. *Was it a victory?* Ralph had to assume he would be dead if it wasn't.

Another voice spoke. Hamu stood there, tall and commanding.

'He say, "You harder to kill than sea cow,"' Thabisa translated.

Ralph started to laugh but the pain was too much.

Hamu reached out his hand. 'Come see Shaka now.'

Ralph almost cried out with pain as Hamu lifted him to his feet, though the agony lessened somewhat once he was upright. Leaning on Hamu's shoulder, he hobbled through the trees towards the singing he had heard earlier.

Huge bonfires had been set and the regiments danced around them in their full ceremonial regalia. They stamped their feet rhythmically, turning in slow circles as they clapped their hands and sang.

'Was the battle a victory?' Ralph asked.

Hamu smiled. 'Not for Ndwandwe.'

He led Ralph between the fires to the one that burned brightest. Shaka was dancing among his *indunas*, his oiled body, now fully recovered, gleaming like iron in the firelight. He broke off as he saw Ralph. For a moment, Ralph felt Shaka's gaze fix on him, probing him like a scalpel.

What kind of man are you? his eyes seemed to say.

Then the gaze moved to Hamu, and it was as if Shaka had not noticed Ralph. The king embraced Hamu. He presented him with a lion-skin cloak, which he wrapped around the *induna*'s shoulders, and spoke warmly. Even without a translation, Ralph understood that the battle was being recounted. Shaka began to act out the events of the battle: crouching down, tensing his arm, looking up at the heights, plunging an imaginary spear through a man's heart. The assembled warriors watched and cheered, shouting their approval each time Shaka struck a new pose.

The parts of the battle that Shaka did not re-enact were the gunshots. It was as if the battle had happened without Ralph. The injustice stung: as bravely as Hamu and his men had fought, they would never have gained the summit without the terrifying effect of Ralph's rifle.

How will I ever make my fortune, if Shaka will not recognise my accomplishments? Ralph wondered. But another voice in his head answered: *Shaka knows.* The knowledge had been there in the king's eyes when he looked at Ralph. *Your reward will come in time.*

While Shaka spoke, Ralph scanned the crowd. Most of the *indunas* shouted their praise wholeheartedly, but a few seemed more reluctant. Ralph was not surprised to see that Dingane barely joined in.

Shaka saw it, too. He turned to his brother and beckoned him forward. Shaka danced around him, jabbing his finger and crowing. Dingane was impassive. His eyes were so narrow that he almost looked asleep.

'What is he saying?' Ralph asked Thabisa.

'Shaka tell him, "You say Ndwandwe mock me. You say it is impossible to punish them. But Hamu, he has done it."'

Shaka roared with laughter. Dingane twisted his mouth into a grin. The *indunas* cheered for Hamu, who gestured to Ralph.

'We not win battle without him. He show big loyalty King Shaka,' Thabisa translated.

Shaka nodded, accepting the point.

Ralph bowed his head. He knew that Dingane was staring at him. And while Shaka's eyes could dominate a man, the hatred smouldering behind Dingane's narrowed lids was more worrisome.

Ralph remembered how the Ndwandwes had been waiting for him on the plateau, almost as if they had been warned the Zulus were coming.

I am not a man, he thought. *My entire life I have been a weapon. Now that I am among the Zulus, they care about one thing – who should wield me, and whom I can hurt.*

Dingane had tried to destroy him, and it had only increased Ralph's power.

This will not be the end of it.

Dingane said a few words in his low, mumbling voice.

'Firestick only frighten birds and children,' Thabisa translated. 'And Ndwandwe.'

The Zulu chiefs stamped their feet and hooted with laughter. Those who had been least enthusiastic shouting Hamu's praises now cheered raucously for Dingane. Marius's words came back to Ralph: *When there's two men wanting the same thing, you always end up taking a side.*

The celebrations subsided. The soldiers drifted back to their camp. As Ralph was about to leave, he felt Shaka's gaze settle on him. The king beckoned him forward to the fire.

'Sit with him,' Thabisa said.

Ralph lowered himself onto a log drawn up near the fire, pushing aside his pain. Shaka sat beside him. He opened his cloak and reached out so that he wrapped it around Ralph's shoulders. Ralph wondered what the Zulus would think of this intimacy, but the *indunas* had all left. Apart from Thabisa, squatting by the fire like a cat, and the king's ever-present bodyguard, he and Shaka were alone.

Shaka put up his hand and touched the scars on Ralph's cheek. He spoke.

'How you get those?' Thabisa translated.

'A battle.'

'Who do you fight?'

'The man who killed my father.'

Shaka accepted this. 'You kill him.'

It was not a question.

'He died.'

'This man, he have children?'

'He had a son.'

Shaka frowned, as if to say that this was what he had feared.

'You kill him too.'

Ralph couldn't tell if Shaka was assuming he had already killed the boy, or asking if he would later, or telling him that he should. He glanced at Thabisa, trying to get a sense of the king's meaning, but she offered no clue.

'The boy is not a threat.'

'Boy always dangerous. That why me, no children.'

'Nor me.'

'Do umGeorge have children?' Shaka asked suddenly.

'No,' said Ralph. It was true, so far as he knew. King George IV had had a daughter, but she had died.

Shaka nodded approvingly. 'umGeorge good king. Good king, no children.'

But who will take the throne when the old king dies? Ralph wondered. He was wise enough not to ask. Shaka's mind had already moved on.

'umGeorge, he have many warriors?'

'Yes. Many.'

'So many as Shaka?'

Shaka shot Ralph a sly look: a man who wanted to be flattered, but also wanted the truth. To tell him how comprehensively the British Army outnumbered the Zulus would be impolitic; but to downplay Britain's strength would give Shaka a false confidence.

'umGeorge's army is no less than King Shaka's.'

'His warriors have firesticks?' Ralph nodded. 'How many?'

'All of them.'

Shaka fell silent. A mind honed in war could imagine what an army equipped with guns might do.

'umGeorge far away?'

'Across the sea.'

'You are *induna* for umGeorge?'

Am I? Ralph wondered. Should he try and represent himself as an emissary of King George, align himself with the power of the British flag? That might give him status and authority.

You always end up taking a side.

'I fought the Ndwandwes for King Shaka.'

The answer pleased the king. 'Fight good.' He spoke rapidly. 'King Shaka say you be *induna*,' Thabisa translated. 'He give you cattle, kraal, wives. Ivory and beads.'

Ralph could have said he did not need the cattle or the beads – only the ivory. Nor did the prospect of a harem of Zulu wives excite him. But he knew he could not reject a king's gifts. He bowed low.

'*Ngiyabonga, Nkosi.*' Thank you, Lord.

Ralph had one task to complete first.

'Tell him I must go back to Nativity Bay,' he said to Thabisa. 'I need more powder and ammunition.'

He expected he would have to explain what those were. But Thabisa did not hesitate. She must have seen plenty of guns and hunting in her childhood in Nativity Bay, and found words that made sense to Shaka. He nodded.

'You go with Hamu. Then come KwaBulawayo.'

Ralph was surprised how easily the king had granted his request. 'If Shaka gives me the ivory, I will take it back to my friends.'

Shaka's eyes gleamed. Once again, Ralph had revealed his desire, his vulnerability.

'Ivory make you slow,' said Thabisa. 'Long way eThekwini. Go, then come back KwaBulawayo for ivory.'

Shaka clearly meant to keep Ralph on a short leash to ensure his return. Ralph knew it was unwise to argue with the king. But he sensed that if he did not insist on some immediate reward, then he would be making the king too much his master – Shaka was capricious, when it came to it he might decide that he didn't feel like rewarding Ralph for taking the Ndwandwes' stronghold.

'If I do not bring them ivory, they will not give me powder and shot. We trade one thing for another.'

Ralph met the king's gaze and stared, the way no Zulu would have dared. *We need each other*, his eyes said. *But it must be a fair exchange.*

Shaka looked away impatiently. He barked an order and made a beckoning gesture. Servants came forward carrying six elephant tusks and laid them before Ralph.

'You take these. When you bring gunpowder to KwaBulawayo, I give you more.'

Ralph examined the tusks, trying not to let his satisfaction show. They were mid-sized, maybe seventy pounds each, but creamy white and not pitted or cracked with age. They would fetch a decent price.

He smiled and bowed low. 'You can rely on me. More ivory, more gunpowder.'

'More war,' said Shaka. 'Many more battles to fight.'

'I will come back.'

Where else could he go?

They travelled slowly to Nativity Bay. From the highlands, where they had conquered the Ndwandwes, back to the coast, was two hundred miles or more, Ralph estimated, though it was almost impossible to tell the real distance. The paths were uncertain, and the pace was irregular with the cargo that they carried. Ralph had to stop often to rest his aching back. Fortunately, the wound was healing well. Thabisa had tended to it expertly. Each day, he felt stronger; each day, his stride lengthened and his stamina grew.

And he felt free – a total, exhilarating freedom. Shaka was like a bright star that drew every planet into its orbit, constantly tugging at them with his invisible force. Only once you broke free did you realise how much he had drained you. Even Hamu seemed to walk taller, speak more easily. In the evenings, they sat by the fire swapping tales. Thabisa sat with them, but gradually Ralph found he needed her translation less and less. Although there were sounds in the Zulu language he would never master – the click on the roof of the mouth; the hum that prefaced many of their words – he could make himself understood. And Hamu was an equally quick study in English.

They crossed the Thukela at a drift and headed south. Ralph's Zulu escort became more wary on the far side of the river. This was contested land, caught between the Zulus and the kingdom of the Mpondos further south. Occasionally, Shaka would send an *impi*, or raiding expedition across the river. They would devastate the land, take captives and cattle, but they did not stay. That was what Hamu had been doing the day they had met by the river.

'How much further?' Ralph asked. It was the second evening after crossing the river.

'Tomorrow.'

Ralph stared into the fire, rubbing his scar absent-mindedly. Even now, the smell of smoke still made it prickle.

He thought of what he would find at Nativity Bay. Had they finished rebuilding the ship? What would he do if they had? Six tusks was better than nothing, but divided with Marius and Jobe and the sailors who had stayed, it would not amount to much.

If we go back to Cape Colony and are caught, we will all dance on the end of a hangman's noose.

The best way to avoid that fate was to amass such a fortune that he could buy a passage anywhere in the world, and bribe anyone who tried to stop him.

And what of Ann – and Harry? The memory of his dream after the battle had faded; the burning he had felt for her then had cooled. At night, he lay with Thabisa. Yet there was still a curious hunger inside him to see Ann again, however often he reminded himself that it was a foolish wish.

I suppose some of our profits will have to go to her, to help her move on with her own life.

He could not leave her and the boy penniless on whatever random, unsafe dock they finally landed.

Ralph's thoughts drifted from Ann to Marius. He remembered the Dutchman's last words to him: *If you try to cheat me, a scorpion sting will seem like nothing against what I will do to you.* What would he think when Ralph returned as the commander of a company of Zulus? If Marius had been sitting idle at Nativity Bay, he would resent Ralph's success. And what of Jobe? Would he be jealous that Ralph had won Shaka's favour, while he was exiled?

Hamu gave Ralph a curious look, as if he had read his thoughts. 'The big *abelumbi* – he is your brother?'

Ralph had to grin at the question. 'Can you not see how different we are?'

'Maybe one father, two wives.'

'You forget, my friend, that in our country a man has only one wife. Blessed by God, only death can break a marriage bond.'

Hamu considered it, as if puzzling over a problem. Then his face cleared. 'One wife, many cattle.'

'We do not buy our wives with cattle.'

'Then how you get woman?'

'Sometimes we marry for love,' Ralph said.

He had spoken to himself, so he did not notice that Thabisa hadn't translated it. Nor did he notice the intense look she gave him over the smouldering coals of the fire.

'I am going to sleep,' Ralph announced.

Thabisa had set out his sleeping mat and headrest a little distance from the fire, within the circle of thorn branches they had gathered to keep out wild animals. It was a cloudy night, and he could not see the stars. He thought of the dream he'd had of Ann the night before. They had been standing on opposite sides of a deep chasm. An enemy was approaching, and if Ralph could not get across, they would kill him. Ann held out her hand, imploring him to jump, but he was unsure of himself – the fissure kept changing, sometimes deeper, sometimes wider. He wanted to jump, but he could not be sure of the timing and the enemy was almost upon him.

He had woken before the dream ended. Had he jumped? And if he had, had he reached her – or had he fallen short and dropped into the abyss?

Ralph heard footsteps approaching. He recognised Thabisa's soft tread. She would sleep nearby, an arm's length away, as if they were in the kraal on their respective sides of the hut.

Except this time, she did not go where he had expected. She lay down beside him, so close that he could feel the warmth from her body warming the narrow gap of air between them.

She put her mouth to his ear. 'Long time no *hlobonga*,' she whispered.

It was true – not since before the battle.

'You know I do not want my wound to reopen.'

She reached across and laid her hand across his hips. 'Wound better. You can do marching, you can do *hlobonga*.'

He felt himself stiffening under her touch. His body swelled with desire, but he fought it back.

'You not like?' She could not understand why he was unwilling. She rolled on top of him. The smooth mound between her legs pressed against his thighs.

His body, starved of intimacy, thrilled to her touch; but still he
resisted. Thabisa was beautiful, but a voice in his mind said this
was not right.

Why? Because you do not love her? jeered another voice.

How many women had he lain with, since his first fumble in
a Cantonese brothel? A few, over the years, had fired his heart,
but most had been brief, functional affairs. He felt more genuine
affection for Thabisa than he had for most of those women. So
why did his soul tell him that this was wrong?

'I do not want you.'

The words came out harshly, unexpectedly vehement. Thabisa
recoiled as if he had slapped her in the face. She drew herself up,
looking down on him with furious eyes.

'Why—?'

Before she could finish her question, light fell over them both.
Thabisa rolled away. Hamu stood over them, holding a burning
brand from the fire.

He was not looking at them. His spear was in his hand, pointing at the darkness beyond the circle of firelight. 'Who is there?'

Ralph heard a high-pitched squeal and the noise of crashing
branches. Was it a warthog, or a wild boar? It stopped at the edge
of the clearing, just beyond Ralph's sight. And then, in a clear
voice, it said: 'What are they doing, Mummy?'

With a shiver of foliage, two people emerged from the bush.
One was a boy with fair curls and bright eyes. The other was a
woman. The last two people he had expected to see so far away
from Nativity Bay.

Harry and Ann.

They built up the fire, and Hamu found portions of mealie porridge. Mother and child devoured it as Ann told them what had
happened at Nativity Bay.

'We fled as fast as we could,' she concluded. 'Marius had told us
of the great city you found. We thought we could find you there.
But we got lost. We have been stumbling around this jungle these
last three days.'

Ralph tried to imagine it: a woman and a child struggling
through the wilderness that had almost defeated three armed

men. What sort of courage had it taken her to make such a journey?

All the time she had been telling Ralph of the atrocities that had taken place in Nativity Bay, she had not met his eye even once. He could sense that she was disturbed by what she had seen earlier. But now she lifted her face and met his gaze. He had forgotten how much strength there was in those eyes.

'Many of the Chunus ran off, but others did not get away. I am sure Marius and Sterling will hunt down as many as possible of those who escaped. We cannot leave them to be carried into slavery. We promised they would be safe.'

'I have given many promises of safety in my life.' Ralph touched the scars on his cheek. 'None of them was ever worth a damn.'

Ann's face contorted. Perhaps she had expected nothing noble of him.

'Marius has captured Jobe. Did you not swear an oath of brotherhood with him?'

'So did Marius.'

'I hoped you might be a better man.'

Ralph had no answer to that. His mind raced. He had once sailed aboard a ship that had called at Rio de Janeiro. Half the ships in the bay seemed to be slavers, feeding the machine that ground human blood and sweat into sugar. He would not forget the stench of misery and suffering that had emanated from them. He had watched one crew clear out the corpses of those who had died on the passage, throwing them overboard like unwanted ballast. He had decided that day that there was one trade that he would never be part of.

'I could speak to Marius,' he said uncertainly.

'You know what kind of man Marius is. You think he will pass up his chance at a fortune, simply because you ask him nicely?'

'What, then?'

'Marius is corrupt and greedy. He has to be forced to confront his wrongdoing and made to set things right.'

'But Marius and I are not enemies,' he reminded her.

'I am his enemy,' she said fiercely. 'Either you set yourself against him, or you set yourself against me and the Chunu.'

Ralph pondered her ultimatum. 'You said Ratray and the slavers were well armed?'

'They all have guns, lots of guns – and the ship has cannons.'

'Then we're powerless.' Ralph felt a stab of shame, but pushed it away. 'Look at what we have. A rifle, without ammunition, and two dozen men armed with spears. Do you know what Marius's guns would do against us? If we were not killed, we would be taken prisoner and added to his haul of slaves.'

He spoke angrily. What right did she have to make him feel guilty? But Ann did not shrink from the heat in his voice. She held his gaze.

'Marius spoke of a great army. Surely with them at your back you could force the slavers to give up.'

'They would not fight for this.' He turned to Hamu: 'What do you do with prisoners of war?'

Hamu shrugged. 'If they are caught, they are *izigqila*.'

Ralph felt Thabisa stiffen beside him. *Izigqila* was a word he had heard before, from her lips. *Slaves.* For a Zulu, it was the natural fate for the people they conquered.

Ralph translated what Hamu had said for Ann's benefit.

'You will not make abolitionists of the Zulus.' He pointed to Thabisa. 'She is a slave herself.'

'I do not pretend to know what her life has been like,' Ann sympathised. 'I am sure she has suffered greatly. But you know this is different. She has not been torn away from her homeland, transported across the ocean like a bundle of goods, and sold to be worked to death.'

Ralph's face grew hot. The scar on his cheek began to throb again. 'What do you expect me to do?'

'Stop them,' Ann said simply.

'It is not possible.'

'Are you afraid of Marius?'

'I fear no one. But that does not mean I want to charge into his cannons.'

'And what do you think Marius will do if you let him get away with this? He has already betrayed Jobe,' she reminded him. 'Do you think the colour of your skin will protect you from his greed?'

Ann's remark made Ralph think. He had taken the measure of Marius's character. The bargain they had struck on Robben Island had endured in large part because all three men had nothing. It survived now because the men were apart, and Ralph had the advantage. But if Marius made his fortune – if he established Nativity Bay as a slave port, with guns and cannon at his disposal – he would become a fearsome presence on the borders of Zululand. He would raid further and further with Sterling's guns – in pursuit of defenceless tribesmen he could sell as slaves. At best, Ralph would be caught between Shaka and Marius. At worst, he would be destroyed.

And there was Ann to think of. However much he tried to dismiss her words, they had struck him in a place he thought was immune to feeling.

Staring at him across the fire, with the flames reflected in his eyes, Ann could not surmise what Ralph was thinking.

'You told me once that you had carried out terrible acts in your life. This is your chance.' Ann glanced at Harry, and Ralph felt his gut twist with emotion.

Did she know?

'Save those people. Redeem yourself.'

When Ralph looked up, the scars on his face seemed to writhe in the firelight.

'I was going to Nativity Bay in any event,' he said. He still needed powder and shot. 'I suppose it will do no harm to spy out what Marius is up to.'

NATIVITY BAY

R alph crouched in the bush that fringed the beach and peered over a rotting tree stump. The settlement at Nativity Bay had grown considerably in his absence, from a castaways' camp to a proper colony. How long had he been away? Months, certainly. A year? He had stopped counting the days.

He studied the new landscape. The village the Chunu had built was deserted, but the occupants were not far away. Inside the stockade, he could hear singing, a low and plaintive lament. The slavers had managed to round up a good number of the fugitives. Soon they would load them onto the *Nanticoke*, which sat at anchor out in the lagoon. Ralph could smell smoke and scorched iron: he guessed the slavers had set up a forge and had begun to shackle the captives. They would take no chances this time.

Guards stood on the corners of the stockade, while more men patrolled the perimeter outside. Almost twenty of them. There were a few faces Ralph recognised from the *Farewell*'s crew, and more he did not, who must have come from the *Nanticoke*. All were armed with rifles – lighter than the one Ralph carried and faster to reload. The *Nanticoke* was anchored at bow and stern, to keep her broadside to the beach. The snouts of her nine-pounder cannons protruded from her side, with men standing nearby. Ralph did not doubt they were loaded, or that the crew would be ready to fire if the prisoners tried to escape again.

The slavers must have brought ashore powder and shot for their rifles. Ralph guessed that they would keep their arsenal in the blockhouse in the middle of the stockade. To reach it, he would have to get through the gates, across the compound and into the house. And out again.

You are insane for even thinking of doing this, he told himself. He could have walked up to the gate and introduced himself as Marius's business partner. But that would have been too dangerous: it was a reckless man who put himself in Marius's power.

And without gunpowder, Ralph was powerless. He began to move, crawling through the bush along the edge of the beach towards the camp until he found the place he wanted, about twenty yards from the stockade gates.

It stank of urine and excrement; the foliage was black and shrivelled from having been repeatedly showered with human waste. In the time he had been watching, Ralph had seen several of the guards leave the stockade and wander over to this place. It was where they had made their latrine.

Ralph had not waited long when one of the guards laid his rifle against the stockade wall and sauntered to the patch of bushes, undid his belt and dropped his trousers.

Ralph waited until he could hear the patter of water sprinkling the bushes. Then he pounced. He had one hand over the guard's mouth, and the other holding a knife at his throat, before his enemy knew what was happening.

'If you make a sound, I will kill you,' Ralph whispered in his ear. 'If you do exactly as I say, you will live. Nod if you understand.'

The man nodded. Soundlessly, Hamu and two of his warriors emerged from the undergrowth. They stripped the man naked, bound his hands, and tied a gag made of braided vines over his mouth. His eyes widened in horror at being held captive by black men, which gave Ralph a great measure of satisfaction.

See how you like it.

'You wait here,' Ralph told Hamu, as he put on the guard's clothes.

Hamu touched his arm and held Ralph's gaze with a frank stare. He was silent, but the concern on his face spoke his mind eloquently enough: *When you go in there, I cannot help.*

'I will be careful,' Ralph reassured the *induna*.

Ralph pulled the guard's wide-brimmed hat low over his face, though with his scars it was not much of a disguise. He peered out at the stockade again, looking for Marius among the guards, but did not see him. He was relying on the men from the different ships not knowing one another well enough to identify a stranger.

The moment he left the shelter of the trees, he was vulnerable. Every step of the walk across the hot sand felt like a death sentence. With his hat low, head down, he could not see if the guards were paying him any attention. Sweat prickled on his skin and ran down his back. His body tensed as he approached the gate, expecting to feel a bullet tearing through his flesh at any moment. If anyone challenged him now, he had no chance of escape.

One of the guards looked up. His shoulders twitched, as if he could sense that something was not quite right. Ralph forced himself to keep still and calm.

'What d'you want?' The man's voice was slurred, his eyes dull. Clearly he had helped himself to the rum barrel.

'The Dutchman told me to fetch powder and shot,' said Ralph. 'He wants to go hunting.'

The man spat on the sand. 'That'll be more game for supper, then.' He cracked the gate open. 'In you go. Don't let them darkies give you no trouble.'

Ralph squeezed through the gate, brushing so close to the guard he jostled his elbow. The man's head jerked up; his startled eyes fell on Ralph, inches away from his face. Surely the man could not fail to see who Ralph was now.

'Watch where you're standing,' Ralph said, stepping quickly through the gate.

'Watch yourself,' the guard snapped.

The gate closed behind him, and Ralph heard the bar drop back into place. He was inside the stockade.

Ralph had seen many gruesome sights in his life, but what he saw inside the stockade was truly abhorent. Captured Africans lay around the edge of the compound, with iron shackles on their legs; some so still they might be dead. Many were women, some pregnant, some nursing starving babies. Even if Ralph closed his eyes, he could not escape the stench. It was like the place the sailors had used as their latrine, but concentrated a thousand-fold, and layered with blood and sweat and desperate misery.

A chill went through Ralph's body. He knew enough of the slave trade to know that the young children would never be put aboard a ship. In the economics of the business, they were worthless – nothing more than extra mouths and extra space.

He picked his way across the open square. The sun was almost directly above him, shrinking his shadow to a pool around his feet. Guards with rifles watched from the walls, ready to fire if the Africans showed any sign of attacking him. But none would try. Even the smallest children, who wandered free because their feet were too small for the shackles, cowered away from him as he passed.

This is what Marius has taught them, he thought. *That a white man is to be feared above all else.* The thought made him sicker even than the stench.

The guard in front of the blockhouse noticed Ralph staring at the Chunus. 'Filthy, ain't they?' he said. 'We'll have to clean 'em up afore we reach Havana, or even the cane planters won't want 'em.'

Ralph felt anger rising inside him. He wanted to tell the man that you could take the grandest British duke or American merchant, and if you brutalised him in this way he would seem as wretched. He wanted to show the man the splendour of the Zulu empire: twenty thousand warriors in the great kraal at KwaBulawayo, singing Shaka's praise songs. He wanted to draw his knife and ram it through the guard's throat.

'Dutchman sent me to fetch powder,' Ralph said, burying his rage.

The guard peered at him. Further from the rum barrel, closer to the prisoners, he had not drunk so much as the man on the gate, and it showed in his sharp eyes.

'Do I know you?'

Ralph gave what he hoped was a careless shrug. 'Dunno. Do you?'

The guard squinted. 'Was you on the *Farewell*?'

Ralph froze. What was the right answer?

If the man was from the *Farewell*'s crew, and Ralph said yes, the lie would be obvious. But if the man was from the *Nanticoke*, he would know Ralph was not one of his shipmates.

Ralph shot the man a quick look. Did he recognise him from the voyage out from Port Elizabeth? Or the muster on the beach, after the shipwreck, when the men had chosen sides? He could not remember.

'I sailed on the *Nanticoke*.'

'Is that so?'

Even as he spoke, the guard's hand was already moving to his gun. Ralph did not wait. He sprang forward, barrelling the man backwards through the open doorway into the blockhouse. Before the man could retaliate, Ralph smashed his forehead ferociously into the man's face. The guard's nose broke with a crack and a spray of hot blood. Dazed, the man reeled away, but two more sharp punches from Ralph knocked him, unconscious, to the floor.

Ralph glanced back through the open door. Half a dozen faces stared at him in shock at what they had just witnessed. But none of them spoke. The Africans chained in the courtyard had already learned one immutable lesson: there was no gain in drawing attention to themselves. They looked away.

None of the guards had seen Ralph's actions. There were no shouts of alarm, or warning shots. The stockade was quiet, only the low singing of the prisoners disturbing the afternoon heat.

Ralph bound the man he had knocked out, gagged him and took his rifle. Now he was armed – but also running out of time. It would not be long before someone noticed the guard was not at his post.

It was dark inside the blockhouse. There was only one window in the mud-plastered walls, covered by a curtain made of scraped animal hide. In the dim light, Ralph saw casks and chests piled almost to the ceiling. He prised open one of the boxes, and saw it was filled with paper cartridges. Sterling's men had brought enough powder and shot ashore to start a war.

What I could achieve with all of this, in Shaka's service, Ralph thought.

He reached out for the guard's ammunition pouch and filled it with cartridges, then stuffed his pockets with a few more.

He grabbed one of the small casks of powder. Taking it was a big risk – but it might tip the odds a little more in his favour.

He glanced at the guard he had assaulted, lying on the floor. The man twitched, groaning. Soon he would regain consciousness. It would be safer to cut his throat and silence him forever – one less enemy to contend with – yet Ralph hesitated. To kill a man in battle, or in anger, was fair. To kill a helpless captive was murder.

That is more mercy than they would show their slaves.

Once before, he had stood over an unarmed man with the chance to kill him. The choice he had made then had shaped his entire life.

Stepping out of the blockhouse, Ralph was temporarily dazzled by the sun; he tensed in expectation of a challenge or a hail of bullets, but strode on blindly.

No one had noticed him.

And no one noticed as he crossed the courtyard with the cask of black powder straining his arms. Even the prisoners flopped in the sun seemed more preoccupied with their own misery than with him.

Still no one paid him any attention.

'Ralph,' called a voice – it was low and cautious.

He spun around, but saw only half a dozen gaunt-faced Africans, squatting on the sand. Most looked at the ground, rubbing every now and then at their ankles, where the chains had chafed them raw. But one had his head up, his eyes focused on Ralph.

'Ralph,' he said again.

Ralph stared. Fixated on the guards, he had not looked closely at the captives. It was Jobe.

'Did you not recognise me?' Jobe's face twisted in a sneer. 'Marius also seems to have forgotten our bargain.'

'I did not see you.'

'Just another slave.' Jobe nodded to the rifle on Ralph's back. 'Marius, I never trusted. But you . . .' The angry stare Jobe gave him made Ralph's soul shrivel in shame. 'I thought more of you.'

'I am not here with Marius.' Ralph glanced over his shoulder. If the guards caught him talking with one of the captives, they would ask questions. 'Ann found me. I came to rescue you.' He saw Jobe did not believe him. 'I swear it.'

Jobe lifted his ankle, making the chains rattle. 'Then set me free.'

Up on the corner of the stockade, one of the guards had stopped moving and was staring at Ralph and Jobe.

'I cannot.'

'You mean you *will* not.'

Ralph felt the weight of disgust in Jobe's voice. 'If I try to save you now, we will both be caught. Even if we escaped, what would happen to the others? Marius would have them moved onto the ship before we could act.'

Ralph saw that Jobe was formulating a rebuttal, but Ralph's answer had taken him by surprise. He followed up quickly:

'Remember the beach at Blaauwberg. I told you then that I would come back for you, and I did not lie. I will come back again.'

'I was not in chains.'

'I will get you out of them.'

'Easy to say when you are walking free.'

It was too late. One of the guards had ambled across from the gate, rifle angled low, and was only a few paces away.

'This Kaffir giving you trouble?'

It would take a single word from Jobe to betray Ralph. Ralph thought he might do it simply because he was so angry – his face was twisted by a bitter fury.

With a shudder, as if something had been torn loose inside him, Jobe turned his eyes down to the ground.

'No trouble,' said Ralph. 'I think he wants some water.'

'Hah.' With a deft movement, the guard reversed his rifle and slammed the butt into the side of Jobe's head. 'Kaffirs get what they're given.' He glanced at the blockhouse. 'Where's Henderson? He should be on watch.'

'Went for a piss,' said Ralph, not looking at Jobe.

'Bloody clap, more like,' said the guard. 'He's tupped half these Kaffir girls already. His cock's probably ready to rot off.'

Laughing, he turned away. Ralph resisted the urge to stick a knife between his shoulders.

At his feet, Jobe lay prone, clutching his head. Blood oozed into his hair from the gash the rifle had left. He gazed up at Ralph, and the space between them yawned like a chasm. Blood dribbled over his temple and ran into his eye.

If a look could have held Ralph there, it would have been Jobe's.

'I will come back for you,' Ralph promised, a whisper so faint he did not know if Jobe heard it.

He wrenched himself away and followed the guard to the gate, leaving Jobe lying on the sand, clutching his wound.

'It is impossible to free them,' Ralph said.

He was standing in a clearing in the bush, with Ann, Hamu, Thabisa and the Zulu company. This was where they had chosen to set up camp. Hamu had posted pickets, but even so, every snapping branch and rustling leaf alarmed Ralph.

'You shoot, we charge,' said Hamu, pragmatically.

'I could not fire that quickly. Nor could you run fast enough.'

Hamu had no concept of what a massed rank of rifles would do to his men. Brave as the Zulus were, Ralph did not believe that they could sustain a charge against Marius's guns, even if they survived the first blast.

'Then do not fight,' said Hamu. 'Why Zulus die for *amaLala*?'

'What is *amaLala*?' said Ann.

Marius's words came back to Ralph: *A cross between an Irishman and a Kaffir*. 'It is the Zulus' word for the people who live beyond their borders. They do not mean it as a compliment.'

The expression made him think of Jobe. *I am amaLala*, the Xhosa warrior had lamented. Why should Ralph expect Zulus to risk their lives to save people they despised?

I will get you out of those chains. I swear it.

Ralph could still walk away. Many times in his life, he had backed out of a fight, and there had not been a time that he had regretted it. But that would be to break faith with Jobe – and with Ann.

He turned to Hamu, trying to marshal his thoughts. 'If you let this happen, Marius will grow rich. With more money, he will buy more guns. With more guns, he will mount bigger raids. Eventually, he will take Zulus as slaves, and when you try to stop him, you will find you have let him become monstrously powerful.'

Ralph could see that what he had said made sense to Hamu. The *induna* frowned, unable to hide his distress at the future Ralph had described for his land and his people.

'You saw how Marius treated King Shaka,' Ralph went on. 'Even when he was alone, he would not bow to the king. Think what he would do with a thousand men at his back, all carrying guns.'

Hamu had seen what one man with a rifle had done against the Ndwandwes. It was easy for him to imagine what a thousand firesticks might do.

'I fight with you,' he announced with pride.

Ralph clasped the *induna*'s arm. 'Thank you.'

'But how?'

The question hung unanswered between them. In numbers, the slavers and the Zulus were more or less evenly matched. But the slavers had a gun each, and the cannons aboard the ship. Ralph and his men possessed a rifle and a small cask of black powder.

'We would need a cannon to stand any chance against them,' Ralph mused. 'But I do not suppose there is one between here and Port Elizabeth, besides those on the ship.'

Ann was thinking. She bit her lip, as if she did not quite trust herself to speak. 'Perhaps there is a way,' she said hesitantly.

Marius wiped the sweat from his eyes and cursed the blacks for what felt like the thousandth time. It had taken Sterling's men days to hunt them down after they fled the stockade, and some were still loose.

'We should have stuck with cattle, hey?' he said to Ratray. 'They are not half so much trouble.'

'But there's not half so much profit.' Ratray stood over a brazier, fanning it with a palm leaf. The coals pulsed red.

'They will not get away again,' said Marius.

It was all the fault of that bitch, Ann Waite. If not for her, the prisoners would be aboard the *Nanticoke* and on the way to Havana by now. She had betrayed her race, and betrayed him, and that was unforgivable.

Marius had thought it would be easy to recapture Ann. A white woman and a small boy could not go far; nor could they survive long in the wilderness. Yet she had eluded him for longer than he had thought possible, even with patrols scouring the bush for fugitives. It had angered him. He would happily have swapped half a dozen of the blacks they had found for the chance to get his hands on her.

It did not matter, he told himself. There was nowhere for her to go. When she was hungry and desperate, she would slink back. She would use all her womanly charms to make Marius forgive her. He chuckled. He would hold out his hand, coaxing and gentle, as if he was calling a rare bird from the forest. He would let her think she was safe. He would put on his smile, so she would see that Marius the stupid Dutchman was simply happy that she had returned.

And then, when he had her in his grasp, he would wring her neck. After he had taught her a few harsh lessons, of course. A lascivious grin spread across his face as he imagined what he would do to her – he could almost taste it – and what his men would do afterwards when he threw them her fragile, starving body.

'You thinking about the darkie women again?' Ratray asked. He pointed to the brazier. The coals were so hot that flames licked out from among them. 'Seems a shame to spoil them like this.'

Marius shrugged. 'It is what we do with cattle.'

He picked up the branding iron. It was a crude implement: a marlinspike from the ship, with its tip bent to make a rough circle, and a wooden handle fitted to the end. As he held it in the coals, his mind turned to Ralph Courtney. The day before, one of the guards had gone missing and another, Henderson, had been attacked and knocked out – not by a prisoner, but by a white man. Henderson had not recognised his assailant, but when he described the tall man with blue eyes and a knot of scars on his cheek, Marius knew at once who it must be.

Ralph Courtney had returned.

The news made Marius furious. But after he had taken out his anger on one of the slave girls, he had become more philosophical. Most likely, Ralph had simply come for more powder. When he had seen Marius's strength – the men and the ship in the bay – he had surely become frightened, and decided to run away with the powder like a thief. That Ralph was able to penetrate Marius's stockade so easily, and in the middle of the day, left a sliver of anxiety in Marius's mind. He would hunt Ralph down. *I will teach you to steal from me*, Marius thought. But first, he had to get the slaves away.

The iron was glowing red-hot now. Marius nodded to the man at the stockade's gate, one of Sterling's crew.

'We're ready.'

The guard cracked the gate open. With shouts and the prod of a sword, Jobe was pushed out on to the sand and driven to the brazier. He was naked, but his hands and feet were still chained, his scalp heavily scabbed from being clubbed by the rifle butt. Marius grabbed his arms and held him tight.

'Keep still,' he grunted. 'It will hurt more if you move, hey?'

Jobe twisted and tugged against Marius's grip, but he had spent too long on starvation rations to break free.

'You are not a man,' he hissed. 'You are a devil. You make promises, and then you sell a man's soul.'

'Kaffirs don't have souls.'

Ratray took the red-hot iron and pressed it into the soft skin below Jobe's shoulder. Jobe tried to keep silent, but even pride could not withstand the pain. He screamed, drowning out the angry hiss of the iron on his flesh. Marius held him fast, until Ratray was satisfied with his handiwork.

Finally, Marius freed his prisoner. Jobe staggered away, his chains restricting his movement, holding him back as he tried to run down to the lagoon. Marius watched him as he fell, scrambled to his feet and fell again. The pain drove Jobe on and he began crawling down the beach until he reached the water and began desperately scooping it over his arm. Jobe screamed again as the salt bit into his raw flesh.

'You need to go faster,' Marius told Ratray as he watched two of Sterling's men grab Jobe and begin to haul him back to the stockade. 'We've dozens of these to do.'

Normally they would have completed the branding several days before embarking, to give the scars time to heal before the slaves were confined in the foetid hold. But after the escape, and Ralph's appearance in the stockade, none of the slavers were in the mood to delay any longer.

The next victim was a young woman, no more than eighteen. Trying to cover herself with her hands, she stumbled forward a few paces – straight into Marius. He looked her up and down.

'No time for that,' said Ratray. He dug the branding iron into the coals, sending up a shower of sparks. 'Hold her still.'

He pulled out the iron and advanced towards the girl. She held herself stiff, refusing to cower as Ratray brought the iron closer to her chest. Only the tremble of her lower lip betrayed her fear.

A shout from the stockade interrupted them. Ratray and Marius looked up, following the guard's outstretched arm to the line of trees where he was pointing. Ralph was walking across the sand, unarmed, his hands in the air. The sight made Ratray lose his grip on the branding iron. It swung down and knocked against his knee with a fizz of scalded flesh. He howled with pain and dropped it onto the sand.

Marius pushed the girl away and wheeled around to confront Ralph.

'So you came back, hey?' he said easily. 'Was the powder you stole yesterday not enough?'

Ralph's blue eyes surveyed the men on the beach, and an amused smile played at the corners of his mouth. As if two dozen men armed like pirates were nothing more than an entertainment.

'I can see you have been busy.'

'Busy making money. Can you say as much?'

'I'm sure you planned to share the profits,' Ralph said. 'But this is not a trade I wish to be part of.'

'Then we have nothing to discuss.'

'I do not wish *you* to be part of it either.'

'That's a shame,' said Ratray. 'Because you ain't one to tell us what we can be doing.'

'Let the prisoners go,' said Ralph. 'Or suffer the consequences.'

'Consequences?' Ratray gave a laugh. 'The sole consequence is that you'll get a thrashing you won't forget. Unless we put you aboard, too.' He jabbed his finger at Ralph. 'There'd be a few pennies to be made selling a good-looking boy like you to the right buyer.'

Marius was blunter. 'I will give you one minute to leave this beach alive. And if you ever come back . . .' He smacked his fist into the palm of his hand.

Ralph didn't move. 'I will be more generous. Five minutes, to free all of those slaves. Otherwise, I will order my men to attack.'

A few of the slavers glanced anxiously at the bush, but most just laughed. Marius advanced towards Ralph.

'What men? A handful of starving Kaffirs with spears? Bring them on. There is enough space in our ship to hold them.'

'As you wish,' said Ralph. He put out his arm and windmilled it up and down.

Nothing happened. Ratray leered at him; Jobe glared at him with furious disappointment.

'Is this a joke?' said Marius.

An explosion sounded from one of the low hills overlooking the bay. All the men spun around and saw a column of smoke rising from the trees, and a plume of spray erupt from the water just off the *Nanticoke*'s bow.

'What the devil?' said Ratray.

'I have a cannon,' Ralph announced.

'That is not possible!' Marius looked as if he was about to explode himself. 'Kaffirs do not have cannons.'

'These do. And they are not Kaffirs. They are Zulus.'

Another shot boomed around the bay. Another spout of water fountained, this time only half a cable from the *Nanticoke*.

Steady, Ralph thought. *You were only supposed to fire once. You will split the old gun in half if you keep that up.*

'My gunners are finding their range,' he said. 'Will you keep talking until they start shooting holes in your ship?'

Across the water, he could see the *Nanticoke*'s crew running about her deck in confusion. They stared at the hills – but the gun was hidden by the bush. All they had to tell her position was smoke rising from the trees, and the squawking of a flock of startled parrots. Even if they had wanted to try their luck, the ship was anchored in a position where her guns could not be brought to bear on the hillside, and there were not enough men aboard to warp her around.

'You see that smoke?' said Ralph. 'That is not just gunsmoke.' Within the drifting white haze, a column of dark woodsmoke was rising into the sky. 'They have a furnace lit. You know what heated shot could do to an anchored ship?'

'Where did you get the cannon?' Marius demanded.

Ralph's grin broadened. 'You should never underestimate the Zulus.'

It had been Ann's doing. She had led them through the undergrowth along the trail that Harry had found, to the clearing with the graves by the ruined house. She had shown them the iron cannon embedded in the ground.

Hamu had stared at it as if it were made of gold. For the Zulus, iron was a scarce and precious commodity. To see so much in one object was like looking at a gold reef.

'How many spear blades you can make from this,' said Hamu.

Ralph had clapped him on the shoulder. 'We can do better than spear blades.'

Ann pulled away the creepers that shrouded its breech and exposed the design she had seen embossed in the metal. The letters *C.B.T.C.*

'Do you know what that stands for?'

Courtney Brothers Trading Company, thought Ralph. *The company my ancestors used to make their fortunes.*

'It must be the foundry mark.'

Ann pulled the creepers back further. Underneath the letters, a date was stamped: 1711.

'So long ago,' said Ann. 'Do you think it still works?'

The barrel must have been there for over a hundred years. If they tried to fire it, the shock of a powder charge might split it in half, or shatter it into razor-sharp fragments that would cut through anyone near it.

But the paint on it was still thick, and when Ralph rapped the barrel, it rang sound and true.

'There is only one way to find out.'

They had dug out the soil around it, then attached vines to the trunnions and hauled the cannon up the hillside to a place where they could see the ship in the bay. Even with two dozen men pulling it, and logs underneath as rollers, it was laborious work.

There was no gun carriage, nor had they the time to build one. Ralph had laid the cannon on the ground, its barrel propped up on rocks, pointing towards the *Nanticoke*. They did not need to be able to change its aim. It had only a single target.

But they would need ammunition to hit it.

'What shall we fire?' Ann had asked. 'We have no cannon balls.'

The Zulus had their spear blades, but that was not enough metal for even a half-sized cannonball. Nor did they have the time, or the skill, to make a forge to melt them.

Ralph had picked up a stone. It was smooth, about the size of his fist.

'This will have to do.'

Ann had stared at it doubtfully. It seemed to her more than likely it would shatter under the force of the powder charge. Even if it did not: 'Will that do any good against a ship?'

'It does not have to sink the ship,' Ralph told her. 'It only needs to make them *think* we can sink her.'

Now Ralph stood in front of Marius, Ratray and their men. Would they believe that he had a cannon on the hill that could sink the *Nanticoke*? Ralph had to make them believe it. Even though there was a good chance that the gun had broken in half with that second shot. And there was certainly no chance they could heat a rock hot enough to set the *Nanticoke* alight, even if they hit her. The fire was a ruse.

Did Marius guess that?

The shots had brought men spilling out from the stockade. They surrounded Ralph, pointing their guns at him, as a man in a crimson coat with bright brass buttons strode towards him. Even if Ann had not described him, Ralph would have guessed who he was by his air of command, and the dangerous look in his eyes.

'Captain Sterling, I presume.'

The two men studied each other: Sterling immaculate in his frock coat and tricorn hat, Ralph in a vagabond's rags. But beneath their clothes, there was a certain resonance between them, like two notes of the same chord. The same strength in bearing; the same sure confidence; the same sense of danger.

Except he has a dozen modern cannon, thought Ralph, *and I have an antique that shoots rocks.*

The captain evaluated the situation at a glance.

'I assume you are the notorious Ralph Courtney.'

'I prefer infamous.'

'What are your demands?'

'Free the prisoners,' said Ralph. 'Sail away, and do not bring your vile trade to Nativity Bay again.'

Marius began to speak, but Sterling waved him to be quiet. 'Why are you doing this?' He nodded to Ralph's ragged clothing and wild beard. 'You do not seem to be a man who can afford to turn down a piece of good fortune.'

Ralph shrugged. 'What I choose is my own business. I do not have to justify myself to you simply because you have a finely cut coat.'

'And how about to me, hey?' The muscles in Marius's chest rippled. 'We had a partnership.'

'Jobe was a partner, too,' Ralph reminded him. 'He does not seem to have profited from it.'

'A bargain with a Kaffir is no bargain at all,' said Marius. 'But you and me . . .'

'We have no bargain,' said Ralph. 'I am dissolving our partnership. We came here for *freedom*. We will not buy it with other men's bondage.'

Ratray's face twitched with hatred, but he did not dare move. Marius was unbowed.

'You think this land is yours? You think you will make yourself a king, hey, when you have driven off every other rival?'

'The land belongs to King Shaka,' said Ralph.

'To hear a white man say such things,' spat Marius. 'You think you can threaten me? You walk in here, no guns and no friends, and think you can tell me what to do?' He snatched a rifle from one of the men and aimed it at Ralph's heart. 'I say we will kill you now, and take our chances.'

Ralph did not move. 'If you kill me, that ship will burn to the waterline.'

'I don't care,' Marius bellowed. 'I am not going anywhere.'

'But I have no intention of staying here.' Sterling's voice, cool and commanding, broke in. 'And I cannot leave without my ship.'

Marius turned on him. 'You bloody coward,' he raged. 'Stand and fight like a white man.'

Sterling's composure did not crack – but two points of crimson flushed on his cheeks.

'It is easy to talk of fighting, when you want to do it with another man's crew.' He turned to the surrounding men. A few of them were survivors of the *Farewell*, but the majority were from the *Nanticoke*. 'Disarm him.'

Ralph's gamble had paid off. Sterling had been convinced that Ralph's cannon could use heated shot to set the *Nanticoke* on fire and cut off any chance of escape. Maybe Sterling fully believed it, maybe he had doubts: but he would not risk his future, and the profits from his voyage, to test a theory.

The guns that had been pointing at Ralph were turned on Marius. A solidly built boatswain stepped forward and pulled the rifle out of his hands. The stockade gates were opened, and the Africans began to emerge to have their shackles knocked off. As soon as they were free, Ralph sent the fittest to the block-house to fetch the rifles and powder and shot. Marius watched on helplessly. Without Sterling and his crew, he did not have the numbers to oppose Ralph.

'This is not finished,' Marius warned. 'We still have business, you and me.'

Ralph nodded. 'After Captain Sterling is safely departed.'

The *Nanticoke* sailed that same afternoon. Sterling had made his choice, and he was not a man to second-guess himself. His stay in Nativity Bay had not proved profitable – it had cost him twenty rifles and a good quantity of powder and shot – better to cut his losses and move on. The brutal truth was that he would find another cargo easily enough.

Ralph stood on the whale-backed promontory and watched as the ship manoeuvred her way out of the lagoon. He wanted to be sure she was gone, and did not plan on returning to ambush them.

As the *Nanticoke* navigated towards the channel, he considered how the bay had been when they arrived, and how it had changed in the months since. The bush had retreated where trees had been felled for timber, or burned to make fields for crops. Hippos no longer wallowed at the river mouth, and the monkeys kept hidden. Even the birdsong seemed quieter. This had been a place of sanctuary, an Eden, and now its soil grew only human jealousy and greed.

We brought nothing that was not already present, he told himself. War, plunder, suffering: the Zulus and their neighbours lived those miseries as well as the incomers. The sole difference was the col-our of their skin – and that was no difference at all. But the thought gave him little solace.

A rumbling drew his attention back to the bay. It sounded like distant thunder, except the sky was a perfect blue. The *Nanticoke* had turned so she was beam-on to the shore – and from her side, the snub noses of nine-pound cannons now protruded.

You did not cross a man like Sterling without retribution. High on the promontory, Ralph watched as a line of flame rippled down the *Nanticoke*'s side like the sparks of a quickmatch. A fraction of a second later, he heard the deep boom of the guns, felt the sound wave like a succession of punches to his chest as each fired in turn.

Sterling's gunners knew their business. The first two shots hit the blockhouse, and turned it into a cloud of splinters and falling logs. Ralph thanked his stars that he had removed the powder and shot from it. After that, the gunners went for the half-rebuilt hull of the *Farewell*, propped up on the beach. Ball after ball smashed into it, dismantling the weeks of work that had gone into making her seaworthy until there was barely a single one of her timbers intact.

The noise echoed around the bay and rang in Ralph's ears long after the guns had finished. With a sharply executed move, the *Nanticoke* came about and headed for the channel. From the steep-sided promontory, Ralph could look straight down on to her decks, see the gun crews sponging out the cannons; and Sterling standing on his quarterdeck, barking orders.

The captain glanced up, saw Ralph and gave an ironic salute. Ralph hoped he would ground his ship on the bar, rip out her bottom and drown his whole crew. But she passed safely over it, and slipped past the point into the open ocean.

By the time Ralph made it back to the wreckage on the beach, the *Nanticoke* was a speck on the horizon. Everyone had gathered around the ruins of the blockhouse, coalescing into three groups that kept a wary distance from one another. Ann and Harry stood with Hamu, Thabisa and the Zulus; the freed Chunus clustered around Jobe; while Marius stood apart with the three sailors from the *Farewell* who had chosen to stay, and now looked as if they regretted their choice.

'What now, hey?' Marius's shoulders twitched with the effort of holding in his fury. He had found his sjambok, and kept methodically coiling it, letting it unravel, and coiling it again. 'Your Kaffir-loving madness has signed all our death warrants.'

Ralph remained silent. He had a knife tucked in his waistband, and he could feel the hilt pressing against his hip. A voice in his mind whispered he should put the blade through Marius's heart now and be rid of him forever.

Across the sand, Jobe could see what was in his mind. The violence in his eyes willed Ralph to do it.

You would be a fool to leave an enemy like that alive.

From the corner of his eye, Ralph saw Harry watching him with horrid fascination. His hand paused, fingers touching the hilt of the knife. Could he commit cold-blooded murder in front of the boy?

His mind hung suspended between the two choices, like a ship in a storm suddenly held still on the crest of a great wave, a churning abyss on either side.

He let go of the knife.

I have enough blood on my hands already.

'Leave this place,' he told Marius.

Marius pointed to what remained of the *Farewell*, the wreckage spread across the beach, some of it still smouldering. 'No one is going anywhere. We will all die here – thanks to you.'

'You can go overland.'

But that, too, would be a death sentence. A lone white man, crossing hundreds of miles of unmapped country populated by fierce local people, would not survive a week.

'You have no authority over me.' Marius's voice was low as he swung his gaze across Hamu's men, his eyes hot with contempt. 'Even if you bring Shaka's whole army, I will fight you.'

Ralph knew that if he left Marius alive, it would not be the end of the matter. If Marius remained in Nativity Bay, sooner or later they would confront each other again. Next time, Ralph might not have the upper hand.

'We had a bargain,' Marius reminded him.

'You broke it.'

'You broke it when you decided to stay with that Kaffir king and sent the rest of us away.'

Ralph turned to Jobe. 'You had an equal share in our bargain. What do you say?'

Jobe was standing near the Chunus, though a little distance from them. Anger twisted his face.

'I say, if you make a bargain with the Devil, you will regret it.'
He pointed to the burned circle on his shoulder. The flesh was
raw and ragged; a black crust had formed around the edges. 'He
has marked me for life, a white man's property. And you let him.'

Ralph touched his own cheek. 'We all carry scars.'

'You promised you would save me,' shouted Jobe.

'And I kept the promise. I came back.'

'Not soon enough.'

Ralph had risked his life to rescue Jobe; he had not expected to
be treated like a criminal for it.

'In any event, you are free now.'

'Freedom.' Jobe made the word sound like a curse. 'Our
Republic of Libertalia. See where that has got us. I am no better
than the Chunus – no home, no people, and nowhere to go.'

'Come with me to Shaka's court.'

'To be laughed at? To be *amaLala*?'

'Shaka respects me. He will respect you, too, if you prove your
worth.'

'At Shaka's court, they respect only Zulus, unless you have guns
and white skin. I would be nothing more than your dog.'

A great sadness swept through Ralph's heart. Looking at
Marius and Jobe, it seemed the bonds that had once united the
three men had frayed away and they had nothing left in common, save hatred.

A lazy gust of wind blew across the lagoon. It stirred the pen-
nant at the top of the flagpole, the flag of Libertalia that Jobe had
drawn and Ann had sewn. The flagpole had survived the bom-
bardment that destroyed the blockhouse. It stood untouched
above the ruins, taunting them.

'Our partnership is dissolved,' Ralph said. 'Let us make a final
accounting of the bargain we made.'

'A reckoning where you take everything, hey?' said Marius.

'The weapons, powder and shot we will divide equally. For the
rest . . .' He turned to Jobe. 'What will you do?'

Jobe squared his shoulders, and touched the little cross tattoo
just below his breastbone.

'I will go with the Chunus. I will teach them the truth of God,
and to beware the lies of white men.'

'Then Marius can remain here,' said Ralph. 'But you will stay south of the river, the Thukela. You will have no trade or dealings with the Zulus. You will not hunt on their lands or steal their livestock. Above all, there will be no slaving.'

'And you?' said Marius. 'I suppose you will make yourself a slave to that Kaffir king.'

Waves lapped on the shore. A rattle sounded from the blockhouse as another part of it collapsed. A heron flapped low across the lagoon.

I have chosen my side, Ralph thought. Even if he'd had any way of leaving, he had nowhere else to go.

'I will serve King Shaka.'

'And what about us?' said Ann.

She had listened in silence to the three men arguing, simmering with her own anger that they appeared to have forgotten her as they carved up their world.

'You are free to choose.' There was more Ralph wanted to say, but not in front of Marius and Jobe. 'Speak with me afterwards.'

He turned to go. But Marius would not let Ralph have the final word.

'What will Shaka do when he gets bored with his new pet? Will his men remain content when they realise that the guns you gave them will kill a white man as easily as a black?'

Ralph ignored the taunt. 'If I see you again, I will shoot without warning.'

'If you see me again, it will be because I am cutting out your heart.'

And looking into Marius's eyes, Ralph could not doubt that if he had the chance, he would make good on the promise.

Again, Ralph's hand drifted to the knife. Again, he wondered if he had made the right decision. If he had known when the day he next saw Marius would come, or what would happen when it did, he might have chosen differently. He might have pulled out his knife and run Marius through at that moment.

But Ralph, like all mankind, was blind to the future.

There was no reason to linger at Nativity Bay. Ralph and the Zulus left that afternoon, with a dozen Chunu porters to carry the rifles and powder, and put several miles behind them before nightfall.

Ann and Harry came, too. Ann had needed little time to make up her mind. Staying at Nativity Bay with Marius and the three desperate sailors would have felt like a death sentence. Marius had revealed his true character, and it terrified her. She could imagine how he would take out his anger on anyone weaker than he was, anyone he could dominate. A woman – or a child.

Midway through the march, she came upon Ralph sitting on a fallen log by the side of the path, pulling a thorn from his bare foot. The Zulus had gone on ahead, pursued by Harry, who was fascinated by them.

Ralph glanced up quickly, saw it was Ann, and looked down again. 'How do you feel?' she asked.

He showed her the splinter. 'It did not go deep.'

'That is not what I meant.'

She kept her gaze on him until he had no choice but to meet it. He held his head at an awkward angle, so that the scars on his cheek were hidden.

'I wish Jobe had come with us,' he said. 'We should have kept together.'

'Would he trust you? After what he suffered?'

'I saved him,' Ralph protested.

'Would you be grateful to someone simply for restoring what was rightfully yours?'

'I might have the grace to say thank you.'

Ann's face softened. 'I did not mean you were wrong. It was a good thing, you did.'

Ralph looked surprised. 'That is the first time I have ever heard you approve of me.'

'I didn't think you cared what I thought.'

Ralph stood, and began walking along the track, treading gingerly on the foot that had been pierced by the thorn. Ann kept pace with him.

'I have not treated you badly,' he said.

'I did not say you have. But you do not put great efforts into making yourself agreeable. Harry, for example. You are always so mean to him, when you know he adores you.'

'He is a child,' Ralph growled. 'When he is older, he will learn better judgement.'

'You should not be so hard on yourself. I think, perhaps, it is because you do not love yourself that you cannot love him.'

Ralph was not sure what she meant, but he had the feeling she was rebuking him.

'Is that what you think of me? That I am unlovable?'

'What am I supposed to think?' The words splattered out, suddenly hot, fired by frustration. 'You have not said a word about yourself. You arrived on the beach like an apparition out of the fog, with a dead woman and a baby – and three years later you walked into that *winkel* with a price on your head. So, you tell me what I should think of you.'

'What do you want to know?'

The bush had gone still. The noises from the Zulus ahead sounded distant and unreal. Ann's mind raced.

'Tell me about Harry. Where did you find him?'

Why had she never asked that before? Partly, it was because she was frightened of Ralph, and anything related to Harry seemed to make him angry. But also, she admitted, a part of her did not want to know the answer. So long as Harry's past was a mystery, she could pretend it did not exist; that he was her own son. Knowing his past meant sharing him.

But she could not hide from the truth forever.

The silence lengthened. Ann decided that Ralph had chosen to ignore her question – maybe the answer was too painful – when he suddenly said: 'We were on a ship. It caught fire. The boy, his mother and I found ourselves in the longboat together.'

Ann stepped carefully over a fallen log. 'What was her name – Harry's mother?'

'Lizzie.'

'You knew her?'

'We met aboard the ship.'

'You are impossible,' she said. 'You hide yourself behind half-truths and silences, and then you wonder why I do not know what to think of you. Why do you not tell me your whole story?'

Ralph would not deny his evasions; he had been doing the same thing for most of his life. There had been a number of people, over the years, who had been curious about his past, wanting to find something they could use against him, or profit from.

'Why do you want to know?'

Ann stopped. 'Because I care for you.' She saw Ralph's raised eyebrow as he turned back. 'I mean, we are so far from anywhere, thrown together by chance, yet we know nothing about each other.'

'I did not ask for you to come here.'

'And I came because I had lost everything and had nowhere else to go. But here we are.'

She stood there waiting as the silence stretched between them. Ralph gazed at her, but his face was a closed book.

What would she do if I told her the truth? Ralph wondered.

He could not reveal the full story, of that he was certain, but to even crack open the door would be to let her into his life, and that could put him in danger. It might put her in great danger too. It was safer for all of them, even Harry, if she didn't know the truth.

But Ann was already in his life, unwanted and uninvited. Almost as if they were destined to be together in this African wilderness.

When he looked into his heart, he found an inexplicable part of him wanted to let her in.

'Where to begin?' Ralph murmured the words, to himself as much to her. He had never told this story before. There was not a man alive who knew even a tenth of it.

His mind drifted to the story of a book he had loved as a child, and that he had rescued from the wreck of the *Farewell* for Ann. *The Adventures of Robinson Crusoe*. A castaway shipwrecked on a dangerous shore, fighting desperately to survive. It seemed apt.

The first line of the story arose to his lips from deep memory, and the moment he said it, he saw Ann smile in recognition.

'I was born in the year 1798, in the city of Calcutta, of a good family, though not of that country . . .'

A good family? He had been brought up to think so. The Courtneys who had settled in India were conquerors, after all; the makers of an empire. Later, after Ralph had made a wider acquaintance of pirates and brigands, he began to understand his ancestors for what they actually were. He guessed that if his father and his grandfather had exercised their talents on a freelance basis, they might have ended their lives on the gibbet. Instead, because they put their greed at the service of the mighty East India Company, they had been hailed as heroes.

'My father died when I was eight years old. It was not a peaceful death.

There was an uprising in India. The local queen lured him to an audience and then set upon him with her army. My father fought bravely, but he was killed in the fighting.'

This was the story that the Company had told their masters back in London, using it to justify their savagery as they slaughtered the queen, looted the diamond-rich kingdom and subjugated its people under their rule. For a time, Ralph had believed it. Later, he had learned that it was not the Indian defenders who had killed his father, but an adventurer named Adam Courtney.

'I did not know my father well.' He had been absent for much of Ralph's life, away on the Company's business looking for new realms to conquer. Perhaps that had made it easier for Ralph to mourn him. 'After he died, my mother and I travelled about India.'

He closed his eyes, reliving those terrible years when they had moved from house to house and city to city all across India. Living off the charity of others: friends, at first, but as they used up their connections, their hosts became less and less familiar until they were virtually strangers. Sleeping alone in unfamiliar rooms, while his mother stayed up late with mysterious men behind locked doors. Even then, Ralph felt the cloud of scandal that followed them. He knew that his mother was doing something shameful. Later, when he was older and understood the nature of the transaction, it disgusted him.

The last of her companions was a ship's surgeon twenty years her senior who drank so much he could barely hold the bone saw straight. The sole benefit to their match was that, at the end, he could give her drugs to ease her pain as she lay in Calcutta, dying of an untreatable fever.

'My mother died. I was an orphan, like Harry.'

Ralph had watched as she slipped away. An unhappy end to an unhappy life. He remembered the feeling of helplessness. She was all the family he had. When the last breath escaped her lips, and her face went still, at that moment he was alone in the world. He had felt as weak and impermanent as a candle flame, as if a single breath of air might blow him out of existence.

'I went to China.'

The surgeon had taken Ralph to Canton on his ship, and died six weeks later from the pox. Ralph, fifteen years old, was abandoned, penniless, in a cruel and decadent city, a no-man's-land between mighty civilisations. He had grown up so quickly, too busy learning the skills he needed to survive on the streets in China to think what he had lost along the way.

'Is China strange?' Ann prompted him.

'Strange to outside eyes. Like England would be to an African. But I suppose to the Chinese it is common enough.'

In his mind Ralph saw sloops sailing up the Pearl River from Whampoa, heard the clack of abacuses and the clink of coins from the shops on Old China Street, and the grunts of sailors from the brothels on Hog Lane. He could smell warm rice and incense in the air, a peculiarly pleasant combination which helped to take the edge off the stinking filth of the river, where the multitude of sampans were moored like a floating city.

Most of all, he could taste the opium on his tongue like the dream of a lover's kiss. The memory threatened to open the chasm inside him again.

He had been speaking for so long, the column had reached their camp for the night. Hamu's men erected a thorn fence to keep out animals, and built the fire. They ate, and after Harry had gone to bed, Ralph continued his story.

He told Ann of his adventures on the Pearl River. Haggling with the Hong merchants and the officials and the river pirates; the cargoes he had smuggled to sustain his habit; his secret visit to the Forbidden City of Peking. Ralph had been young and fearless, driven by the need to find release in the opium dens that were strung out along the river – no cargo was too dangerous, no journey too risky. He spoke about how he had escaped with his life and a fast ship; how he had traded all across the China Sea and the Bay of Bengal, building a glittering fortune. Until a chance encounter brought him to a ship called the *Tiger*, and her captain, Adam Courtney.

He did not tell Ann about Adam Courtney.

'It was always my dream to return to England. To buy a house in Devon and settle down.' Ann could hear the longing in his heart. 'I had made my own fortune and was able to never work again. I gave up my former life and bought passage on a ship from Bombay to London – the ship that caught fire. My fortune ended up at the bottom of the ocean. I was left with another man's son, his dead wife – and this.' He touched the scars on his face and smiled, mocking himself. 'The rest of my story you already know.'

He wondered if she could sense the evasions. Nothing he had told her was false – but he had deployed facts like shields, protecting the greater truth that lay behind them. The real story of his life remained hidden.

Why not tell her everything? Unburden himself, confess the guilt he carried. Would it not lift the weight from his heart?

Ann was looking at him in a peculiar way: a tenderness in her gaze. If he told her what had actually happened – described the events as they had occured, laid out the facts before her – he would lose her affection. It was folly to think that she would absolve him. The crimes he had committed were unforgivable.

'I suppose you think I got what I deserved,' he said gruffly.

The words stung her. 'How could you say that, Ralph?' she asked, with something like contempt in her voice.

'I have not lived a good life.'

'I cannot imagine what you have suffered.' She reached across and stroked his scarred cheek gently.

Their eyes met, and in that moment it was as if she saw him clearly for the first time. He became vividly real, as if everything until that moment had been a bad dream and now she was awake.

Ralph and Ann were alone. Hamu's men were long asleep on their mats. The fire had died down, the orange glow from the embers lit up the branches and leaves that reached out above them, sheltering them from the stars that glittered, cold and distant in the ebony sky. He stared at her, noticing every detail: the fine hair on her bare arms; the sheen of moisture like diamond dust on the skin above the bodice of her dress; her wine-red lips.

This was a new feeling for Ralph. His desire for Ann was so intense that he could feel his heart racing in his chest. He stretched out his arm slowly, not sure that she would welcome his advances, then drew her to his chest. She came willingly.

It was morning in southern Africa. The sun climbed above the lip of the Indian Ocean, painting the earth in a swirl of pinks, amber and gold. Around the camp, the spreading trees were silhouetted black against the glowing sky, intricate as lacework. Birds in their thousands sang from the branches. The air was cool and fresh with night dew.

Ralph opened his eyes, realising immediately that he was not alone under the blanket.

Ann. He caught her scent – smoke and musk – as he hugged her tightly. The memories of the night before, echoes of their climax, came to him, arousing him again.

Then Ralph felt her tense against him and was suddenly afraid of losing her. He had had many lovers in his life. For the most part, passion had flared and then been extinguished; sometimes it had burned hotter and brighter, and left more permanent marks, but he had never cared so much as he did now with Ann.

'What is it?' he asked her gently.

Did she regret their union? Waking in his arms, her head against his disfigured cheek: was she disgusted?

Ann pulled away a little from Ralph. She turned to him, brushing a strand of hair from her face.

'The night I found you.' She looked nervous, struggling to find the right words. 'The woman you were with . . .'

'Thabisa?' *What was the proper word for her? Servant? Translator? Lover? Slave? All those were correct, but none were quite true.*

'It was not what it seemed,' he said.

'Oh, Ralph, do you think I am so innocent?'

He rolled away, staring into the depths of the forest while his heart squeezed tight enough to burst. 'You see that scar on my back?' he said. 'It's from a Ndwandwe spear. When I thought I would die of the wound, it was you I wanted to see. Not Thabisa.'

His answer seemed to satisfy her – or perhaps she wanted to be convinced. Her hand touched his shoulder and turned him towards her. She kissed him.

Overhead, the sky changed colour from gold to azure blue. The rising sun fell on his face, bathing him in light. Ann lay beside him with her head on his chest, so he could feel every beat of his heart under her.

'What are you doing?' said a voice.

A silhouette had appeared above them. It was Harry, his hair a mop of wild curls and his eyes as blue as the sky. If the sight of his mother in Ralph's arms troubled him, he gave no sign of it. He simply looked curious.

If Ralph had thought that opening his soul to Ann would free him, that her love would let him look at the boy without shame, he had been wrong. Even now, at the moment when he was at his happiest, the guilt weighed upon him.

You did not tell her everything. He silently reprimanded himself for being a coward.

Could she forgive him if she knew the truth?

'Will you play with me?' Harry asked.

How many times must I save your life before you will leave me alone?

Ralph got to his feet. It was bright daylight, the dawn had passed, and a glance at the flawless sky, clear of any clouds, told him of another hot day ahead. 'We had better make a start at once,' he said.

The long days of marching that it took to return to KwaBulawayo were some of the happiest of Ralph's life. Hamu and his contingent of warriors ran ahead at their usual fearsome pace, while the Chunu porters laboured behind with their loads of powder and shot. For most of the time, Ralph was alone with Ann and Harry.

Every day, he walked beside Ann, telling her tales of India and China and his adventures on the high seas. They were extraordinary stories, but Ralph preferred listening to Ann speak about her childhood. Her life had been simpler, at least until she came to Africa, but to him England was as exotic as any oriental empire. He devoured everything she had to tell him: the grey hills of the Pennines where she had grown up, purple with heather in summer and in winter dusted with snow; the green pastures, and the rain that fell so often.

'That is where I will go, when I have made my fortune with Shaka.' Ralph gave her a glance, then looked away as he saw Harry holding her hand.

How can I be with Ann, if it means being with the boy?

For her part, Ann wondered: *Could I go with him?*

When she was with Ralph, talking on the road or together at night, she felt a sense of completeness that she had rarely felt before. Not even with Frank, though it felt like a betrayal to admit it. It was easy to imagine spending her life with Ralph.

Though when she thought of it, she did not see them in England. It was here in Africa, a small homestead on the red soil. The thought surprised her. Leaving England had not been her choice, and since coming to Africa she had known nothing but hardship. Yet something about the country had bewitched her, creeping into her heart. She did not love it – it was too hard and capricious for that. But she could not imagine leaving.

Would Ralph be willing to stay here? If not, would she follow him? And what about Harry? Every time she saw the two of them together, the boy and the man, a worm of dread turned inside her. She sensed – without knowing why – that they were a terrible danger to each other. She knew that there were things that Ralph still had not told her.

And there was Thabisa. She must have sensed what had happened between Ann and Ralph, but she never said a word. Even in their small group, she managed to keep out of sight, always walking a few paces behind. Yet Ann never forgot her presence, or the feel of Thabisa's gaze prickling on her back. Ann had been quick to accept Ralph's assurance that Thabisa had no claim on him – perhaps she had been too quick to trust him?

After five days, they came to the top of the same ridge where Ralph had arrived a few months earlier, under the same euphorbia tree. Spread across the opposite hillside, Ann caught her first glimpse of the Zulu capital. She gasped at the sight in front of her. Though she had heard Marius and Ralph describe it in extravagant detail, the reality of the city was overwhelming.

'KwaBulawayo,' said Ralph.

There was no great ceremony taking place that day. Women worked in the fields, or outside their huts, while herdboys grazed the royal cattle on the surrounding pastures. Ralph's party were taken to the royal enclosure, where Shaka sat on his chair outside the great hut. His eyes widened in astonishment when he saw the rifles and barrels of powder being carried in. Dingane merely scowled at them.

Ralph commanded the porters to lay the weapons before Shaka.

'*Bayete*,' he saluted him.

Shaka nodded. He spoke rapid-fire sentences that had most of his courtiers nodding approval. Too quick for Ralph to understand, despite his progress with the language. He waited for the translation.

'King Shaka say, you good friend,' Thabisa translated. 'Zulus with firesticks, wash spears in the blood of *amaLala*.'

It should have been a triumphant moment, but Ralph felt uneasy. To his right, Dingane's narrowed eyes took in everything, observing Ralph and watching his reaction to the king's words.

Perhaps I should not have brought the guns. They made Ralph a player in the game of Zulu politics, and he did not know the rules. *There are too many currents here I do not understand.*

'Shaka will reward you,' said Thabisa.

The king raised his hand and made a gesture with his stick. Servants scurried to open the gates. How much ivory would those guns be worth?

A procession of boys came marching into the enclosure. But they were not carrying elephant tusks. Instead, they carried piles of furs and animal skins – which, when they held them up, turned out to be clothes. There was a kilt made out of pleated monkey tails, arm and leg bands of billowing ox-tails, and a necklace of sharp claws strung on a leather thong.

Shaka stepped from his throne. Ralph tried not to look underwhelmed.

'Take off your clothes,' said Thabisa.

Ralph looked around uncertainly. 'Here?'

'Here.'

There must have been fifty or sixty people gathered outside Shaka's hut that afternoon. Ralph felt their eyes on him as he pulled off his shirt, revealing the scar that was still fresh on his back. Self-consciously, he undid the rope that served as a belt and dropped his trousers. He stood naked in front of Shaka and his court.

Shaka said something that made the *indunas* laugh. Thabisa did not translate.

'Are they going to give me those clothes?' Ralph asked.

He knew the Zulus were more careless of nudity than Europeans, but even so he had begun to wonder if this was Shaka's idea of a practical joke.

'You dress now.'

The boys came forward. One wrapped the kilt around Ralph's waist and tied it on. Two more attached the ox-tails around his biceps and his calves. Finally, Shaka himself slid a brass ring onto Ralph's arm, and fastened the necklace around Ralph's neck. The claws pricked into Ralph's chest.

Shaka stepped back and looked at Ralph.

'*Induna*,' he said, and Ralph felt transformed. The ox-tails tickled his limbs, while an unfamiliar breeze blew between his legs.

He caught Ann's eye, thinking she must be struggling not to laugh at how he looked. But her face was solemn, while Harry was staring at Ralph with something like awe.

Shaka spoke again. 'Now, reward.'

All faces turned to the open gate.

More boys came through the gate. Again, they did not carry ivory: instead, they drove in a herd of cattle.

Shaka held out his arms.

'This is your reward,' said Thabisa.

It took a tremendous effort for Ralph to hide his reaction.

'That is a very generous gift,' he said. The cattle were still coming in, trudging past like an army on parade. There must have been over a hundred of them, some tawny red, others with mottled black and white coats, all with wide-spreading horns and wet black noses. 'But I have nowhere to keep them.'

'Shaka give you kraal. Talala kraal, near Thukela. Good land.' Shaka leaned forward and added something more. 'Big kraal. Space for many wives.'

'I do not have any wives.'

Shaka considered that. For the first time, he seemed to notice Ann. 'She not wife?'

Ralph and Ann shared a quick glance. 'No.'

Was it his imagination, or did Thabisa's eyes narrow at that. Shaka pointed to Harry. 'And him? Son?'

'Not mine.'

'Then you need wife. Shaka find.'

'I do not need a wife. Shaka has given me more than enough.'

He saw Shaka's frown. But before the king could respond, Dingane spoke.

'Have you forgotten that the Talala kraal belongs to me, brother?' he said in his stony voice. 'You cannot take what is mine and give me nothing in return.'

No one else could have spoken to Shaka that way and remained alive. Even for Dingane it was surely an enormous risk.

That is how much he despises me, Ralph thought. *He cannot hide it even if it means defying the king.*

But Shaka did not bristle, as Ralph had expected. He looked away, and said curtly: 'What do you want?'

'Give me her.'

Dingane pointed at Thabisa.

What is he doing?

Ralph's mind raced. His command of isiZulu was not nearly good enough to manage alone. Without Thabisa, he would not be able to understand the customs of the court, the king's orders, he would not be able to make himself understood when he needed to. He would be helpless.

'Please, *Nkosi*,' Ralph said to Shaka. 'How can I serve you well if I cannot understand what you command?'

Ralph could see the calculation behind Shaka's eyes. He could not take back the rewards he had given Ralph without looking weak. But he did not want to publicly humiliate his brother.

Shaka flicked his stick, like a man shooing away a fly.

'Take her,' he said to Dingane.

'No!' cried Ralph. All eyes turned to him. He saw triumph on Dingane's features, the satisfaction of a bully who has found a weakness. 'I need Thabisa.'

'I will give you another servant,' said Shaka.

'What is happening?' Ann asked.

Thabisa began to walk towards Dingane, eyes downcast. From the age of eight, she had been a slave, to be passed from owner to owner. She did not believe that a different life was possible for her.

The sight filled Ralph with rage. *Is there nothing I can do to save her?*

He felt his powerlessness like a void inside him. The fine clothes he had put on scratched his skin; the necklace weighed like a yoke on his neck.

Shaka looked away, his attention already turning to other matters. 'If there is something you can do for her, then for God's sake do it,' said Ann.

She had no reason to love Thabisa, but she could not look at Dingane's face without feeling, deep in her body, what Thabisa would endure. She would not wish that on any woman – and she would not forgive Ralph if he let it happen.

'There is something,' Ralph murmured. The seed of an idea had begun to grow. 'But it would have consequences.'

'Do it,' Ann said firmly. 'Do it now.'

'Wait!' Ralph called out, so loudly it silenced the surrounding courtiers. He felt the power of Shaka's attention descend on him again.

'You said an *induna* must have a wife.'

Shaka nodded.

'I will marry Thabisa.'

The words died away without translation. Thabisa turned to stare at him in disbelief.

Ralph could not bring himself to look at Ann, though he could feel the agonising heat of her gaze on him. His hand touched his cheek. Once before in his life, he had given up what he desired most to do what he felt was right. He had lived with that ever since.

Ann looked at Ralph; the colour had drained from her face, she felt breathless. *Perhaps this is what he wants*, she thought, and thinking it made the pain easier to accept. She remembered how she had found him in the forest with Thabisa, naked. *Perhaps*

I am the serpent in the garden. Perhaps they were in love, and I tempted him away.

More likely, she concluded, Ralph had never cared about her as much as she had imagined. That sparked anger in her heart, and though it seared her, it was better than what came before. She nursed it, using it to fight the pain. To a man like Ralph, so hard and coarse, one woman was like any other. *No wonder I was so afraid to open myself to him. I knew the danger.* Yet even as she tried to cling to her anger, she could feel the ache of loss in her heart. She told herself it was her shame at having been deceived.

I was a fool.

Thabisa still had not spoken.

'Tell him,' Ralph said to her.

Thabisa spoke a few short, quiet words.

Shaka was uncharacteristically quiet. Dingane stepped forward, stomach pushed out, peppering his brother with an angry tirade. Thabisa did not translate it, but Ralph could guess the gist.

I cannot let him win the argument.

'How many cattle does it take to buy a bride?' he asked at the top of his voice, interrupting Dingane.

If Ralph's intervention had given Thabisa hope, she did not show it. She translated the question in a low, flat voice, as if it was irrelevant to her. She was beside the point. The real currency was not cattle or women or slaves: it was power.

'Nine cows,' said Shaka.

Ralph gestured to the herd of animals he had been presented with earlier.

'I will pay Dingane twelve cows to have Thabisa as my bride.'

Dingane started to object – he did not want to sell – but Shaka cut him short. He spoke briefly.

'What did he say?' said Ralph.

Thabisa looked at the ground. 'umRalph give Dingane twelve cattle. Dingane give Thabisa wife.'

Shaka thumped the butt of his stick on the ground to emphasise the point. The matter was closed. He bared his teeth in a smile that said any more dissent might be fatal.

'Everyone have what he want,' he announced.

FOUR YEARS LATER . . .

TALALA KRAAL

The *induna* sat in judgement.

The trial had been going on all day – and the day before, in fact – but that did not dim the litigants' enthusiasm. The two men stood opposite each other, arguing as vociferously as ever. A great crowd gathered around them. Some were there to offer testimony as witnesses, others as supporters of one side or the other. Many had come for the entertainment, and the chance of a free meal.

A Zulu trial was a boisterous affair, more like a boxing match than the hushed proceedings of the Old Bailey. As the claimants argued, the crowd around them would nod and murmur agreement, or shake their heads and hiss through their teeth if they were unconvinced.

None of the participants showed the least interest in the fact that the judge was not a Zulu. The novelty had worn off long ago. Over the past four years, they had grown used to having a white man as their chief. In their minds, Ralph was an *induna* in reality as much as in law.

Ralph's mind often wandered during these disputes. He did not need to be a judge of facts, only a judge of men. The people would decide the merits of the case. The *induna*'s job was to read their mood until there was a consensus, and then reflect that in his judgement. It left plenty of time to think.

The scar on his back was not the only mark time had left. His limbs carried their own stories written in scar tissue: an elephant tusk, a wild dog, a knife. And some marks that notched the passage of time with less violence: the lines around his eyes, the crease across his forehead. His thirtieth birthday had been and gone, though he could not have said when. He marked time the Zulu way, moon by moon and season by season, with the great first fruits ceremony as the linchpin of the year. He had no concept of the date according to European reckoning, except that if four years had passed, it was probably 1828.

When he told Thabisa about his birthday, she did not understand. When he tried to explain, she stared at him like he was an idiot.

'Why celebrate get older?'

Ralph had no good answer. It was just what people did. But that wasn't true – the Zulus didn't do it. It was just what he had grown up with. 'Because I am wiser,' he tried.

Thabisa's face had told him what she thought of that. 'Old man no good.'

Four years we have been married.

The wedding, he remembered as a blur of details: Thabisa with her hair pulled up into a topknot, caked with red ochre; the short spear she had pointed at him as they danced; his feet fumbling as he tried to repeat the steps that Hamu had taught him, and the watching Zulus roaring with laughter.

The night before the wedding, he and Ann had spoken under the bushwillow that stood outside the kraal. Everyone was asleep; the moon shone through the tree's purple leaves and turned them silver.

'You know this is not a true marriage,' he had said. 'It is only to save Thabisa.'

He had longed to touch her, but Ann had held herself away. 'Thabisa thinks she is marrying you.'

'What does that matter?'

'It matters to her.'

'Zulus have many wives.'

She shook her head. 'You are not a Zulu. And nor am I.'

'Then why did you let me do it?'

She had reached out then and cupped her hand against his cheek. Her palm was cool. 'You have made your choice. Now we must both live with the consequences.'

'I am always living with the consequences,' he had wanted to say. But he had stood there, until at last she took her hand away and found her fingers wet with his tears.

That was the last time she had touched him. For four years since then, they had held themselves apart, even though she and Harry lived in his kraal. Sometimes, Ralph spotted her looking away hastily when his gaze caught her; sometimes, he knew, he did the same. When they spoke, she was polite and formal. Many times, he had wanted to shout at her: *Why do you not go away? Leave me in peace?* But he had never said it. He feared that she might take him at his word. When he returned from court, or from war, hers was always the first face he looked for. Even though he knew when he saw her, it would only hurt him.

He did not know why she had stayed. *What is there to keep her among the Zulus?* She showed no interest in taking a husband, and she could not participate in the rituals of the Zulu women. Harry was old enough now to look after himself during the day. Ralph had the impression Ann was waiting for something, biding her time.

Perhaps it was simply that she had nowhere else to go.

Ralph forced himself back to the trial in front of him. He scanned the crowd, noting who had fallen silent; whose eyes were downcast; who stood straighter and spoke more loudly. He could understand their speech almost perfectly by now, but body language told him more about who'd had the better of the argument. Many of their faces were familiar to him: the headmen of various kraals that were built on his land, their families and retainers. He had been accepting their service, taking their tithes, settling their disputes and leading them in battle for four years.

A new face at the back of the crowd caught his eye. He smiled in recognition. He did not see Hamu often these days, but when they met it was always with the warmth of old friends.

It was time to draw the proceedings to a conclusion – he had made his decision. The crowd fell silent as Ralph stood.

'You, Gouzi,' he said to the man on his right. 'You say that Mbikwana has built his kraal too close to yours, and your cattle do not have enough pasture to graze.' He turned to the other man. 'But you, Mbikwana, you say that Gouzi's kraal was yours, before, and that you have the right to live there, too.'

He tipped back his head, so that his eyes slanted down, and glanced around the assembly. It was a gesture he had copied from Shaka and used many times.

'The kraal was granted to Gouzi by King Shaka. Therefore, it belongs to Gouzi, and all the land he needs for grazing,' announced Ralph. Murmurs of agreement from one side, disappointment from the other. 'But Mbikwana should be properly compensated. I will give you the fields by Inkwenkwe, in the next valley, to build a new kraal.'

Gouzi smiled; Mbikwana bowed his head. The men around them nodded approvingly. It was a just decision.

'We will eat as friends,' Ralph declared, picking up his spear.

A cow was led into the centre of the kraal. It was so tame, it stood still, even as Ralph walked to it and plunged the spear into its shoulder. This, too, he had done many times. He had learned that if he stabbed too deeply, he could pierce the heart at once and kill the beast outright. This was poor form, for the Zulus believed that if the animal did not bellow loudly when it was killed, it reflected the ancestors' displeasure. If it died without making a sound, another cow would have to be offered up, and that was wasteful. The trick was to hurt the animal enough to make it cry out, and then swiftly end its ordeal.

The cow bellowed and then fell dead. In minutes, it had been skinned and butchered, while girls knelt around it with basins to collect the blood. It was vital that not a drop be left on the ground, lest a wizard find it and use it to make medicines and spells against the village. When the cow's entrails had been removed, Ralph cut out the *inanzi*, the fourth stomach, with its characteristic folds that always reminded him of the nautilus shell, and which the Zulus held sacred. He carried it into his hut, together with other choice cuts from the cow's shoulder blade and abdomen. Some of the meat was mixed with the yellow flowers of the *impepho* plant and thrown on the coals to burn, filling the hut with a thick smoke that smelled to Ralph like liquorice and molasses. The rest of the offering was laid on a damp hide and covered in branches, where it would be left overnight for the spirits of the ancestors to lick at and satisfy their hunger.

Are my ancestors watching? Ralph wondered. His father and his grandfather had both been conquerors, grinding India's complex, ancient civilisations under the heel of white rule. *What would they say if they could see me now? What would they think of my actions?*

His European clothes were long gone. He wore a kilt made of black and white ox-tails woven together in the Zulu style. He went bare-chested, save for the necklace of lion claws that Shaka had given him. His body was bronzed by the sun and honed by many hours of hunting and exploring. His hair had grown so long that he wore it in a plait down his back, which amused the Zulus greatly. All that remained of the man he had been were those piercing blue eyes, and the mesh of scars on his cheek.

Black smoke licked the air as the beef began to sizzle over the fire. Ralph moved through the throng of people, exchanging greetings and pleasantries, until he found Hamu near the gate.

'*Yebo*,' Ralph greeted him, with a broad grin.

'*Yebo*.'

'You look well,' said Ralph.

'You look too thin. Thabisa does not feed you enough.'

'I feed him plenty. He does not eat.'

Hamu's arrival had brought Thabisa out of her hut. She gave Hamu a shy smile as she presented him with a bowl of beer. It reminded Ralph how rarely he saw her smile these days.

Hamu glanced between the two of them. He could not have missed how they kept apart and rarely looked at each other. He had long since stopped asking when Thabisa would bear children.

It had not been a successful marriage. Thabisa understood why Ralph had taken her as his wife, but she was still lithe and beautiful when they married, and Ralph had been a young man. They had lain together before, why not again? But on their wedding night, when she had opened her thighs to him, he had gently pushed them closed. The hurt and shame on her face had pained him, but he did not relent.

'I will not have children,' he had told her.

For a while, Thabisa had thought he might change his mind. She knew men, she knew what they liked and Ralph was, after all, just a man. One way or another, he would succumb to her charms. But he never did. Instead, the more she tried, the more he resisted and the more she got hurt.

'No children, why wife?' she had shouted at him, during one of their frequent fights in the early days of their marriage. 'Why marry? Why not leave me in *isigodlo*?'

I married you to save your life. That was the only reason. But Ralph never spoke those words. He was not so cruel, and in any case, she knew it as well as he did.

'Uncle Hamu!' Harry came running up, beef fat smeared over his face. Thabisa scowled. 'Did you bring me a present?' the boy asked.

Hamu squatted down and tousled Harry's hair.

'You speak our language better than umRalph,' he said.

The boy was bilingual and could make the uniquely Zulu sounds – the tongue-click, the hum – that still made Zulus laugh when Ralph tried them.

'Did you bring me a present?' Harry asked again. He had learned from experience that Hamu would not arrive empty-handed.

Hamu lifted off the necklace of red glass beads he wore and put it around Harry's neck. Harry fingered it in delight. In this, too, he was a proper Zulu.

'You spoil him, Hamu,' said Ann, coming out from behind one of the huts. Ralph had not seen her all day: the sight of her now lifted a weight from his heart that he had not realised was there.

'Do you bring nothing for me?' she asked Hamu, pretending to be offended. She, too, spoke in Zulu. She still dressed in the English fashion, but had picked up certain mannerisms from the Zulu women. In particular, she had perfected the scornful toss of the head and impatient roll of the eyes that said a man was barely worth her time.

'How could I forget you?' Hamu protested, with the ardour of a young Zulu wooing his bride. He beckoned forward one of his servants, who presented Ann with a large fabric bundle.

'Oh,' she cried. She shook it out, revealing a long bolt of blue calico cloth. 'This is a priceless gift, my dear Hamu.'

Hamu beamed to see how happy he had made her. The fact was that ingenuity and constant darning had been all that held Ann's clothes together for years. Cloth was almost unknown to the Zulus, who used grasses and hides for their clothes. Even a simple wool blanket was a fabulous luxury to them, which the king might wear as a ceremonial cloak when he desired something more exotic than his leopard and lion skins.

'Where did you get that?' Ralph asked Hamu.

'Are you jealous?' Ann teased him as a crowd of Zulu women gathered around her, touching the fine fabric and marvelling at its quality. Ralph left them to their chatter and moved away to the edge of the kraal.

'Did I do wrong, to give her the cloth?' Hamu asked, following Ralph. He could see that his friend's mood had darkened.

'You can give her what you like. She is not my wife.'

'Not your wife, no. But she is not your sister, either.'

'She would not marry me for a hundred cows.'

'But would she marry any other man?'

'What she does is her business.' Ralph changed the subject. 'Where did you get the cloth? And the beads you gave Harry?'

'From the king.'

'Where did he get them?'

Hamu shrugged.

'Those are English beads,' Ralph explained. 'Not the second-rate goods you get from the Portuguese. And the cloth is from India.' He looked at Hamu, to see if he had understood. 'Shaka has been trading with the *abelumbi*.'

Hamu's face remained impassive. 'It is possible.'

'If there is another Englishman coming to this kingdom, I need to know.'

'The king trades with whoever he likes.'

'He should tell me.' Ralph thought for a moment. 'Did this person give him firesticks? Rifles?'

Hamu burst out laughing. 'Are you frightened? You are like a woman who thinks her lover will find a more beautiful wife.'

'Other *abelumbi* may not be as loyal as I am.'

'Then Shaka will smell them out.' A shadow crossed Hamu's face. Ralph wondered what it meant. 'But you are not a poor man. How big is your herd, now?'

'More than a thousand head of cattle.'

Ralph had made himself wealthy – and not just in livestock. Buried in pits beneath his kraal was a huge trove of elephant tusks that he had been given as gifts for his various services to Shaka.

'Then you have nothing to fear.' Hamu swept an arm across the landscape: the river valley below them, dappled with trees and meadows; the distant wooded hills. 'You have land, cattle, kraals. You are *induna*.'

'I am an *induna*,' Ralph agreed.

I am living the life that Marius dreams of, he thought with a wry smile. A homestead, a herd of cattle and a woman to keep a fire in the house. Though he doubted whether Marius's dream included serving a mighty African king and his empire.

'You should take more wives,' Hamu chided him.

'One woman is plenty.'

'No man is rich if he has only one wife.'

This was not a new thread in their conversation.

'It would make Thabisa jealous.'

'It would make her *happy*. You cannot be the great wife if you are the *only* wife.'

'This is women's talk.' Ralph glanced back to the cooking fires. 'It is time to eat.'

When the feast was over, and the crowds had returned to their own kraals, Ralph and Hamu sat on the hilltop, looking down into the river valley. The sun was setting. The herdboys were driving the cattle into the enclosure for the evening. Hamu watched them admiringly, commenting on each beast with the rich and varied vocabulary the Zulus had for describing their cattle. These were only a small fraction of the animals that Ralph owned; the rest were distributed among various kraals on his lands. In exchange for keeping them, the headmen were given the cows' milk, and allowed to eat any of the beasts that died.

'Why did you come?' Ralph asked at last. 'Was it to eat my beef?'

Hamu put tobacco in his pipe and lit it with a grass spill.

'Shaka will dance the *amaGaqa* again. He will summon the *impi*.'

By now, Ralph knew what that meant.

'Who will he go to war with this time?'

'King Faku of the Mpondo.'

The Mpondos were a tribe to the south, beyond the Thukela frontier.

'That is a long way away,' Ralph observed.

'King Shaka soars higher than the eagle. His shadow falls to the ends of the earth.'

Ralph glanced at Hamu, wondering if there was a deeper meaning behind the words.

'How is the king?'

'He is as determined as the rhinoceros.' Hamu sighed. 'But I think his skin is not so thick.'

That, too, Ralph had heard. Ever since the assassination attempt, the king had become increasingly withdrawn and prone to fits of temper. Ralph tried to keep his distance from the court, and tend to affairs on his own land. Yet he could not avoid the king completely. Everything he had in his life, he owed to Shaka.

'You will come?' Hamu asked.

You did not deny the king what he wished for. He would need the riflemen Ralph had trained for the campaign, and in return there would be more ivory and cattle to swell Ralph's coffers. This was the bargain they had made, each reliant on the other, for Shaka would not trust any of his other *indunas* to command the riflemen.

I must find out who this other white man he has traded with is, Ralph thought. *Could it be Marius?*

Ralph had not been back to Nativity Bay in four years, though he sometimes sent men across the river to spy it out. From their reports, he knew that Marius and his associates still occupied the camp by the lagoon. Word of their settlement had got out, and a few more adventurers and desperate men had trickled in to swell their numbers. They made a living by hunting, and occasionally a ship would brave the bar and enter the lagoon to trade with them. Though it could not be an easy or luxurious life, Ralph supposed it gave Marius the freedom he craved above all else.

So far as Ralph knew, the ultimatum that he had given Marius that day on the beach had held. He had kept to his side of the Thukela.

I am rich and he is free. Which of us got the better of the bargain?

As for what had become of Jobe, he knew nothing.

Now Shaka's campaign threatened the fragile truce. The march against the Mpondos would take Ralph closer to Marius than he had been in years. If Shaka defeated King Faku, then Nativity Bay would fall into Shaka's new territory. Whether either man wanted it or not, Marius and Ralph would find themselves thrown together.

For four years, Ralph had lived in comfort, amassing his fortune in cattle and ivory. Now, he felt as if he stood on the edge of a cliff, hearing the stones move under his feet.

Hamu saw his worry but misread the reason.

'The Mpondo are weak,' he assured Ralph. 'They fall over like blades of grass if a Zulu even breaks wind. They will flee like children when they hear your firesticks.'

'I hope so,' said Ralph.

Hamu's confidence made him feel foolish. He was an *induna*, a mighty lieutenant of the most powerful king southern Africa had known. What did he have to fear from anyone?

But in his heart, he could hear the rattle of stones trickling away beneath his feet.

MPONDOLAND

Two weeks later the army marched south. Twenty thousand warriors beating a path through the long grass two hundred yards wide. The pride of the Zulu nation.

Ralph had not gone so far beyond the Thukela frontier in years. He had no map, and the country was unfamiliar, but he knew that they must be near Nativity Bay, and Marius would surely remember his grudge. Ralph marched with his gun loaded.

On the third night, the Zulus halted in a kraal whose chief had hastily proclaimed his loyalty to the Zulu empire. Next morning, Ralph went to see Shaka.

'Those are very fine beads,' said Ralph, indicating the string of red and white glass beads the king wore.

Shaka looked down. His cheeks puffed out with satisfaction. Like many men, he had grown more vain as he got older.

'Where did you get them?' Ralph asked.

They were the same kind of beads – probably from the same factory – as the ones that Hamu had given Harry. Ralph had noticed them everywhere since: around the necks of the *indunas*, on favoured wives and serving girls in the *isigodlo*, and now on Shaka himself.

'My brother gave them to me.'

Dingane. Ralph's misgivings deepened. For most of the past four years, he had been able to avoid Shaka's brother. He saw him at festivals, and when the army gathered, but he always kept his distance. Time had not made Dingane any fonder of Ralph. Every time they were together, Ralph saw those lidded eyes gazing at him implacably.

'It is a generous gift,' said Ralph.

'My brother loves me.'

Ralph remembered a conversation they had once had around a campfire. *Boy always dangerous*. He remembered the fate that had befallen Shaka's own father.

'He loves you as a son loves his father.'

He saw in Shaka's eyes that the king understood his meaning. 'If I cannot trust my brother, who then?'

Ralph bowed his head. 'You can always trust me.'

Shaka considered for a moment. Then he snatched the beads off his neck and threw them at Ralph. They stung his palm as he caught them.

'Are these what you want? Take them! Do my people go hungry when Shaka provides? I am the bull who feeds the nation, until even the vultures have full bellies.'

For a moment he held a defiant pose: shoulders squared, his chest puffed out, face pointed to the sky. Then his shoulders slumped, and his face shrivelled with self-pity.

Ralph knew how dangerous Shaka was in this mood. He tossed the necklace back to him. It was an expensive gesture; he could have traded it for ten cows.

'I serve you because I respect you,' he said. 'Because you are the king, the *Nkosi*. But I fear what Dingane may do.'

He saw Shaka's face soften. 'Dingane is fat and lazy,' Shaka declared, his confidence returning. 'He can do nothing.'

'Where did he get the beads?' Shaka didn't answer. 'He has been trading with white men. Did you give him permission?'

'Dingane is not like other *indunas*.'

No, Ralph thought. *He is far more dangerous.*

'If he can trade for beads, he can trade for other goods. Guns, for example.'

Shaka ignored the warning. 'You are faithful,' he declared. He beckoned Ralph closer, held up the beads and placed them over his head. 'I will reward your loyalty.'

This time, Ralph accepted the gift. 'I would rather you watch your brother.'

'Speak to me after we have defeated the Mpondo, when we have burned their kraals and put their cattle to pasture in our own fields. All the world will see then that no one can stand against King Shaka.'

Ralph knew it was true. As long as Shaka kept conquering, rewarding his *indunas* with the spoils of war, they would be content, and his throne would be secure. That was why he had launched this latest campaign. The greatest threat to his power was not war or invasion, but peace.

Yet even warriors could grow tired of war. Ralph had seen it in the men's faces as they marched south, fatigue creeping in where previously there had been only strength. They had been fighting every year of Shaka's reign.

Shaka was right, Ralph told himself. Victory would make them forget their doubts. He picked up his rifle and his cartridge bag.

'Where are you going?' Shaka asked.

'To hunt.'

'Alone?'

'I will take a boy with me.'

Shaka wagged a finger at him. 'The way you hunt is foolish. Very dangerous.'

This was an old argument. For the Zulus, hunting was second only to war for the numbers of men it involved. Thousands of warriors would fan out across miles of countryside, beating the forest and closing in a circle until they had trapped the game in a killing ground. Though the king received the spoils and the trophies, he kept away from the animals. Ralph preferred to go alone, or at most with a single attendant who could fetch bearers to retrieve his prizes later. The life of an *induna* meant being surrounded by retainers and servants every day, dawn to dusk. Hunting gave Ralph precious moments of solitude.

Shaka did not see it that way. Ralph saw concern in the king's eyes.

'It is the animals who need to be careful.' Ralph grinned.

Shaka did not smile. 'A man thinks what he will. The lion has his own ideas.'

Two hours later, Ralph had reason to remember those words. He had not seen anything since he entered the forest, and he was starting to grow impatient.

'Where are the animals?' asked the bright-eyed boy trotting behind him. His name was Bheka, the son of a headman who kept one of Ralph's cattle kraals. He was only ten, not even as tall as Ralph's rifle, but he stood as proud as an *induna*. To be taken to hunt with Ralph was a mark of honour.

'They do not want to be found today,' Ralph murmured.

Bheka shivered and touched the amulet around his neck. 'There is bad magic in this place.'

'Maybe so,' said Ralph.

More likely, the animals had been shot out. They were not far from Nativity Bay here; Marius and his men would no doubt have scoured the forest for game.

Thinking of Marius sent an unpleasant shiver through Ralph. Perhaps bad magic was not so far off the mark.

'Go back,' he told Bheka. 'I will follow soon.'

He knew it was probably pointless, but the hunter in him refused to go home empty-handed. There must be water nearby. If he could find it, there would be some fowl at least, maybe even big game coming down to drink.

Bheka handed Ralph the second rifle he carried and scampered away through the trees. Ralph moved easily through the forest. He passed a wild plum that rose tall as a ship's mast, with vines stretching out from its crown like stays and halyards. Then the *umNeyi* tree – red ivorywood – with its bark stripped where porcupines had eaten it; and the *isiFice* tree whose leaves were prized by the rhinoceros. Ralph was in his element.

He reached the top of a ridge, where the trees fell away, and he could see across the valley to the next hill. The forest thinned: open water glittered in a ravine that split the valley floor. Meadows opened on either side of it, and in the long yellow grass he could see brown shapes gathered around a cluster of rocks. It was a herd of impala, heads down, grazing.

That is what I have come for. Ralph could almost smell the sweet impala meat roasting over the fire that he and Bheka would build back at the camp, the boy so tired from skinning the animal that he would fall asleep as soon as his belly was full.

The sight lifted Ralph's spirits. He followed the ridge downwind, then worked his way into the valley until he found the edge of the river. It flowed lazily through a ravine it had cut out of the cracked earth. Dragonflies buzzed over the surface. On the mudbanks, Ralph saw the splayed-toe prints of crocodiles.

He followed the riverbank, keeping a wary distance from the water, until he entered the meadow he had seen. He crouched low, stalking his prey. When he risked a glance at the impala, he could see their tawny backs breaking the line of rippling grass a hundred yards ahead.

He unslung one of his rifles and checked the priming. He had learned from experience that the quantity of powder that would put a ball into human flesh was not nearly enough against the hide of African game. He measured an extra dram of powder when he filled his cartridges. The first time he had tried it, the ball had flown a foot above the target and the kick had almost dislocated his shoulder – but he had learned to compensate. More than once, the extra powder had saved his life.

The bullet was rammed home snug, and the pan was primed, brimming with powder. He knelt on one knee, put the rifle to his shoulder and stood, rising smoothly out of the grass, searching instinctively for the nearest target.

The animals sensed the movement. They raised their heads and turned to look at him. These impala had long snouts and small ears; black noses and downturned mouths. One opened its mouth, yawning, revealing a pink tongue and four enormous fangs.

That was the moment Ralph realised his mistake.

It was not a herd of buck. It was a pride of lions, at least twenty of them. Some lazed on their sides on the warm rocks; others sat up on their haunches, or prowled about through the long grass. And one – the male, with a white-flecked muzzle and a thick mane framing his face – stood twenty yards away, staring at Ralph.

Ralph did not hesitate. The rifle exploded with smoke; the butt slammed into his shoulder. At that range, he could not miss. The bullet hit the big male in the jaw. Even as Ralph twisted away to absorb the recoil, he was already reaching for the second gun on his shoulder. He took it, aimed and fired at a second target – a lioness who had been sitting on one of the rocks. But the sound of the first shot had frightened her into motion; the bullet went wide.

Ralph reloaded both guns swiftly, with a series of precise movements. This was the moment of greatest danger. If the lions attacked him now, he would not be able to fend them off.

He rammed home the bullets in both guns, driven on by adrenaline, his mouth dry, the breath sawing in his throat, but when he looked up, Ralph saw that the shots and the smoke had spooked the lions. The pride had fled in terror.

Ralph ran after the lions, picking a target to follow at random. The big male, he could come back for later.

He followed the spoor, checking his surroundings in case one of the lions circled back to attack him. After so many hours of frustration, he relished the hunt. A few times he glimpsed a shape moving in the distance, and tried a shot, but he never had clear sight. The animals had scattered.

He continued along the trail the lions had taken. It led deep into thick bush and then into a forest. Still he saw them, a flash of brindled fur through the dense foliage; he could smell them too – the stink of rotten flesh heavy under the thick, leafy canopy. But now hunting was more difficult. The trail began to dwindle until Ralph could no longer tell if he was still on it. Were the lions ahead of him or behind him? Were they outflanking him? Ralph had used up almost all of his cartridges. It was time to turn back.

The sun was past its zenith by the time Ralph returned to the meadow. The carcass of the male would be too heavy for him to carry by himself, but he could skin the animal and take its hide. That, too, was something he had become practised at.

He pushed through the long grass until he reached the place where he had killed the lion.

But to his astonishment, it wasn't there.

This was definitely the right spot. He could see the cluster of rocks where the pride had gathered, the flattened dents in the long grass where they had lain. Blood still covered the grass where the big male had taken his bullet.

Had it somehow managed to drag itself down to the water? Ralph walked to the edge of the ravine to check. Here, the river broadened out into a wide pool, almost a little lake. He scanned the banks all around it, but there were no marks in the soil, and the surface of the lake was smooth and undisturbed. Where could the lion have gone?

A low growl sounded behind him.

Ralph spun around, just as the lion sprang.

I thought I'd killed it, Ralph's mind protested, before a quarter of a ton of lion flesh collided with him. The crushing impact forced the air from his lungs and punched him backwards off his feet – over the edge of the ravine.

He felt a second of weightlessness, as lion and man fell through the air. Then they hit the surface with a fountain of water. The lake was deep – much deeper than Ralph had expected. Even with the bulk of the lion driving him down, he did not touch the bottom. Now he had to fight not just with the wounded animal on top of him, but with the river, too.

Man and beast pawed their way to the surface. Ralph kicked out, trying to escape the lion, but his arm was caught in its mouth. As they struggled in the water, Ralph realised that his bullet had shattered the beast's teeth and torn away its cheek and part of its nose. Its face was only inches from his own, bloody foam boiling from its mouth as it struggled to breathe while keeping hold of its quarry. He tried to punch the beast on the nose, to kick it in the stomach, but he was pinned.

Ralph caught a blow to the head, feeling the jagged remnants of the lion's teeth tear into his arm as he was driven underwater. Was the beast trying to drown him? He felt its powerful legs churning the water next to his, lifting them both up, but as soon as Ralph's head broke the surface, the lion's paw hit him again, another skull-shuddering blow that drove him back down into the river, mud and blood churning around him.

He is bobbing me like an apple, Ralph realised, short of breath, the pain in his arm unbearable.

But without a foothold the lion could not keep him under-water. Ralph drew in a deep lungful of air as the beast gave up on drowning him and began to search for a way out, pawing the water, circling the edge of the lake. The earth banks were high and steep on both sides and Ralph could feel the lion begin to tire, but the grip on his arm never slackened. Dizzy, waterlogged, racked with pain, an even more terrible thought struck Ralph. What if the lion drowned with its jaw clenched shut and pulled him down to the bottom of the river? No one would know what had happened to him, unless in some drought, years in the future, a hunter found their skeletons in the dried-up mud.

The lion attacked him again. A claw raked his face and cut open his cheek. There was still strength in its limbs, enough to rip Ralph apart if it could find leverage.

Something brushed past Ralph's side. He thought it must be the lion's hind legs, but even as it happened he realised that whatever it was felt different. Something long and scaly, more potent than the lion's flailing limbs.

The water erupted. A pair of flashing jaws gaped wide, brandishing an impossible number of teeth. For a second, Ralph stared down the monster's gullet. Then the jaws snapped shut, biting deep into the lion's shoulder.

It was a crocodile, drawn by the blood in the water. The lion tipped back its head in a deafening roar of pain, twisting around to fight its new enemy.

The moment it opened its mouth, Ralph's arm came free. The water churned around him, a boiling maelstrom of teeth and claws and thrashing muscle. One more blow from the lion would have knocked him out and drowned him.

Ralph kicked off, desperate to get away. The two great beasts, locked in their death struggle, ignored him – but there would be other crocodiles nearby. He splashed towards the bank, his injured arm flapping like a broken wing; he had to grit his teeth and use all his strength to keep from spinning in circles. His progress was agonisingly slow. Behind him, he could hear the water roiling as the two beasts fought.

He reached the edge of the lake. The steep cliffs made progress almost impossible, but he found a place where a vine hung down from one of the trees above. He wrapped it around his arm, ignoring the shooting pain from the bloody holes the lion's broken teeth had punched in his flesh. One-handed, he hauled himself up the bank.

With a final effort that made him scream out with pain, Ralph slithered out onto the rim of the cliff. Behind him, the water had gone still. Ralph guessed the crocodile had triumphed, dragging the lion down to the depths.

I must not tell Shaka about this, he thought through his pain. The Zulus believed that the spirits of the ancestors spoke through animals. The death of a lion, torn apart by a crocodile, was an omen that needed no interpretation.

Ralph lay still, drawing breath and gathering his strength. His arm was bleeding, while his face and torso were covered in wounds from the lion's claws. An open cut across the top of his scalp leaked blood down his temples and into his mouth.

How far had he come from the camp? Several miles, at least, through thick forest. Weak from his ordeal, still bleeding, he would be lucky if he could find his way back. The pack of lions had scattered, but they would come hunting when night fell.

Shaka was right, he thought ruefully. *I should not have come alone. I should not have sent the boy away.*

Ralph imagined the king mocking him, hunching into a ball to mimic a man cowering in terror while his courtiers rolled with laughter.

I will not let Shaka have the last word.

Ralph pushed himself to his feet and looked up to the ridge he had descended earlier that day. In his current physical state, it loomed as steep and high as Table Mountain.

His only other option was to give up and die. Half stumbling, half crawling, he found a game trail that led up the hill. Every movement was agony. Once, he tripped, threw out his arms to break his fall and lost consciousness from the pain. He tried not to think about the blood he had lost, a trail that every lion and hyena in the forest would follow as soon as the sun went down.

Pain and loss of blood made him dizzy. When the wind rustled the grass around him, he imagined he saw the shadows of vast monsters lurking to devour him. In his mind, he was back in the open boat with Lizzie Courtney and Harry, enduring endless days of ravaging thirst and hunger. Now the shadows in the grass were the men who owed him vengeance, stalking his tracks. A Chinese pirate, the first man he had ever killed. The boy at KwaBulawayo, murdered by Marius to prove a point with the rifles. Warriors from the different tribes he had fought over the last four years. And most terrifyingly of all, far off in the undergrowth, half hidden, the ghost of Harry's father.

The phantoms drove Ralph onwards until, at last, he looked back and realised he had reached the top of the ridge.

The sun was sinking behind him. Shadows pooled on the valley floor, hiding the lake where he had fought the lion. He still had miles to go.

He stumbled on, ignoring the voice in his head that insisted the effort was futile, that he would never find his way home. He had to keep going until he escaped or died. It would be a lonely death, but he did not feel alone. The ghosts of his past spoke to him constantly.

The Zulus are right. The ancestors are always watching.

Ralph could not tell what was real anymore. Even the pain in his arm seemed to somehow be outside of him – a constant raw tearing that lit up the night with showers of red-hot sparks. When he heard a voice, ahead through the trees, he assumed at first it was another one of his ghosts.

But something about this voice was different. He paused, listening. The voice was real, a living human being, and not far off.

A rush of relief went through Ralph. He was saved. He opened his mouth to shout for help—

But a cautionary instinct held him back. This was a contested country, between the frontiers of the Zulus and the Mpondos. A man in the forest might lead you to safety, or he might stick his spear in your guts.

Ralph sank to his knees and crawled closer to the voice, trying not to make a sound. He came up against a fallen log covered with moss and lay there, listening. The people must have been only a few yards away, though the thick bush hid them from view.

The man he could hear was speaking in Zulu. It should have reassured him – but it did not.

'Shaka will not go with the army,' the voice said. 'He will stay near this place, until the battle has been fought.'

The percussive monotone, the sibilant hiss as the speaker sucked air in through the gap between his front teeth: it sounded like Dingane.

'Shaka will not go with the army.'

The same words again. Had the speaker repeated himself, or were the words simply echoing in Ralph's fevered head? Though this time he had heard them in English.

'He will stay near this place until the battle has been fought.'

It *was* an English voice. And different from the one before, deeper and richer. Yet – impossibly – familiar again. It sounded like Jobe.

Ralph clenched his eyes shut and shook his head. Panic stirred inside him.

Am I losing my mind?

A third voice answered, and Ralph knew he must be either in the depths of a nightmare, or wide awake and in mortal danger. A man he feared more than any lion or crocodile.

'Shaka's a bloody coward, hey? How many men will he keep with him?'

Marius.

Jobe translated the question.

'A thousand,' Dingane answered.

'That is too many to fight at once,' said Marius.

'Not all of them are loyal to him.'

Marius chuckled. 'I suppose not.'

Ralph got up on his knees and raised himself until his eyes were above the level of the tree trunk. Marius, Dingane and Jobe stood around a small clearing, forming a rough triangle. They kept apart, which was why they had to speak so loudly: their need for secrecy was evidently less than their distrust of one another.

It was four years since Ralph had seen Marius and Jobe. The interval had not been kind to Marius: he had grown thinner, making his enormous frame seem more grotesquely oversized. Any softness that had been present in his bullish face was gone; all that remained was an ugly gaunt strength. As for Jobe, Ralph could not guess where he had been, but it seemed to have agreed with him. Always tall, he had grown big in every other direction, with a full face and a swollen paunch sagging over his woven belt. He wore a chief's cloak, copper rings on his forearm and three strands of glass beads around his neck. The same new beads that Ralph had noticed among the Zulus.

Jobe's cloak was draped over his shoulder, hiding the mark that the slavers had branded into it, but it was surely still there. *What could have brought him together with Marius now?*

'Does Shaka suspect?' Jobe asked.

'Shaka fears all men, always,' Dingane answered. 'The more he fears, the more he kills. The more he kills, the more men hate him.'

'What about when the army comes back?'

'The army serves the king,' said Dingane. 'When they return—' He broke off suddenly. 'What is that?'

Ralph had been straining to listen and had leaned forward, putting his weight on the branch he was kneeling on. It snapped, sending a crack like a gunshot through the twilight of the forest.

All three men in the clearing looked around. The forest diffused the sound, making it almost impossible to tell where the noise had come from. Dingane and Jobe looked this way and that. Marius had keener instincts. He stared at the tree where Ralph was hiding.

Ralph fought the urge to duck away. Marius had a hunter's eye that would seize on any movement. Instead, Ralph made himself stay still. Leaves shadowed his face; his skin was smeared with mud and blood. He must be almost invisible.

Marius took two steps towards him. His eyes raked over the undergrowth.

He has not seen me yet.

Another pace. Any closer, and he could not miss Ralph.

If I had a rifle and two bullets, Ralph thought, *I could end a great deal of mischief this moment.*

It was a vain thought. He had lost both his guns in the struggle with the lion, and his ammunition pouch was soaked through. Marius had two pistols in his belt, and a long-barrelled rifle slung on his shoulder.

Something seemed to catch Marius's eye. He pulled out one of the pistols and levelled it towards Ralph's hiding place. Now all three men were looking towards him.

'You see someone?' Jobe asked.

Marius fired. Ralph flung himself to the ground, at the same moment that the bullet ploughed into the tree trunk.

If he moved, he would get a bullet in his back. He cowered behind the tree trunk, bracing himself for Marius to fire again. But through the ringing in his ears, he heard Marius say: 'That should flush out any nosy Kaffirs.'

Marius had not seen him. It had been a feint, to scare Ralph into revealing himself. Instead, the pistol smoke had blinded Marius for a moment, so he had not seen Ralph duck away.

Ralph crouched behind the tree trunk, keeping his breath as shallow as possible. He listened as the after-effects of Marius's shot echoed through the forest. He heard beating wings and swaying foliage as birds left their perches; rustling undergrowth from creatures scuttling away. Distant animal cries and calls of fear.

And, closer, snapping branches and running footsteps; and then Marius's voice shouting: 'I knew we would find him.'

What does he mean?

Ralph heard the rapid movements of a struggle, a slap, a high-pitched voice crying out, and then the thud of someone falling to the ground.

'Who are you?' Marius demanded.

'Who sent you?' Jobe asked in Zulu.

Who would be so far out in the woods? Someone from the local tribes? A lost hunter? Or had Shaka suspected Dingane's treachery and sent a spy to follow him?

'Who sent you?' Ralph heard Jobe repeat his question, then a dull thump that sounded like a boot kicking flesh. A moan, and whimpering.

'I was looking for game,' said a small voice in Zulu.

Ralph knew that voice. It was Bheka, the boy he had brought hunting.

I sent you away, he raged. *Why did you come back?*

'Are you one of Shaka's boys? Did he send you?'

Jobe translated the question.

Do not mention my name, Ralph willed him. *That will only bring you pain.*

All three men's attention was surely on the boy now. Ralph risked putting his head above the log. Bheka lay on the ground, naked like all Zulu boys. Marius and Jobe stood over him, while Dingane watched from a distance.

Let him go, Ralph willed. *He is innocent.*

Bheka had spent most of his life in Ralph's kraal, away from the intrigues of Shaka's court. Even so, he recognised the king's brother. Confronted by these three men, he did not know what to say.

Marius crouched beside Bheka. He stroked the boy's face.

'You're frightened, hey? You have nothing to fear. Did Shaka send you to see what his brother was doing? Did he ask you to listen, in case his brother was in trouble?'

His voice was soothing and steady. 'You're a good boy, hey? You do what you're told. Are you hungry?'

He reached into his bag and pulled out a strip of smoked meat, which he tossed to the boy. Bheka tore off a chunk in his teeth and chewed eagerly.

'Who sent you?' asked Jobe.

'Shaka,' said Bheka, through a mouthful of biltong.

Marius nodded. 'I thought so.'

In a single motion, Marius took one step back, drew his second pistol and fired it into Bheka's skull. The boy's head exploded in a shower of blood and bone; his body jerked and went limp. A half-eaten strip of biltong fell from his lifeless hand.

Ralph bit his lip until it bled; his muscles quivered with the effort of keeping still. Even with his wounds, dizzy from blood loss, it took all his strength not to fly at Marius. But that would be suicide.

Dingane gazed on Bheka's corpse, his face expressionless.

'You should not have killed him so fast. He could have told us more. What Shaka knows, what he suspects.'

'In a week, it will not matter what Shaka suspects,' said Marius.

Dingane was still studying the body. 'I have seen this boy before. He is a servant of umRalph.'

Marius raised his head. 'Ralph Courtney's boy?' He kicked the corpse. 'If I had known that, I would have skinned him alive to make him talk.'

'We should go,' Jobe interrupted them. 'We are not safe here.'

The other two nodded. 'When will you strike?' Marius asked Dingane.

'I will make plans.' The prince's eyes were emotionless, but a frown creased his broad forehead. He pointed to Bheka. 'This is a bad sign. If Shaka suspects . . .'

The three men disappeared into the trees, leaving Bheka's broken body unburied. Ralph waited in his hiding place until the sound of their footsteps crashing through the bush had died down. He was so dazed and exhausted, he couldn't stand, so instead he crawled to the centre of the clearing and dug enough rocks out of the ground to cover the boy's corpse. It did not take many.

Ralph lay by the grave and wept. Bheka must have come to look for his master when Ralph did not return. He would have heard Marius's pistol shot, and assumed it was Ralph's rifle. Right up to the moment that Marius shot him, he would not have understood what he had found.

Do I understand it?

The conspirators meant to kill Shaka: that much was clear. Without him, Dingane would be king; and if any *indunas* or regiments remained loyal to the old regime, Marius's guns would change their minds. In exchange for Marius's support, the new king would bestow trading privileges and hunting rights.

So why is Jobe with them? From his poise and conditioning, it looked as if he had thrived among the Chunus since leaving Nativity Bay, made himself a chief. *What could induce him to make common cause with Marius, the man who had tried to enslave him, and branded him for life?*

If Shaka's campaign was successful – if he extended his grip south of the Thukela – he would encroach on the lands the Chunus had settled. He would threaten Nativity Bay, too. That was what had driven Jobe and Marius together again. They would help Dingane take the throne, and in return he would leave them to build their own kingdoms.

Ralph's head throbbed and his arm was agony, but one thought overwhelmed everything.

I must warn Shaka.

Afterwards, Ralph could not fathom how he had managed to get back to the kraal. Every movement was excruciating, each step so difficult that he thought he could not go any further. But still he kept moving forward.

By the time he caught the smell of woodsmoke, and saw the glow of fires from between the trees, dawn was not far away. The sentry who found him was amazed that Ralph was alive. He summoned three others, and between them they carried him to the hut he had been assigned in the kraal where they were staying. Ralph felt unconsciousness dragging him down, but he fought it back.

'I must speak to Shaka,' Ralph said.

The king had retired for the night some hours earlier, appropriating for himself the headman's hut at the top of the kraal. Ralph had to swear at the guards, using every Zulu curse he knew, before they dared wake Shaka. He came out of the hut, naked, his dark body gleaming almost blue in the moonlight.

'I told you, one man hunting is dangerous,' Shaka said, delighted to have been proved right. 'I sent your boy to find you because you did not come back.' The smile faded as his eyes adjusted to the dark, and he was confronted with Ralph's mutilated body held up by two of his guards. 'What have you done? Did you fight a lion?'

'A lion and a crocodile. But they were not the most dangerous beasts in the forest.'

'You need the sangoma.'

'Later. The boy is dead. I must talk to you alone.'

Waves of pain washed through Ralph; he spoke every word through clenched teeth. The urgency of what he had to say was plain.

'Go,' Shaka told his men.

The guards laid Ralph down on the swept earthen floor of the kraal and retreated to the fence. Shaka knelt and put his head close to Ralph's.

'What happened?'

'I saw your brother in the forest.' Ralph told Shaka what he had witnessed. The king frowned.

'He should not be there speaking with strangers. What foolishness! I will talk to him.'

Ralph wondered if he had made himself clear. 'He was not speaking with strangers. These men are your enemies. He plans to kill you and make himself king.'

Shaka drew back. His eyes narrowed. 'How could he do such a thing?'

'It almost happened once before.'

'And the ancestors protected me. No spear will pierce my heart.'

'Dingane will bring white men with guns.' Ralph had to make him understand. 'They killed my boy, Bheka, because they feared he would betray them.'

Shaka flicked his hand, as if to say *a boy is nothing more than a fly*. 'Did Dingane say he would kill me? Did he say he would be king?'

Ralph tried to remember the exact words. 'No. But . . .'

Shaka pointed to the long cut across Ralph's scalp. His mouth twisted in mockery. 'I think the lion cut out your brains.'

Ralph wondered if Shaka was right – if loss of blood had made him lose his senses. At Shaka's court, even the suspicion of treason meant certain death. He had seen men dragged away and executed because their attention had wandered during one of Shaka's speeches, and that was enough proof of disloyalty. Yet now, Shaka acted as if what Ralph had seen was nothing.

'Why do you not listen to me?' Ralph asked. 'Are you frightened to strike?'

Shaka jerked away and stood, towering over Ralph. Light from the fire flickered over his gleaming torso.

He turned to one of the guards, raising his voice: 'Who do you say I am?'

'*Nkosi*, you are the one who always leaves the battlefield unharmed. The one whose spear sheds more blood than all others,' the guard said loudly, chanting the praises in a sing-song rhythm. The other guards repeated them, stamping and clapping.

'Can one man overthrow me?'

'No man can overthrow you.'

Shaka looked back at Ralph. 'You hear what they say? Who can come against me?'

'Marius has guns,' Ralph murmured – but quietly. He knew Shaka would not hear it.

A commotion sounded by the kraal gate – raised voices. Shaka tensed; the guards readied their spears. For all Shaka's bravado, perhaps Ralph's words had made him think again.

Dingane came hurrying into the compound, waddling so fast his enormous stomach wobbled like a flummery.

'*Bayete*,' he saluted the king. He gazed at Ralph's wounds. 'What has happened?'

Shaka regarded his brother coolly. 'umRalph went into the forest today.'

At that, even Dingane's inscrutable mask slipped. His eye twitched, and Ralph could almost see the thoughts racing in his brain. Where had Ralph been? What had he seen?

'The forest is dangerous for a man by himself,' Dingane said.

'*Impela*.' Indeed. 'He fought three wild animals,' Shaka said, and Ralph did not correct him. 'A lion, a crocodile and a snake.'

The two brothers' eyes locked. Dingane took a half step back. 'He is lucky to be alive.'

'The three animals devoured one another.'

Ralph lay on the ground and watched, forgotten.

Shaka knows, Ralph thought. *He understood me. So why did he argue with me?*

Did he think Dingane could be brought to heel? Was he hiding his knowledge, to keep Dingane off balance? Or was it that after all the bloodshed and murder that had put him on the throne and kept him there, Shaka at last recoiled from killing his own brother, his last family?

Dingane's cold gaze flitted back to Ralph. 'Did he bring trophies from these beasts? I would like to see them.'

'They drowned.' Ralph's voice came out as a hollow rasp. 'I did not have the chance to skin them.'

'It is easy to be a great hunter when you do not bring back evidence,' Dingane sneered.

'His wounds prove his story,' said Shaka. 'He has no reason to lie.'

Dingane looked between Ralph and Shaka. Again, Ralph saw Shaka's genius for manipulation. He would keep Dingane guessing about what he knew, dropping hints that might mean everything or nothing. This course of action offered Dingane an opportunity – whatever he had done or planned, he could still abandon it without penalty – but if he wanted to press forward with his plans it would also slow him down. He would be paralysed with doubt. What did Shaka really know? Which of his men were truly loyal? How was Shaka obtaining his information?

It was a dangerous strategy.

'I have reviewed my plans for the campaign,' Shaka announced. 'I will go with the army myself.'

Dingane was caught off guard. 'Is that wise?'

'Am I so old that I cannot fight?' Shaka gave his brother a severe look, then burst out laughing. 'My soldiers have become fat and lazy. With their king watching, perhaps they will fight like warriors.'

'I look forward to seeing it.'

'You will go back to the capital.' Shaka gave a grin. 'Someone must keep the *isigodlo* in order.'

In other words: *your place is with the women.*

'I should be at your side,' Dingane protested.

'I know you are always with me, brother. In spirit.'

With a nod, Shaka dismissed Dingane. The prince backed away and marched out of the kraal.

Shaka watched him go, then turned to look down at Ralph, as if he had only just remembered him. Like sun chasing off a rain shower, his face softened into concern.

'We have spoken too long while you are hurt. Bring me the sangoma,' he ordered his guards. 'We must heal his wounds. I will need my most loyal *induna* for the battles ahead.'

You will, Ralph thought, but he was filled with fear. Shaka might think he could keep Dingane in his place, and Ralph had kept Marius away for four years, but if the two men made an alliance . . .

What if the crocodile had not attacked the lion? What if, instead, they had both attacked me?

Ralph felt a sudden, overwhelming urge to flee. The thought shamed him. He tried to ignore it, but it would not leave his mind.

I could not even get myself out of this kraal right now, he told himself. *And Shaka will never let me go while he is at war.*

But it was too late. He had seen the future, and it terrified him. Wheels were turning; events had been set in motion that even Shaka could not control.

If I am to get out of here alive, I must go soon.

TALALA KRAAL

Ann examined her patient with dismay.

'You have been in the wars again,' she exclaimed. 'Look at you! I do not know if I will be able to mend you this time.'

Her patient squirmed. 'We won.'

'I am glad to hear it. But there is no point winning a victory if you hurt yourself so much you cannot fight again.'

'Maphitha hit me on the knuckles,' Harry complained. Ann knew that this was considered cheating. 'Sothobe and I climbed the hill where they couldn't see us. We charged and they ran away.'

Ann half-listened as Harry prattled on, telling her in detail about the battles he had fought that day with his friends. She cleaned out his scrapes and grazes and rubbed a decoction of buffalo thorn leaves onto his bruises to ease the pain. Most of his cuts were already scabbing over, but one needed a bandage. She wondered why she bothered. Tomorrow, he would have new wounds. And again, she would tend them and bind them, and kiss them better. She could not do otherwise.

In the beginning, she had tried to keep him in Ralph's kraal. But the boy was not meant to be penned up. The first day they were there, he found a way to slip out of the gate when her back was turned. She found him halfway down the hillside chasing a cow, just as he had seen the herdboys do.

After that, he went where he chose. Often, he disappeared with the first morning light, when the cattle went out to graze, and did not return until sunset. By the end of their first week living among the Zulus, he had become friends with a group of boys. They tended their cattle, trapped and hunted small game, and roamed the countryside fighting miniature battles. Ann fretted, but she could see it was good for Harry. It was the first time in his life he'd had the company of boys his own age, and he embraced their companionship, drinking it up like a desert plant after a drought. Every day, Ann could see the changes in him. He seemed to grow a foot taller, walking with a confident strut. He glowed with happiness. And if he came home with bruises on his arms and legs, or a cut on his knee, or a black eye, he never complained.

Eight years old, she marvelled. It seemed impossible that the bawling baby she had pulled out of the boat at Port Elizabeth had grown into this strong, opinionated child. At night, when she read him stories from the battered volume of Daniel Defoe that Ralph had rescued from the *Farewell*, he would look into her eyes and tell her seriously: 'When I am grown-up, I will go on adventures.'

'You have already been shipwrecked like Robinson Crusoe.'

'Then I will explore Africa, like Captain Singleton,' he said.

And she believed him.

Of course, she worried about him. Not just about the scrapes and bruises, but about the boy he was becoming. She tried to school him in the things an English child should learn, but she had few resources and Harry was a poor pupil. From memory, she tried to teach him the kings and queens of England, and passages from the Bible, but he got distracted by the least thing – the hornbills that squabbled in the kraal, the lizards that scurried in the thatch – and was constantly slipping off the moment she looked away. She spent hours trying to get him to read, drawing letters in the dirt and getting him to sound them out, but each time they came back to them he seemed to have forgotten what he had learned in their previous lesson.

'Don't you want to be able to read *Robinson Crusoe* for yourself?' she encouraged him.

He looked at her as if she was mad. 'But I know it all already.'

He hadn't seen the inside of a church since they had left Paradise Valley, and Ann did not know his birthday, even if she had kept a calendar.

If he goes back to England, they will think he is a perfect savage, she worried.

But what was England to him? He showed no interest in learning about it: it was no more real for him than the stories from the Bible, and considerably less real than the adventures of Daniel Defoe. Harry was perfectly content living with the Zulus: their country was his country, their ways his ways. Everything in his life was entirely normal and natural to him. And if he noticed that his skin and hair were different from those of his playmates, he never thought it worthy of comment.

This cannot last, Ann thought. *He cannot be what he is not*. But she could not see how things would change.

Perhaps she envied Harry his simple, certain place in the world. For though she lived in Ralph's kraal, and Ralph played the part of the *induna*, Ann had no place in Zulu society. She was not a wife, or a grandmother, and she had no interest in getting married again. Ralph's duties took him away for days or weeks at a time, hunting or at war, or visiting the kraals that Shaka had given him. That left Ann alone with Thabisa.

To Ann, it was like being back at sea on the *Farewell*. She felt that she was useless and always in the way. She did not want the Zulus to wait on her like servants, but when she tried to help with the cooking, Thabisa glowered at her, so she retreated to her hut.

Observing what the other women did, Ann noticed they spent much of their time weaving baskets. Their work was fantastically intricate and decorated with beautiful patterns – diamonds, triangles, whorls – created from palm leaves dyed in a riot of different colours.

Ann had no palm fronds, and she did not dare ask Thabisa, so one day she picked rushes by the stream and left them in the sun. When they were dry, she began to plait them together as she had seen the other women do. The rushes constantly pulled apart, and she could not get them to hold their shape. After hours of labour, all she had to show was a misshapen ball of grass.

Thabisa had come into the kraal, unnoticed, and looked at Ann's handiwork. She had wrinkled her nose.

'I am practising,' Ann said.

Thabisa had knelt beside her. She took a handful of the rushes, pinched them in a star shape and began to wrap them together. In less than ten minutes, she had created a loosely woven bowl.

'I will learn.'

Ann had wished Thabisa would go away. What did she want to prove by humiliating Ann?

But Thabisa did not leave. Instead, she had unpicked her handiwork until the fibres were separated into a sunflower shape. She held it out to Ann.

'Do like this.'

Slowly, so that Ann could see, she wove one of the fronds in between two others. Then she passed it to Ann.

'You try.'

And so Ann had learned to weave. The two women could sit beside each other for hours working on their pieces. Thabisa's were so tightly woven that they could hold gallons of beer or water without leaking a drop; for a long time, Ann's creations would not take the weight of a mealie without falling apart. But eventually her hands learned how to twist the fibres so they held, how to bend the flat fronds to form curves, and how to shape those curves into baskets and bowls. In the same way, the cold silence between the women became a companionable silence; the few words they exchanged became sentences, and finally conversations.

Though there were still many things they did not know about each other.

'When you marry Ralph?' Thabisa asked one day.

Ann laughed, to cover her embarrassment. 'I am not his wife.'

'The boy?'

'He is not Ralph's son.'

Thabisa shot her a disbelieving look. 'Who is father then?'

At last Ann understood her hostility. If Thabisa thought that Ann had arrived as the mother of Ralph's child, his wife or – Ann shuddered at the word – mistress, no wonder she saw her as a rival. Though Ann was happy to be ignorant of what happened in the privacy of Ralph's hut, she could draw her own conclusions from the fact that Thabisa had not borne a child in four years of marriage to Ralph. She could see how much it hurt Thabisa, both her pride as a wife and her maternal instincts. If Thabisa thought Ann had mothered a son for Ralph, that would make Ann both a rebuke and a threat.

So Ann told Thabisa her story. Thabisa listened in silence, the only sound was the scratch and rustle of her fingers weaving the fibres of the basket she was making. She barely looked at it, but kept her gaze focused on Ann until her tale was complete.

Was there a hint of sympathy in her eyes? Thabisa's face, schooled by years as a slave in the *isigodlo*, was impossible to read.

But Ann thought she detected a slight softening in the young woman's attitude, perhaps an understanding.

It was as close as she had come to friendship in months. She did not want to let the feeling go.

'How did you learn such good English?' she asked. Surely Ralph could not have taught her so much in the few months he had been there before she arrived.

'In the place you call Nativity Bay,' Thabisa said. 'From white people.'

Her hands had stopped working on the basket. She gazed into the distance as she told the story she had told Ralph: growing up with the white household who lived at Nativity Bay, the attack, and her capture by the Zulus. Ann listened, rapt, thinking of the ruined house she had discovered in the woods, and the five graves in the clearing. At last she could put names to them – Gert, Susan, Mary, Peter, Rachel – and imagine the life they had lived there. It must have been idyllic – until it ended in fire and slaughter.

'What was the name of the family?'

Thabisa didn't understand. Ann tried again. 'I am Ann Waite. Ralph is Ralph Courtney.'

'Courtney,' Thabisa repeated.

'Yes.' Ann was pleased she understood. 'But what was the family who lived in Nativity Bay?'

'Courtney.'

'Not Ralph's name. Gert and Susan and their children. The people in the house.'

'Courtney.' Thabisa gave Ann a look as if she were the dullest child in the schoolroom, so sharp that Ann felt a fool for not having understood sooner. Except that it was impossible.

'Their name was Courtney?'

'Yes.'

It was so incredible Ann did not want to believe it. And yet, deep in her heart, she could feel it must be true. It explained so much. That was how Ralph had known the hidden entrance to Nativity Bay – not because he had a map, but because the people who settled it were his family.

Why had he never told her? What else had he kept from her?

A horrible thought began to grow in her mind.

'Did Ralph ever come there?'

Thabisa shook her head. 'No. Not Ralph.'

'Thank God,' Ann breathed.

She had few illusions about Ralph. He was a dangerous man who had lived a violent life. But if he had been responsible for those graves at Nativity Bay – the deaths of an innocent family – she could not have stayed there another minute. She would have walked out of his kraal, all the way back to Cape Town if she had to.

She realised Thabisa was staring at her with a crooked gaze. 'What?'

'You love Ralph.'

The words came as a shock. In Thabisa's flat voice, Ann was not even sure if it was a question or an accusation.

'No,' Ann protested. The outrage in her voice was genuine. The thought appalled her. There had been those few nights when she had shared his bed, true, but they were a terrible lapse of judgement she preferred not to dwell on. 'Why would you think such a thing?'

She thought Thabisa would answer. But either she did not know the words, or she decided not to say them. She gazed at Ann, with that same knowing look as if Ann was the most dunderheaded person she had ever met.

Ann pulled herself to her feet. The brief moment of confidence between them had gone.

'I do not know what you may think . . .' She sounded prim as a schoolmarm – she knew it – but she could not change the way the words came out. '. . . but the sole reason I am here is because I have nowhere else to go.'

That was the bitter truth. There were just two ports within a thousand miles that she could leave by: the Portuguese settlement at Lourenço Marques to the north, and Nativity Bay to the south. The way north was blocked by a faction of the Ndwandwes who had escaped Shaka's war and made a new home: it would be beyond perilous to try and make her escape that way. But Marius controlled Nativity Bay, and she feared what would happen if she put herself and Harry in his power again.

And even if I managed to get aboard a ship, what then? She had no money, no family and no prospects. She might persuade a kind-hearted captain to take her as far as Port Elizabeth or Cape Town, but how many truly kind-hearted captains plied their trade in these waters? What might they ask in return? And even if she could trust them, if they kept their word and deposited her on the beach at Port Elizabeth, where could she go from there? She would be in exactly the same position as she had been when she had walked into the *winkel* all those years ago.

'Mother!' Harry came tearing up the hill, breaking into her thoughts. 'Uncle Ralph is back.'

Ann ran to the gate. Thabisa put aside her basketwork and ran after her. They both watched as Ralph climbed the path towards the kraal, resplendent in his headdress of crane feathers. Twenty bearers came behind with his luggage, and behind them, boys driving dozens of cattle.

'They have a victory,' said Thabisa.

Ann, whose eyes were on Ralph, was not so sure. The headdress could not hide the long pink-white scar that ran across the top of his head; and he seemed to walk more slowly than she remembered.

Ralph entered the kraal, greeting Thabisa with the respect that was due to her as his wife and setting his rifle against the pallisade.

'What has happened to you?' Ann asked. By now, she knew every line and scar on Ralph's body – more than a few of them she had sewn up herself. The mass of scar tissue on his arm was new, as was the weal across his scalp. 'Was the fighting so terrible?'

Ralph took the bowl of beer Thabisa presented to him and gulped it down. 'The fighting was brutal. But that was not the worst of it.'

He left the servants to attend to the cattle and the baggage and went into his hut. Thabisa came in and took down his sleeping mat, headrest and spoon. Like any Zulu wife, she had hung them on the wall while he was away. Ralph lay down on the mat, while Thabisa and Ann squatted opposite on the women's side.

'Was it a victory?' Thabisa asked.

'Shaka calls it a victory.' Ralph frowned, marshalling his thoughts. 'It does not feel like one.'

The Zulu army had advanced in strength across the Mzimkhulu River, into Mpondo territory. They found many kraals, and plenty of cattle – but the kraals were deserted, and the cattle scrawny and underfed.

'These do not belong to the Mpondo king,' Hamu had said. 'He lets the birds peck for grains from the chaff, while the ripe corn is gathered safely in his storehouse.'

As they went deeper into Mpondo country, the army grew more restive. Faku, the Mpondo king, would not meet them in open battle. Instead, he tormented them. The long Zulu column, moving at the pace of its cattle train, made an easy target for an ambush. At any moment, a volley of Mpondo spears might be launched out of the forest. They painted their spears black on one side, white on the other, and smeared poison from the *isiFice* tree on the tips. The Zulus quickly grew to fear the sounds: the humming of the spears in the air, the thud as they struck flesh, and then the screaming. Each time, the Zulus would charge into the bush, but the Mpondos would have melted away.

The losses did not concern Shaka.

'They are like flies stinging the buffalo,' he said, when the *indunas* raised it at a council. He turned to Ralph. 'The smoke from your firesticks will drive them away.'

Ralph had trained a small corps of riflemen, equipped with the guns he had taken from Marius at Nativity Bay. In peacetime, the gunmen hunted for him, and in times of war they fought under his command. Each man had become a skilled marksman, but their real strength remained their ability to shock. Against people who had never faced guns, the thunder of gunpowder did more damage than the most accurate bullet. Many times, Ralph's men had broken the enemy's will so that Shaka's spearmen could charge in and finish them.

Yet they did not have the same effect against the Mpondos. Occasionally, one of his riflemen might hit a man who dared to show himself, but the roaring of the rifles did nothing to deter their attacks. The Mpondos kept their discipline and continued to harass the column.

One day, they captured a Mpondo warrior alive. Ralph managed to speak to him before Shaka had him executed.

'Why do you not run from the firesticks?' he wanted to know.

The man had bared his teeth in defiance. 'You think we are cowards?'

'I have seen brave men terrified by them.'

'We are Mpondo. We are not afraid of the white man's magic.'

His words intrigued Ralph. 'Have you seen white men before? The men from the north?'

They were a long way from Nativity Bay, but it was possible that Marius and his companions had hunted this far south.

'Not from the north. The men in red skins, across the river.'

Ralph was sure he must have misunderstood.

'You mean the British?'

'The men with firesticks who live in a stone kraal.'

'You have fought these people?'

'Sometimes, they cross the river.'

The northern frontier of Cape Colony was the Fish River, where the British maintained a garrison. Ralph had always known that if you travelled south far enough from Shaka's kingdom you ought to reach the frontier, but he did not know how far it was. The area between had not been mapped.

'Does the Mpondo kingdom stretch to the river?' The prisoner nodded. 'Is there a road?'

'Not for the enemies of King Faku.'

'But if a man was a friend, and brought gifts for the king?'

'Yes.'

Ralph had stored the information away for the future. At that moment, he was more worried about Shaka than the enemy. The meeting he had witnessed the day he fought the lion preyed on his mind constantly. He kept close to the king, watching every man who came within ten feet of him. At night, he slept nearby with a loaded gun at his side.

Whether Shaka's change of plans had thrown off the conspirators, or if Dingane had been frightened away, no one made an attempt on Shaka's life. After a month on campaign, the Mpondo king had sent an ambassador with a tribute of cattle, and the offer of peace.

'You see?' Shaka had exulted, 'All the *amaLala* kings are dust beneath King Shaka's feet.'

But afterwards, when Hamu and Ralph were alone, Hamu said: 'Faku will *konza* to Shaka, pay him homage and call him his lord. But after Shaka has gone away, Faku will laugh, and say that Shaka is like a father who sells his daughter for one old goat.'

Ralph had pointed to the herd of cows they had accumulated from their raids.

'We have done better than a goat. There must be ten thousand head of cattle there.'

'They will keep the *indunas* content for a little while. But soon they will be hungry again.'

Ralph had not mentioned to Hamu what he had witnessed in the forest between Dingane and Marius.

'Do the *indunas* speak against Shaka?'

'Of course not. They do not wish to die. But what is in their hearts . . .'

Ralph gave his friend a sharp look. 'What is in your heart?'

'To sit in my kraal with my wives, my children and my cattle,' said Hamu. 'The same as every man.' But though he smiled as he said it, his eyes were grim.

'Is Shaka in danger?'

An alliance between Dingane and Marius was worrying enough. If the *indunas* turned on Shaka, nothing could save him. And though Ralph might talk and dress and act like a Zulu, he had no illusions how the others saw him. He was Shaka's creature. If the king died, Ralph would not live five minutes.

'Shaka is the king.'

Ralph gripped Hamu's arm. 'If anything is going to happen, you will tell me?'

'If a man knows where the spear will strike, he does not stand there,' said Hamu. 'It is what he does not know that he must fear.'

Ralph had pondered those words on the march back to the Thukela. Shaka might have proclaimed the campaign a victory, but you could see in the army's slumped shoulders and scowling faces that they did not believe it. Fighting long campaigns, year after year for diminishing gains, had exhausted their appetite for war. For the young men, it meant other hardships, too. They entered their regiments at the age of sixteen and were not allowed to marry until they had completed their service. In previous times, that had been no more than a year or two, but under Shaka it had stretched to the best part of a decade. Ralph hoped that when they returned, Shaka would dismiss the *impi* and give the young regiments permission to marry. Men who were enjoying the delights of their new brides would have no appetite for war and plotting.

Now, back in his hut, Ralph turned to Thabisa.

'I need you to go out among our villages and find me a hundred or so strong men to serve as porters.'

She pouted. 'You have just come back.'

'And now I need porters.'

Ralph felt a sudden, overwhelming weariness. After weeks on campaign with only the company of his fellow soldiers, having to justify himself to Thabisa seemed a ridiculous imposition. Irrationally, it enraged him.

'Just do what I tell you,' he said brusquely.

Thabisa stared at him, eyes smouldering.

'Go,' he said. 'You will not come to my hut tonight.'

Thabisa turned her head sharply away and ducked out of the hut. Ann started to follow.

'Wait,' said Ralph.

'What?' He could see she was angry. 'Why should I listen to you when you are so cruel to your own wife?'

'I am leaving here.' The words tumbled out in a rush. 'If I sounded harsh, it is because I did not want to say it to Thabisa now.'

Ann paused by the doorway. 'Where will you go?'

'To Cape Province. There is a way through Mpondo territory that leads to the frontier.'

'Is it safe? Will Shaka let you go?'

'We are at peace with the Mpondos for now, and King Faku will not want to risk war again so quickly. As for Shaka . . .' Ralph poked the embers of the fire. 'I will tell him I am coming back.'

'You do not intend to return?'

He shook his head. 'It is not safe for me here – or you.'

That made her laugh, though it was not a happy sound.

'Was I ever? Safe, I mean?'

'It is different, now. I saw Marius.' Briefly, he described what he had seen in the woods.

Ann shuddered to think of Marius. 'But he has so few men, and you are óne of the mightiest *indunas* in Zululand. What could he do against you, let alone King Shaka?'

'A great mischief, I fear.'

A disaffected prince and a penniless Dutchman should be nothing more than pests against the full might of the Zulu empire, flies buzzing around a bull's tail. And yet . . . Ralph struggled to find words to make her understand the dread in the pit of his stomach, but he could feel it, the way a man knows when a curse lies on him.

Perhaps I have become more a Zulu than I credit.

'Dingane is Shaka's weakness. He gets away with things a lesser man would have his neck broken for. However many times he steps into the noose, Shaka will not pull it tight. And Marius is as cunning as the devil. Between them, there is no telling what they could do. As for Jobe, any cause that can unite him with Marius must be hard to resist.'

He plucked an ostrich feather from his headband and twirled it between his fingers. 'There is a strange mood in the court. Even Hamu is oblique and will not give me straight answers.'

Ann shuffled back and sat down on the women's side, tucking in her legs so they kept away from Ralph's. Even after four years, she took great care not to touch him. It would be inappropriate; he was a married man, and she did not want to give him any cause to think she might still harbour feelings for him.

'If Shaka is in danger, should you not be with him?'

'This is a matter for the Zulus. If it came to a civil war, I would be caught between two fires.' His hand strayed to the scar on his cheek. 'I have been burned enough. And I would not wish to see any harm come to you, or the boy.'

'Or to your pile of ivory.'

He gave a weary sigh that made Ann feel she had said something unworthy. 'I will leave with my fortune. But that is not *why* I am leaving.'

'Will you take Thabisa?'

Ralph shook his head. 'She deserves a better husband. A man who can give her the station she deserves. Hamu will help her.'

Abruptly, Ralph threw the feather into the fire. 'But what will you do? Would you come back with me to England?'

'As what? As your concubine?'

'If that was what you wanted.' Ralph smiled. 'Or in a more regular state, if you preferred.'

He said it so casually, it took Ann a moment to realise he was proposing to her. It took her so much by surprise, she could not think what to say.

'You are married,' she objected.

'Not according to the laws of England.'

'In the sight of God.'

He laughed. 'You think a priest would consider what I have with Thabisa a marriage?'

'I did not say in the eyes of the Church. I said God.'

'I doubt our God interests Himself much in the affairs of the Zulus. Nor they in Him.'

In the dim firelight, Ralph's face glowed like amber. Ann knew she should find him hideous, with the new cut across his scalp added to the old mesh of scars on his cheek and those firm, unyielding eyes. Yet he looked handsome, in a strange and savage way.

She shook away the thought. 'Harry and I will come with you as far as Port Elizabeth.' They could not stay alone in Zululand; and though she was too proud to ask, she knew Ralph would not let her starve. He would use some of his store of ivory to give her the money she needed to make a new life. 'Then we can each follow our own destinies, and this strange acquaintanceship we have had will be gone from our lives like a dark dream.'

They faced each other across the domed hut. The fire crackled; Ann could hear the beat of her heart throbbing in her ears. She had the feeling of an enormous gravity pulling her towards Ralph, tugging her across the thin line of polished earth that divided man from woman in the Zulu sphere.

Ralph seemed to feel it, too. His eyes were so full of desire that Ann could hardly bear to look at him. He raised his hand and reached towards her, but then, suddenly he mastered himself. The hand dropped to his side.

'As you wish,' he said. His eyes glowed with firelight, while the edges of his mouth turned up in that devil-may-care smile that had become so familiar. 'If you can stand my presence that long, we will leave within the week.'

The next day, Ralph made the journey to Shaka's capital. This, too, had changed: it was not the city that Ralph and his companions had entered in their rags after the wreck of the *Farewell*. That city, KwaBulawayo, no longer existed.

A Zulu capital, Ralph had discovered, was impermanent. It survived on the king's whim. If the needs of government or strategy or cattle grazing demanded it, he would not hesitate to move the entire settlement elsewhere. When KwaBulawayo no longer served his needs, Shaka had it burned to the ground and moved his court – the regiments, the *indunas*, the *isigodlo* and of course the cattle – to another place. He had established his new capital in rolling hills behind the mouth of the Thukela, no more than fifty miles north of Nativity Bay. He called it KwaDukuza.

In form, it was the same as the old capital. Fences made two concentric circles, the inner for the cattle and the outer for the people. Ralph had counted over fifteen hundred huts, plus more in the upper quadrant, where tightly woven fences eight feet high screened off the *isigodlo*. It was an exact duplicate of KwaBulawayo, so that anyone who had known the old city could have found their way unerringly to the same place in the KwaDukuza.

It is like me, Ralph thought. *The same, but changed.*

He had come to see Shaka in private. To his surprise, he found the city busy: the whole army had been assembled in the great enclosure. The men were still weary from the campaign and the march back from Mpondo territory, but they were in better spirits than Ralph had seen them for weeks. The prospect of demobilisation, a chance to return to families and sweethearts, had put them in happy spirits. Beer had been passed around and there was singing, and excited chatter.

Ralph went to the head of the kraal and found Hamu among the other *indunas*.

'What is happening? Why is the army here?'

'Because the king commands it.' Ralph saw tension around his eyes. *He does not know either.* 'The red ox bellowed in the night.'

Ralph knew better than to ask what that might mean. Depending on your point of view, it meant either that the ancestors had spoken – or whatever Shaka wanted it to mean.

As usual, the king was in no hurry to explain himself. The army waited for hours in the hot sun. The celebratory mood dulled to an anxious silence. The *indunas* grew restless.

At last Shaka appeared, followed by Dingane. The king had put on his full battledress: his dark skin gleamed like oiled iron, while his headdress sprouted so many feathers he seemed to be transformed into a giant bird of prey.

The *indunas* squatted down and shouted out the salute: '*Bayete, Nkosi!*'

Shaka acted as if he had not noticed. He threw a curt, imperious glance around the assembled men.

'I told you to gather my army,' he said to Dingane, loud enough that everyone could hear. 'All I see here are dogs and old women.'

A chill went through Ralph. He had seen Shaka in this mood in the past. He wanted to melt away to the back of the crowd, but instead, he was trapped at the front, where he could feel the heat of Shaka's anger on his face.

'I heard the bellow of an ox,' the king announced. 'My ancestors spoke to me, Senzangakhona and Jama and Zulu himself. They said my *impi* would rather eat beef and grow fat than let their lips go red from drinking the blood of our enemies.'

He tipped back his head. 'Gather your spears and bring out the shields from the storehouse. Arm yourselves, and march to the country of the Balule.'

Murmurs and groans sounded from the army.

'Where is Balule?' Ralph whispered to Hamu.

'North.'

'Far?'

'Very far.'

One of the *indunas*, a man called Umsega, stepped forward. 'Why are we being sent away, *Nkosi*? The men should be taking wives and building their own kraals.'

It took a brave man to challenge the king in this mood, but Umsega feared nothing. Squat and strong, he had fought in every battle Ralph had witnessed, usually leading the regiment at the centre of the line. Like many warriors, he wore a necklace strung with a carved piece of wood for each man he had killed in battle. It covered his broad chest almost to his belly button. If any man had earned the right to question the king, it was Umsega.

Shaka nodded his head. Without further prompting, two guards rushed forward, and grabbed Umsega's arms. Umsega's face was grey, but the discipline of a lifetime did not break. Neither fighting nor faltering, he let the guards march him away. Ralph marvelled at his courage.

Every man gathered there knew where Umsega would be taken: to the knoll outside the city, where a thorn tree grew and the ground was black with blood.

Did he know what would happen when he spoke? Ralph wondered. Was it suicide, or a terrible misjudgement? Ralph had spent years among the Zulus, and yet sometimes he felt he had but a rudimentary understanding of the complexities of their civilisation, let alone the intricacies of their hearts.

The crowd were impassive. Umsega had been a popular and famous champion, but no one breathed a murmur against his fate. Perhaps they knew that any sign of dissent would see them follow him to the execution place. Or perhaps months of such moments, so many victims, had dulled their horror of it.

'Are there any more cowards in my *impi*?' Shaka demanded.

His gaze moved around the enclosure. To every one of the thousands of men standing there, it felt as if the king's eyes rested on him and him alone. Challenging, searching, threatening.

Shaka turned his attention to the *indunas*. They were brave men who bore the scars of many battles, but they cast their eyes down like the soldiers.

'You,' said Shaka.

The king's hand was extended, and for a terrible moment Ralph thought it was pointing at him. But the power and malice of Shaka's eyes was turned to Hamu.

Ralph stiffened: *what had his friend done?* On the long, frustrating, bloodthirsty campaign against the Mpondos, he had not once seen Hamu anything less than loyal. Every man in every *impi* knew that Hamu was the king's man to his core.

Hamu stepped out. If he felt any fear, he kept it hidden deep inside. He stood as straight as the shaft of his spear, his head held proudly on his long neck, then he knelt before Shaka.

'You led the army south against King Faku,' Shaka reminded him.

'We captured many cattle.'

'But your spears remained dry.' Shaka's voice dripped contempt. 'Who told you to come back so soon?'

Hamu could have answered that it was Shaka who had given the command. But those would have been the last words he spoke. He bowed his head and remained silent.

'You will lead the *impi* north. Sweep up all the rubbish and take them with you, even old men with bad knees. That is the army you deserve.'

Hamu's head slumped. It was sorrowful to watch, this proud and loyal captain being humiliated.

'*Yebo, baba.*'

Shaka turned. 'And you, my brother, you will go with the *impi*.'

Dingane, who had been gazing nonchalantly at the crowd, suddenly jerked to attention.

'Me?'

'If any man forgets the name of his king, you will remind him.'

Perhaps that is what this is about, Ralph thought. *Shaka has not forgotten what I saw in the forest. He wants his brother away.* It was a good idea, but it filled Ralph with dread. *His distrust is pushing the army to breaking point. If they turn against him . . .*

He shook off the thought. If Shaka was laying up trouble for the future, Ralph would be gone before it manifested.

Shaka continued his speech. It was his usual mesmerising performance, his voice rising from the softest whisper to a bellowing roar; he stamped his feet, gyrated his body and jerked his head about, so that no man knew where his gaze would fall next. Sometimes he seemed so angry, Ralph feared he would drag a man from the crowd and cut his throat. At other times, he shrank into a melancholy that had his warriors on the verge of tears.

At last, with a furious barrage of insults, Shaka let silence descend. He raised his spear and held it out, pointing down the valley. The message was clear. The army would leave at once.

'*Yebo, baba,*' Hamu murmured humbly.

He shuffled back on his knees until the crowd swallowed him. Then he stood and began walking away. His men fell in behind him. They rolled up their shields and followed their general towards the gate. It seemed as if the whole army was being punished.

Ralph waited until the enclosure was empty, then he went to the gate to the palace quarters. A part of him said he should stay away, that it was dangerous to approach Shaka in this mood, but urgency overrode his caution. He had to leave the Zulu kingdom as soon as possible.

He found Shaka alone, hunched on his wooden chair, staring at the fire. The flames cast deep shadows, so that the lines on his face seemed almost bottomless, and there was no longer the overwhelming strength in his gaze that Ralph remembered from their first meeting. The fury that had possessed the king in front of the army had drained away.

'I have come to ask permission to go back to my people,' Ralph said.

This was the first time that Ralph had spoken of this plan to the king, but Shaka nodded as if he had expected it.

'You will go across the water?'

'First across the land, then the water.'

'To umGeorge?'

'Yes.'

That was a lie. Ralph had no intention of seeing King George – nor any of his representatives. There was a warrant for his arrest in Cape Town, and plenty of zealous Crown servants ready to enforce it. Even passing through on a ship carried risks.

Fewer risks than staying with Shaka.

Ralph could not tear his eyes away from the play of the fire across the leopard-skin headband Shaka was wearing; somehow the flames seemed to make it writhe like a snake.

'Tell umGeorge he must send men. Many men, with firesticks. Say King Shaka will send him ivory for this.'

'Of course.'

Ralph considered what would happen if he did what Shaka asked. He imagined the colonial government's reaction to a stranger arriving at Cape Town castle, demanding they send men to a black king in a distant country. Or – if by some miracle they agreed – the strange sight of redcoats parading in the cattle enclosure of KwaDukuza, marching in close order and exercising their guns. It seemed ridiculous, laughable; no intelligent man could imagine it ever happening.

But not so long ago, it would have been impossible to imagine those redcoats marching through Bombay or Madras or Cape Town. If there was profit to be made, they would come in the end. Even if they arrived with modest intentions, they would soon realise their power. And when a man had power, however noble his motives, eventually he would use it.

The thought of it filled Ralph with dread. The Zulus were not saints. They were violent and capricious, yes, but no more or less than any other race. And they were also generous and exuberant, and in love with their land. He would not want that crushed under a British regiment's boots.

'You do not need umGeorge's men,' he told Shaka. 'You have the finest regiments in the world. Who can stand against you?'

It was a sentiment he had heard Shaka repeat many times when addressing his troops. Yet now Shaka bowed his head; the lines on his face stretched deeper.

'Who will stand with me?' he murmured. There was an emotion in his voice that Ralph had not heard in all the years he had known Shaka, so unprecedented that he needed a moment to identify it. *Fear.* 'My men are weak as grass, while the *indunas* whisper against me. Even my own blood . . .'

Ralph knew what he was thinking. 'You were wise to send Dingane away.'

Shaka looked him in the eye. 'You are the one soul left in my life who I can trust now.'

That is because I will be nowhere near you.

Shaka leaned forward. 'I wish I could have had you as my son.'

There had been times, in the past years, when Ralph had thought that he must be the loneliest man in Zululand. Now he realised that he had been wrong. Shaka had forged himself a crown using his iron will and ruthless ambition, but at a terrible cost. No wife, no children, no parents; only a half-brother whom he could not trust, and the constant terror of being stabbed in the back.

I am not the son he always wanted because he cares for me, Ralph thought. *I am that son because I am the one man in this kingdom who does not threaten his throne.*

Shaka had lost faith with his people. That was why he wanted Ralph to bring foreign soldiers. It was his new hope for the survival of his kingdom.

'Like a son, I will return,' Ralph lied. He had to get away, before Shaka's mood changed and he insisted Ralph stayed with him. 'When I do, I will bring a whole regiment of the King's dragoons.'

Shaka nodded. He did not offer an embrace or warm words; he waved his hand, indicating Ralph was dismissed.

Ralph bowed and retreated. He felt a shiver of foreboding, but he told himself it was nonsense. Shaka had been good to Ralph, and it felt wrong to deceive him, but now he had his own path to follow.

'Wait.'

As Ralph was about to pass through the door, Shaka stood. He took three paces towards Ralph and lowered his voice as if he were about to impart some fearful secret.

'I have heard umGeorge has medicine that can turn white hair black.'

Ralph did not know what Shaka meant. 'Medicine?'

Shaka mimed rubbing ointment in his hair.

'Macassar oil?'

Shaka nodded. 'You can bring this?'

'Yes.' It was easier than bringing a regiment of dragoons. 'Of course, it is not cheap.'

'I will give you ivory to trade,' Shaka promised. 'Four tusks.'

Ralph marvelled at this stroke of luck. *If I had known, I would have bought up the supply from every barber in Cape Town and made myself a fortune years ago.*

'I will bring a boatload of it,' he promised.

It was not the biggest lie he had told in his life – not even the biggest lie that night. He had learned, long ago, that honesty was an extravagance that few could afford. Deceit was the way of the world, no cause for guilt. And yet this small untruth, promising an insecure man a tonic for his greying hair, made him feel ashamed.

'I will be back in six months,' he said.

Almost certainly, he would never cross paths with Shaka again, but chance was a strange mistress. There were any number of people in the world that he had thought gone from his life whom he had encountered months or years later. Who was to say that some twist of fate would not bring him back to Shaka one day?

With a final bow, Ralph backed out of the hut.

Ralph wanted to depart at once, but that proved optimistic. The new war that Shaka had declared made porters hard to find. Most of the men had gone away, and the few that remained were fearful they would be branded as cowards if they drew attention to themselves. It took Ralph the best part of a month to find the bearers he needed. Then the ivory he had patiently accumulated had to be dug out of storage and parcelled into loads they could carry. Supplies had to be prepared for the bearers – cows had to be slaughtered and the meat hung to dry; dried mealies had to be taken from the stores and pounded into meal. Every day, Ralph chafed at the delay.

Thabisa sat by her hut and watched sullenly. Ralph had kept up the lie that he meant to come back to her – he was never sure how much he told her might make its way to Shaka – but he doubted she was fooled. She saw how thorough his organisation was, how completely he had packed up his life. She also saw that Ann was going with him, and drew her own conclusions.

I have not treated you as you deserved – as the wife of a great induna, Ralph thought. The knowledge was like a splinter digging into his conscience. *But what else could I have done?*

Finally, everything was ready. Ralph stood by the gate of his kraal, watching the sun set, and surveyed the landscape for the last time. The hills with their stands of trees, giant *umzimbeet* with their wide-spreading crowns, wild plums and tall mahoganies; the folds of the hills and the thin line of the track that led to KwaDukuza. The Zulu kraals like circles printed on the landscape.

It feels like leaving home.

The idea surprised him. He had never expected to stay, but he had also not given much thought to leaving. He had not counted the days and months as they passed, yet now, when he added them up, he realised he had lived here longer than anywhere else in his life.

'Will you miss us?' Thabisa asked. Ralph had not heard her come up beside him.

'I will. Until I return,' he added hastily.

'And me?'

'You will manage the kraal while I am gone.' He should have spoken of this much sooner to Thabisa, but she had been avoiding him, and he had put it off. 'You know the journey will be long. I will travel through dangerous country. Perhaps I will not come back. If I do not, after a year you should consider yourself free. My kraal and all my cattle will belong to you.'

For a woman who had grown up as a slave, it was an extraordinary change of fortune. Thabisa's smoky eyes gazed at him, unmoved.

'You are still young,' Ralph said. 'You can find a man who will make you his great wife and give you children. You will be a proper *umfazi*.' *All the things I could not give you.*

Thabisa turned away. Frustration welled in Ralph.

I only want you to be happy, he thought. But he could not say it.

The cattle were being brought in, and the purple haze of dusk filled the valley. In the distance, Ralph heard the yelp of a jackal, and in his imagination it became the cry of a seagull calling him back to the sea.

'Who are they?' Thabisa asked.

Ralph looked where she was pointing, down the hill to the earthen road that ran not far from the kraal. It ought to be empty: Zulus did not like to travel at night. Yet dust was rising from it as two dozen warriors tramped southwards.

Ralph felt a strange foreboding. The army should be away on campaign for months – and these did not look like returning soldiers. They trudged slowly, no order or discipline. No one sang.

He ran out of the kraal and down to meet them. The leader, an *induna* with many beads and brass rings around his arms, raised his weary head to greet him.

'Hamu?' Ralph said in shock. 'I thought you were away on campaign?'

'I came back.'

Hamu stepped out of the road, letting his men march by. In the dusk, Ralph could see his friend had changed. There was a stoop in his proud bearing. His face had grown gaunt, his body hunched.

'Has the army returned?'

'Only a few. The rest are still in the north.'

'Was it a victory?'

The slump of Hamu's shoulders gave the answer. 'I have come to tell King Shaka.'

'You know what that means?'

Even at the best of times, Shaka was not tolerant of generals who suffered defeats. In the king's present mood, there could be no doubt as to Hamu's fate.

'I will do what must be done.'

'This is Shaka's fault,' Ralph said. 'He should never have sent the army so far, so soon after the last campaign.'

Normally, the army might undertake one such campaign every two or three years. To send them to another war hard on the heels of the first, at the opposite end of the kingdom and without time to tend their wounds or recover their strength or see their families: it was pure cruelty, an exercise in power.

The injustice of it sparked a rage in Ralph's heart. 'You should not suffer for his mistake. Come away with me.'

'I cannot.'

Ralph would not have believed that Hamu could face his own destruction so calmly – except that he had seen many examples of the Zulus' extraordinary stoicism over the years. To show fear in the face of the king was worse than death.

Ralph knew he would not dissuade him. Hamu's course was set. Ralph gripped his friend's arm, so that the thick brass rings that both men wore chimed together. He wanted the *induna* to know how much his friendship meant, how much Ralph felt for him. But he did not have the words.

'*Sala kahle*,' he said: Stay well.

The normal response would be *hamba kahle* – go well – but Hamu did not say that. He stepped back.

'You remember the day we met?' His voice softened. 'The sea cow charged at you but you did not flee. You stood your ground and faced it. I knew at that moment what sort of man you were.'

Ralph grinned at the memory. 'I would not have survived it without your spear.'

Hamu nodded. A smile flickered on the edge of his mouth, like a ray of sunlight escaping from storm clouds. Then he was grave again.

'The next time the beast charges, you should run.'

Hamu's words unsettled Ralph. All through the night, and the next morning as they made their final preparations, he counted the passing hours, wondering how long Hamu had to live. He considered going to KwaDukuza to beg Shaka for Hamu's life, but he dismissed the idea. It would humiliate Hamu, and change nothing. In Shaka's eyes, a defeat had to be punished.

When Ralph's column assembled, it amounted to nearly two hundred people. He went to his ammunition store and chose four well-oiled rifles, with powder and shot for hunting when the food stores ran out.

'You know I would not run,' he said, to no one in particular. He hoisted down an extra cask of powder. 'But I will be ready.'

'When are we going to go?' demanded a small voice.

Ralph saw Harry eyeing up the guns. The boy lifted one of them and slung it over his shoulder, as he had seen Ralph do. The weapon was bigger than he was, but Harry stood straight and proud as a colour sergeant.

'Put that with my baggage,' Ralph told him. 'And do not let your mother see you.'

For Ralph, teaching the boy to handle a gun was merely sensible, but he knew Ann hated it. As Harry grew older, her tone became sterner and less indulgent. Harry playing at soldiers, or fighting with the other boys, or sneaking into the weapons store: they always ended with her dragging him away, berating him furiously. Though that never stopped him from doing it again.

The sun shone, the Zulu porters sang, and everyone was in high spirits as they set out. The column stretched a quarter of a mile, the full measure of the fortune they carried. The only person who did not smile was Ralph. He walked at the front, frowning in thought.

'Are you missing Thabisa?' Ann asked. She had come up beside him, while Harry slipped back to terrorise the cows.

'She is better off where she is.'

The words came out sounding harsh. Without another word, Ann dropped back, leaving him alone again.

He had not wanted Ann to think him sentimental or feeble, but now she must think him heartless. He walked on quickly until he had left the column some distance behind him. Ahead, a line of trees marked the ridge where the land sloped down into the broad Thukela valley, where the muddy river would be winding towards the sea. A herd of *nhlegane*, tiny deer, no bigger than hares, grazed on the lush green grass.

When I get back to England, I will find some Devon girl with ten thousand a year and no knowledge of who I have been, he promised himself. Ann, Thabisa, Harry: he would leave them behind and forget them. It would be a new beginning.

A dark shape plummeted from the sky. The herd of *nhlegane* scattered, but not all escaped. The eagle climbed back into the sky, clutching one of the animals in its talons. Ralph heard the creature shrieking until the grip of the bird's claws broke its neck.

If I were a Zulu, I would think that was a terrible omen.

He chuckled, and pretended not to notice the unease that had crept into his bones.

He waited to let the rest of the caravan catch up. The river was running high, and he wanted to supervise the crossing to make sure that nothing was lost. It would be a long trek to Port Elizabeth, and he had to accept there would be some wastage. But each tusk, every head of cattle, represented a battle he had fought, a man he had killed, a mile he had walked. He would fight with all his strength to keep his fortune intact.

At the back of the convoy, he noticed a commotion. Had one of the cows escaped? Someone was running up the line, barging porters and herdboys out of the way.

Thabisa.

Her short braids were swinging as she ran. Did she want to come to England with him, after all? But that would not explain the urgency. Her body was streaked with sweat and dust, her chest heaving from the effort. She must have run all the way from the kraal.

A knot began to tighten in his stomach.

Thabisa halted in front of him, bent double with cramp, drawing deep breaths before she could speak.

'Shaka is dead. They have killed him.'

Ralph stared at her as if she had announced that the sun had fallen out of the sky. He did not want to believe it.

'How do you know?'

Rumours always outpaced the truth. Perhaps Shaka had only been wounded.

'I could go to Shaka,' he said uncertainly. The news had already spread along the column. Some of the porters threw down their loads and ran off at once; others squatted down, wailing and tearing at their hair. 'I cured him before. Maybe I could save him again.'

'He is dead,' said Thabisa more emphatically, looking as if she wanted to shake sense into him. 'Now they kill you.'

'Who?'

But he knew who 'they' were. The three men he had seen conspiring in the forest: Marius, Jobe and Dingane. Whoever had wielded the weapon, it would have been their hands guiding it.

I warned you, Ralph raged silently. *Why didn't you listen to me?*

But Shaka *had* listened. He had sent Dingane away on campaign. A new and terrible thought began to grow in Ralph's mind. Why had Hamu returned so early, in defiance of his orders? What if he had brought Dingane with him?

Is there no one I can trust?

By sending his army away, Shaka had played into his enemies' hands. A few cut-throats from Nativity Bay, armed with guns, could easily secure the new king's power. Dingane would buy their loyalty cheaply: ivory, trading concessions, land. Only later would he find out what it had really cost him.

Marius's words, their first night in KwaBulawayo: *What if we became kings here ourselves? Overthrow this Shaka, take his kingdom and live like lords.*

Now he had done it.

'What is happening?' Ann had arrived at his side, clutching Harry's hand. She had not heard the news, but she could see it was something terrible.

'They killed Shaka.'

Harry's eyes went wide. 'Does that mean you will be the king?'

'They will kill me next. And you, too,' he added to Ann.

It sounded brutal, but even that downplayed the true threat. Ralph knew what Marius would do to her if he caught them.

'Where can we go?'

Ralph stared at the brown waters of the Thukela, the great artery of the Zulu kingdom, flowing to the ocean. How long had it been since Shaka had died? How long had it taken for the news to reach Thabisa, and for her to find him? How soon before Marius and Dingane sent out their men to hunt him down?

He remembered Hamu's parting words: *The next time the beast charges, you should run.* The general had known what was coming. He had tried, in his way, to help Ralph, to warn him.

By now the greater part of his column, almost two hundred porters and drivers, had melted away. Some would hurry to the capital to pledge loyalty to Dingane; others would go back to their families or their kraals, and pretend they had never heard of Ralph Courtney. Ralph had been a mighty *induna*, but he was always an outsider. He had no family to protect him, no clan that might make a vengeful king hesitate to move against him. All his power had come from Shaka. Now that the king was dead, Ralph was nothing.

From Ralph's vantage point on the banks of the Thukela, the rolling hills of Zululand seemed to stretch in every direction. But it was an illusion. The road south was impossible. Even if Ralph evaded Dingane at KwaDukuza, his column of porters and cattle would never survive the hundreds of miles to Port Elizabeth. Dingane and Marius would overtake and slaughter them. To the north, the remnants of the Zulu army would be called back from the campaign, and what better way to prove their loyalty to the new regime than to capture one of Dingane's bitterest enemies?

'We will try to slip past the Zulus and make our way to Nativity Bay.'

In the chaos of the succession, he would have to gamble that the Zulus would be too busy fighting one another to look for him. If Marius had come north to support Dingane, Ralph might find a ship before he returned. He might even manage to bring some ivory with him.

There were still many things that could go wrong, but he ignored them. This was the best of his bad options.

The remaining porters were looking at him expectantly.

'Across the river,' he ordered them.

Once they got into the forest, they would have a fair chance of avoiding capture.

Assuming Marius is more interested in plundering Shaka's kingdom than revenging himself on me.

But the porters stayed where they were, still staring at Ralph. Or rather: not *at* him, but past him. Ralph turned, to see what they were looking at.

His plan had already failed. On the far side of the Thukela, a company of armed warriors had appeared, spread out in a line as they advanced towards the riverbank.

Ralph grabbed his rifle. The river was too wide for a spear throw, but a shot would carry. He could probably hold the ford long enough for the others to get away – though the sound of gunshots would certainly draw attention. And they would still be trapped on the wrong side of the river.

One problem at a time. He levelled the rifle and aimed, squinting through one eye to seek out the leader. But as he ran the gunsight across the approaching force, he noticed something. They were not Zulus. Their war dress was different, with loincloths wrapped around their waists and white leather greaves on their calves. Their shields were cut in an 'X' shape, and the spears they carried had long, broad blades like palm leaves.

Ralph lowered the rifle and looked with both eyes. One of the oncoming warriors had pulled out ahead of the others and marched right up to the riverbank. He wore a red cloak over his shoulders and his fat belly protruded over his loincloth. The sun sparkled on the strands of red and white beads around his neck.

'Jobe?' Ralph had to shout to make his words carry across the wide, brown waters.

Jobe halted, arms folded across his chest. 'You did not think we would meet again?'

Ralph could not think what to say. He was aware of the river flowing by, the eagles circling overhead, yet his chest pressed so tightly on his lungs that he could hardly breathe.

'Is this your doing?' he said at last.

'It is the Lord's doing.'

'Is Marius with you?'

From across the river, Ralph saw the white of Jobe's teeth as he smiled. 'He is nearby. You are lucky that I found you first.'

'I never thought I would see the two of you make common cause together.'

'Even the lion may lie down with the lamb.'

Ralph could feel the seconds of his life trickling away. Down-river, a crocodile slithered off a mudbank and submerged itself in the water.

'What has Dingane promised you in exchange for your help?' Ralph called.

Jobe's smile widened. 'The reason we came here in the beginning. Freedom.'

It was as Ralph had suspected. Dingane would pull back and leave Jobe in peace to enjoy the kingdom he had built with the Chunus. Marius would have the run of Nativity Bay. And Ralph would be dead.

I chose the wrong side.

He rubbed his finger along the stock of the rifle. Jobe's men had gathered at the water's edge but made no effort to cross. Ralph still had the advantage of range.

'Are you going to kill me?'

Jobe shook his head. 'Once, you saved my life. Now we will be even.'

Was that the truth, or merely a ploy to keep him waiting until Marius arrived?

'Will you let me through to Nativity Bay?'

'I cannot. If Dingane learned that I let you cross the river, he would not forgive it.'

'Then where can I go?'

Jobe stretched out his left hand. 'Go inland. Follow the river. I will tell Dingane you went another way.'

The river flowed between them, continuing its inexorable path to the sea.

The water has no choice where it goes, Ralph thought, *and neither do I.*

'You will have to leave behind your baggage,' Jobe called. 'You must flee quickly.'

Ralph looked back. The cows had begun to roam off the road, pulling up grass, while the ivory lay where the porters had abandoned it. Four years' patient accumulation, four years of Ralph's dreams for the future, left scattered in the road like so much dung.

And Jobe will sweep it up.

A part of Ralph had to admire Jobe's cunning. He had played his partners against each other, building alliances. With the ivory he collected, he could make himself a still greater chief.

Ann, Harry, Thabisa, and the few remaining porters were waiting for his decision. He pointed upriver.

'We will follow the river that way.'

'What is that way?' Harry asked.

Ralph had only been there once, on the campaign against the Ndwandwes. He remembered the river they had crossed and his surprise when he had learned that it was the same as the one that now flowed in front of him. And beyond it, the rampart of mountains that walled off the horizon, a barrier even the Zulus did not cross.

'We will find out.'

While Jobe watched from the far bank, Ralph took some of the food bags and attached leather thongs to them, so that they could carry them on their backs. He gave one to Ann, and one to Harry, who struggled with the weight but did not complain. When he came to Thabisa, he paused.

'Thank you for warning me,' he said. Looking in her eyes, he felt a remorse that he wished he could voice. *I know I gave you little reason to love me. I know I treated you badly. And now you have saved my life.*

'What will you do?' he asked.

She took one of the packs and slung it on her shoulder, a defiant look in her eyes. 'I come with you.'

'Dingane will try to kill me,' Ralph warned.

He did not believe Jobe's assurances that he would mislead Dingane. Even if he did, the new king would learn quickly enough where Ralph had gone.

Thabisa shrugged. 'He will kill me also.'

That was doubtless true. In Zulu eyes, she was Ralph's wife. If the new king caught her, he would inflict horrors on her over long and excruciating months.

Ralph looked at her again. *You did not have to warn me*, he thought. *You could have run, hidden yourself away before Dingane's men came for you. You might even have been safe.*

There was no regret in her eyes, only impatience.

'We must go.'

The rest of the porters – the few who had stayed – Ralph let go. The supplies that they could have carried would have been useful, but more people would slow him down. And no kindness would be shown to them if Dingane's men found them in Ralph's service.

He took a length of rope, a traditional Zulu hand axe, four rifles and as much powder and shot as he could fit in his bag. Ann looked surprised.

'What do we need those for? You are the only one of us who can use a gun.'

'By the time we finish, we may all have to fight for our lives.'

He tossed her one of the rifles. Ann looked as if she wanted to throw it in the river, but she put it over her shoulder without complaint.

She bent forward to pick up one of the small hippo tusks that lay on the ground.

'Leave it,' Ralph said. He wanted no reminders of what he had lost.

'If we get to Cape Town, we will need something to trade for our passage,' she said. She tied it on top of her pack and slung it over her shoulder.

Ralph could not help admiring Ann's refusal to give up. Elizabeth Courtney had been like that as well, in the boat after the *Tiger* had sunk. When he had despaired, had contemplated drowning his pain in the ocean, she had refused to accept defeat. She had remained strong for her son, and so she had saved Ralph, too.

For the second time in his life, Ralph found himself cast adrift with the boy, and a woman determined to protect her child. He did not like his chances, but they had delayed long enough. Ralph slung the skein of rope over his shoulder, picked up the axe and the rifles and started to walk, while behind him Jobe's men splashed across the river to gather up the fortune he had left in the dust.

Ralph left Zululand in the manner he had arrived: with a few companions, little food, and almost no sense of where he was going. Except when he came, he had had two armed men with him; now he had two women and a child, and a whole kingdom snapping at his heels.

Dust thou art, and to dust thou shalt return. Ambition was folly; riches withered like grass in the dry season. Ralph had spent years building himself into one of the most powerful men in the kingdom, a trusted and respected *induna*, and in the space of a heartbeat, he had lost all of it. He had come with nothing, and he was leaving with nothing.

You were never a Zulu, he reminded himself. *You wore their clothes and spoke their language, but they were not fooled. They tolerated you, because you had Shaka's favour. Now he is gone you are nothing to them.*

These words replayed themselves in his mind. They were not pleasant thoughts to accompany the long trek ahead.

Their progress was slow. Ann could not keep up the pace Ralph set. Thabisa was strong, but she had spent most of her life around Shaka's palace. She tired as the march went on. As for Harry, for long stretches he seemed immune to fatigue. He would tear ahead, scrambling over rocks and leaping down gullies like a goat, then race back to show them some pebble or beetle he had found. But after a stretch, all the energy suddenly drained out of him. His head would go down, and then he would drag his heels and hang back, so that Ann had to take his hand and tug him along.

For Ralph it was slow torture, trapped between the danger behind that never receded, and a hope that seemed to never grow nearer. After four years hunting and fighting across Shaka's king-dom, he could march like a Zulu; travelling with the others was like dragging a boulder behind him. He should be running for his life. Every minute, the frustration tightened in his chest until he could hardly breathe.

When it grew dark, Ralph did not make a fire in case their pursuers saw it. He stayed awake until dawn, clutching his rifle against the predators that might come in the night.

'How can you be sure they are following us?' Ann asked. It was the third day, and they had seen no sight of pursuit. Dark circles rimmed her eyes and her skin was sallow; all of them were exhausted. Ann's dress was in rags, while their feet were blistered and raw. 'Jobe said he would send them the other way.'

'I would not trust Jobe's word,' Ralph said bitterly. 'Even if he did as he said he would, Dingane will quickly realise his error. And Marius will not rest until he knows that I am destroyed.'

It was four years since he had last confronted Marius, but the Dutchman's parting words still echoed in his mind: *If you see me again, it will be because I am cutting out your heart.*

Even working the farm in Paradise Valley, Ann had never been so exhausted. Each time the wheat crop failed, she had managed to find the strength to go on, but now she felt almost complete despair. She knew she was holding Ralph back and would never be able to go fast enough for him.

'You should leave us behind,' she said. It was the fifth night, and they were huddled together on the open plain. 'You and Thabisa are strong. You will make better progress without us.'

'You would die,' he said. 'Either Dingane will catch you, or you would starve.'

'The new king has no quarrel with me or Harry.'

'It would be enough that you lived with me. Unless . . .' He considered the import of what he was about to say. 'Unless you could come to an arrangement with Marius.'

She shuddered. 'No.'

'I know a life with him would not be gentle,' Ralph acknowledged. 'But . . . you would live. And so would Harry.'

'Never!' The word sprang out fierce and loud, filled with energy Ann did not know she still possessed. Harry stirred. His eyes blinked open.

'Is it time to go?'

'No, my heart.' Ann stroked his cheek. 'Back to sleep.'

She glanced at Ralph with a look so full of fury that he was lost for words.

I only want you to be safe.

As Ann's shock ebbed, she could see the sense of what Ralph had suggested. Caught between the wilderness and the pursuing Zulus, throwing herself on Marius's mercy might be the only way to keep Harry alive. But being with Marius every day would be a living death. She could not do that – even for Harry.

'I would rather die than surrender to Marius.'

Ralph nodded. 'Then most likely we will all die together.'

The next day they came to flat lands where the riverbanks opened into a broad plain. They trudged across it, mile after mile with no sense of progress. No one spoke, each alone with their thoughts. Even the usually chatty Harry was sombre.

Every day they had travelled more slowly and halted sooner. On the plain, the heat was unbearable and the dust stuck to their bodies, caking their eyes and mouths and noses. Late that afternoon, without a word, they all stopped where they were and sank to the ground. Ann's throat was raw and she was desperate for some water, but she did not even have the strength to stagger the fifty yards to the riverbank.

She did not realise she had fallen asleep until a gunshot woke her. How long had she been sleeping? She rubbed her eyes and looked around.

A little distance away, she saw Ralph kneeling beside Harry. Harry was holding the rifle, almost overbalancing as he tried to get the long ramrod down its barrel.

'What are you doing?' she cried. 'Put that down!'

'Ralph is teaching me to shoot,' Harry said.

'Not to shoot,' Ralph corrected him. 'To load.'

'If you can load, you can shoot,' Harry pointed out.

'If you tried, you would break your shoulder.'

Harry peered at the rifle more warily – until Ann snatched it out of his hands.

'Leave my son out of this.'

'He is in this whether he wants it or not.' Ralph took the gun from her, slammed the ramrod home, then primed the pan. 'And when Dingane's men catch us, our lives may depend on how quickly he can reload. You should learn, too,' he told her.

'I want to fight,' said Harry. 'I want to fight like Ralph.'

Exhausted, only half awake, Ann had her hand half raised to slap him before she realised what she was doing. Horrified, she snatched it back.

What have you done to me? she wanted to scream. *What are you doing to Harry? Why is there violence wherever you go?*

'He is a child,' she told Ralph.

'That will make no difference to Dingane and Marius.'

'Maybe they are not coming.' She was almost incoherent now, unable to contain her emotion. 'You have dragged us here for nothing, so we can die in the wilderness, or else walk forever, or . . .'

Ralph wasn't listening. He stared over her shoulder, looking back down the broad valley. In the distance – maybe twenty or thirty miles away – a brown smudge rose against the evening sky. A column of dust, thrown up by marching feet.

'They are coming.'

No one could think of rest after that. They marched almost until dawn, snatched a few hours' sleep, then carried on. Too often, Ann looked back, scanning the horizon for the telltale cloud. At first it was not there, and she dared to hope that what she had seen the evening before had been an illusion. But as the sun climbed and the ground dried, it appeared again, like smoke from a brush fire creeping towards them.

The flatlands ended at a place where the river divided. Both forks were as wide as each other: it was impossible to tell which was the tributary, and which the main course. Ralph asked Thabisa, but she had never been so far inland and did not know.

'Does it matter?' Ann asked.

Every moment they delayed felt like a minute on the hangman's scaffold.

'The Thukela leads to the mountains. The other . . .' Ralph shrugged. 'We cannot afford the time to find out.'

'Then we cannot afford the time to wonder about it,' Ann replied. She glanced between them, then – on impulse – stuck out her right hand. 'That way.'

So they went right. The river entered a narrower valley, flanked by steep hills that hid the dust cloud from sight.

I almost preferred it when we could see them, Ann thought. *At least then we knew where they were.*

As they wound through the valley she sensed they were climbing. The valley gave out onto another plain, then more rugged hills, then flatlands, each higher than the last. It was as if they were ascending the country in a series of giant terraces. Without meals or sleep to mark time, days fell into one another, uncounted. Even Harry no longer had the energy to complain, but trudged along with his head down.

But despite everything, every hour they progressed gave them optimism. They could see the mountains rising in the distance, the great rampart that Ralph remembered.

'Is there any way up?' Ann asked.

'There must be,' said Ralph. He gazed at the long ridgeline. Ahead, to the right, there seemed to be a gap where the river issued out. 'We will try that place.'

Before they reached the mountains, there was one more plain to cross. By now, Ann could barely keep her eyes open. Head bowed, she stumbled forwards. She did not notice the tug on her shoulders, until she heard Ralph shouting urgently.

'What?'

Her eyes focused as she saw blood running down her arms. In her daze, she had walked into a thorn bush without realising, and was now deeply tangled in it.

She stood and wept, tears mingling with the blood that welled from a scratch on her cheek. She could not go any further.

'Don't move,' Ralph called.

She felt pressure on her wrist, smooth and firm. Ralph held her arm while his other hand pulled out his *isizenze*, the hand axe he had taken from the baggage train.

'Keep still,' he murmured.

He cut the branches away from around her, carefully extracting every thorn that had pierced her flesh before removing the branch with the razor-sharp axe. She knew this was costing them time, yet he worked patiently, speaking reassuringly all the while.

At last she came free. She staggered out of the bush, but her dress, already ragged, had been torn to ribbons. She grabbed at it to try and cover herself, but it was pointless.

Pulling the garment from her body, Ann threw it to the ground and stepped away. She stood there, naked, and gave Ralph a look of fierce defiance. He averted his eyes. She felt a renewed energy.

'Give me your knife,' she demanded.

She cut off the largest piece of fabric that remained intact from the dress, just enough to go around her waist and cover her hips. She tied it in place with another strip of cloth.

'If Zulu women dress like this, why shouldn't I?'

Ralph had no answer.

'We must go on,' said Thabisa.

She pointed back. A figure had appeared on a kopje, five miles or so behind them. He stood outlined against the sky, staring across the plain. A second figure joined him.

Ralph swore. 'Dingane's scouts. The others must be near.'

They left the fragments of Ann's dress hanging from the thorn bush. There was no time to disguise their trail, and no point now. It was a foot race to the mountains.

'And when we reach there?' Thabisa asked. 'What then?' She had come up alongside Ralph, while Ann and Harry followed. 'We will be against a wall.'

'Not if there is a way through.'

'If we go through, they can follow.'

'They cannot go on forever.'

'They do not need to go on forever. Only until they catch us.'

'Then we will continue until they do,' Ralph said forcefully.

By the size of the dust cloud behind them, the Zulus had added to their numbers. If they overtook Ralph's party on open ground, the battle would be over before it began. Ralph's only chance was to get into cover, where his rifles might be able to hold off the Zulus for longer.

That was a faint hope. They would surely run out of bullets before the Zulus ran out of men.

They walked in the glare of the sun, and when night fell they continued by moonlight. But even with Dingane's men on their heels, they could not go entirely without rest. Some time in the depths of the night, clouds built up and covered the moon. A soft rain began to patter on their faces. All of them licked at it greedily.

'We will halt here for an hour or two,' Ralph declared. 'We cannot move in this darkness, and we will make better progress after some rest.'

Thabisa, Ann and Harry laid themselves on the ground. Thabisa could nap anywhere, and Harry had a child's ability to fall asleep in seconds. Ralph sat cross-legged, clutching the rifle across his body, and stared at the dark horizon. His mind picked shapes out of the night – the monumental outlines of mountains and kopjes – though he could not tell if they were real or phantoms in the darkness.

Grass rustled behind him. He craned around, already raising the rifle. Had Dingane's men caught them so soon?

'It is me.' Ann's voice came out of the darkness. She was naked, apart from her thin skirt; her pale skin seemed to glow in the darkness.

'You should sleep.'

'I could not.' She sighed. 'Every minute of the day I am exhausted, but when I close my eyes I cannot rest. I feel I am being chased by demons, and if I drop my guard for even one minute they will devour me.'

'I have felt that way all my life.'

Ann sat down beside him. 'What have you been running from?'

Ralph hesitated. Afterwards, he could not say why he spoke: if it was a condemned man's need for confession, or one last weight to discard after he had jettisoned everything else. Perhaps, after all they had suffered together, he simply wanted Ann to know the truth.

'The man who killed my father was called Adam Courtney. He was Harry's father.'

The words died into the darkness. *Perhaps I always knew*, Ann thought, *that it would come back to Harry*. It was a mystery that had haunted her ever since she had lifted the baby out of the longboat.

'So, Harry is your . . .' She tried to think what the relationship would be. 'Nephew? Cousin?'

'He is my blood.' Ralph shrugged. 'I do not know how, exactly.'

'Then how do you know you are related?'

'Many years ago, two brothers set sail from England. One settled in India, and one in Africa. They quarrelled, and from that day to this the two halves of the family have been at war with each other. Harry is the last descendant from one line, and I am the last from the other.'

'Surely no one could bear a grudge all that time.'

'You do not know what my family are capable of.'

The words chilled her. 'The family who lived at Nativity Bay, the graves I found . . . Thabisa said they were Courtneys.'

'They were Harry's family.'

'What happened to them?'

'My father went to Nativity Bay and destroyed it. But all he found there were old men, women and children. Adam Courtney was away, serving in the Royal Navy. And so he survived.'

Ralph paused. 'Adam learned what had happened and came to India for revenge. He came to my house. I was Harry's age then, and to me he was like a god. Handsome, strong, a navy captain. The first man who was ever kind to me.' A silence. 'Then he seduced my mother and murdered my father.

'For a long time, I believed every misfortune in my life began that day. Later, I saw my fate was written long before that, even before I was born. I decided I must end the cycle of vengeance and violence once and for all.'

Ann reached across and touched his arm. 'It was the right decision. To walk away – to refuse revenge.'

He shook her off as if her touch scalded him.

'I did not choose to forswear violence. I decided to end it by killing them all.' His head slumped. 'Even the children . . . So that finally there would be no one left to continue the fight.'

'You wanted to kill Harry?' Ann covered her mouth with her hand to stifle her gasp. 'But you saved his life.'

'I dedicated my life to destroying him. I vowed I would become so rich and powerful that no one would be able to stop me avenging my father.' He drifted off. 'It was not easy, but I did it. I found Adam Courtney.'

'The story you told me. The fire on your ship – how you rescued Harry.'

'It was true – to a point. The irony of it is that I had grown so rich, and Adam Courtney had eluded me for so long, that I had almost given up on my revenge. I took my ship to London.

Then, making for the Cape, we fell in alongside a ship, the *Tiger*. Adam Courtney's ship. He did not know who I was. He invited me aboard for dinner. I met his wife, still nursing their infant son. And that night, I led my crew aboard to kill them.'

Ann saw that Ralph's hand had crept up his cheek.

'As you can see, I failed.'

'What happened?'

'We took them unawares. But a Courtney is always ready for a fight, and Adam was one of the best of them.'

In his mind, Ralph heard the ring of steel, panicked shouts and the screams of dying men. He smelled the blood in the scuppers, and tasted the powder on his lips. And as always, in his memory, thick choking smoke.

'We fought our way through his men, but at terrible cost. The *Tiger* caught fire. My crew tried to cut our own ship free, but she was tangled in the boarding lines. The fire spread to her, too. All the treasure I had gathered was in her hold. It ended up at the bottom of the ocean.

'At last, I came face to face with Adam Courtney.' The face appeared through the flames in his memory: deep brown skin, the tousled hair and those piercing dark eyes, muddied with confusion. 'This was the moment that I had dedicated my life to. His crew were dead, his ship lost. He stood by the stern rail, holding me back, while his wife tried to lower the longboat. She wore the baby tied to her chest in a blanket.

'Adam fought me off. We duelled the length of the ship, while the world burned around us. I was a strong fighter, and younger, but he was defending his family. He disarmed me. I was helpless.

'Then fate intervened. The ship broke in half. A burning spar fell to the deck and pinned us both beneath it. That was how I got these scars on my face. I managed to get free, but Adam was not so lucky.

'I went back to Lizzie in the stern and stood over her and the baby. In that moment, I could have ended everything. But . . .' A shudder went through him, a deep convulsion of the soul. 'I could not. My sword would not strike. I looked at Harry in his mother's arms, and all I saw was an innocent child and his frightened mother.

'The *Tiger* sank. Adam died. My own crew deserted me, and whether they managed to save themselves or drowned, I do not know. When dawn broke next morning, there was no sign of any other boat. I was left with another man's widow, and the child I could not kill. The rest you know.'

He fell silent.

'I do not expect you to forgive me,' he added. 'I know what I am.'

Ann shook her head. 'You saved Harry. And everything you did – however dreadful it may have been – is what brought him to me. I know I should hate it, but I cannot.'

She lifted her arm. She had meant to reach out, but Ralph cowered as if she was going to strike him. Or perhaps he wanted her to hit him, so the pain might somehow absolve him of his sins.

She lowered her hand. Ralph straightened.

'I should not have told you that.'

'I am glad you did.'

'You must never tell Harry,' Ralph said. 'He must never know.'

He saw conflict in her face, but when Ann spoke her voice was firm. 'I cannot hide Harry's past from him. When he is older, he will need to know the truth. Then he can make his own decision.'

Ralph wanted to tell her that it was a mistake: it would lead only to bloodshed and death. But it was too late for that. By telling her, he had made his choice. The secret was no longer his.

While they had been talking, the rain shower had passed, and the clouds had cleared. The moon shone clear and full, lighting their way.

'It is time to move on,' Ralph said.

As the new day broke, the river funnelled into a steep-sided valley, winding ever upwards. The valley walls hid their surroundings, so they could no longer see the mountains, though Ralph could feel the wild immensity of them all around. They picked their way over rocks where the slopes had collapsed; elsewhere, thick bush came down so close to the river that they had to wade through the shallows by its bank.

The higher they climbed, the more Ralph dared to believe that he might have found the way he was looking for. Perhaps the river had carved a pass that would lead him through the mountains.

Then he reached a bend and realised it had all been in vain.

The land broadened out into a vast bowl, surrounded on three sides by a ring of mountains packed so close they merged into a single wall. Its face rose out of the valley, two thousand feet of sheer rock that reared above shreds of cloud like the ramparts of Heaven itself. And over it came the river, plunging off the mountain in a billowing white ribbon that seemed to fall for an eternity.

There was no way through. No pass, no cleft, no river gully. After so much effort, Ralph had led them into the bottom of a sack. They were trapped.

He glanced back, and saw his worst fears confirmed. A party of Zulus was climbing up the valley behind them. They must have marched at a blistering pace to whittle away Ralph's head start, yet they showed no sign of fatigue as they leaped from rock to rock.

But one of the men moved with more deliberate purpose. He stood almost a head taller than any of the others, able to stride over the gaps between the rocks. You could tell by his silhouette he was not a Zulu: he wore trousers instead of a kilt, a baggy shirt and a straw hat. The long barrel of a rifle protruded from over his shoulder where he had slung it.

Marius.

Ralph had never imagined the Dutchman would come himself. He had assumed he would stay close to the throne, guarding his stake as Dingane consolidated his power.

He must be desperate to make sure I am dead.

Or, Ralph thought, *perhaps Jobe had persuaded Dingane to send Marius to do the job, so that Marius and Ralph would destroy each other. The final piece of his revenge.*

Rage flooded through Ralph. Marius was the reason all this had happened. He had shattered the alliance with Ralph and Jobe by trying to make Jobe a slave; he had given Dingane the backing he needed to overthrow Shaka.

The bowl under the mountains was so huge it was almost a world in itself, divided by ridges and outcrops knotted into fantastical shapes. Ralph could not see where the waterfall met the ground, but it seemed to him that the river had somehow carved and twisted the rock over centuries.

In the shadow of those enormous cliffs, the lesser formations seemed mere ripples in the landscape, though in reality each was a formidable hill in its own right. Ralph scanned the landscape until he found a kopje, the top of which was divided by a cleft. The slopes in front of it were steep, loose scree, giving anyone who held the summit a wide field of fire.

'There.'

Ralph and his companions floundered up the slope, often losing their footing in the shifting stones, expecting at any moment to feel the impact of a bullet. Ralph could hear their pursuers' shouts behind him. Something clattered off the rocks to his left – a spear or a falling rock, he did not see. He pushed onwards. His legs burned with the effort; his hands were raw from scrabbling over the rocks, but he forced himself to keep going.

He rolled over the lip of the slope into the shadow of the *krans* at its summit. Thabisa was almost at the top, but Ann was lagging behind. Harry had stumbled and fallen; she was trying to help him up, but he kept sliding away from her on the loose stones.

Three Zulus ran out at the foot of the slope. Two carried short stabbing spears, but one had a javelin. He dropped into a crouch, arm cocked to throw. Not an easy throw, against the slope, but Ralph had seen the Zulu hunters hit targets over greater distances many times.

Ralph brought up his rifle and fired. The spearman fell back, clutching his ribs, while the other two retreated.

'Harry,' Ann screamed.

Ralph looked down. Harry should have gained the top by now; instead, he was skidding down the slope. The sound of the shot had surprised him. He had lost his grip and was slipping further and further away.

More Zulus were gathering at the foot of the slope. Soon Harry would slide right into their hands. Ralph had no time to think. With a curse, he vaulted over the lip and plunged after the boy. He stumbled, half leaping, half sliding, so fast he thought he would break his neck.

Harry had managed to grab a tree stump midway down the slope and slow his descent. Ralph almost flew past him. He dug his heels into the ground to stop himself, then grabbed the boy's shoulder, almost wrenching his arm from its socket.

'Come on!'

Inch by inch, he dragged Harry back up. His feet were slipping as he tried to climb. He could hear Ann shouting warnings to him from the top of the kopje. He knew men were coming up behind him. The stones he dislodged tumbled on to the Zulus, battering their hands and heads, but one warrior was more agile than the rest. He sprang up the slope and Ralph, dragging Harry, could not outrun him.

A shot rang out. The Zulu was thrown backwards. He lost his balance and cartwheeled down in a welter of blood and flailing limbs. Ralph saw Thabisa at the top of the escarpment, holding a smoking rifle.

Never underestimate a woman's resolve, he thought to himself.

With a final effort, he tucked Harry under his arm and staggered into the lee of the cliff.

Ann handed him another rifle. She had loaded it: the pan was primed and the hammer cocked. As soon as her hands were free, she wrapped Harry in an embrace that almost crushed him.

'In there,' Ralph shouted, pointing to the cleft in the rock. The mouth of the fissure was wide enough that two of them could stand shoulder to shoulder, while the others sheltered further back.

Four of the Zulus were still climbing up. Ralph sent one sprawling with a well-aimed shot; Thabisa managed to hit another in the thigh. The other two scrambled back down the slope.

Smoke hung in the air. Ralph's ears rang with the noise of the gunshots so that the world seemed distant and muted. For a moment, a strange silence descended.

The Zulus gathered at the bottom of the slope. A sapling on the edge of the bush shuddered as Marius pushed past it and came out into the open. He stared up at the kopje, hands on his hips.

'You led us quite a chase, hey?' He looked gaunt. His cheeks were hollow, fringed with a ragged beard. But he was still tall and broad, and his limbs had lost none of their restless power. 'Now we have you.'

'You should have let me go,' Ralph called back. 'Stayed and got rich with your new master. No doubt he will reward his lapdog well.'

He had chosen his words to wound.

'No Kaffir will ever be my master,' Marius snarled. 'He has his kingdom, for now. But things change.'

Ralph wished the Zulus could understand what Marius said. If only they knew what he really thought of their king.

'If we fight, many of you will die,' Ralph said loudly, switching to isiZulu so that the warriors could understand. 'This is not your fight. It is between me and the *abelumbi*.'

The Zulus gazed back impassively. They had followed Ralph relentlessly for days: it was foolishness to hope he could change their minds now. Even so, he could not believe they wanted to die here, like this.

He ran his eyes over the row of faces below him. Dingane would not have sent his most trusted men: he would have needed them close at hand. He would have sent men who had served Shaka faithfully, who would know that they must prove their loyalty to the new regime or be deemed traitors.

Sure enough, among the faces was one he recognised. A slim, wiry man with darker-than-average skin and finely drawn cheek-bones. He wore a white eagle feather in his hair and carried a shield of brown and white hide.

'I see you, Sibebu,' Ralph called. 'We fought alongside each other at eZindololwane. My firestick saved your life that day. I have no quarrel with you.'

Sibebu would not meet Ralph's gaze. He stared ahead, gripping his spear.

Marius laughed. 'You have no authority now,' he jeered. 'These men will do whatever I say. If I give a good account of them to the king, maybe he will give them some of the lands that were yours.'

'Dingane will already be plotting how to get rid of you,' Ralph warned. 'I would go back now, before you find Nativity Bay burned to the ground.'

Marius shook his head. His mouth twisted in a grin. 'I have come too far for this.'

'There is no profit in it.'

'There is always profit in claiming a debt.'

Marius barked a command to his men. He must have learned enough Zulu to make himself understood, for Ralph did not hear the echo of a translation. The Zulus stamped their feet and readied their weapons.

'Are they going to attack?' Harry had crawled forward to peer over the edge. His face was alight with excitement. 'Will we fight them?'

'Do you remember how to load a gun the way I showed you?' said Ralph.

Harry nodded.

'Then stay behind me. Every time I fire, you have another gun ready.' Ralph looked at Ann. 'You can reload for Thabisa?'

'Yes,' she said. She looked as if she was about to be sick.

All the hours they had struggled under the weight of the guns were worth it now. Ralph took his rifle, checked the priming carefully, and then looked for Marius. For all their bravado, he did not think the Zulus wanted to assault his position. Without their leader, they would probably slink back to Dingane. They would say that they had killed Ralph, and no one would be able to contradict them.

But Marius had retreated into the shelter of the trees, and Ralph could not get a clear shot. He counted at least a hundred Zulus.

'Do we have enough bullets?' Ann asked.

'We are about to find out.'

With a great shout, the Zulus charged.

On a level battlefield, Marius's men would have overcome Ralph before he could have fired his third shot. Here, fighting the slope and the ever-shifting footing, the odds turned against them. Ralph waited until they had advanced twenty yards up the hillside, then began to fire. The first man he hit fell into the man behind and knocked them both back. His second victim went down and tripped one of his companions. Thabisa blasted away beside him. Some men panicked and turned away, colliding with those coming up behind them and causing more chaos. The line buckled.

Ralph took no pleasure in it. It was like shooting game that had been driven into a trap – except these were men, forced to fight because of a grudge they had no part of. He shot them down in the grim knowledge that if he did not, they would massacre him and his companions.

The Zulu charge petered out and the survivors scrambled down the slope to regroup. Ralph heard Marius shouting angrily, damning them as dogs and cowards. He counted seven dead, and as many again nursing wounds.

'Have we won?' Harry asked.

'No.'

There were still too many Zulus. And they would not underestimate the power of the guns again. Ralph could see them studying the landscape, working out where they could outflank the defenders.

Eventually, they would find a way to get up onto the *krans* behind Ralph. He looked behind him. The cleft where they had lodged themselves went deeper into the kopje and vanished around a corner. *Was it a dead end?*

'See where that goes,' he told Harry.

Harry scampered down the rocky passage. He was gone longer than Ralph expected, and when he returned, it was with triumph on his face.

'It goes all the way through,' he announced. 'It comes out the other side.'

That was good – and bad.

'It gives us a line of retreat,' said Ralph, 'but it also means they could come up behind us.'

'They are coming now.'

Thabisa had been keeping watch on Marius's men, who had reformed and were advancing again. This time they divided into three groups: two skirting either flank of the slope while a third came up the centre, crawling on their stomachs. Marius loitered in the trees, directing operations with jerks of his gun. Still Ralph could not get a clear shot at him.

'This will be harder.'

The Zulus might not be used to facing gunfire, but they learned quickly. They came spread out in a long line, plenty of space between them. Ralph managed to knock two back, but Thabisa's shots, less practised, went wide. The further the Zulus climbed, the more Ralph and Thabisa had to lean out of their redoubt.

'Do not get too far in the open,' Ralph cautioned Thabisa.

To see her enemies, she had come well forward from the cliff. Up on one knee, squinting down the barrel, she would make a tempting target for a throwing spear – or for Marius, still prowling at the foot of the slope with his rifle.

Thabisa ignored Ralph. She fired again, passed the musket to Ann and took the reloaded gun. Ralph had no time to see what she had hit. He was firing as fast as he could, alternating between the men on his left flank and those coming up the middle. Each time he managed to check one party, the other came forward.

Every yard they advanced, his advantage was reduced. He had relied on the shock power of the guns to break the Zulus' spirit, or else to inflict so many casualties at a distance that they gave up. Now, however frantically he fired his gun, he could not hold them back.

Something sharp scratched his cheek, cutting into the scar tissue. He turned. In the rock face next to him was a small crater where a bullet had hit, throwing off the stone splinters that had grazed him. An inch higher and he would have lost his eye. It must have been Marius. Ralph could not see him through the smoke, and he had not noticed the shot above the din of his own firing.

'Be careful,' he called to Thabisa, pointing down the slope. He doubted she heard him. He could barely hear himself. The roar of the guns was deafening.

The Zulus on the left had been pushed back, but those on the right had come up so close to the cliff that the defenders no longer had a clear shot at them. The group in the middle had found a shallow depression in the slope, where they could hide from the bullets if they pressed themselves flat.

For a moment there was a lull while they gathered their strength. Ralph glanced back. Harry crouched behind him, laying out spare cartridges on a flat stone as neat as toy soldiers. His lips were pursed in concentration.

The sight sparked a rage in Ralph. The boy should not be fighting for his life. His eyes met Ann's, and he could see she was thinking the same thing.

I will not let him die here. He wanted to say the words to comfort her, but they would not come.

'Where is the rest of the ammunition?' he asked.

'This is all of it,' Harry said.

From the foot of the hill, Marius fired again. The bullet passed wide of Ralph, but that was not its purpose. It was the signal for the Zulus to attack.

They rose as one and charged. The moment they were up, Ralph and Thabisa opened fire. At that distance they could not miss. Several men went down, but there were more to take their place. The gap closed.

Seeing their objective so close spurred the attackers on. If Ralph had been a remote observer, he would have been in awe of their courage, charging head first into a fusillade of gunfire. Instead, he could only fire, pass the weapon back and fire again.

The row of cartridges Harry had lined up grew shorter.

The first of the Zulus reached the top of the slope and gave a triumphant shout. Ralph discharged the gun at him point-blank. The bullet shattered his skull, spraying blood everywhere. Ralph did not bother passing the gun back to Harry – there was no time. The next attacker was already on him. He swung the weapon round and smashed the butt into the man's chest. It knocked him back over the edge and down the slope.

A spear was thrust at him. Ralph caught it on the gun barrel and beat it aside, then jabbed the man in the ribs. But this was the kind of fighting the Zulus excelled at. His opponent rode the blow, then swung at Ralph with his shield. Too quick for Ralph. The hide slammed into his arm with such force that he dropped the rifle.

He was defenceless. He looked up at his adversary and realised it was Sibebu, the man he had seen earlier.

I fought alongside you for Shaka, Ralph wanted to plead, *and now you will kill me for Marius?*

It was grotesquely unfair. But in the heat of battle there was neither pity nor recognition on the Zulu's face. He pulled back his spear, ready to drive it into Ralph's belly.

A gun exploded so close to Ralph's ear he lost all hearing. In dumbshow, he saw a gout of flame from Thabisa's rifle muzzle erupt from over his shoulder into Sibebu's face. A hot breath scalded Ralph's cheek. The flame licked the eagle feathers in Sibebu's hair and set them alight. In an instant, the fire spread to his hair. He fell away, his head burning like a Roman candle.

Ralph was too astonished to move. If another man had come at him then, he would have been skewered like a pig.

But nothing came. The Zulus had held firm in the face of the rifles for longer perhaps than even well-drilled British redcoats, but it had taken its toll. The sight of Sibebu with his head on fire terrified them. They abandoned their position and streamed away down the hill.

Ralph could have taken the opportunity to fire a few parting shots, but he simply watched them go.

A puff of smoke at the foot of the hill reminded Ralph that standing out in front of the cliff made him an easy target for Marius. Still deafened, he did not hear the shot, nor where it struck. He kicked one of the Zulu corpses away, then retreated hastily into the shelter of the crevice.

'We must go,' he croaked. Powder smoke had left his throat parched, while the ringing in his ears made his voice sound muffled and faint. 'They will come again.' He glanced back. 'What is wrong?'

Ann was staring at him in horror. She had blood on her face and hands. Had she been wounded?

Then he looked down, and saw the blood was not Ann's. Thabisa lay on the ground, clutching her side. Her left leg was skewed at an unnatural angle, and blood pooled around her thighs. Her mouth moved; she was groaning in agony.

Marius's last shot had missed Ralph, but it had still found a target.

One glance told Ralph that the bullet had shattered Thabisa's hip. Even in the best of circumstances, she would not be able to walk for weeks, if ever. In that place, she probably had less than an hour to live.

They could not staunch the bleeding. Ann took off her skirt and tried to cover the wound, but the blood soaked through almost at once.

'What are we going to do?' Harry asked.

The question hung unanswered. They made a desperate group: Ralph, covered with blood and powder burns; Ann, naked without her skirt; Harry, who looked if he was going to be sick; and Thabisa, bleeding to death on the ground.

It was Thabisa who had the strength to say what no one else would.

'Leave me,' she said through gritted teeth. 'Leave me and go.'

'Won't she die?' Harry asked.

'I die anyway,' said Thabisa. She spoke harshly, forcing Ralph to accept what they had to do. 'A spear is a quicker death than running.'

'I will not abandon you,' Ralph insisted.

He reached to lift Thabisa up – Harry came to help him – but the moment they moved her she let out a howl of agony.

'You are hurting her, Ralph,' Ann said. 'Let her go. There is nothing we can do.'

'You leave me,' said Thabisa. 'You must.'

Thabisa reached out an arm towards Ralph's gun, lying where he had dropped it on the ground.

'I fight. You go.'

Ralph did not trust himself to speak.

'How many bullets do we have left?' Ann asked.

Harry had been scavenging through the ammunition pouches. He laid out five cartridges. All were battered; some had torn open and leaked powder.

It was all they had.

They carried Thabisa out and laid her on her stomach on the ridge overlooking the slope. She had to bite her lip to keep from screaming, but she did not complain. Ralph loaded all four guns and laid them beside her. She pushed one away.

'You take it.'

Ralph took the gun. Only one bullet, but if he could put it into Marius's heart he might die content, knowing that he could not harm anyone else.

At the bottom of the slope, he could see the Zulus reorganising themselves. Yet he still could not bring himself to leave Thabisa.

He saw the expression on her face that he knew so well. The twitch of her mouth, the crease of her forehead and the glint in her eyes. She smiled.

'Go,' she said.

He kissed her head and turned away.

They entered the narrow passage that the crevice made through the rock. On the far side, they came out again into the great bowl of the mountains, and the impenetrable cliff face towering over everything.

'Where can we go?' Ann asked.

A gunshot rang out behind them, the sound echoing through the crevice. Ralph could not tell if it was Thabisa opening fire, or Marius signalling another attack. It made little difference.

He looked down into the valley. Some way below, he could see the river winding white through the channel it had carved. It was like a string through a labyrinth that he had followed for hundreds of miles, from its mouth almost to its source. But he had done so with false hope. He remembered the falls he had seen, the river dropping almost half a mile over the great mountain cliff. There would be no way up there.

Only the flanks of the mountain offered any hope, if they could get there. To his right, above the river valley, a game trail led across the hillside in a broadly north-westerly direction.

Another gunshot made up Ralph's mind.

'That way.'

The trail brought them into thick forest, mercifully shaded from the sun. Little streams gave them fresh cool water to drink. More gunshots echoed up the valley. Ralph counted five, then – after a pause – one more. Then nothing.

The trail twisted and turned, following the curve of the hills. Soon Ralph lost all sense of direction. They might have gone in a circle and be blundering back towards Marius, but the bush was too thick to break off the path.

Ralph's hopes faded the further they went. Rather than climbing, the path dipped down through another stretch of trees with the sound of flowing water growing steadily louder.

Then the trees ended, and he gave a cry of despair. They had not escaped the river after all. The game trail had brought them up the valley, and now back to the Thukela.

They were trapped. Their pursuers would by now have discovered their exit and would be tracking them – they could not go back. To their left, the river descended in a series of drops and deep pools back the way they had come. To the right, it flowed out of a gorge between rocky cliffs – still only foothills of the true mountain face, but high enough that there was no hope of climbing them. The gorge was so narrow that the sides almost touched together at the top. The waterfall that they had seen as they entered the giant stone bowl must find its end on the other side of the gorge.

'Can we get through there?' Ann asked.

The water was not deep, but the current was fast and strong. Floods had worn the sides of the passage glassy smooth, while the tight-pressed cliffs left no bank to walk on. If they lost their footing on the riverbed, there would be nothing to cling to. They would be carried all the way back to Marius's waiting spears.

'We have to try.'

Ralph abandoned the rifle and his *isizenze* in a stand of ferns. He could not keep the powder dry in the water, and he needed both hands free. The river was ice-cold and the strong current constantly tried to knock them over. Ralph took the lead, testing every step on the slick stones underfoot. Ann brought up the rear, while Harry went between them, holding each of their hands.

The river gradually grew deeper as the cliffs squeezed it tighter. Now the two sides met, creating a tunnel that had been shaped round and smooth by aeons of floodwater.

Ralph came around a bend, balancing himself against the wall, and stopped. The river had been calm, but now he was confronted with boiling rapids coming down over a tumble of rocks.

'We cannot get up that,' said Ann.

Ralph didn't answer. Beyond the rapids, he could see daylight where the cliffs opened out again. If they could get up there, they might find a way out.

The churning water chattered away, echoing and re-echoing off the tunnel until it became a roar. Ralph pushed on, fighting his way towards the rapids, leaving Ann and Harry behind him. Spray blinded him. He closed his eyes, launched himself off the bottom and lunged forwards with two powerful kicks. The current drove him back, but he flung out an arm and his hand closed around firm rock.

He hauled himself forward. He began to ascend the rapids, hand over hand and step by step. The river battered his body. Each time he lifted one of his arms or legs, Ann thought he would lose his grip completely and be dashed back down. She could see the muscles rigid across his back, the fearsome effort needed for every movement.

A chilling thought struck her: *Is he going to abandon us? Is he going to disappear over the top of the falls, into the daylight, and never return?* She glanced back. *How long would it be before Marius found them?*

Ralph reached the top of the rapids. His legs buckled – for a moment, Ann thought that the water would pluck him off – but then he sprang forward, onto a rocky ledge that protruded from the cliff just out of the water. He lay there for a moment, gasping.

Then he turned back.

'You can come up,' he called.

Ann shook her head. There was no way she could fight against that churning torrent – let alone Harry. The water would drown them.

'Quick,' Ralph insisted. 'There is no time.'

He slithered off his ledge, back into the water. Ann thought he would go over the rapids, but he found a hollow and managed to plant his feet behind a stone. He leaned out, took the skein of rope off his back and began to pay it out to her.

'Come on!' From down the tunnel, she heard a man shouting, close enough to be unmistakable even over the roar of the river.

She thought of Thabisa. Better to die fighting than surrender. Her hand circled Harry's small wrist and she swam as best she could towards the foot of the rapids.

Grabbing the rope, Ann wrapped it around her arm, just as she had the day that the *Farewell* had come over the sand bar at Nativity Bay, the day that Ralph had saved Harry from the sea.

She felt the rope snap tight as Ralph began to haul them up the rapids, like a fisherman landing a catch he refused to release. Even having seen Ralph's efforts, nothing prepared her for the sheer force of the water coming at her. The moment her foot came off the bottom she felt herself being pushed backwards. She was weightless, entirely insubstantial.

The water slammed against her, filling her mouth and nose, trying to sweep her legs from under her. Harry clung to her back as Ralph pulled them through the white water, his unyielding strength drawing them up and over the boulders that stood in their way.

Then, suddenly, Ann felt something take a firm grip on her arm. She blinked her eyes, and through the water running down her face she saw Ralph's face peering down. She had never thought she would be so glad to see him.

Her chest and belly scraped raw from being dragged over the rocks, Ann flopped onto the ledge, bruised and bleeding. Harry collapsed next to her. She thought she would never move again.

'I have to rest.'

'Not yet.'

Ralph tried to loosen the rope, but the water had shrunk the knot too tight and he had no time to undo it. He could only pull up the end and leave it coiled on the ledge. At least Marius would not be able to use it to climb the rapids. Then Ralph pointed the way they had come. Reflected light made golden ripples on the ceiling, but now the pattern was broken by a looming shadow coming quickly up the tunnel.

Ralph dragged Ann and Harry forwards, around another bend. The cliffs that had hemmed them in now spread apart; warm sunlight fell on their faces. They could see the mountains soaring above them, close now. The river became shallow again, though the roar of water did not lessen.

They had reached the end of the gorge – but it had one last trick to play before it let them go. It ended in a deep pool cupped between rock walls, which the river poured over in a waterfall. It was not high – maybe only five or six feet – but the rocks had been worn so smooth there was no way up. Ralph swam to the cliffs and tried his luck, but he could find no handhold or purchase.

'Perhaps I could lift Harry up,' he said.

But what would that do? An eight year-old boy could not haul them over the cliff. And even if he got away, he would never survive on his own.

'Maybe Marius will not brave the rapids,' said Ann.

Her hair streamed out behind her in the water, while below the surface her naked body gleamed pale in the sunlight. The water was cold, but fear and desperation pulsed so strong in her veins she did not feel it.

'He has followed us this far. The rapids will not stop him.'

Ralph looked around, searching for anything he could use to climb out – a tree root, a creeper, even a crack in the rock he could pry his fingernails into. Nothing. He wished he had managed to bring the rope.

He thought of all the animals he had hunted over the last four years, driving them into his traps. Was this how they had felt, knowing death was upon them? He thought of the ivory he had accumulated, and how he had left it scattered in the dust at the roadside by KwaDukuza for Jobe to take.

He would not surrender his life as well.

He swam closer to the waterfall, examining its sides for a ledge or an outcrop.

Were his eyes tricking him, inventing things because he wanted them to exist? Or did he see darkness behind the waterfall, where there should have been nothing but rock? He swam closer, wiping spray from his eyes. The cascading water made an almost solid curtain, but where it broke the surface, he thought he could glimpse the hollow of an opening.

There was only one way to be sure. He ducked under the water and launched himself forward, holding his breath. If there was a cliff behind the waterfall, he would smash his head into it; but if he did not go full tilt, then the current coming off the falls would drive him back.

He felt water churning all around him as he swam under the waterfall. His head popped up above the surface. Blinking water from his eyes, he peered at his surroundings.

He was on the far side of the waterfall. It was not a proper cave, but part of the riverbed that had been covered by a slab of rock, creating a hollow underneath. The river ran over it like a mill race.

Ralph moved to the entrance, right behind the waterfall. He planted his feet on rocks either side, then stuck his head out through the wall of water, taking the full weight of the cascade on his back and making an arch between his legs.

The water hammered down on him. The noise drowned out everything, but he knew their pursuers could not be far.

'Hurry!' he called to Ann.

She and Harry swam towards him. He reached forward and dragged them in, almost losing his balance, then shepherded them between his legs.

As soon as they were through, he pushed himself back behind the falls and disappeared from sight. Not a second too soon. Through the curtain of water, he saw the blurry outline of a man coming around the bend out of the gorge. He stopped on the edge of the pool opposite, surveying the scene. It was impossible to make out any detail through the water, yet Ralph was certain it was Marius. His height, his breadth, the arrogant stance: there was no one else it could be.

Had he been quick enough? Or had Marius seen him disappear behind the water? The Dutchman turned about, his bull-headed brain trying to comprehend how a man could vanish from this dead end. Surely it would not take him long to work it out.

Then the chase would be over. In a strange way, Ralph was glad of it. He had been running all his life. Now at last he could stand his ground, an old bull elephant brought to bay, weary of life but with one charge left in him.

Ralph had abandoned his rifle and his *isizenze*, but he still had his knife. Even if Marius had a gun, there was no way he could have kept his powder dry clambering over the rapids. If Marius came close enough, Ralph could spring out from behind the waterfall and surprise him. He would not escape the army of Zulus waiting downstream, but at least he could take his enemy with him. Perhaps they would let Ann and Harry live.

How unfathomable life is, he thought. For the first part of his life, he had devoted himself to seeing the boy and his family dead. Now, he desperately wanted to save Harry and Ann.

The water which seeped through cracks in the ceiling ran over his shoulders and streamed into his eyes. The noise deafened him. Jammed shoulder to shoulder in the tiny space, Ann hugged Harry to her while the boy covered his face.

It was a fantasy for Ralph to think he could spring out through the waterfall, like a thief emerging from a dark alleyway. The water would knock him down and push him under. By the time he resurfaced, Marius would be ready. The only chance would be for Ralph to swim underwater and grab him like a shark. But for that to work, Marius would have to be right in front of the falls.

Marius waded deeper into the water. He moved tentatively, sensing a trap, yet uncertain of what it was. A few paces closer. His head turned towards the waterfall. Ralph held his breath. If Marius could have seen through the falling water, he would be looking straight at Ralph.

Marius did not see him. He looked away again, up at the cliffs, seemingly trying to calculate if it was possible for a man to climb them. By now he was into the pool, almost floating in the deep water. Ralph gripped the knife more tightly. With Marius's attention elsewhere, Ralph would have the vital half-second he needed for his attack.

But the current was strong. In the moment that Ralph tensed himself, it pushed Marius back. Now he was out of range again, in the shallows where he could stand easily.

I am a farmer, Ralph remembered him saying once. *Give me solid ground under my feet.* He would not enjoy being out of his depth in the water. He would only approach the waterfall if he was certain there was someone there.

Could Ralph draw him closer? Or would that give too much warning? He would have to wait for Marius to look again. He could see the big Dutchman turning his head, considering his options, puzzling over how Ralph had disappeared.

Marius looked back down the gorge. Had he heard something? Had one of his men called him? Deafened by the waterfall, Ralph could only guess at what had distracted Marius. He glanced at the falls again, then back down the river. *Come on*, Ralph urged him. Marius looked again, straight at him. A spark of light flashed from his hand, the sun bowing off a blade. He was also armed.

The sound Marius had heard came again. He looked back a second time, turned and splashed through the shallows back the way he had come.

A wave of despair swept over Ralph. Marius had been in front of him, finally vulnerable, and he had not taken his chance. But he could follow Marius, catch him before he descended the rapids. Man to man, knife to knife – he would have an even chance. And whether he killed Marius, or died himself, he would not regret it.

He gripped his knife and drew a deep breath, ready to plunge under the waterfall. But as he was about to submerge, a hand gripped his shoulder. Ann tugged him back.

Ralph pulled away. 'I must stop him.'

She put her lips against his ear. 'We have escaped.'

'He will come back.'

'Can you not accept it? Or must you wish your own destruction?'

It was as if she had snapped him out of a dream, a waking nightmare of vengeance. Ralph's hand went to the scar on his cheek. As the river poured over his head, he felt not water, but the hot lash of flames. He had pursued revenge before, and what had it achieved?

She was right. Fate had offered them this one reprieve. For all their sakes, he should take it.

Their bodies huddled together in the frigid water, waiting for the ominous shadow of movement beyond the waterfall. Time passed agonisingly slowly, but Marius did not return. If his men had found a different trail to follow lower down the valley, or if Dingane had summoned them back, or if he had simply given up and left Ralph to die in the wilderness – Ralph had no way of knowing.

He could not wait any longer. Without the energy of the chase and motion to warm them, the freezing mountain water had started to bite. Harry had lapsed into a lethargy; Ann was alabaster pale, and Ralph shivered constantly.

'Wait here,' he shouted in Ann's ear. 'I will see if it is safe.'

He forced his way out through the waterfall and let the current push him across the pool. Where it funnelled out to the rapids he had climbed, a jumble of boulders made a small tongue of dry land. Ralph was so weak the river almost swept him past it, but he managed to grab a rock and haul himself out.

The stones were warm from the sun. He lay there for a moment, letting the heat sink into his bones. His eyes fluttered closed, and it would have been easy to fall asleep, perhaps accept death there, but he could not abandon Ann and Harry. He forced himself to stand and look down into the ravine, where the river cascaded into the tunnel they had climbed through.

There was no one there. The Zulus had gone.

'Did you think I would give up so easily, hey?'

The words echoed off the surrounding cliffs, so it seemed that it was the air itself whispering around him.

Ralph turned. Marius stood in the shadows on the opposite side of the river, his face in darkness except where a blade of sunlight came through the ravine and cut across his eyes.

How long had he been waiting there? He has the patience of a hunter, Ralph thought. He cursed himself for forgetting that.

'You have wasted your time,' he said. 'By now, Ann and Harry will be far away.'

Marius grinned. 'Not so far, I think.' He jerked his head to the waterfall.

He had known everything, all along. Instead of taking his chances in the water, he had waited to draw Ralph out onto land. While Ralph had been shivering in the cold water, Marius had regathered his energy.

Now they confronted each other across the narrow headwaters of the Thukela.

I was willing to let go of my revenge, Ralph thought bitterly. *Why could you not do the same?*

'When we made our partnership on Robben Island, I did not think it would end like this.' Ralph had no plan, except that the longer he kept Marius talking, the more strength he might recover.

The words affronted Marius. 'We could have been kings. I gave you chances, and every time you chose the Kaffirs instead of your own race.'

'Black or white, I would rather live with honest men.'

Marius sprang at him. The river was only a few feet wide: he cleared it in a single bound, driving the point of his knife towards Ralph's chest. Ralph brought up his own blade to parry it.

The weapons clashed. Ralph had expected the attack, but he was not ready for the overwhelming force in Marius's arm. His knife was dashed from his hand and into the water.

Ralph was disarmed. Marius bared his teeth and gave a howl of triumph. While he was gloating, Ralph attacked. Marius had not expected an unarmed man to come at him; his reflexes were a fraction too slow. He brought the knife around, but Ralph was already inside his guard. Ralph threw a punch to his ribs, and another to Marius's jaw that sent him reeling.

Marius teetered on the edge of the cataract. The knife flailed wildly, but Ralph had to risk it. He flung himself at Marius. On the wet rocks, the Dutchman lost his footing and slipped backwards.

Locked together, the two men tumbled down the rapids in a welter of water, rocks and limbs. Ralph was battered from so many directions he did not know where the hits came from. He clung to Marius, using his enemy to break the jarring blows.

It is like wrestling the lion, he thought, a moment before he hit the bottom of the rapids with a shuddering impact. They had landed in the channel where the river flowed away: too shallow to cushion their fall, but deep enough to drown them. Ralph's head went under; he was pinned down, and whether Marius intended it or not, the Dutchman was on top.

Marius's weight crushed Ralph against the smooth stones. Ralph struggled to push himself up, but the effort only provoked Marius. Ralph felt those meaty hands close around his throat, holding him prone, throttling him even as he drowned. Pain exploded in his skull. Shards of white light lanced his eyes. He thrashed and fought, but he was too weak.

Ralph's life ebbed out of him. As he stopped struggling, urgent thoughts drifted through his mind.

What will happen to Ann and Harry?

There was no way they could escape. When Marius had finished with him, he could do as he liked with them.

The injustice kindled one last ignition of resolve. Ralph pushed against Marius with all the power he could summon. He bucked his back; he kicked off against the riverbed.

It was not enough. Marius's weight was too much. Ralph had failed.

Ralph stopped struggling and let himself go still. He felt surprisingly peaceful. He no longer felt the chill of the water, only the motion of the current, pushing against his body like a summer breeze against a leaf. Bright light spread in front of his eyes.

And suddenly the weight lifted off him. Ralph felt himself rising out of the water. For a moment, he thought it was his soul leaving his body, but when he put out his arms, he felt firm rock underneath. He pushed up and met no resistance.

Water sluiced off him as his head broke the surface. He gulped in a great mouthful of air, with such pain in his chest he thought his lungs would burst.

He was not dead. Nor was he alone. He could hear Marius thrashing about behind him.

Why did he let me go?

Swaying like a drunk, Ralph rose to his feet and turned.

Marius was standing in the tunnel, bent over, clutching his leg in agony. A red cloud blossomed in the water where he stood, spinning out in thin tendrils as the current washed it away. The bone handle of a knife – Ralph's knife – stuck out from the back of his thigh.

Harry stood behind Marius. His mouth was open, his young eyes wide in terror and wonder. His hand was covered in blood.

Marius roared, the outrage of a wounded alpha animal. He grabbed the knife handle and yanked it out of his flesh. A stream of fresh blood pumped out of the gaping hole, but he did not seem to notice it. Nor did he think of Ralph. His instinct was to destroy the creature who had hurt him.

He towered over Harry, his head almost touching the rocky ceiling. Harry stood his ground, staring up defiantly.

Ralph flung himself at Marius. He crooked one arm around the Dutchman's neck to pull him back, while with his other hand he tried to wrestle away the knife. Marius jerked backwards, struggling to keep his balance with Ralph on his back. He staggered three steps down the tunnel.

Ralph kicked his heel against the bleeding wound in Marius's leg, making him howl in agony, but the Dutchman's grip on the knife stayed tight. Ralph could not pry it out of his monstrous hand.

Ralph was still desperately weak from his ordeal in the water. With a shrug of his mighty shoulders, Marius dislodged him. Ralph had to spring away, or he would have been dumped in the river again.

The two men faced each other down the tunnel. Marius lunged with the knife, and in the tight confines there was no space for Ralph to dodge it.

But halfway through his stride, Marius suddenly stopped as if he had hit an invisible wall. Harry had dived forward and wrapped his arms around the Dutchman's leg. Marius toppled forward like an oak tree. Ralph stepped aside, and as Marius crashed past him, he grabbed the Boer's arm and bent it backwards over his knee. The arm snapped; the knife dropped from Marius's grasp.

It never touched the water. Ralph caught it left-handed, transferred it to his right, and stabbed it into Marius's back. He felt it slide past the vertebrae, between the ribs and deep into the cavity of Marius's heart.

Marius's body jerked, then went limp. He floated face down in the water; air bubbled up around him. Ralph wondered why the river did not carry the corpse away, until he realised he was still clinging to the dead man's shirt, holding him in place.

He rolled Marius over. He had driven the knife in so far, the point had come out through his chest. Blood seeped from the wound and washed away in the current. Marius's dead eyes stared up, wide open: the eyes of a man who had seen what he most craved – and had lost it all.

You wanted this land for yourself, Ralph thought, *but it is not yours to own. It never was.*

He released his grip. The body drifted away, gathering pace, until it vanished into the sunlight.

In Ralph's mind, he saw the body making its last journey along the Thukela. Down the valley, across the plains and hills they had struggled over. He saw it spinning in the lazy current where the river broadened by KwaDukuza, past basking hippos and crocodiles sunning themselves on the banks, until at last it reached the ocean. The same ocean from which, eight years earlier, a man had staggered out of the fog while a boy slept in his new mother's arms.

Harry picked himself out of the water and stood beside Ralph. Together, they stared down the tunnel. The sun filled the space with a golden light that shone off the surface of the water and rippled across the stone ceiling.

'Is he dead?' Harry asked.

'Yes.'

Harry nodded. 'Did I kill him?'

'No.'

A shudder went through Ralph that had nothing to do with the freezing water. In that moment, he understood with the clear force of an epiphany that he must keep Harry from that path. The boy must grow up innocent, free from the stain that Ralph carried.

'I killed him. You saved my life.'

Harry grabbed Ralph's hand and Ralph held him tight, feeling the strength in that small body.

'What will we do now?' Harry asked.

'We had best find your mother.'

They met Ann trying to scramble down the rapids using the rope that still hung where Ralph had tied it. Ralph wondered that she had been so slow to come after Harry, until he realised how quickly the fight had unfolded. It had been a matter of moments that Harry had been there, though it felt like a lifetime. Ann hugged Harry close. The water had already washed the blood off his hands.

They followed the river back through the tunnel and the gorge, sliding down the rapids on their backsides, until they reached the stony shingle where the river met the forest path. At every turn, Ralph tensed himself for an ambush – but there was no one waiting. Without Marius, the rest of the Zulu company had retreated.

They laid themselves out on a dry stone where the sun still lingered, drawing heat into their chilled bodies until Harry's teeth had stopped chattering. Ralph gathered branches and ferns to make a rough shelter.

'We will be quite *intimate* in there,' Ann observed.

'I can sleep outside.'

She laughed – the prettiest sound Ralph had heard in weeks. She and Harry were naked; Ralph still wore the remnants of his kilt, but it was torn to shreds and hid nothing.

'I think we are past caring about modesty.'

Ralph untied his kilt and tossed it to her. 'This will cover you.'

Ann gave him a surprisingly frank look that lingered between his legs. 'That may preserve my shame. But it hardly protects my sensibilities.'

It was such a prim sentiment, delivered with such a wicked grin, that Ralph could not help smiling back.

'We are like Adam and Eve.'

Ann had thought herself in Eden once before, in Paradise Valley. It reminded her of Frank, and everything she had lost since then.

Ralph saw her face cloud over. 'Do you regret this?'

'Regret?' She shook her head.

Ralph moved to pull away, but Ann grabbed his wrist and pulled him close, so his face was only a few inches from hers.

'Every step that brought us here has been attended by tragedy and death,' she reminded him. 'It is not the path I would have chosen.' She saw the hurt in his eyes, felt him tugging away from her again. She would not let him go. 'But now that I am here with you, there is not one single thing I regret.'

She leaned forward and kissed him. Her cheek still carried the chill from the river, but her lips were warm and soft. The moment Ralph touched her, he had a flash of the feeling he'd had in the river: a blissful release, the burden of life lifting from his soul. Except then, he had thought he was dying; now he felt he was waking up to a new life.

'Harry is watching,' she murmured in his ear. 'We will have to continue this later.'

They separated – but even apart, Ralph felt her warmth living on in him. Ann picked up Ralph's kilt and tied it around her waist.

'We will have to find some more clothes,' she said.

'And food.'

This was not Eden; the trees would not give up their fruits so easily. Even if the Zulus did not come back, Ralph, Ann and Harry would be lucky to survive.

'What will we do?' Harry asked. In the hush of evening, his words sounded very small, lost in the landscape around them.

Ralph pointed over his head, to the great mountain cliffs that towered over them. The rock face was in shadow, but a thousand feet up, a few last rays of sunlight still touched the summit and turned it golden.

'We will have to find a way to get over that.'

Harry craned his head to look up at it, so far he almost fell over. 'It is a long way.'

'It is,' Ralph agreed. 'But we will go there together.'

'And what is on the other side?'

Ralph put one arm around Harry, the other around Ann, and squeezed them close to him.

'Adventure.'

WILBUR SMITH

THE POWER OF ADVENTURE

DISCOVER THE BIRDS OF PREY SEQUENCE
IN WILBUR SMITH'S EPIC COURTNEY SERIES

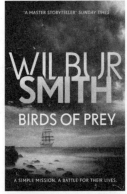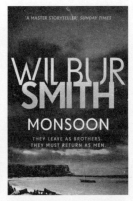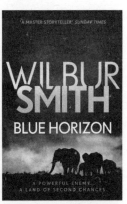

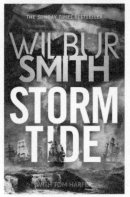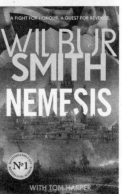

The earliest sequence in the Courtney family adventures starts in 1667, amidst the conflict surrounding the Dutch East India Company. In these action-packed books we follow three generations of Courtney's throughout the decades and across the seas to the stunning cliffs of Nativity Bay in South Africa.

AVAILABLE NOW

THE MASTER
OF ADVENTURE
RETURNS TO EGYPT

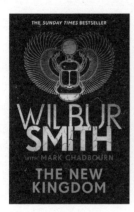  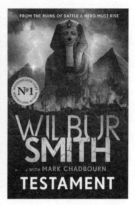

Gods and men.
Magic and power.
Glory and salvation.

The fate of Egypt hangs in the balance in . . .

THE NEW KINGDOM
TRILOGY

Find out more at:
www.wilbursmithbooks.com/books

or join the Wilbur Smith Readers' Club to be the
first for all Wilbur Smith news

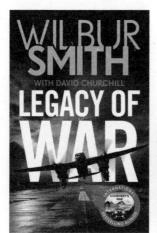
 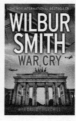 

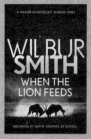

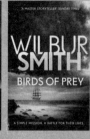
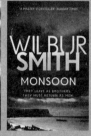

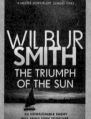

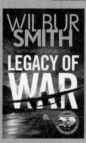

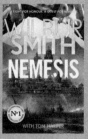

DISCOVER
THE COURTNEY SERIES
ADVENTURES